THE

COLLECTED

SHORT

STORIES

Volume 2

Fiction Titles by P. C. Wren

Dew and Mildew. 1912
Father Gregory. 1913
The Snake and Sword. 1914.
Driftwood Spars. 1916
The Wages of Virtue. 1916
The Young Stagers. 1917
Stepsons of France. 1917
Cupid in Africa. 1920
Beau Geste. 1924
Beau Sabreur. 1926
Beau Ideal. 1928
Good Gestes. 1929
Soldiers of Misfortune. 1929
The Mammon of Righteousness. 1930 (U.S. title: Mammon)
Mysterious Waye. 1930
Sowing Glory. 1931
Valiant Dust. 1932
Flawed Blades. 1933
Action and Passion. 1933
Port o' Missing Men. 1934
Beggars' Horses. 1934 (U.S. title: The Dark Woman)
Sinbad the Soldier. 1935
Explosion. 1935
Spanish Maine. 1935 (U.S. title: The Desert Heritage)
Bubble Reputation. 1936 (U.S. title: The Cortenay Treasure)
Fort in the Jungle. 1936
The Man of a Ghost. 1937 (U.S. title: The Spur of Pride)
Worth Wile. 1937 (U.S. title: To the Hilt)
Cardboard Castle. 1938
Rough Shooting. 1938
Paper Prison. 1939 (U.S. Title: The Man the Devil Didn't Want)
The Disappearance of General Jason. 1940
Two Feet From Heaven. 1940
The Uniform of Glory. 1941
Odd—But Even So. 1941

The

Collected

Short Stories

of

Percival Christopher Wren

Volume 2

Edited

by

John L. Espley

Riner Publishing Company
Riner Virginia
2012

ISBN
978-0-9850326-1-6

Contents

"Soldats de la Légion,
De la Légion Étrangère,
N'ayant pas de nation,
La France est votre Mère." . . .

PREFACE

The Collected Short Stories of Percival Christopher Wren (hereafter *The Collected Short Stories*) began as a desire on my part to make the short stories and articles written by P. C. Wren more available to the reading public. His novel, *Beau Geste*, is usually recognized by most of the book dealers I have met over the years, but his other works are not so easily remembered. In my opinion, his short stories are some of his best work and worthy of greater recognition.

I have been collecting P. C. Wren for almost fifty years now, and have been working on a comprehensive bibliography for almost as long. Hopefully, the bibliography will be published later this year (2012), which is the 100th anniversary of Wren's first published work of fiction, *Dew and Mildew*.

The text of the 116 short stories published in the seven Wren collections, *Stepsons of France*, *The Young Stagers*, *Good Gestes*, *Flawed Blades*, *Port o' Missing Men*, *Rough Shooting*, and *Odd—But Even So* were easily obtained from copies in my own collection. For that collection, I certainly need to thank the hundreds of used book dealers I have purchased items from, but I need to thank by name, Steven Temple, David Mason, Walt Barrie and, especially, the late Denis McDonnell for the advice and help they have provided over the years.

For helping me obtain the text of the remaining items in *The Collected Short Stories*, I need to acknowledge the assistance and guidance of the "chums" of the Fictionmags listserv and specifically Mike Ashley. My friend, Lane Rasmussen, was able to obtain a copy of the article, "Wonderful Egypt", through the Inter-Library Loan department of our local university. My friend, Robert Maxwell, from Brigham Young University went beyond the "call of duty" when over one weekend he was able to find (after a search in the stacks for a potentially lost item) a copy of the rare periodical *Prediction*, in which the article "I Saw a Vision" appeared. The book dealer, Bevis Clarke, of Clearwater Books, is owed a great deal of thanks for making the manuscript available of the unpublished short story "Broken Glass".

Mr. John Venmore and Mr. Philip Fairweather, both descendants of the late Mr. Richard Alan Graham-Smith, Wren's stepson, and the executor of Wren's estate, have both been very helpful in providing information about Wren. Based on information provided by Mr. Venmore and Mr. Fairweather attempts have been made to contact their relative, Elizabeth Jane Ellen, the person last known to own the works of P. C. Wren. It is presumed that Ms. Ellen is deceased, but I have been unable to verify that. It has been over seventy years since the death of P. C. Wren (November 21, 1941), and it is assumed that his works have passed into the public domain.

I also need to acknowledge the help and guidance of the members of my family: my daughter and son-in-law, Dawn and Andrew; my son and daughter-in-law, Jared and Claudia; and my long-suffering wife, Cathy. Thank you.

In conclusion, I need to thank Percival Christopher Wren for the many years of great enjoyment that his stories have provided. I know that Wren is not a literary or critical success, but, at least for me, he is one of the great storytellers of the early twentieth century.

John L. Espley
Riner, Virginia
July 4, 2012

INTRODUCTION

Percival Christopher Wren is best known as a novelist, publishing twenty-eight novels from 1912 to 1941, the most famous of which being *Beau Geste* (1924). Wren also published seven short story collections: *Stepsons of France* (1917), *The Young Stagers* (1917), *Good Gestes* (1929), *Flawed Blades* (1933), *Port o' Missing Men* (1934), *Rough Shooting* (1938), and *Odd—But Even So* (1941). These short story collections contained a total of 116 stories. There were also two omnibus collections published, *Stories of the Foreign Legion* (1947) and *Dead Men's Boots* (1949), containing stories taken from *Stepsons of France*, *Good Gestes*, *Flawed Blades*, and *Port o' Missing Men*.

Wren was a man of mystery in that the more popular biographical statements about him seemed to be more fiction than fact. A typical biography has him born in Devon in 1885, educated at Oxford, and having a career of world traveler, hunter, journalist, tramp, British cavalry trooper, legionary in the French Foreign Legion, assistant director of education in Bombay, and a Justice of the Peace. Most of the above biography, however, has not been verified. Wren was born Percy Wren November 1, 1875 in Deptford, a district of South London on the banks of the Thames. He did attend Oxford University, graduating in 1898 with a 3rd class honours in History leading to a Bachelor of Arts degree. He attained his "M.A." in 1901. In those days, a person acquired a "M.A." after a certain number of years (three in Wren's case) and purchasing it.

After leaving Oxford he was a teacher at various commercial schools until 1903 when he and his family left England for India. He married Alice Lucie Shovelier in December 1899 with whom he had a daughter, Estelle Lenore Wren, born in February 1901. From 1903 to approximately 1919 Wren was employed as an educator by the Indian Educational Service (I.E.S.). During that time he published a number of educational textbooks, some of which are still in use in Indian schools today. It was at this time that he started using the name Percival C. and Percival

Christopher on the textbooks. From 1905 to 1915, he also served in the Volunteer Corps (Sind and Poona) in India (see the novel *Driftwood Spars*), and was appointed a Captain in the Indian Army Reserve of Officers, the 101st Grenadiers of the Indian Infantry, in November 1914. He probably saw action in the East African campaign of World War I (see the novel *Cupid in Africa*), and resigned from the Indian Army Reserve of Officers in November 1915.

Wren's first novel, *Dew and Mildew*, was published by Longmans, Green in 1912. His first novel of the French Foreign Legion, *The Wages of Virtue*, was published by John Murray in 1916 (written in 1913). One of the many questions about Wren, is whether he actually did serve in the French Foreign Legion. Given the chronology of his documented biography it is hard to see where he had time to actually serve in the Legion. Wren himself always maintained that he had served, and his stepson, Richard Alan Graham-Smith, who died in 2006, "strongly maintained that Wren had indeed served in the French Foreign Legion and was always quick to refute those who said otherwise."[1]

The Collected Short Stories is an attempt to bring Wren's shorter fiction back into print. Twenty-six of the 116 stories published in the seven collections have been identified as being first published in the newspapers and fiction magazines of the early twentieth century. Many of the other stories were probably published in the newspapers and fiction magazines but information about these appearances is limited since the indexing of the fiction in the newspapers and magazines of the early twentieth century is incomplete. A bibliographical history (as known as of 2012) is included in each introductory commentary to each story.

The order that the stories are presented is primarily chronological, but there are some discrepancies in order to keep some stories that were presented within a frame together. The original spelling, punctuation, and grammar have been preserved as found in the latest editions/printings of the stories during Wren's lifetime (1875-1941). The footnotes within the individual

---

[1] http://en.wikipedia.org/wiki/P._C._Wren

stories are also found in the original source material.

In addition to the 116 stories published in Wren's short story collections there are some additional items. "At Oxford: Innocent Ernest and Artful Eintz" is a short story originally published in 1919 in an obscure fiction magazine. "The Romantic Regiment" and "Twenty-Four Hours in the Foreign Legion" are "factual" articles originally published in magazines. "Wonderful Egypt" is an article (more a photographic essay) originally published in *The Strand Magazine*. The article "I Saw a Vision!" originally appeared in a rare psychic magazine, *Prediction*. There is also an interesting article found in an Australian newspaper, "Meaning of Dreams", where Wren relates a couple of dreams he had experienced. Finally there is "Broken Glass", an unpublished short story.

Volume Two

Volume two of *The Collected Short Stories* contains eighteen short stories and two non-fiction articles originally published between 1928 and 1933. Twelve of the eighteen stories come from the collection, *Good Gestes* (1929), and the remaining six from *Flawed Blades* (1933). One of the articles was originally published in a fiction magazine, *Soldiers of Fortune* (December 1931), and the other article first appeared as a BBC radio broadcast.

The stories from *Good Gestes* either feature one or more of the Geste brothers or are tales related to them by other legionnaires. Two of the stories, "What's In a Name" and "Dreams Come True", are the third and fourth longest of Wren's short stories. A number of the stories from *Flawed Blades* feature characters from Wren's novels *Soldiers of Misfortune* (1929) and *Valiant Dust* (1932).

All of the stories from volume two are interesting, but particular favorites of the editor include "The Devil and Digby Geste" (from *Good Gestes*), and "Mastic—and Drastic" (from *Flawed Blades*).

WHAT'S IN A NAME

"What's in a Name" was the first story in the collection Good Gestes *(1929), which as the title indicates features stories of the Geste brothers from* Beau Geste *(1924). "What's in a Name" is the third longest of all of Wren's short stories, and is really two connected parts, that were originally published as two separate stories in fiction magazines in 1928. The first part is a pathetic (Wren calls it "absurd") story about how a young man embarrasses himself in front of his commanding officer. The second part is about how a young Englishwoman comes looking for her fiancé who is hiding in the Legion. "What's in a Name" was first published in the magazines,* Hearst's International *combined with* Cosmopolitan *(June and July 1928) and* Pall Mall Magazine *(August and September 1928) under the titles "Betrayal" and "What's in a Name?". The stories were combined and published as "What's in a Name" in* Good Gestes *(1929),* Stories of the Foreign Legion *(Murray 1947), and* Stories of the Foreign Legion *(Macrae-Smith, 1948).*

I

The three brothers sat in a solemn row upon Beau Geste's bed by the window in their barrack room, enjoying the blessed peace of a Sabbath afternoon.

John Geste yawned cavernously, and the pot-shot made by his brother Digby, with a small piece of soap, was entirely satisfactory—to Digby.

"The child seems bored," observed Beau Geste; "he must do more Arabic. Yes," he continued, "and I think I must institute a course of ethnological studies, too."

"Oh, splendid," agreed Digby, "I shall love that. What is it?"

"What I mean," continued Beau, "is that it would be rather interesting to see how many different nationalities we can discover in the Legion; how many different trades, professions, and callings, and—"

"And all that," said John, having completed another yawn.

"How is Beau like Satan?" asked Digby.

1

"How's he *un*like him?" interrupted John, ere Digby answered his own question with the statement:

"Because he'll find some mischief still for idle coves to do. They'll make him a sergeant, if he's not careful."

"Why mischief?" asked John. "Ethnology isn't mischief, is it?"

"It would be, my lad, if it took the form of going about asking personal questions of *les légionnaires*. They'd *do* you a mischief, too," was the reply.

"That's just the point," observed Beau. "No questions to be asked at all. See who can get the finest collection of nationalities, professions, home-towns and all that, without asking anybody *anything*. No vulgar curiosity. . . . All diplomacy, suggestion, induction, deduction . . ."

"Then production," murmured Digby.

"Quite so, my dear Watson. The one that gets the biggest bag, to give the other two a present. Splendid idea. Keep your young minds active. Train the faculty of observation."

"When do we compare notes?" asked John,

"When I think I've got the biggest list," replied Beau.

"And what if the same feller appears in more than one list?" inquired John.

"Cancel him out, or toss for him, or find who discovered him first, fathead."

"I'm afraid the idea's too late to save *you*, John," observed Digby—"mind dead already."

One evening a month later, the three brothers, sitting in a row as was their wont, with their elder and leader in the centre, adorned a broad, low divan in Mustapha's café.

"Well, pups, how's ethnology going?" inquired Beau, as he put his clay coffee-cup on the floor beside him.

"Fine," said Digby. "I'm a great man with a great mind. A diplomatist is lost in me."

"*Is* he?" inquired Beau, in some concern. "Let's get him out."

"No; you don't understand, Beau," observed John. "He means he *is* a diplomatist. He's right, too. Nobody but a clever diplomatist could hide the fact that he *is* a diplomatist so well as Digby does."

"Anyhow, I bet I win," said Digby triumphantly. "All

2

authentic, too."

"Then you'll give us each a present," pointed out John. "Shall I choose a fiddle, or a free excursion-ticket, single, to—to—Brandon Abbas? Read out yours."

"No, we'll declare ourselves in order of merit," interposed Beau. "I've got a grocer, Bingen; a shipping-clerk, Barcelona; an officer of the Imperial Guard, St. Petersburg; a valet, Paris; a surgeon, Vienna; a commercial traveller, Hamburg; a vendor of unpostable post-cards, valued and respected citizen of Marseilles; a stevedore, Lisbon; a street-corner fried-bean merchant, Sofia; a teacher of languages, Warsaw; a fig-packer, Smyrna; a perfectly good, nice-mannered, bloody-minded brigand, Bastilica—"

"There isn't any such place," interrupted Digby. "Where is it?"

"Nothing to be ashamed of in honest ignorance, my lad. It's right in the middle of Corsica, fifty miles from Ajaccio—according to the brigand," replied Beau.

"Isn't that where Napoleon Bonaparte was born?" inquired John.

"Bastilica?" replied Digby. "Why, of course; I remember the place quite well now."

"A restaurateur from Ancona; a rock-scorpion from Gibraltar; a Japanese barber from Yokohama—he speaks English with an American accent, he understands Russian, I know, and I'll bet you he could not only drill a battalion but handle a brigade or a division."

"Oh, you mean that chap Yato," interrupted Digby. "I've got him. He's a wonderful tattooer, too. He's going to do portraits of you two on my back, so that I can't see them."

"Will he, too, tattoo, two, to . . ." murmured John sleepily.

"Cancel him out, then," said Beau.

"I've also got a Portuguese cove from Loanda. That's in Angola, Portuguese West Africa."

"Well, we know that, don't we?" complained Digby.

"No," answered Beau and continued: "A Swedish sailor from Göttenburg, and two frightful asses from Brandon Abbas."

"Rotten list," commented Digby; "barely a score."

"Well, how many have *you* got?" asked his brother.

"Oh, in round numbers, about a hundred."

"*Round* numbers? All round the truth, I suppose?"

"Well, listen and don't be jealous," answered Digby, producing a paper. "I've got a Russian banker from Odessa; an Italian opera-singer; a Dutch bargee; an Austrian count—or discount, perhaps; a Munich brewer's drayman; a Spanish fisherman; a Goanese steward; a Danish farm-boy; a beastly, bounderish, bumptious, Byzantine blackguard; a French actor; a schoolmaster from Avignon; a gambling-hell keeper from Punta Arenas—wherever that may be; a bank-clerk from Rome; a lottery-ticket seller from Havana; a hybrid Callao *maquereau*; another cosmopolitan gent from Sfax, who, on being asked his trade, always says, '*Je faisais la mouche*'—"

"But no questions were to be allowed," interposed Beau.

"I didn't ask any, clever; I overheard, see? . . . A Dutch Colonial soldier, a Bowery tough; a Dresden—"

"Shepherdess," murmured John.

"Wrong again," said Digby—"street-scavenger; a Finnish—"

"Time we got to the finish," murmured John again.

"Bloater-paster, or salmon-smoker—"

"Funny stuff to smoke," commented Beau, "but probably better than this French *caporal* tobacco."

"A colonel of Don Cossacks."

"From Donnybrook?" inquired John.

"Yes, and Donegal—or perhaps Oxford," replied Beau.

"A bootblack from Athens; a poor *fellah* from Egypt; a boatman from Beirut; and two frightful asses from Brandon Abbas. . . . Oh, and a lot I haven't written down. Tinker, tailor, soldier, sailor, rich man, poor man, beggarman, thief; painter, pander, pedlar, parasite, printer, professor, prize-fighter, *procureur*, prefect, priest, pro-consul, prince, prophet-in-his-own-country. . . . Oh, lots. Get you all the names and addresses by and by."

"What have you got, John?" inquired Beau, turning as with bored distaste from the loquacity of his twin.

"I've got another Jones," replied John, alluding to Digby's *nom de guerre* of Thomas Jones.

"What *is* a Jone, by the way?" inquired Digby. "I ought to know, as I am some."

"Dunno. Anyhow, this is the only other Jones," replied John.

"He's an Englishman—public-school, Oxford, and all that. Indian Army, too, poor beggar. In a rotten state, living on his nerves. Sensitive sort of chap. Shoot himself one of these days. This is about the last place in the world for a man like him."

"Sounds as though it *will* be the last place in the world for him," observed Digby. "Let's get hold of him and shed the light of our countenances upon him, thus brightening his dark places. Does he seem to be a criminal, like Beau?"

"No, nor a moral wreck like you."

"Moral wreck!" commented Digby. "Better than being an *im*moral wreck anyhow." And his look was accusatory.

"Neither criminal nor moral wreck," continued John. "Simply a gentleman, like me."

"Oh, a gentleman like you, is he?" remarked Beau. "Then I don't think we'll associate with him."

"Yes, we will. I'm bringing him here to-morrow night, to meet you two. He's simply longing to talk English to people of his own kind. And I'll tell you something else. Unlike most people here, he wants to talk about himself, too. He's in a queer state of nerves—neurotic."

"Poor chap, we must see what we can do for him," agreed Beau; and Digby nodded.

A lean haggard man, his sensitive young face a mask of misery, old and lined, haunted and hopeless, arrived with John the following evening at Mustapha's café. That he was in a terribly nervous condition was all too evident—a reserved and reticent gentleman, devil-driven to be garrulous, talking the harder the more he was ashamed of talking. He seemed literally dying to express himself, to make a clean breast of something terrible, something that still stung and scorched and branded him.

His story, told in a swift rush and a curious metallic voice, without break or hesitation, greatly interested the sympathetic, silent brothers. It interested them yet more, next day, when they learned that, for some reason not divulged, he had shot himself during the night.

Five minutes after his introduction by John to Beau and Digby, he told them that his meeting with them was a godsend, for there was something he *must* get off his mind.

And a pitiful thing it was, to the listeners, prepared as they were to hear a dark story of vice, crime, ruin and downfall. . . . Pitiful, pathetic, tragic and ridiculous, like a torrent in spate, the absurd story came.

"Looking back and considering the affair again in all its bearings," he said, "I am still of opinion that I did my painful duty and nothing more; that I acted as a man of conscience should do, and that I have nothing whatever wherewith to reproach myself.

"Only the fool or the moral coward says, 'Am I my brother's keeper?' For what had my dear mother trained me, and my dear father in God developed my sense of responsibility to my neighbour and myself, but that I should act precisely as I did in that affair?

"I suppose it is the Devil himself who is the *fons et origo* of those foolish, unworthy and sinful doubts that do sometimes try to raise their poisonous heads in my disordered mind when I look back upon the little incident.

"However, I will tell the exact truth as to what I thought and said and did; and you shall judge as to whether any high-minded, conscientious and morally courageous person could have done otherwise than I did.

"I was brought up by the best mother a man ever had, a human saint, and by a priest whose chief regret, I think, was that burning at the stake has become unpopular. No, he didn't want to burn anybody; he wanted to *be* burnt—for his faith. He sought a martyr's crown and found a comfortable living, much honour and preferment. Finding also that honour is not without profit save in its own country, he determined to go abroad and find profit to his soul among the heathen—and possibly the martyr's crown beneath the solar topi—it would look odd on top of one.

"And I went to India to join the Indian regiment into which I was exchanging, by the same boat that took him to join the holy army of martyrs, if he could contrive it. It was a great joy to my mother that I was to travel with the good man and not be left to stray alone into the detrimental atmosphere of Gibraltar, Malta, Port Said, Aden, Bombay or other such colourful, and therefore wicked, places.

"And on that accursed boat I saw my new colonel's young

wife kiss another man. I saw him with his arms about her waist. I saw him go into her cabin, when the colonel lay snoring in a *chaise longue* upon the deck.

"When I heard them *plotting together to go off*, at Port Said, on Christmas Day, my terrible struggle with my conscience was ended. My conscience had won, and I knew I must tell the colonel the horrible truth, however agonizingly distasteful and obnoxious this hateful duty might be. Yes, I was a Young Man with a Conscience. . . . But let me tell the facts in sequence as they occurred.

"My new colonel (of the regiment to which I was going), returning from leave and his honeymoon trip, was a grey, stern man; a typical dour Scot, very unapproachable, and the last man in the World with whom one would attempt to jest or trifle.

"His bride was a beautiful young girl who might well have been his daughter—as merry, frivolous and gay as Colonel Gordon-Watts was sober, hard and dour. Opposites attract—and it was plain that he worshipped her.

"I admired her greatly, and she was very kind to me on the one or two occasions on which I spoke to her. Sometimes I felt I would rather be promenading with her, sitting beside her deck-chair or playing deck-quoits and bull-board with her than eternally walking and talking with my good and kind mentor.

"But I was far too much his spiritual child, his acolyte and disciple, to think of breaking away from his control. You see he had educated me from childhood until I went to Oxford, and he had settled there, with those admirable Fathers irreverently known to undergraduate youth as the Cowley Dads, and continued to exercise his powerful influence upon my character. I was with him daily and much of every day, and, as you hear, even now that I was in the army—with a university commission, as my mother would never hear of my going to Sandhurst—and *was* going abroad into the wide and wicked world, he was with me still. Yes, I was a Young Man with a Conscience.

"No, I did not make any attempt to desert my mentor and cabin-companion in order to bask in the society of the colonel's wife; but while my ear listened to my spiritual father and my tongue replied to him, my eye undoubtedly followed her.

"Nothing happened until we reached Marseilles and the

7

overland passengers came on board. When I went on the promenade deck that evening, one of them already sat beside her, and I was very sorry to see her accept a cigarette from him and smoke it. He was, like herself, young, and again like herself and most unlike the colonel, merry, frivolous and gay.

"They had evidently made friends very quickly and they were always together. Certainly they made a splendidly matched couple, and certainly she seemed far more merry and bright in his company than in that of her husband."

"*How* they laughed together!

"And the colonel seemed content. He would sit in the writing-room scribbling away, all the morning, at some military text-book or other that he was compiling; sleep all the afternoon; scribble again in the evening; walk violently round and round the deck, for exercise, before dinner, and go to bed quite early. I confess that I envied the handsome, laughing youth and that I often longed to talk to someone other than my spiritual father— someone like this merry, frivolous girl, for example.

"And on the second day out from Marseilles I received a terrible shock.

"Coming suddenly round the corner from the music-saloon, I almost ran into her deck-chair as she withdrew her hand from that of her new companion with the words:

"'You are a darling, Bobby; you shall have a hug for that'— and, as I dodged the foot-rest of her chair, her eye met mine, even as she spoke. Did she look confused, uncomfortable, guilty? Not she! Her gaze was utterly untroubled, and it was evidently nothing to *her* that I must have heard every word she said.

"Perfectly shameless!

"And as for *him*—he had the effrontery to murmur quite distinctly, 'Hold up, old hoss!' as I stumbled and blundered past.

"Of the three, it was certainly I who would have struck an observant onlooker as the guilty one, as I flushed to the roots of my hair and hurried away, not knowing where to look.

"*Think of it!* Married a month, and the man had not been on the boat three days! I trembled from head to foot, and went straight to my cabin, feeling shocked to the point of physical sickness.

"Should I tell Father Staunton?

"Ought not I to tell her husband? Was not I an accessory after the fact, almost an accomplice, practically compounding a felony, if I stood by and said nothing? Was I my brother's keeper? I knew I was. I knew it was my duty to save the Colonel from shame; to save this woman from ruining her life; to save this young man 'Bobby' from himself.

"But I knew I was not brave enough to do it. And the devil tempted me with whisperings of *'Most un-gentlemanly of you to tell tales of a lady!' 'Gross impertinence!' 'Colonel Gordon-Watts will refuse to believe you, but not to kick you downstairs.' 'Mind your own business, you young fool,'* and even: *'Make love to her yourself, since she's of such an oncoming disposition'*— whereat I jumped with horror and told myself I would do my painful, dreadful duty.

"That evening, while Father Staunton was undressing in the cabin, I went on deck. It was a glorious moonlight night. As four bells rang and the lascar look-out replied with his sing-song cry of *'Ham dekhta hai'* to show that he was awake and watchful, I was moved with an idle inclination to go right up into the bows and watch the phosphorescence as the knife-like stem churned up the sleeping waters.

"I ran down the companion, crossed the well-deck, and climbed the iron ladder to the fo'c'sle.

"*He* and *she* were there, leaning on the bulwarks—and his arm was around her waist!

"Going up on deck early next morning, I saw them meet— *and kiss!* During that day, as on previous days, the young man (his name was Mornay, by the way) cultivated the society of other young women a good deal, presumably as a blind. But, as I sat reading in the lounge before dinner, Mornay and Mrs. Gordon-Watts came and sat down close behind me, and they made their arrangements for going off together, on Christmas Day, at Port Said!

"They spoke with shameless openness and lack of decency; and I distinctly heard Mornay say: 'Slip away while he's writing, then,' and a few minutes later: 'Bring *all* the cash you can scrape together, mind! You'll want it at . . . and I am nearly broke. I can't keep—' and her reply, with a heartless giggle: 'Suppose he comes after us!'

9

"I sprang up, and leaning over, said: 'Pardon—I am hearing much of what you say, and I shall—'

"With brazen effrontery, Mornay interrupted with, 'Right-o, old thing! Sorry if our artless prattle disturbed you,' while Mrs. Gordon-Watts stared at me as though she thought me eccentric.

"I rushed to my cabin.

"How shall I tell of the agonies of indecision, cowardice and self-contempt that I suffered, as I wrestled with my conscience once more. I *ought* to stop this thing. It was my bounden duty to warn the Colonel. Was I my brother's keeper? And so on, *ad nauseam*.

"And a thing which somehow, and strangely, seemed to make it all worse, if that were possible, was the fact that she was not the only woman that he pursued. He was a perfect Don Juan and made up to every pretty girl and woman on board, married or single.

"'An arrant flirt,' thought I, 'a lady-killer; a heartless, conscienceless scoundrel.' And yet I could not deny that he was popular with all on board. He was in the greatest demand, always and everywhere—in fact, 'the life and soul of the ship,' as Mrs. Gordon-Watts truly said.

"And while I sat on my berth, and suffered, Father Staunton entered and I laid the matter before him. I weakly suggested that he, a priest, was the fitter person to intervene.

"'No, my son,' said he, 'I go to no man with a tale about a tale. . . . And I shall leave it to your own conscience. Do what you think right, but be no self-deceiver. Be very sure of your motive before you act or decide not to act.'

"And I read this to mean, 'Do not stand by and see this happen because you are a coward while you pretend it is because you are not a busybody. . . . Do not shirk your duty because you have told yourself that this is not your business and that you have no duty in the matter at all!'

"I had no sleep that Christmas Eve. I tossed from side to side, a prey to doubt, fear, self-contempt and indecision. I was stretched upon the rack of my Conscience.

"But in the morning, the glorious Christmas morning, I arose, calm and decided, and dressed as one dresses who goes to execution. Conscience had triumphed and I was going to do the right thing at any cost to myself—and the right thing in this case was, believe me, a loathsomely distasteful thing for me to do. I would go through with it, however—and I would do it openly and fairly, sparing myself nothing. I would tell Colonel Gordon-Watts, in the presence of his wife and her lover.

"There would be no backbiting, no 'tale about a tale,' no hole-and-corner sneaking about *that*.

"As the passengers trooped up from breakfast, I followed the Colonel, with whom were his wife and Mornay, on to the deck; and with beating heart and dry mouth, I went up to him and said:

"'May I have a word with you, sir, on a matter of the most urgent and vital importance—and may Mrs. Gordon-Watts and Mr. Mornay be present?'

"The Colonel stared, looking more like a cold volcano than ever.

"'What the dev—' he began, and I could feel my knees turning to tape and my heart to water, as Mornay interrupted with:

"'If it's to form a syndicate for a bet on the day's-run sweepstake, on the strength of a tip from the engine-room, let us congeal ourselves and hist.'

"Mrs. Gordon-Watts giggled. If Mornay and she guessed at my business with the Colonel, they acted cleverly, I thought. There was no trace of guilty confusion. No; they did not *dream* of what was coming.

"'Well? Out with it,' growled the Colonel.

"He had vile manners, as I had already discovered in my brief and rare encounters with him on board.

"'It would be better for all concerned, if we were alone—we four, I mean,' said I.

"'Let's go up on the bridge and ask the captain to clear out for a while,' suggested Mornay. 'He won't mind.'

"The lady laughed again.

"'I am very much in earnest, sir,' continued I to the Colonel, ignoring Mornay.

"He saw from my manner, and probably from my appearance, that I certainly was very much in earnest.

"'Come in here,' he said, indicating the empty smoking-room. All the passengers were crowding forward on the starboard side of the deck, to watch Port Said rising out of the sea.

"Sir,' said I, 'it is my unspeakably painful duty to tell you, before this man, Mornay, that I have seen him *embrace and kiss your wife*, have heard him address her in terms of intimacy and endearment, and have heard him *arranging to go off with her*— and with what money she could secure—at Port Said. I have said it and done my duty. My conscience is clear. . . .'

"The Colonel's eyes blazed. His wife and Mornay stared at me open-mouthed. Thus we hung for seconds that seemed like years, without sound or movement—till suddenly Mornay threw himself down upon the couch behind him and buried his face in a cushion; the Colonel raised a hand—not to strike, but to cover his poor twitching mouth; and Mrs. Gordon-Watts burst into wild hysterical screams of distraught laughter.

"And *I* had made this ruin!

"But I had obeyed my Conscience. . . .

"And *then*—and *then*—the Husband turned, first to the Wife, and then to the Other Man, and said:

"'Is this thing true? If so, you are not to waste more than ten pounds in the shops, Lilian. And if you, Bobby, have been kissing your *own* sister for a change, it's a change in the right direction!'"

II

"I say," said Digby as he entered the Barrack Room, a few days later, and strode across to where Michael and John, sitting on the latter's bed, industriously waxed and polished belts, straps and pouches. "Did you see the draft that came in this afternoon from Colomb Bechar or somewhere?"

"No," replied Michael. "Why?"

"Well, they've got about the ugliest lad I've ever seen, among them. . . . *Awful* face."

"Worse than John's?" asked Michael.

"Well, you can't very well compare them," replied Digby. "John's ugliness is what you might call natural. He was born like it. This other fellow's is artificial. Been made like it."

"Got an artificial face, has he?" inquired John.

"Not exactly that either," replied Digby, pushing John off his bed, and seating himself by Michael. "It's the ugliness that's artificial. It's as though I didn't like your face—which I don't, of course—and set to work with cold steel and red-hot iron to improve it, or at any rate to change it."

"Wouldn't *any* change be an improvement?" asked Michael, looking up from the pouch that he was polishing.

"Well, I gather it wasn't so in this man's case," replied Digby. "His *escouade* seemed quite proud of his face, and one of them was telling me about it. He's an Englishman. It seems he got a poisoned foot and couldn't get his boot on. He fell behind, as they were doing a forced march to relieve a threatened post, and couldn't stop for anything or anybody. They hadn't even any mule or camel *cacolets* for the sick and wounded. He kept going, with the utmost pluck and endurance, sometimes hopping, sometimes using his reversed rifle as a crutch, and at last going on all fours . . . When he completely collapsed and couldn't even roll, the tribesmen who had been watching the Company and stalking this straggler, came down like a wolf on the fold and gathered him in—not without loss to themselves as they rushed him from all points of the compass.

"Well, it seems they were so annoyed with him, for shooting frequent and free, that they had a bit of fun with him, then and there, before taking him up to the *kasbah* or caves, or whatever it was, in order to let the ladies torture him properly.

"Apparently they slit his cheeks perpendicularly and threaded twigs through the latticework, so to speak, and did something similar with his forehead. An argument then arose as to whether the girls would mind if he were handed over to them without ears, nose, lips and eyelids. Some murmured '*Place aux dames*,' while others said, 'There will be plenty of him left for them.'

"Like the sensible fellers they are, they compounded and compromised and split the difference and said they'd just have his ears for luck, and for something to send in to the Commandant of the nearest Fort, on his birthday, or for Christmas or something.

"Well, one nasty man had just grabbed this chap's right ear, and had just begun to cut with a rather blunt knife, when round the corner came a policeman, and the boys had to run for it. In other words, along came a half-troop of Spahis who were following the Company.

"I gather that the Spahis were divided in their minds as to

whether it would be kinder to shoot him, or to save him up, when the *vile corpus* or vile body sat up and said that if anybody shot him, he'd punch him on the nose. He said this in English, a language understanded of the *sous-lieutenant* of the Spahis, so they pulled most of the brushwood out of the latticework which was his face, tied his ear on with string, mopped him up a bit, and put him up behind a trooper."

"Poor devil," murmured John. "He must be a stout lad."

"Yes, let's go and call on him," suggested Michael. "He might like to have a jibber with fellow-countrymen."

"We will," agreed Digby. "Better look him up tomorrow, as he may be among those of the draft who are being sent to Arzew to recuperate."

"Where's that?" inquired John.

"You're an ignorant lad," replied Digby. "It's a health resort, on the coast, about one hundred miles west of Oran. Didn't you even know that much? I learnt it this afternoon."

The brothers found *le légionnaire* Robinson to be a pleasant English gentleman with a most unpleasant face, hideously scarred, and rather terrible to behold. It was obvious that he was still most painfully self-conscious.

As the four chatted, Robinson sat with his hand across his face, as does a weak-eyed person in a strong light. Although it was easy to see that the poor fellow was very uncomfortable among strangers, the tact, charm, sympathy and *savoir faire* of the three Gestes won upon him, and put him at his ease. Before long he was laughing and telling them the story of his ghastly experience.

"I suppose I'm a *légionnaire* for life," he smiled wryly and whimsically, "now that my face is my misfortune . . . This home of the Soldiers of Misfortune is the best place for it . . . the only place. Can't go about scaring women and children . . . Might get a job at a sort of Barnum's Show, I suppose.

"Rather hard luck," he added. "I had only four months more to serve. . . ."

"Rough luck," murmured Michael, "but look here, you know . . . I think you make too much of it. . . . What I mean to say is . . . it'll get a great deal better in course of time . . . scars do, you know, and these are very recent. . . . And then these great surgeons can do most marvellous things."

"Why, yes," agreed John. "It's astonishing what they can do in the way of grafting new flesh, and that sort of thing. I knew of a man whose nose was most hideously smashed . . . flat with his face . . . bone all gone—and they built him up a perfectly good nose."

"Sort of thing he took off at night with his wig and false teeth?" inquired Robinson grimly. "I shouldn't care to wear a mask."

"Nothing of the sort," objected John. "This fellow's nose was not detachable. It was built up under its own skin, so to speak. I believe they inject molten paraffin wax, and mould it to the required shape as it cools—something of that sort."

"Yes," added Digby. "I distinctly remember reading of a great Viennese surgeon who practically rebuilt the shattered face of a man whose gun burst as he was firing it. According to the account they even made him a new jawbone, and grafted on to it skin which they took from his leg. There was a portrait of him, and he looked perfectly normal, quite good-looking.

"Why not take your discharge, and go to the best surgeon in the world? Costly job, I suppose, but if a loan . . . we should be . . ."

"Oh, I've plenty of money *now*, thanks," replied Robinson. "Reminds one of the Spanish proverb, '*God gives nuts to him who has no teeth.*' I hadn't a bean in the world. Partly why I came to the Legion. . . . But the day I came out of hospital—and had a good look at my face—I got a letter from home. Plenty of money, now."

"Well, that's all right then," observed Michael, "and you can spend some of it to good purpose."

"My dear chap, it's hopeless. You know it is. It's most kind of you to be consoling and encouraging, and all that, but the damage is done, and it's irreparable. If the marvellous surgeon had been on the spot, I've no doubt he could have done something and made, at any rate, a tidier job of it than Nature and my comrades' dirty paws did. It's far too late now, and I'll spend the rest of my young life where nothing matters—thanks all the same."

"Well, anyhow," replied Michael Geste, "you see if I'm not right. Things will improve enormously in time. The scars will lose all colour and cease to be livid. They will become mere seams and lines . . . hardly noticeable."

"That would be a pity in a way, too," smiled Robinson. "My *escouade* would be disappointed. They would miss my face. Perhaps some sniper won't—if I can get on active service again."

§2

"Where's Beau?" inquired Digby one afternoon, a couple of months later, as he joined John at the trough in the *lavabo* where they washed their white uniforms.

"Dunno," replied John, "but he'll be in for evening *soupe* all right. Why?"

"A job, my little lad! . . . A *geste* . . . a deed . . . a do. . . . You know that dear fellow, Klingen. He was telling his gang an extraordinary yarn while we were peeling potatoes this morning. . . . Reminded me of that lass who chased the Crusader home."

"What lass was that?" inquired John.

"D'you mean to say you don't know *that*, you uneducated worm . . . you worm that dieth not. No, that was a sharp-headed worm, wasn't it? Nothing sharp-headed about you, John Geste."

"We were talking about a girl," interrupted John coldly. "Who was she?"

"How the devil should I know?" replied Digby. "It's you who ought to know useful things of this sort, so that you can be helpful to Beau and me."

"You don't mean Mrs. à Becket by any chance, do you?"

"That's it, my lad," said Digby, smiting his brother with his wet tunic. "Why couldn't you have said that at once, without all this jibber. Thomas à Becket went to the Crusades and there picked up with a Saracen lassie."

"But I thought he was a turbulent priest, and a perfectly good Archbishop of Canterbury," observed John. "I think it was T. à Becket Senior. Old Mr. Gilbert."

"No, no," replied Digby. "It was Tom Cantuar all right, and all this happened when he was young and merry and bright, before he had found grace. . . ."

"*Was* her name Grace?" asked John. "I thought it was Zuleika or Zenobia or Aggie."

"Will you shut up and listen, and improve your mind!" admonished Digby. "He took up with this young woman, and they were walking out . . . keeping company . . . *you* know . . . when T. à Becket's time expired, or else he was due for leave and furlough, and in the hurry of packing his kit and getting his papers signed and proving to the Quartermaster that he was a liar . . ."

"*He* was—or the Quartermaster was?" asked John.

". . . he quite forgot, or else mislaid, Grace or Zuleika or Zenobia or Aggie—and in any case he couldn't have taken her aboard the transport as she wasn't married to him 'on the strength.' Well, there it was. T. à Becket safe in England and poor Grace walking up and down the Pier or the beach at Acre or Joppa or Jaffa or Haifa weeping and wailing. . . ."

"Whaling?" queried John. "From a pier or a beach?"

". . . and Grace's Pa making kind inquiries for T. à Becket with a thick stick."

"How *do* you inquire with a stick?" asked John.

"I'll show you in a minute," promised Digby, and continued:

". . . When Grace found that Thomas had done a bunk—and she having nearly filled the bottom drawer and all—two of everything and all hand-stitched—she up and had an idea. Drawing her savings from the Post Office, she left Pa and Ma to scratch for themselves; she went down to the shipping office and just said 'Single, London,' and went straight aboard a perfectly good fifteen-ton lugger or yawl or scow or junk or barge or battleship and 'proceeded' to London, which she knew to be Thomas's home-town, as she had seen it on his washing.

"Safely arrived, she took a room in a perfectly respectable boarding-house in Bloomsbury, patronized entirely by clergymen's daughters, had an egg to her tea, and then went out to look for Thomas. . . .

"Now the artful dog, Thomas, had never given her his proper name and address, and she only knew him as Thomas, Tommy and Tom, and there were quite a lot of gents so named in London Town. However, she worked clean through the London Directory and the Bars and Night-clubs of the Shaftesbury

Avenue district, and in the end, probably the West End, she met her own True Thomas, who promptly said he was just having a last drink before setting out to look for her, having been engaged hitherto in getting a home together. Whereupon they married and were happy ever after. . . . She was housekeeper at the Palace when he settled in at Canterbury as Archbishop, because you know how people talk and all that, when celibate clergymen . . ."

"But my poor dear excellent ass," interrupted John, "what's all this got to do with the unspeakable Klingen and the deed we have to do?"

"Nothing, probably," replied Digby, "and then again, you never know. As I was saying when you interrupted, he was telling his gang an extraordinary yarn while we were peeling potatoes this morning.

"It appears that, last night, as he was strolling down the Rue de Tlemçen, a beauteous maiden stopped him and asked him if he was English. I gathered that he behaved precisely as Klingen would behave in the circumstances, and that she cleared off with her chin in the air, followed by Klingen with his mind in the gutter—until she went into the *Hôtel de l'Europe* and thither he could not follow her. Then up spake a lad whose name I don't know, and said he'd had a similar experience. A pretty girl had stopped him near the hotel, and, with blushing apologies, asked him if he were English. Apparently this chap behaved like an ordinary decent person—said he was sorry but he wasn't English. The girl then explained that she wanted to find an English *légionnaire*. Her idea seemed to be that her best plan was to find *any* Englishman, as he would be more likely to know *the* Englishman."

"Of course, the chap she wants will have changed his name, and her only chance—if the man has been transferred from Sidi—is to meet somebody who can identify him from her description," said John.

"Clever lad," approved Digby, "you've got it. Here's a girl looking for her Thomas, and hasn't got the vaguest idea as to what he now calls himself. She can't even go about like Grace or Zuleika asking for him by his Christian name, and, even if he's in Sidi, it's like looking for a needle in a haystack; and if he's in Morocco or the Sahara or the Sudan or Madagascar or Tonkin, she'd never find him at all. He may be here, of course. . . ."

"And that's where we come in," said John, wringing out the shirt that he had washed. "By Jove," he added, suddenly straightening himself up, "it couldn't be Isobel!"

"Of course not, you fat ass. That's what I thought the moment Klingen spoke. But it was only yesterday you had a letter from her. And if she came here, she'd have no need to stop strangers in the street and ask if they spoke English. She'd only have to send a card round from the hotel to the Barracks addressed to *Légionnaire* John Smith, No. 18896, saying that she was at the Hotel."

"Of course," agreed John sadly. "I spoke before I thought."

"People who never think, inevitably do that," observed Digby loftily.

"Now stop both thinking and talking and listen," he continued.

"La Cigale, who was standing there, peeling away as though he'd been a hotel scullion all his life, instead of a military attaché and ornament of Courts, suddenly said:

"'Why! That must be the lady with whom I had so charming and delightful an adventure last night.'

"You know how the poor old dear talks. He went on:

"'I was sitting in the Gardens, not feeling very happy, when a lady came and sat down on the same seat. She was young, beautiful, and a gentlewoman. She paid me the compliment . . .'

"And here the poor old dear bowed most gracefully toward me—

"'. . . of asking me if I were English. I replied in French that I was not, but that I could speak the language quite well, and we had quite a long talk. I promised to mention to all the Englishmen whom I knew, that there was an English lady looking for a compatriot. But the whole matter had gone completely out of my mind until Klingen spoke just now. It must be the same lady. . . . This absent-mindedness is terrible. . . .'

"And the old chap went off into apologies and regrets that he'd forgotten to tell us."

"Hullo, here's Beau," interrupted John. "Beau," he added, "get some mutton-fat, or dripping or something, and make your hair extra beautiful. We're going calling on a lady this evening, at the *Hôtel de l'Europe*."

Beau's eyes opened a little wider as he looked from John to Digby.

"Claudia here?" he asked.

"No," replied John. "Nor Isobel."

"Oh no," added Digby. "It's Grace or Zuleika or Zenobia or Aggie or somebody," and he proceeded to tell Beau that there was an English girl who had the courage to walk the streets of an evening and stop passing soldiers, to inquire if they were English or knew any Englishmen in the Legion.

"We must go and put ourselves at her disposal," said Michael Geste.

§3

Helen Malenton, sitting at "tea" in her room, and honestly endeavouring to detect any remotely tea-like flavour in the luke-warm liquid that trickled reluctantly from a grudging coffee-pot, was losing heart and hope, if not faith and charity. From the day that Barry had disappeared, leaving only a letter of passionate renunciation of her, and even more passionate denunciation of himself, she had kept a stout heart, high hope and profound faith.

Being a firm believer in the great truth that Heaven helps those that help themselves, she had done her utmost to merit the help of Heaven, but hope had been deferred and undoubtedly her heart had grown sick—with apprehension, disappointment, and the feeling that the expected help had not been forthcoming.

She rose and went to the window that looked across a dirty street to a dusty garden, and, turning from the familiar and unsavoury prospect, began once more to pace the more familiar and less savoury room—hideously ugly as only the sitting-room of a provincial hotel can be.

"I *won't* give up," she said. . . .

"Faith as a grain of mustard seed . . . I *know* he's alive, because he could not die without my being aware of it. . . . My heart would die too. . . . Only believe and . . . if you want anything hard enough it comes to pass. Effort is never wasted."

Seating herself on an unbelievable sofa of stamped velvet, she stared unseeingly at the incredible carpet, her tense hands clenched on either side of her drawn face.

"Oh God," she whispered aloud. "*Do* help me. Life isn't a welter of blind chance. . . . Oh, how long? . . . If there were a ray of hope. . . . A sign. . . ."

She sprang from her seat as the door opened and a dirty nondescript garçon of no particular nationality, and arrayed chiefly in a green baize apron, entered bearing an envelope in his grimy hand—an envelope addressed "To the English lady staying at the *Hôtel de l'Europe*."

Murmuring that this was apparently *pour mademoiselle*, the youth explained that three soldiers were waiting below, for an answer.

Tearing the envelope open with trembling fingers, Helen Malenton read:

"Three English *légionnaires* would like to inquire whether they can be of any help to you; and, if so, will be delighted to put their services at your disposal."

Foolish and irrational hope sprang up in her heart.

An answer to prayer? A gleam of light in her darkest hour, the darkest hour before the dawn?

"Where are they, these soldiers?" she asked eagerly.

"Below in the *fumoir*, madame."

"I will come down," said Helen quietly, and endeavoured to conceal the excitement that surged up within her, and caused her limbs to tremble.

Three handsome youths, obviously Englishmen, rose and bowed as she entered the stale and dingy lounge.

"Good evening. Will you allow our excellent intentions to excuse our intrusion?" said one of them. "I am—er—William Brown and these are my brothers Thomas Jones and John Smith."

Helen Malenton gravely shook hands with her visitors as Digby remarked:

"Same family, but different names. Curious, but quite simple—like us."

"Yes," agreed John. "William is curious and Thomas is simple."

"I think I understand," replied the girl. "My name is Helen Malenton, and I'm most grateful to you for coming. I most thankfully accept your offer of help. I have just discovered that a friend of mine—my fiancé, in fact—is in the Legion, and I've come to look for him. He disappeared suddenly. Nothing wrong; he is absolutely incapable of doing anything base or mean."

Her voice trembled.

"Look at *me*, Miss Malenton," smiled Digby. "You have but to glance at my countenance to be assured that I could do nothing wrong, and am absolutely incapable of anything base or mean. Yet I disappeared suddenly, and am in the Legion. And, in a lesser degree, this applies to my brothers—who also disappeared suddenly."

The girl smiled, and with regained self-control, continued:

"I am sure you all understand."

"Absolutely," murmured Michael. "We are in a position to do so, and may I add we quite understand that a man who is your fiancé must be an honourable gentleman."

"Oh, he's one of the noblest and bravest of men who ever lived," said the girl impulsively. "He hasn't a fault or a failing, except that he is headstrong and rash, and yet very sensitive really. You know how such a person can be beautifully good-tempered and yet—well—at times *hot*-tempered."

"Oh, rather," agreed Digby. "They are the best sort. Pure gold from the furnace—and with the warmth of the furnace still in the heart of them—noble, brave and generous. I'm like that myself," and smiled infectiously.

Helen Malenton laughed for the first time in many months.

"Oh, we'll find him all right," he added. "What's he like? Is he like me in face as well as character?"

"No," smiled Helen. "He's a very handsome man. . . ."

Michael and John grinned appreciatively, and Digby looked sad, modest and embarrassed.

". . . but as dark as you are fair, I was going to say. Tall, broad-shouldered and spare. Extremely handsome—almost too much so, for a man—large eyes, silky black hair with a lovely wave in it, aquiline nose, small moustache, rather small mouth, a cleft chin. He had a complexion like a girl's. I used to chaff him about it, and tell him it wasn't right. He would laugh, and say it was due to his having been brought up solely by his mother, for his father died when he was a baby."

An awful thought struck Michael Geste. *Jones!* Of course it must be the poor chap who called himself Jones! Poor devil! . . . And oh, this poor, poor girl! The unhappy, overwrought, devil-driven Jones, too sensitive, highly-strung and introspective even for ordinary life—much more so for life in the Legion—the very last place in the world for a man of his temperament.

Had they done their best for him? What more could they have done? They'd been most kind and friendly of course, and they had only got to know him on the day he committed suicide. It was Digby who had discovered him and brought him along. Had he said anything about a girl, in telling them his tragi-comic piteous story?

And he had shot himself.

The poor girl was just too late. . . . Ghastly . . . Oh, this was terrible.

He glanced at his brothers, and realized that the same thought had entered their minds. Digby was eyeing him apprehensively and he generally knew what his twin was thinking. John was looking very grave and thoughtful.

"You haven't told us his name," he said, for the sake of saying something while he considered the best way of breaking the terrible news to the girl, should his fears prove justified.

"Chartres," was the reply. "Sir Barry Chartres; but I don't suppose he would use his own name."

"I know the name perfectly well," remarked Beau, and added, "No, he wouldn't use it in the Legion. You don't know what he calls himself now, of course."

"No," replied the girl.

"I wonder if he called himself Jones," said John, eyeing Michael.

"Quite likely," replied the girl. "Do you know an Englishman of that *nom de guerre*?"

"We *did*," admitted Michael.

"Did?" queried Helen Malenton quickly. "Is he . . . ?"

"Was Sir Barry Chartres ever in the British Army? Did he ever go to India?"

"Yes, yes, he did. He transferred from his County Regiment to the Indian Army, in the hope of seeing some active service."

The girl rose to her feet and faced them with shining eyes and parted lips.

"What is your friend like? You said '*did*.' Does that mean he has gone away from here? Where, where . . . ? Oh, it must be Barry! There wouldn't be *two* Englishmen here, who had both been in the Indian Army. Oh, *please* tell me quickly where he has gone?"

Seldom had the three brothers felt more miserably uncomfortable.

John and Digby looked to Beau for the next move, feeling that the situation could not be in better hands, and, while prepared to help him in every way, thankful that he was leader and spokesman.

What could he do? This was going to be really painful.

"Look here, Miss Malenton," said Beau Geste. "Suppose you leave everything to us. We are complete strangers to you, I know, but you can trust us absolutely. . . ."

"Rather," chimed in Digby and John.

". . . and we will do our best for you; we should love to. What I suggest is that you go back to England at once and we'll carry on. Do! I'll write to you immediately, when there is any definite news. It must be wretched for you here, and we three can do all sorts of things that are impossible for you. Go home tomorrow, and leave it to us."

"I don't know how to thank you," replied Helen Malenton. "But I couldn't, I simply couldn't. I *had* to come here, the moment I discovered that Barry had joined the Legion, and I must stay here until I am absolutely convinced that he is not in Sidi-bel-Abbès. And I shall only leave this place to go to some other in which he may possibly be."

"Suppose, for the sake of argument, he were dead," said Michael gravely.

"Oh, he isn't, he *couldn't* be," the girl protested.

"I want you to answer my question," replied Michael. "Suppose it."

The girl smiled through gathering tears.

"Why then I could—and should—follow him, of course," she answered. "I don't want to talk wildly, and be melodramatic, but I am going to find him, either in this world or the next."

A silence fell upon the four. Digby wiped the palms of his hands with his handkerchief.

Suppose it had been Isobel looking for *him*.

"Please don't," murmured John, with the slight nervous cough which his brothers knew to be an expression of deep embarrassment at deep feeling.

Suppose it had been Isobel looking for *him*.

"Well, then," said Michael, "if you won't go home and won't leave here till you have a clue leading elsewhere, just remain quietly here, and let us work for you. We'll hunt out every English *légionnaire* in Sidi, and do our utmost to find out what has become of all those who have been here during the last five years. It'll be quite simple, for there are very few Englishmen in the Legion. We shall be able to eliminate most of them from the list very easily."

"Yes, but where *has* this friend of yours gone, please?" interrupted the girl. "You don't tell me. It is almost certainly Barry. I'll follow up this clue just as soon as I'm sure that Barry himself is not here—and that should be easy, now that you three are going to help me. I thank you a thousand times."

"Not at all. Pray don't speak of it," replied Michael. "It is both a duty and a great pleasure. My only fear is lest we fail or—or—have to bring you bad news. We'll go now, and start work at once."

And the brothers rose to take their departure.

"Where *did* your friend *go*, please?" repeated the girl as she extended her hand to Michael.

"That's what we're going to find out," was the reply.

§4

"A brave and charming gentlewoman," said Beau as they marched down the street from the *Hôtel de l'Europe*.

"Yes," agreed Digby. "If only the late Mr. 'Jones' had been as brave, and had stuck it out a little longer! How are we going to tell her he blew his brains out just before she came?"

"We aren't," replied Michael.

"You mean we're going to say he died fighting bravely beneath the Legion's flag?" asked John.

"I'm not sure we're going to tell her he's dead at all," was the enigmatic reply.

"Enlighten us, Uncle," said Digby.

"I'm not at all certain that poor old Jones is the man. I've got an idea."

"So have I," said John.

"The Man with the Face?" asked Michael.

"Clever lad," he approved.

"By Jove!" ejaculated Digby. "Of course! *Of* course! Brainy birds! I never thought of that. He fits exactly, and of the two it's far more likely that *her* man would be the one who didn't commit suicide. I don't believe it was poor old Jones at all. Oh brains, brains! I somehow feel certain it is the Man with the Face."

"So do I," agreed John. "Her description of the long-lost lover suits him even better than the late Jones. I got the impression of a big chap from her description, and Jones wasn't enormous."

"No," observed Michael, "but he wasn't by any means a small man, and I wouldn't build much on that particular point. I imagine that any average-sized man is a fine huge hero to the girl who loves him."

"Yes, I suppose even we are," agreed Digby, his thoughts at Brandon Abbas.

"Yes," said Michael and John simultaneously, their thoughts in the same place.

"Still it really is an idea and a clue—and a hope," said Digby, "and we'll follow it up for all it's worth. I vote we now palter with the truth, and say that the ex-Indian Army man, to whom we referred, is at Arzew, and that we are on his trail."

"It isn't paltering with the truth so much as switching it over," said Michael. "A line of inquiry that was to lead us to the Legion Cemetery in Sidi-bel-Abbès, now leads us to the Convalescent Camp at Arzew."

"I say," broke in John. "There isn't very much time to lose, is there? Didn't the Man with the Face say his time was up, and that he was going to re-enlist? Pretty rotten for Miss Malenton if he did so, just before we told her we'd found him!"

"Yes, and that raises another snag," said Michael loftily. "A point upon which I have been wisely and profoundly pondering while you and your brother jibber and jabber and gabble."

"A snag isn't a point, may I observe?" commented Digby

coldly. "A point is that which has no parts nor magnitude."

"Like your brain, my lad," answered Michael. "You call this unfortunate gentleman 'the Man with the Face.' Well, does it or does it not occur to what we must call your mind, that if he *is* the man, he is certainly not going to bring his poor carven face and lay it before his best girl?"

"By Jove!" said Digby. "I never thought of that."

"What a ghastly position!" murmured John.

"But surely," he added, "the girl wouldn't turn him down because he's hideously disfigured. Not if she really loves him."

Would Isobel turn *him* down if his face were so slashed and scarred that he was unrecognizable? She would not.

"But it's not of the *girl* that I'm thinking at all. It's the man, my good little asses. I believe she'd stick to him if he'd lost both eyes, both ears, both lips, and both nose. *He*'ll raise the trouble, not she."

"You're right, Beau," said Digby. "He will. I've got the impression that he is the sort of person who'd do just that. I believe he'd sooner meet anybody in the world than the woman he loved."

"I can quite understand it too," agreed Beau. "He'd feel that she'd be repressing shudders the whole time, and fighting a desire to scream. He'd be afraid that, purely out of loyalty and decency, she'd swear she not only still loved him, but couldn't *live* without him."

"While, all the time, life was a purgatory to her—a hideous nightmare," added John.

"Depends on the woman, of course," said Digby. "There are women who'd honestly and truly love their man all the more because he was a bit chipped and cracked. Want to make it up to him, and mother him."

"Yes," agreed John, "there are. And then again there are equally fine women who simply could not bear it—literally could not stand the sight of a face like that, without being physically sick."

"And that's what poor old Carven Face will think, I'm afraid," said Michael. "He'll write and tell her he's not the only pebble on the beach and beg her to acquire a nice round smooth pebble that has not been carved—by Arabs. We'll do our best, anyhow, and we shall have to be careful and clever."

"John, *you*'ll have to be careful," stated Digby.

§5

Le légionnaire Robinson had returned from Arzew, his intention of re-enlisting confirmed by an offer of promotion to the rank of Corporal if he did so. He realized that he would probably regret the step when it was too late, but after impartially studying his terrible face, with the help of a good mirror, he decided that the best place for such a work of art was a desert outpost at the ultimate Back of Beyond.

"A pretty picture," he smiled grimly, as he regarded his reflection. "A picture which should certainly be hung," and he smiled again.

But only *le légionnaire* Robinson knew that the facial contortion was a smile.

Seated alone in a dark corner of the canteen, on the night of his return to Sidi-bel-Abbès, his hand, as usual, across his face as though to shade his eyes, he saw an Englishman enter the room and approach him. Pulling his *képi* well down over his face, he turned away and appeared to fall asleep.

"Discouraging," murmured Beau to himself as he turned to the zinc-topped bar, and procured a bottle of wine and a couple of glasses.

Seating himself beside Robinson, Beau Geste poured out two glasses of wine, coughed slightly, somewhat in the manner of John, and remarked:

"As you say, Robinson, this is an unwarrantable intrusion."

"I haven't said anything," growled Robinson.

"No, not aloud," agreed Michael. "Very nice of you, but I am butting in nevertheless, and I apologize—and my reason is my excuse. I've got a most important message for you."

"Oh?" grunted Robinson, evincing no interest whatever.

"From a lady," added Michael.

"Yes?" growled Robinson, with the complete indifference of one who received messages from ladies every few minutes.

"From *Miss Helen Malenton*," enunciated Michael, slowly

and distinctly.

Robinson's hand, extended to raise his glass, knocked it off the table.

"Ah?" he murmured, in the tone of one who was more than a little bored by Miss Malenton's attentions.

Watching the man's face as closely as was possible, Michael decided that it had shown no faintest sign of any feeling whatsoever; no slightest flicker of emotion; no shadow of change of expression, as he spoke the girl's name. But, as he told himself, he could not see the eyes properly, and the rest of the face was hardly calculated to register emotion of any sort. In fact, it was not a face at all, but a mask, a mask of tortured flesh, probably incapable of showing what its unfortunate owner felt, even when he wished it to do so.

Yes, decided Michael, *le légionnaire* Robinson was well entrenched behind the double defence of the mask he wished to wear and the mask he *had* to wear. Only his hands betrayed him, as so often they betray the man who has perfect facial control.

This was going to be a difficult job, and Robinson was going to behave exactly as they had feared.

"She is here," he said quietly. "Here in Sidi-bel-Abbès."

"Yes?" was the discouraging reply, in a voice as cool and quiet as Michael's own.

"She wants to see you, Robinson," continued Michael.

"To *see* me?" asked Robinson. "Five *sous* a peep, or something like that? Have you gone into the impresario business, or what?"

The man was certainly bitter.

"Don't *you* want to see *her*?" said Michael patiently.

"Not the faintest desire, thanks," was the uncompromising answer.

Michael sighed, and picking up Robinson's glass, he refilled it.

"Let's drink to her health," he suggested.

"With pleasure," growled Robinson. He raised his glass, muttered something unintelligible, and drained it.

"She's an amazingly brave, staunch, loyal woman," observed Michael.

"I'm sure she is," agreed the other.

"And she's in a pretty bad way, too," added Michael somewhat sharply. And—

"Look here, Robinson," more sharply still, "at the risk of your considering me an impudent meddler, I really must say this— When a girl has suffered on a man's account as Miss Malenton has done on yours—and when moreover she has travelled to Sidi-bel-Abbès to look for him—I do think it's up to him to see her."

"Yes," agreed Robinson politely.

"Well, don't you think it's the very least he can do?"

"Oh, quite," agreed Robinson again.

"Then you *will* see her?" said Michael promptly.

"No, Mr. What-is-your-name, I will *not*—and we'll now close this somewhat boring conversation," yawned *le légionnaire* Robinson, as he arose and departed thence.

§6

"Ah, this is a job that wants brains, of course," observed Digby at the conclusion of Michael's account of his discouraging interview with *le légionnaire* Robinson. "Leave it to me; do as I tell you, and all will be well.

"D'you mind if I visit Miss Malenton unhampered and unhindered—I mean, unaccompanied and unsupported, by your two silly faces?" he added.

"Quite hopeless, my dear chap," said John, "even if Miss Malenton were not absolutely wrapped up in her lost lover. And, in any case, she would prefer a visit from the nicest of us."

"We must try and keep him out of the sun, Beau," urged Digby, surveying his younger brother compassionately; "and while he keeps out of the sun I'm going into the shadows—of the *Hôtel de l'Europe* to propound a scheme to Miss Malenton."

"And why this sudden desire for a tête-à-tête?" inquired Beau. "If you feel you have a Mission and a Message and that we are neither worthy nor competent . . ."

"Well, it's only partly that," smiled Digby. "But I feel you'd be much more competent to play your little parts in my plan, if you knew nothing about it."

"Quite probably, I should say," observed Michael. "What are our parts?"

"Merely to lend your countenances and your money to my scheme. It's a dinner-party. We are going to dine and wine Mr. Robinson. A dinner to mark the occasion of his coming promotion and re-enlistment—a most hilarious celebration and all that."

"Where?" inquired John.

"At the *Hôtel de l'Europe*," was the reply.

"He'd never go there," objected Michael. "He literally wouldn't show his face in a crowded café like that."

"We shall have a private room," said Digby. "He'll come all right. He's very fond of me—naturally."

"And if he does, what's the idea? Make him drunk and get his word of honour that he will at least consent to an interview with Miss Malenton before he re-enlists?"

"Wrong again," was the answer. "Now ask no more questions, but be prepared to dine and wallow in the wassail on Sunday evening with Robinson at the *Hôtel de l'Europe*. This is Friday, isn't it? I'm going to see Robinson to-night and Miss Malenton to-morrow, and thereafter you shall behold the wondrous works of your Uncle Digby."

As one man, his brothers emitted a loud derisive grunt.

The charming Digby charmed, and the morose and bitter Robinson succumbed, on learning that the dinner was to be held in a private room, and that absolutely nobody but the three Englishmen was to be invited to it. "It's extraordinarily nice of you fellows," he growled, "and I can't refuse."

§7

The dinner went extremely well, for the Gestes were what they were, and Robinson strove to be what he once had been, a gay and debonair gentleman. The warmth of their kindly friendship unfroze the once genial current of his soul.

No mention whatever was made of Miss Helen Malenton, and when, at the wine-and-walnut stage of the feast, she entered the room, neither Michael nor John was greatly surprised.

The four men rose to their feet, and Robinson stared, his mangled face utterly expressionless.

Helen Malenton, her eyes shining, her countenance transfigured with emotion ineffable and uncontrolled, gazed at him for a moment, uttered a little gasping cry, rushed to him and flung her arms about his neck.

"Oh *Barry*, *Barry*, my darling!" she sobbed.

Seizing her arms in his hands, Robinson removed them from about his neck and gently but firmly pushed her from him.

"I don't know you," he said.

"Oh my own *darling*, my *dearest*!" cried the girl. "Your friend told me that your face had been wounded. . . . I was prepared for it. . . . My sweetheart, it is *nothing* to me."

"I don't know you," repeated Robinson, his outstretched hand between them.

"Barry my *love*, my *darling*, don't be so foolish! If such a thing be possible, I love you all the more! . . . How can you possibly think I should shrink from you? Why, my darling sweetheart, I used to think you were far *too* handsome for a man. . . . You were *pretty* almost. I swear to God that I like you better like this, even though I couldn't love you better."

The man's hand fell to his side in a gesture of resignation and acceptance, and the girl's arms were again clasped about his neck.

"I am *not* Barry," he groaned, and as, with the laugh of a mother humouring her child she drew his head down until their lips met, his arms went about her and crushed her to him.

Except for themselves, the room was empty.

§8

"Once again, good-bye, and God for ever bless you," said *le légionnaire* Robinson, wringing the hands of the brothers, as the four stood at the barrack-gate.

"You'll keep your promise and visit us on the island that we are going to buy—one of the Islands of the Blest, of which we shall be the sole inhabitants, and where no one but her will see my face. . . . God! To think that to-day I should have re-enlisted and gone back into hell instead of going off into Paradise with this noble and wonderful woman. How can I ever *begin* to thank you?"

"No need," replied Beau Geste. "It's been the most

tremendous pleasure. We shall always be happy to think that we brought you and Miss Malenton together again."

"You didn't bring us together *again*," smiled Robinson.

Surprised, the Geste brothers stared uncomprehendingly.

"I never set eyes on her in my life until last night," he said, and as he turned away added, "*But she won't believe it!*"

IF WISHES WERE HORSES . . .

Digby Geste is one of four legionnaires sitting around a campfire, one of whom asks the others what is the one thing they would wish for. The main part of this powerful story is told by a Pole of what happened to his family during a Russian pogrom. "If Wishes Were Horses" was first published in the magazine, Hearst's International Combined with Cosmopolitan *(September 1928). It saw its first book publication in* Good Gestes *(1929) and was reprinted in* Stories of the Foreign Legion *(Murray 1947).*

§1

The full moon, a great luminous pearl, and the incredible tropic stars—palely blue diamonds scattered over darkly blue velvet—looked down upon four weary, dirty men who lounged around a small camp-fire beneath a stunted, crooked palm beside a puddle of slimy water, rock-circled, thing-inhabited, malodorous.

One of the men was fair, huge, with huge moustache, a great laugh, great hands, and gross appetite. He looked too dull to be wicked, or successful. Drink had washed him into the Legion.

The second was dark, tiny, the ideal gentleman-jockey in build; pretty, small of mouth, and large of eye. He looked too clever to be trustworthy or determined. Racehorses had carried him to the Legion.

The third was grey, tall, spare and gaunt, a light-cavalry type. His craggy face was sad and weary, bitter, and somewhat cruel. He looked too cynical to be very intelligent or helpful. Vengeance had driven him to the Legion.

The fourth was Digby Geste, typical English gentleman. Brother-love had led him to the Legion.

Around them stretched to the horizon, on every side, the illimitable desert plain, still, mysterious, inimical, its dead level of monotony broken only by an occasional bush or boulder. A select small company of vultures formed a large circle around them, and took an abiding interest in their risings up, and their lyings down—particularly the latter.

A more select and smaller company of human vultures had made their camp a mile or so distant—by the simple process of lying down in their tracks, eating dates, and going to sleep—while one of their number, having wriggled like a snake with incredible flatness, speed and skill to within view of the men around the little camp-fire, squatted behind a boulder and also took an abiding interest in their risings up, and their lyings down, and particularly the latter.

To the vultures, the chance of a meal was something to follow up for days, and to the human vultures the chance of a rifle, worth its weight in silver, was something to follow up for weeks. Should the watcher, one night, see the sentry nod, sit down, lean back, sleep—he would wriggle near, satisfy himself, and then flee like a deer to his fellows. There would be a quick loping run, a close recognisance, a sudden swift rush, a flash of knives, and soon the meal, ready jointed, would await the other vultures.

§2

"Suppose the good Archangel Gabriel suddenly alighted here, with easy grace, and, folding his wings, granted us each a wish, what would you have, Zimmerman?" the dark little man suddenly asked the huge, fair one.

"Eh? . . . Me? . . . Grant me a wish? . . . Like those people in the Grimm fairy tales?" replied Zimmerman, a harmless, worthless waster—once.

"Oh, I don't know. . . . Pick up a diamond as big as my fist. . . . Strike for Berlin, home and beauty then. Take a suite in the Hotel Adlon in the Pariser Platz, do the *Weinrestaurants*, *tanzlokals*, theatres, beer-halls, night-cafés of the Kurfürstendamm, for a bit. Look up all the boys—and the girls. . . . Oh, ho! Champagne . . . fresh caviare . . . feasting . . . races . . . the tables . . . Peacock Island, Grunewald; Charlottenburg, night-clubs . . . Ho, ho! When I drove my girl down the Unter den Linden, every one would turn and look at us. Then I'd take her down to Monte Carlo, by way of Paris. Nothing wrong with Paris, and Monte Carlo, after you've picked up a diamond as big as your fist. Yes, I'd give her a time she'd remember. Let her see all the shops in Paris and Monte. . . . Let her see me win a pile of hundred-franc notes at the Casino. . . . Let her see me shoot the pigeons."

"She'd *love* that, I'm sure," observed Digby Geste.

"Yes, she would so! . . . *Gott in Himmel!* I'd melt that diamond down. . . .

"What would you do, Gomez? . . . Madrid, a Senorita, and the bull-ring? . . . Carmelitas . . . fandangos, guitars, wine of Oporto and Xeres, serenades?"

"Not a bit of it. I should make straight for England. Get another string together, and train 'em myself."

"Win the Derby, Oaks, and the Grand National, all in the same year, what? . . ."

"Yes . . . I'd have my stables all white tiles, mahogany, porcelain and silver plate—the talk of the countryside—and my horses the talk of England, the talk of the world. . . . Ascot . . . Goodwood . . . Newmarket . . . Longchamps . . . Auteuil . . ."

He sighed heavily.

"Well, thank the good God for tobacco, even French tobacco, until Gabriel comes," guffawed Zimmerman.

"What would be *your* line, Jones," he added, turning to Digby Geste.

Digby took his pipe from his mouth, slowly blew a long cloud of smoke, and gazed at the great ball of gentle light that hung from the velvet dome of the low sky.

What boon would he ask, if one were to be granted to him?

It cannot be said that his thoughts turned to Brandon Abbas, for they were already there.

What would be the loveliest thing his mind could possibly conceive? What about a drive in the high dogcart with Isobel?— through the glorious Devon countryside; the smart cob doing his comfortable ten miles an hour; harness jingling; hoof-beats regular as clockwork; Isobel's hand under his right arm; Devon lanes; Devon fields and orchards; Devon moors; glorious— beyond description.

But then he would have to keep at least one eye on the horse and the road, and that would leave only one eye for Isobel. . . . When one is driving a horse, one should drive him properly, with the care and attention which is one's courtesy to a horse that is worth driving. . . . Well up to his bit, with watchful eye and ready hand . . .

No, not a drive. What about two long chairs in the Bower, side by side, but facing opposite ways, so that he would have a full view of Isobel's face . . . nothing for his eyes to do but to watch every change of expression in *her* wonderful eyes, and lovely face . . . nothing for his ears to do but note every change and inflexion and sound of her sweet voice?

Or what about asking something bigger—something really big? . . . Why not ask that time be pushed forward a few years, and that the three of them be distinguished officers? Beau a Colonel, John and he Majors, going home on leave after a glorious campaign; home to Brandon Abbas and Isobel . . . Isobel . . . Isobel's arms about his neck . . . the little church in Brandon Park . . . the Chaplain at the altar . . . Beau should give her away . . . John should be best man. . . . Oh, too wonderfully beautiful . . . too terribly glorious . . . too unthinkable. . . .

He turned to Zimmerman.

"What would *I* like best in all the world?" he said. "Oh, I should love, beyond expression, beyond the power of human speech . . . to hit a very bald man on the head with a very long cucumber."

His companions pondered this ambition.

"No, no! Not a bald man. Not just any bald man. It's *l'Adjudant* Lejaune one would like to hit on the head with a long cucumber," said the Spaniard. "Now, that really would be a deed worth doing! . . . *Smack!* . . . Just when he's bawling his foulest insults. . . . One could die happy after that. Yes, a really great conception, Jones. Can you beat it, Budiski? What would you like?"

"I? . . . I'd ask for nothing better than two minutes with a certain Russian gentleman I know . . . a perfect little gentleman. A General, in fact," replied the grey-haired, grey-faced man.

"I've followed his career with interest ever since he was quite a junior officer. . . . I have shot him *once*. . . . That's why I am here. . . .

"He came with his half-company to our village when I was a lad . . . long, long ago. . . . It was *pogrom* time, and everybody was accusing everybody, when they weren't shooting them instead. . . . And our Russian masters were 'pacifying' that little corner of our country by the excellent Russian method.

"Any Lieutenant was the equal of Julius Cæsar in respect of his complete ability to 'make a solitude and call it peace' . . .

"They banged on our door one night, because ours was the biggest, and most comfortable house in the neighbourhood. . . . Ostensibly, because there was a blood-stained hand-cart in our stables. Of course there was. . . . It had been put there by the worthy soul who had used it to remove bleeding carcasses from where they were inconvenient, to where they were useful evidence against his enemy. . . . Probably—in proof of his hatred of all evil-doing, and his love of all Jews and Russians—he had shown the dripping push-cart to the Russian police.

"Anyhow, there it was, and there were the Russian soldiers round our house, in which slept my father and mother in a front room; my sister Wanda—a lovely girl of about eighteen—in the next room, and I and my young brother in a big room at the back. . . .

"He was a good boy, that young brother of mine. I was rather fond of him. Perhaps some of you can understand that?"

Digby Geste nodded his head.

"And we both adored Wanda. She was one of those simple, gentle, kind natures who, knowing no evil, are slow to think there is any in others, and imagine that all men—and women are like themselves. Not clever, you know, nor accomplished, nor advanced, nor up-to-date, but just merely simply something to thank God for, in a world like this."

"Marguerite, before Faust came on the scene, eh?" said the big German.

The Pole regarded him absent-mindedly, and continued:

"I suppose there is a God of Love—a beneficent Deity?"

"Of course there is," observed Digby Geste. "Didn't he create your Wanda?"

"And didn't he watch what followed? . . . I pulled on an overcoat, and ran downstairs as my father opened the front door to the soldiers. In five minutes they were all over the house, and they brought Wanda and my mother and my young brother down into the big living-room where the Lieutenant, his drawn sword in his hand, lolled in a chair, questioning my father, or rather abusing and bullying him and shouting accusations to which he would hear no answer.

"I can see that *intérieur* now, the impudent hard-faced rascal in my father's chair. A Sergeant and half a dozen grey-coated, flat-capped soldiers at attention behind him. Other soldiers replenishing the fire, lighting more lamps and candles, ransacking the place for food, drink, and loot . . .

"For the sake of his wife and children, my father was humble, meek, conciliatory, deprecating. It did not take the brave Lieutenant, who was prosecutor, witnesses, judge and jury all in one, many minutes to try the old man, find him guilty, and sentence him to death.

"'Remove the prisoner,' said he, having delivered sentence. 'Bind him, and take him outside—under a tree with a suitable bough.'

"As my mother and Wanda threw themselves on their knees before this upright judge, a Corporal and four men seized my father, tied a rope round his body, so that his arms were bound to his sides, and led him out into the snow, over which the cold, grey dawn was beginning to break.

"Smiling evilly on the two imploring women, the gentleman leant forward. With his left hand he gave my mother a rough thrust that sent her sprawling, and then, cupping Wanda's chin in his palm, he turned her face up to his, and kissed her on the lips.

"The brave rash boy, my brother Karol, sprang forward, before his two guards could stop him—and even as I shouted, 'Don't, you young fool,' and, with bursting heart, firmly controlled myself for the sake of all of us—he struck the Lieutenant heavily between the eyes, sending that hero over backwards, chair and all.

"Leaping to his feet, as the guards sprang upon my brother, and on me, this brave Russian officer put his sword-point to my brother's throat—and *thrust* . . .

"I fought like a madman . . .

"I hear my mother's screams to this day . . .

"Wanda had fainted.

"The Lieutenant gave orders that she should be carried to her bed, and tied to it securely. Also that I and my mother should be bound.

"'Take the old hag out to her husband,' he ordered, as they tore her from my brother, who lay bleeding to death among their feet.

"I lost control.

"'Yes,' I shouted. 'You foul dog! You cowardly, inhuman devil! You *Russian*! Bind an old woman, lest she hurt you! . . . Bind her, and feel safe, you miserable swine!'

"And I contrived to spit on him.

"Calmly he wiped his face, and sat himself down again.

"'Bring the woman back, Sergeant,' he ordered quietly, 'and send a man to tell Corporal Kyriloff to fetch the old man back, too. . . . Bring the next prisoner before the Court.'

"I was dragged before his chair, my arms roped to my sides, and my ankles bound together. He eyed me very coldly.

"Always beware of those who, while a seething hell of rage boils within them, eye you coldly, and speak quietly.

"'You have resisted, insulted, and attempted to kill a Russian officer in the execution of his duty,' he said quietly. . . . 'You are condemned to death. Your father has already been condemned to death. Your brother has been put to death. . . . But the Court is merciful. Like your ruler, the Great Czar, whom I have the honour to serve, and against whom you Polish scum treasonably plot and rebel, the Court is just—but it is merciful. . . .

"'Of the five of you, but two shall die, and one is already dead. . . .

"'Or, at any rate, the dog is dying,' he added, stirring my brother's body with his foot, 'so but one remains.'

"My mother's mind rose triumphant from the abyss of horror, woe, grief, and fear into which it had sunk while they held her back from the body of her dying youngest-born.

"'*Me! Me!*' she cried. 'Kill *me*! . . . They are innocent, innocent . . .'

"'Gag her, if she speaks again,' growled the Lieutenant, pouring himself out a glass of vodka.

"'But one remains,' he repeated, smacking his lips. 'Yes, in my mercy, I will hang but one.'

"'The one who spat upon you,' I said. 'The one who will surely kill you some day, somewhere, somehow, unless you hang him now.'

"'*No, no*, my son!' shrieked my mother, and a soldier clapped his great hand upon her mouth.

"'The Lieutenant will hang me,' said my father with calm dignity.

"'No, the Lieutenant will *not* hang you,' replied that Russian dog, 'but hanged you shall most assuredly be.'

"And turning to me, he asked in that cold, cruel voice, so suave and quiet now:

"'Do you love your dear Mother?'

"'In a way you could not begin to understand,' I answered.

"'And that nice, plump, pretty little partridge, your Sister?' he continued.

"'To a degree that no foul *animal* could begin to understand,' I replied, hoping to turn all his wrath to me.

"What less could one do?

"'Ah, that is good,' he smiled. 'Most excellent. . . . And you would save that dear Mother, and beautiful Sister, at any cost, eh?'

"'From what?' I asked.

"'Wel-l-l,' he drawled, 'from a certain—unpleasantness. . . . Your Mother from dying of cold and hunger in a Warsaw prison cell, or perhaps in the Loubianka dungeons, or, possibly, on that little stroll to Siberia. . . . Who shall say? . . .

"'And the nice plump partridge . . . from being "*the little friend of all the soldiers*" when she begins to bore me. . . .

"'They *do* bore one, you know,' he drawled, 'even the prettiest of girls—in time. They mope, most of them, and fail to realize their good fortune; or else they are spit-fires, and one has to take—er—*disciplinary* measures.

"'Well, what about it? Would you like to save them, and your own life, too?'

"'Yes,' I replied.

"'Ah, then you *shall*.'

"My little Lieutenant smiled.

"'When you've done a small job for me, that is,' he added.

"'How do I know that you would keep your word?' I asked.

"'I always keep my word,' he replied. 'It is the word of a Russian officer.'

"'That is the trouble!' I remarked. But nothing could anger him now—outwardly, that is to say.

"'What do you Polish boors know of the word of a gentleman?' he continued, and then rose to his feet.

"'Come—we're wasting time,' he said briskly. 'You wish to save your Mother from death, and your Sister from shame, I understand. . . . *Then come and hang your father for me.*'"

§3

The others stared aghast at the old man's twitching face. Like most of his countrymen he was a good raconteur, and could dramatize a tale as he told it.

"'*Hang your father'?*" murmured Digby Geste. "Did you say . . ."

"Yes, my friends," continued Budiski. "The Russian Bear stood declared, in all its shocking savagery. Fang and claw were revealed. My little Russian gentleman had dropped his semi-transparent mask of civilization. He had been struck by a man, and now he was about to strike back as a beast—the most terrible, relentless, savage, and hypocritical of beasts—the Bear.

"Have any of you ever stood face to face with the bear, and seen it change—change from a rather absurd, stupid, earth-bound thing, somewhat ridiculous—into a monster, a great and terrifying Thing reared upon its hind legs, towering above you, capable of removing your face with one wipe of its paw, capable of removing the front of your body with another? . . ."

The speaker paused, and stared into the embers of the dying fire.

"You hardly believed your ears when I told of it," he continued, turning to Digby Geste.

"Judge then whether we believed our ears when we heard those words, '*Come and hang your father for me.*'

"We thought it was a joke—a typical Russian joke. . . .

"It was—but it was a *practical* joke.

"'Fetch the girl again,' said my Lieutenant to the Sergeant, and the great brute, a huge Siberian, strode off and returned in a minute with my poor Wanda—weeping, half-fainting in his arms.

"'Aha, our little plump partridge! . . . Bring her here,' said this officer and gentleman; and, as Wanda sank to the ground, when the Sergeant put her down beside the chair, he added:

"'Here, wake up, my dear, don't be alarmed. . . . Your brave brother is going to save you,' and he shook her, tearing the shoulder of her nightgown.

"'Oh, thank God,' she said, and, realizing that her father had been brought back, uttered a cry of joy, and scrambled to her feet to rush to him.

"The Lieutenant pulled her back, tearing her nightgown the more.

"'Gently, gently, *golubtchick*,' he said, as he drew her to him. ' Your brother hasn't saved you *yet*. . . . He's going to rescue you and dear Mamma from the naughty men, by doing a little job for me.'

"Wanda raised trusting and grateful eyes to the face of this nobleman—this true *boyar*. My Lieutenant smiled at her, and cupped her chin again.

"'Yes, sweet child,' he added, as he kissed her.

"'*He's going to hang Papa*' . . . and this time his words became real to us.

"We understood.

"'*No!*' my mother screamed. '*No!*'

"'*What?*' shrieked Wanda.

"'*No, no, no*,' screamed my mother.

"'Very well,' smiled my Lieutenant, and turning to the Sergeant gave the order:

"'Take the old woman to the Guard Room just as she is, and the girl to my quarters. Let *her* dress, and take what clothing she wants."

"'Stop!' cried my father, as the Corporal and a couple of men began to hustle my mother from the room, and the Sergeant seized Wanda.

"'Stop. . . . *You will save your mother and sister, my son*,' said our brave old father, a picture of noble dignity. 'You have never disobeyed me, and you will not disobey me now. Do not hesitate for a moment. Are we Russians that we should save ourselves by sacrificing our women? I will show these scum how a *man* can die, and you will live to protect your mother and sister. . . . And perhaps to avenge me ' . . .

"'*No, no, no!*' screamed my mother. 'Take *me*! Take *me*!'

"Wanda shrieked in the Sergeant's arms.

"'Quick, my son,' urged my father. 'How could we live and face each other . . . *afterwards*? . . . How *could* we? . . . I order you to save your mother and sister. . . . How can you hesitate?'

"I turned to the grinning Lieutenant.

"'End this joke, I beg of you, your Excellency,' I prayed. 'See, you have killed my brother. If we have done wrong, you have punished us enough. . . . You do not make war on women and old men. . . . Hang me, and let them go. . . . You said that two would be enough—two out of five, and they are innocent. We have never plotted, nor talked sedition, nor raised a hand against the Government. . . . Be merciful. . . .'

"'Wel-l-l, wel-l-l,' drawled the Lieutenant, 'Mercy is undoubtedly a beautiful thing. I will allow my soft and kindly nature to triumph once again. . . . Yes, yes, my heart shall rule my head. . . . Your adored Mother, and worshipped Sister, shall go free. . . . Your well-beloved and revered father shall *not* be hung.'

"'God bless you, sir,' I whispered.

"'No, he shall not be hung, since you intercede for him so movingly,' he continued. '*He shall hang you, instead!*'

"I stared this monster in the face, incredulous—though subconsciously I knew that he meant what he said. . . .

"And for the moment I was even thankful that my mother and my sister were not there.

"'Well? . . . Come, hurry up! . . . I can't spend the whole night here. Either hang your father, or let him hang you, and thank me for my mercy,' he yawned.

"'Yes, my son, *hasten*,' said my father. 'Your mother will die of cold . . . And Wanda will . . .'

"Oh, my God. . . .

"'Father,' I cried, 'let *me* die.'

"'Silence, my son,' replied the old man. 'Show now of what stuff we sons of Poland are made. . . . You are young and strong, and I look to you to protect your mother and sister—to work for them . . . to comfort them . . . to save them . . . And to *remember* . . . I am old and feeble, and near my end. . . . It is a strong man they need. . . . Obey me for the last time, as you have always obeyed me.'

"And the terrible knowledge grew in my heart that I must drink of this cup. How could I thrust this burden upon my father—this crushing burden, this unbearable cross for him to carry to his grave? For, through every day and hour and minute that he lived, he would have the burning, corroding thought of the deed that he had done. Death would be nothing to it.

"I would choose the harder part. . . .

"But some day I would meet this devilish Russian, face to face. . . .

"'So be it,' I said. 'Give me your blessing, my father.'

"And the brave old man thanked, praised, and blessed me.

"I turned to the Lieutenant.

"'If it is possible that you can do this thing,' I said; 'if you *can* look forward to remembering this night upon your death-bed; if your own soldiers will not prove to be human beings, tear you limb from limb, and stamp you into the mud where you belong—I will save my mother and sister.'

"The Lieutenant smiled.

"'Ah,' he remarked silkily. 'I doubt if *you* will ever spit upon a Russian officer again . . . any more than your dead brother will strike one!'

"He sent two men with orders that my mother and sister be brought back forthwith.

"By the time they arrived, my father was standing beneath the 'suitable' tree, the noose about his neck, the rope dangling from the branch above.

"And God was merciful, for my mother, with a terrible cry of '*Jan! Jan!*' sank down senseless upon the show.

"I glanced from my mother to Wanda, and saw that her body was hanging inanimate in the arms of the big Sergeant.

"Her eyes were closed.

"'*Now*, my son,' said my father in a firm voice. . . .'"

A GENTLEMAN OF COLOUR

"A Gentleman of Colour" is the story of a Japanese legionnaire, Yato, and his enemy, a fellow legionnaire, Klingen. Yato is accomplished in many occupations, including hand-to-hand combat, drawing and tattooing. "A Gentleman of Colour" was published in the February 1929 issue of Hearst's International Combined with Cosmopolitan *and the March 1929 issue of the* Pall Mall Magazine *under the title, "Geisha Girl." The story was also published in book form in* Good Gestes, *which was also published in February 1929. It was reprinted in the Murray (1947) and Macrae-Smith (1948) collection,* Stories of the Foreign Legion. *Sections three, four, and five of "A Gentleman of Colour" were published in* High, *the* TALL *Magazine for Men (February 1958). The entire story was recently (2011) reprinted in* The Big Book of Adventure Stories.

§1

Le Légionnaire Yato was one of the quietest, most retiring and self-effacing men in the Company, and one of the most modest. It seemed to be his highest ambition—an ambition which he almost attained—to escape notice, to blush unseen, and to hide his light beneath a bushel.

And yet, to those who had the seeing eye, he was an extremely interesting person, and for many reasons. He greatly intrigued the Geste brothers, and in spite of his meek, self-effacing humility, they took note of him from the day he arrived, and watched him with interest.

At first sight, and to the casual eye, he was a poor specimen—small, narrow-shouldered, weedy, with yellowish face, a wiry scrub of short hair, and a silly sort of little straggling moustache, the loss of one hair of which would have made an obvious difference.

The mere look of him caused Sergeant-Major Lejaune to feel unwell, and he made no secret of the fact. Indeed, he promised to stuff the little man into a slop-pail and to be ill upon him.

Never had the Geste boys, who were watching the arrival of

this batch of recruits, seen so hopelessly dull, stupid and apathetic a face in their lives, as that of this recruit, while Sergeant-Major Lejaune regarded it; never had they seen one more acutely intelligent, expressive, spirited and observant as Sergeant-Major Lejaune passed on.

"See that?" chuckled Digby to his brothers.

"Yes," replied Beau. "If I were Lejaune I think I'd let that gentleman alone. Wonder what brought him here."

"He's come 'for to admire and for to see,' I should think," said John, "and come a long way too." And as the line of recruits turned to their left and marched off, he added, "His shoulders have been drilled too, and I'll bet you any amount he's worn a sword and spurs."

Other interesting facts transpired later. The mild little man could cut your hair and shave you beautifully, and he could speak your language if you were English, French, Russian or German. He could also sketch rather marvellously, and do pictures of surpassing merit in water-colour and in oil. He preferred to do these drawings and pictures out in the open air—the more open the better—and he had done some beauties of the country round Quetta, for example, and the Khyber Pass, showing all the pretty forts and things.

His manners were delightful, and he gave offence to no man, least of all to those set in authority over him.

To their surprise, the Geste boys—who, during his early recruit days went out of their way to help this lonely little stranger in a strange land—discovered that he knew England fairly well, particularly Portsmouth, Plymouth, Weymouth, Rosyth, Aldershot and Chatham.

For the most part, *le légionnaire* Yato's inoffensiveness, humility, excellent manners, and blameless conduct, kept him out of almost all trouble, official or private—but not entirely. Although a man may camouflage himself with a protective colouring of drab dullness and uniformity, which does indeed protect him by hiding him from general notice, it may not always suffice to hide him from particular notice. His very quietness and mild meekness may be his undoing through attracting the eye of those who need a butt for their diversion, and even more urgently need long-suffering meekness and mildness in that butt.

Two such were Messieurs Brandt and Haff, men who, themselves the butt of their superiors for their stupidity, slovenliness, and general worthlessness, must find someone to be their butt in turn. Almost a necessity of their existence was someone upon whom they could visit the contumely heaped upon themselves. Subconsciously they felt that, for their self-respect's sake, they must stand upon something lower than themselves, or be themselves the lowest things of all.

And this recruit, Yato, seemed so suitable to their purpose, so dull and stupid, so unable to protect himself, so harmless, helpless and hopeless, so proper a target for the shafts of their wit.

So they put thorn-brush in his bed, and unpleasant matter in his *képi* and on his pillow; stole his kit; put a dead mouse in his coffee; arranged a booby-trap for his benefit; fouled his white uniform after he had washed and ironed it; gave him false information, messages and orders, to his discomfiture and undoing; hid his brushes just before kit inspection; stole his soap; cut his bootlaces and generally demonstrated their own wit, humour and jocularity as well as his stupidity, harmlessness and general inferiority to themselves.

One day, Beau Geste and his brothers entered their barrack-room and discovered the cringing Yato ruefully eyeing *les légionnaires* Brandt, Haff, Klingen and Schwartz—four huge and powerful men, who were proposing to toss him in a blanket, having first denuded him of all clothing. The bright idea had been that of Brandt. He had proposed it; Haff had seconded it; and the two, realizing with their wonted brilliance that a blanket has four corners, had impressed the services of the delighted and all-too-willing Schwartz and Klingen.

"Where shall we do it?" roared Schwartz, a great bearded ruffian, strong as a bull, rough as a bear, and sensitive as a wart-hog.

"You won't do it at all," said Beau Geste, advancing to where the four stood about Yato's disordered bed, from which they had dragged a blanket.

"I do not like to be touched and handled," said Yato quietly, in the silence that fell upon the surprised bullies. "Please leave me alone."

"They are going to leave you alone," said Beau Geste.

"Yes! Watch us!" shouted Brandt, and sprang at the cringing little Jap as the mighty Schwartz turned upon Michael Geste, his great hands clenched, his eyes blazing, and his teeth bared. But as he raised his fist to strike, he swung about as something, or someone, fell against him from behind.

It was Brandt.

Using his right arm as though it were an axe, of which the side of the hand from little finger to wrist was the edge, Yato had struck Brandt an extraordinary cutting chopping blow on the neck, below and behind the ear.

As Brandt fell against Schwartz and to the ground, apparently dead, the Jap seized Haff by the collar of his tunic, where it fastened at the throat, and jerked his head violently downward, at the same time himself springing violently upward, so that the top of his bullet-head struck Haff between the eyes with tremendous force.

The huge Schwartz, changing his line of attack, as he turned about, sprang upon Yato, as might a lion upon a gazelle. The gazelle threw itself at the lion's feet—but not in supplication. Before the astonished Gestes could come to the rescue, they saw Yato fling his arms about Schwartz's ankles, causing the upper part of his body to fall forward. And as it did so, Yato astonishingly arose, hugging Schwartz's ankles to his breast.

The result of this lightning movement was that the big man pitched upon his head so heavily that nothing but its thickness saved him from concussion of the brain, and it seemed impossible that his neck should not be broken. And, almost as the body of Schwartz reached the ground, Yato sprang at Klingen, who was in the act of drawing a knife.

Seizing the wrist of the hand that held this ugly weapon, the Japanese wheeled so that he stood beside Klingen, shoulder to shoulder, and facing in the same direction. As he did so, he thrust his left arm beneath Klingen's right, and across his chest, at the same time pulling Klingen's straightened right arm violently downward. There was a distinctly audible crack as the arm broke above the elbow.

Where four burly bullies had gathered about a cringing little man, three lay insensible and one knelt whimpering with pain.

49

"I do not like to be touched and handled," smiled Yato.

"I don't think you will be, to any great extent," smiled Digby Geste in return.

§2

But a man may be touched without being handled, and it was the dominating desire of Klingen's life to "touch" Yato.

It became essential to his continued existence that he should avenge his broken arm, his humiliating defeat and utter overthrow.

For Klingen was a conceited man, devoid of pride, but filled with self-esteem.

He was handsome and he knew it. But "handsome is as handsome does," and Klingen had done most evilly. It was, in fact, by reason of his last and most treacherous love-affair that he was hiding in the Legion.

He was big and strong and bold, and he had been made to grovel groaning at the feet of a man one-half his size. He hated pain, and he had been made to suffer agony unspeakable.

And so he was obsessed with thoughts of vengeance, and lived for the day when the Japanese should make full payment for the insult and the injury he had put upon the bold and brave, the hardy and handsome Klingen.

Meanwhile, a certain poor satisfaction could be obtained by lashing the unspeakable Oriental verbally; for, curiously enough, the Japanese did not resent such abuse—apparently. So when Klingen came out of hospital he poured forth upon his quiet shrinking enemy all the choice epithets, insults and injurious foulness that he had perpetrated, polished and perfected during the miserable leisure of his enforced retirement.

He assured Yato that he was a yellow monkey, a loathsome "native," a *coloured* man, if indeed he were a man at all. Klingen explained fully and carefully that he had always drawn the colour line, and had drawn it straight and strong; also that it was, to him, the very worst aspect of life in the Legion that one was forced to herd with coloured men, natives, that foul scum (or sediment) of humanity which is barely human. He explained that while he hated niggers, abhorred Arabs and detested Chinese, words utterly failed him to express the loathing horror with which he regarded Japs. Brown was bad, black was worse, but what could be said of yellow? That vile bilious colour was disgusting in *anything*—but in human beings it was . . . !

One could be but dumbly sick, and whenever his revolted eye fell upon *le légionnaire* Yato, his revolting stomach almost had its way, and in crude pantomime Klingen would express his feelings.

And Yato would smile.

Furthermore, the good Klingen was at infinite pains to indicate the private and personal hideousness of Yato as distinct from his national bestiality. He would invite all present to contemplate the little man's unspeakable eyes, indescribable moustache, unmentionable nose, unbelievable hair, and unutterable ugliness.

And Yato would smile.

But it was noticed that Klingen never touched the Japanese, nor sought physical retaliation for his broken arm. Nor did Messieurs Haff, Brandt and Schwartz. In fact, these three appeared to entertain feelings rather of reluctant admiration and sporting acquiescence, than of hatred and vengeance, and when Klingen proposed various schemes for Yato's undoing, they would have none of them. They were quite content to regard him as a freak of nature and a human marvel.

Of him they had had quite enough, and it was their firm intention to leave him severely alone.

Not so Klingen. If Klingen were to live, Yato must die; or, better still—far, far better still—suffer some dire, ineffable humiliation, life-long and worse than death.

*　　*　　*　　*　　*　　*　　*

Seated in a row, on a bench in the Jardin Publique, Beau Geste in the middle, the three brothers contemplated the Vast Forever without finding life one grand sweet song.

Life was hard, comfortless, small and monotonous; but quite bearable so long as it yielded a lazy hour when they could sit thus, smoking their pipes in silent communion, or in idle and disjointed conversation about Brandon Abbas. Frequently

Michael would speculate upon Claudia's doings; Digby and John upon those of Isobel.

"Here comes old Yato," murmured Digby. "I'm going to hit him, one day," he added.

"What for?" inquired John.

"Fun," replied Digby.

"Fun for whom—Yato?" inquired Michael.

"Yes," replied Digby. "I want to see what happens to me."

"You won't see," asserted Michael. "You'll only feel."

"Well, you two shall watch and tell me exactly what happens," said Digby. "Then I can do it to you two."

"Good evening, gentlemen," said Yato, with a courteous salute. "Excuse that I approach you."

The brothers rose as one, saluted the tiny man, and invited him to be seated with them.

"Excuse that I intrude with my insignificant presence, gentlemen, but I would humbly venture to do you the honour, and pay you the compliment, of asking a favour of you. You are *samurai*. If one of you gave assent with no more than a nod of his head, it would be a binding contract. . . . Will you do something for me?"

"Yes," replied Beau Geste.

"You do not stop to make conditions, nor to hear what the request may be. You do not fear that it may be something you would not like to do."

"No," replied Beau Geste.

"Ah," smiled Yato, "as I thought. Well, I'm going a long walk one day soon, and I may want something done for me by a friend, after I have gone. I do not *know* that I shall, but it is quite possible. . . ."

"We shall be delighted," said Beau Geste, and his brothers murmured assent.

Yato bowed deeply.

"Honourable sirs," he said.

"Better not tell us anything about your—er—long walk," said Beau Geste. "We shouldn't give you away, of course, but we're not good liars I'm afraid."

"Oh," smiled Yato, "tell them anything and everything that you know, should you be questioned. The honourable authorities will be entirely welcome to me—if they can catch me."

And he rose to go.

"I will leave a note under your pillow or in your *musette*," he continued, addressing Beau Geste. "Goodbye, gentle and honourable sirs. May I have the distinction of shaking the hands?"

"Queer little cove and great little gentleman," observed Digby when Yato had departed.

"Yes," agreed Michael. "A very good friend and a very dangerous enemy, I should say. I suppose he's in the Japanese Secret Service."

"I don't think I will hit him, after all," mused Digby.

§3

Colonel the Baron Hoshiri of the Japanese General Staff, and of the French Foreign Legion (in the name of Yato), made his way along the Rue de Daya with, as he would have said, a song in his heart. There was no smile upon his grim lips, nor expression of joy in his eyes nor upon his face. They were, in fact, utterly expressionless.

But he was very, very happy, for he was returning to his heaven upon earth, at the feet of Fuji Yama—the land of the cherry blossom, the chrysanthemum, the geisha, and the Rising Sun. He was leaving this land of barbarians devoid of manners, arts, graces and beauty.

Also, he had found a little friend, and she gave the lilt to the song that was in his heart.

A Flower from Japan.

Soiled and trodden and cast aside by these barbarian brutes, but still a Flower from Japan.

A pitiful little story—heart-breaking—but the little flower, picked up from the mud, dipped in pure cleansing dew, and set in a vase of fair water, was reviving.

He would take it back to Japan and it would bloom again and live, a thing of beauty and of joy.

Yes, a pitiful little tale.

Her parents had taken her to the *yoshiwara* to earn her dowry. There she had met her future husband, and thence she had been taken—rescued rather it seemed to her—by this man who so earnestly begged her to become his wife. He seemed a nice kind man, and her heart did not sink very much when he told her that they were going to travel to the wonderful West—for he was a merchant, and his business lay in Marseilles.

This was quite true, and in Marseilles, where his business lay, he sold her—in the way of business. Mr. Ah Foo (born in Saigon of a Chinese woman and a French Marine) did very well out of his little bride Sanyora—as he did out of all his other little brides, for he was what one might call a regular marrying man, and had entered the bonds of matrimony scores of times, and each of his wives had entered a bondage unescapable.

From Marseilles, Sanyora had been sold to a gentleman who travelled for his house, in Algiers, and had been taken to that house. Thence she had been appointed, without her knowledge or consent, to a vacancy (created by death—and a knife) in Oran. From there she had been sold into an even fouler bondage in Sidi-bel-Abbès.

Could she do nothing for herself? Yes—fight like a tiger-cat until drugged, and scream appeals for help—in Japanese, the only language she knew.

And, in that language, Colonel Hoshiri had heard her cry to God for death, as he passed below the open shutters of a house in a slum of the Spanish quarter. He had entered, asked for the Japanese girl, made his way to her room, addressed her in Japanese, and told her he only wished to be a friend and deliverer.

And now Sanyora had her own pretty room in a private house in a respectable quarter, and the Colonel had a haven of rest and peace—a refuge and quiet place in which he could take his ease and hear his own language from beautiful lips. Between them, they had made it a tiny corner of Japan, and, day by day, Sanyora grew more and more to be the dainty, charming and delightful geisha, wholly attractive mistress of the arts that delight and soothe and charm the eye and ear—and heart.

*　　*　　*　　*　　*　　*　　*

As usual, *le légionnaire* Yato was watched and followed by

his bitter and relentless enemy, Klingen. A stab in the back, as he passed through some dark alley, would be simple enough, but it would be *too* simple. To a devil like Yato, it would have to be a death-stroke, and he might die without knowing who had killed him. That would be a very poor sort of vengeance.

What Klingen wanted was to hurt him, and hurt him, and *hurt* him . . . humiliate him to the dust . . . disgrace and degrade and shame him . . . torture him to death . . . but a long, slow, lingering death. . . .

One night Yato might go to *le village Nègre*. Anything could happen there. There was no foul and fearful villainy that one could not buy, and a very little money went a very long way in *le village Nègre*. One could certainly have a man waylaid, knocked on the head, gagged and bound and tied down on a native bedstead in a dark room in a native house. One could hire the room and have the key. One could visit one's victim nightly, and taunt him throughout the night. One could let him starve to death, or keep him alive for weeks.

The things one could do! What about that lovely trick of inverting a brass bowl on the man's bare stomach . . . a rat inside the bowl . . . some red-hot charcoal on top of the bowl. . . .

How long does it take the rat to eat his way into, and through, the man? Might it not be too quick a death? No, that was the whole point of it—a good sound slow torture.

Klingen licked his lips and followed the distant figure of Yato with his eyes.

Going to the same house again, was he? A pity he did not go to *le village Nègre*. What could be the attraction here? A woman, of course.

Klingen pondered the thought. There might be something in that . . . especially if he were fond of her. An idea—of dazzling brilliance. Jealousy! No vengeance like it—for a start. Get his woman from him. Was there a girl alive who would give a second glance at that hideous little yellow monkey when the fine big handsome swaggering swashbuckling Klingen was about? What an exquisite moment when the girl (seated on Klingen's knee, her head on Klingen's shoulder, her arms round Klingen's neck) turned languidly to Yato as Yato entered Yato's own room, and said to him in accents of extremest scorn, "Get to hell out of this, you dirty little yellow monkey. The sight and the smell of you make me feel sick in my stomach."

That would be a great moment. And these women could be bought.

*   *   *   *   *   *   *

Ah, yes . . . the little yellow devil was turning into the same house again. It *must* be a woman.

Klingen reconnoitred once again. The usual type of house with a common stairway leading up from a gloomy little basement hall to a rookery of rooms, apartments and flats occupied by hard-working poor people of the better sort.

Klingen hesitated, and for the first time entered the house and looked round the dingy entrance-hall, stone-floored, stucco-walled, gloomily lit by a smoky oil-lamp hanging against the wall, and by the rays that shone through iron-barred window-spaces from a street lamp.

Should he climb the bare, wooden stair that led to the floors above? Why not? Anyone might enter the wrong house by mistake when searching for a friend. Still, it was a pity Schwartz, Haff and Brandt could not be persuaded to come along and have some fun at the expense of the yellow monkey.

Footsteps. . . . Someone coming down the stairs. . . . A little man in seedy European clothing. . . . An idea . . .

"Excuse me, Monsieur," said Klingen, as the man reached the bottom of the stairs. "Can you tell me which is my friend's room? A *légionnaire*—a little fellow—Japanese."

The man shrugged his shoulders and made a gesture with his hands which showed that he was a Spaniard; also that he did not understand a word of what was being said to him.

Klingen mounted to the first floor, a bare landing, around three sides of which were closed, numbered doors. Should he tap at each in turn, and inquire for some non-existent person? And what should he do if one of them were opened by Yato? Suppose the yellow tiger-cat attacked him again? His mended arm tingled at the thought. What was he doing here at all? This longing for vengeance was driving him mad. . . .

Klingen turned back, descended to the street, and took up his stand in a doorway from which he could keep watch upon the porch of the house in which was his enemy.

Another idea! . . . What about waiting until Yato left the house? He could then go in and knock at every door and ask:

"Is my friend *le légionnaire* Yato here—a little Japanese?" If one of the doors were opened by some woman who replied, "No, he has just gone," he would know that he had found what he sought, and would get to work forthwith. He would soon show her the difference between a Yato and a Klingen. And if Klingen knew anything of women, and he flattered himself that he most certainly did, there was a bad time coming for the yellow devil. . . . He could almost hear the very accents in which she should say:

"Get out of my sight, you filthy yellow cur. I've got a *man* now!"

"Yes, and Klingen would have his knife ready too, and this time he'd throw it, if Yato made trouble. And he also flattered himself that he knew something of knife-throwing.

*　　*　　*　　*　　*　　*　　*

Ha! There he was. . . . Blister and burn him!

The retreating form of Yato turned the corner of the street, and Klingen darted across into the house. Running lightly up the stairs he knocked at the first door. No answer. He knocked again, and laid his ear against the wood.

Silence.

He knocked at the next. A fat, slatternly woman, candle in hand, opened the door and eyed him hardily.

"Well?" she inquired, running her eye contemptuously over his uniform.

"Monsieur Blanc?" inquired Klingen.

The woman slammed the door in his face.

The third and fourth rooms were apparently empty.

A child opened the door of the fifth, and seeing a *légionnaire*, shut it instantly. Hearing a man's deep growling voice within, Klingen passed on.

To Klingen's inquiry, at the sixth room, as to whether Monsieur Blanc lived here, the woman who occupied it replied that he did, but was at the moment in the wine-shop round the corner!

"Then may he sit there till he rots," observed Klingen, and climbed the second flight of stairs, and, arriving at a landing similar to the one below, repeated his strategy and tactics.

The first door was opened by a tiny dainty Japanese girl, and Klingen thrust his way into the room, closed the door behind him, locked it, and removed the key.

He had found what he wanted.

The girl stood staring, between terror and surprise. This man was in a similar uniform to that which her lover wore. He must be his friend, otherwise how would he have known she was here? But her beloved had only just gone. Had something happened to him, and why had this man thrust in so roughly, uninvited. But they were rough and rude, these Western barbarians. Why had he come? Did he think this place was like one of those dreadful houses in Marseilles, Algiers and Oran? And she shuddered at the thought.

Oh, if she could only understand what he was saying and make herself understood by him! He seemed to be speaking of someone named Yato. Was it conceivable that he might understand a word of Japanese?

"I am the servant of the Colonel Hoshiri. What do you want?" she said in her own tongue.

And, for reply, Klingen snatched her up in his arms and kissed her violently.

Well, this was a fine *affaire*! . . . This marched! . . . She might, or might not, be Yato's girl, but most certainly she was. A Japanese would hardly be visiting a house in a Sidi-bel-Abbès side-street in which there was a Japanese woman, unless he were visiting her. Japs were not so common in the African hinterland as that. . . . But anyhow, and whoever she was, this was still a fine *affaire*, for here was Klingen the irresistible, locked up in a room with as pretty a little piece as he had ever clapped eyes on. And a very nice room, too, if a little bare. Bed, cushions, hangings, flowers in vase—yes, all very nice indeed.

And now for the little woman. A pity they could not understand each other's language, but the language of love is universal. He could soon make himself understood all right.

When *le légionnaire* Klingen let himself out of the room an hour or so later, he left a sobbing girl lying upon the bed weeping as though her heart would break; moaning as though it were already broken.

But Klingen, as he walked back to barracks, smiled greasily as he licked his lips, and encountering Yato in the barrack-room, laughed aloud.

Yato was sitting on his bed engaged in *astiquage*—the polishing of his belts and straps.

Having whispered his story, punctuated with loud guffaws, to a little knot of his friends who evidently enjoyed the joke hugely, Klingen went over and stood in front of the Japanese, his hands on his hips, and, rocking himself to and fro, from heels to toes, leered exultingly. Without looking up, Yato continued waxing and polishing a cartridge-pouch.

Suddenly he stopped—remained perfectly still, and stared at the floor between himself and Klingen.

Beau Geste drawing near, and watching carefully as he polished his bayonet, thought that Yato sniffed silently, as though trying to detect and capture an odour. Yes, decided Beau, Yato could smell something, and that something puzzled him. Rising to his feet, his hands behind him, and moving slowly, the Japanese approached Klingen, his head thrust forward, his nose obviously questing.

"What the hell!" growled Klingen, as Yato, his face not very much above the big man's sash, deliberately smelt at him.

Yato returned to his cot without remark.

But it seemed as though a shadow crossed his face. It was almost as though he changed colour.

§4

Le légionnaire Klingen, smart in his walking-out kit, a red *képi*, dark-blue tunic with green red-fringed epaulettes, red breeches and white spats, tightened his belt a little, pulled his bayonet frog further back, and swaggered from the barrack-room.

It was "holiday" (pay-day) and he intended to expend on wine the entire sum of 2½*d*. which he had received. Thereafter, being full of good wine and good cheer, it was his intention to see how the little Japanese girl was getting on, and to cheer her loneliness with an hour of his merry society. He would watch the yellow monkey go in, and wait till he came out, and if the girl had locked her door, he would tap and tap and knock and knock without saying anything until she did open it.

What a fighting little spit-fire she was. But that was nine-tenths make-believe, and the other tenth was ignorance of French.

From his seat on a barrel, in the corner of a dark wine-shop which commanded a view of the street in which the girl's house stood, Klingen saw Yato approaching. Pulling down the vizor of his *képi*, and bending his head forward, so that his face was concealed, he waited until the Japanese had passed, and then abandoned himself to the pleasures of drinking, anticipation, and thoughts of revenge.

He was absolutely certain that the girl was Yato's, and, as he rolled his wine upon his tongue, he rolled upon the debauched palate of his mind the flavour of the lovely vengeance that combined the enormous double gratification of deep enjoyment to himself and deep injury to Yato. He honestly agreed with Klingen that Klingen was a great man, and never greater than in this manifestation of his skill—that made his own pleasure his enemy's agony at a time when his enemy's agony was his own greatest pleasure.

On the whole, it had turned out to be quite a good thing that Schwartz, Brandt and Haff had declined to take any further hand in baiting Yato. Any vengeance, obtained with their help, could only have been crude and obvious, and have contained but the single satisfaction of injuring Yato.

But this was subtle, private, worthy of Klingen.

"Yes, my friend," he mused, sucking the wine-drops from his moustache. "I hurt you by delighting myself, and you add immeasurably to that delight by being hurt."

And he laughed aloud.

A couple of thieves and their women, a fat person clothed from head to foot in brown corduroy, and an obese dealer in old clothes who wore a tarboosh (or fez), a frock-coat, a collarless blue shirt, football shorts, and a pair of curly-toed slippers, all turned to stare at the big soldier who laughed loudly at nothing.

"Mad," said a thief, and shrugged his shoulders.

"Drunk," growled the other.

"Mad *and* drunk," said a lady.

"*Que voulez-vous? C'est la Legion!*" observed her sister in joy, and drank to the health of *le légionnaire* Klingen, in methylated spirit. As his tenth *caporal* cigarette began to singe his moustache, and the last glass of his third bottle began to exhibit sediment, Klingen again pulled his cap over his eyes, and dropped his chin upon his chest. A small figure in the uniform of the Legion was passing on the other side of the road.

Two minutes later, Klingen was knocking at the door of the room in which dwelt the Japanese girl. To his first knock no answer was vouchsafed; to the second, a thin, high, childish voice replied unintelligibly. It might have been in invitation or prohibition.

Klingen turned the handle and, to his surprise, found that the door was not fastened. Entering the room, he saw a little figure on the remembered bed, its back toward him, its head and shoulders covered by a silken shawl. Turning, he locked the door, and slipped the key into his pocket.

The figure on the bed moved slightly and did not turn to him.

The little hussy! What was the game? Perhaps-I-will-perhaps-I-won't? Or was she pretending she hadn't heard him come in? Going to make a scene, perhaps, in the hope of extorting payment. Well, she'd be a clever girl if she got money out of Klingen! The other way about, more likely.

With quickened breathing, gleaming eye, and smiling lips, Klingen took a couple of steps in the direction of the bed, and from it, casting off shawl and covering, sprang Yato, lightly clad, his face devilish in its ferocity.

Klingen's right hand went to his bayonet and Yato's right hand, open, shot upward, so that the bottom of the palm struck Klingen beneath the chin. As it did so, Yato heaved mightily upward, as though hurling a sack of potatoes which was balanced on his hand. It was as if the Japanese lifted Klingen by the face, and flung him backward off his feet. But even as his enemy was in the act of falling, Yato flung his arm about him, and turning him sideways, fell heavily with him—Klingen being face downward. Instantly Yato, whose knee was in the small of

Klingen's back, his right hand on his neck, seized Klingen's right wrist, and, dragging the arm upward and backward with a swift movement, dislocated his shoulder, and, as the prostrate man yelled in agony, Yato, with a similar movement of dexterous and powerful leverage, dislocated the other.

As Klingen again roared with pain, Yato hissed like a cat, and, with a grip of steel, dug his thumb and fingers into his victim's neck, with a grip that changed a howl to a broken whimper.

Five minutes later, Klingen's wrists were bound behind him with steel wire, his ankles were fastened together with a strap, and he was bound down upon the bed with a many-knotted rope, in such a manner that he could not raise his knees, nor his head, nor change his position by so much as an inch.

A large handkerchief or rag completely filled his mouth, and a piece of steel wire, passing round his face from beneath his chin to the top of his head, prevented him from ejecting it. In fact, the so-recently active and joyous *légionnaire* Klingen could now move nothing but his eyes, could only see and hear—and suffer.

What was this yellow devil going to do with him? Mutilate him as the Arabs mutilate *les légionnaires* when they fall into their hands? And Klingen shuddered, as he thought of the photographs that hang in every Legion barrack-room for the discouragement of deserters . . . photographs of the remains of things that have been men.

Was Yato going to carve and fillet him? Blind him? Cut his tongue out? Torture him with a red-hot iron? Cripple him for life? Destroy his hands, and so his livelihood? Or merely leave him there to die a dreadful lingering death of thirst and starvation?

He thought of what he himself had hoped and intended to do, if he could have had Yato waylaid in *le village Nègre*.

And he could not utter a word of supplication or remonstrance, nor make offer and promise of impossible reparation and bribe.

What was the cruel, wicked devil doing now? Heating an iron, sharpening a knife, boiling some water? These cursed Japs were artists at fiendish torture, and had a devilish ingenuity beyond the conception of simple, honest Westerners with their kindly hearts and generous natures.

What was he doing? *O God*, what *was* he doing? Something unthinkable . . . something unimaginable.

But, strangely enough, Yato was merely engaged in the exercise of one of his many peaceful and lawful pursuits. Seated comfortably beside *le légionnaire* Klingen, to whom he addressed no remark of any sort, he was making a selection from a number of small objects neatly packed in a sandal-wood box. A faint, but pleasing odour came from this; also a small oblong cake of some black substance, in the powerful delicate fingers of the Japanese. Taking a tiny saucer from the box, he poured into it a little water from the flower-vase, and in this placed the end of the black cake, that it might soak while he dispassionately studied the contorted face of his enemy. Anon, taking the cake in his fingers, he sketched broad lines of the deepest black upon Klingen's forehead and cheeks. Klingen, expecting either burn or slash, winced and shuddered as the substance touched his face. Settling down to his work, unhurried, methodical, and calm, Yato rubbed and dipped, rubbed and dipped, until the face of Klingen was as black as soot—even to the eyelids, lips, ears, and throat.

Having completed this portion of his task to his satisfaction, Yato again considered the contents of the box, and selected another small stick. With this he most carefully continued his work, a keen and conscientious craftsman.

And then, changing his tools, Yato, with patient artistry, laboured long and well, to render indelible his striking effects. With a long-handled brush, whose bristles were needles of steel, he tapped and tapped and tapped at forehead, cheeks and chin, until the blood began to ooze. With separate and single needles, he worked faithfully and well, in the places where the broader tools would fail of full effect. . . .

And at last he rose, an artist satisfied, fulfilled, and gazed upon the face of his enemy.

§5

Le légionnaire Yato was not seen again in the barracks of the Legion. But, three days later, Beau Geste received a letter which reminded him of his promise to help his humble Japanese comrade. All the latter had to ask was that his honourable friend would proceed, forthwith, accompanied by his two honourable brothers, to a described house, and there, having asked a certain man for the key, go to room No. 7, and give freedom and assistance to an unfortunate man confined therein. Should they fail to do this, the poor fellow would starve to death. . . .

Michael, Digby and John did as they were asked.

"*Good God!* Yato!" ejaculated Michael, as they gazed upon Klingen.

"The wicked *devil!*" murmured John.

"What they call a 'gentleman of colour,'" observed Digby,— for, until the worms devoured it, the whole face of Klingen would be a deep blue-black, save for the nose of glowing red.

DAVID AND HIS INCREDIBLE JONATHAN

"David and His Incredible Jonathan" is a story related by La Cigale about two legionnaires who are polar opposites in personality, but also the closest of friends. During a quarrel one of them is mortally injured. "David and His Incredible Jonathan" first appeared in Good Gestes *(1929), and was reprinted in the British magazine* Argosy *(September 1930) and in* Stories of the Foreign Legion *(Murray 1947).*

§1

"Ready, pup?" inquired Michael Geste, turning to where his brother John was endeavouring satisfactorily to arrange his hair by means of a brush originally intended for quite other purposes, and a mirror so small that the work had, as Digby observed, to be done by sections—if not by numbers.

As the three brothers looked each other over, in turn, with a view to avoiding unpleasantness at the gates, where a crapulous and arbitrary Sergeant of the Guard would turn them back if it were possible to find the slightest fault with their appearance, La Cigale approached them.

La Cigale, the Grasshopper, a nobleman of ancient family and once an officer of the Belgian Corps of Guides, was a kind and gentle madman, whose mental affliction had hitherto in no way interfered with his soldiering. At times he was quite mad, and at others appeared quite sane.

Returning to the depôt at Sidi-bel-Abbès, from a long tour of foreign service, he had re-enlisted for the third time, a veteran soldier *de carrière*. With the Geste boys he was a favourite, as well as a source of wonder, admiration and respect. Michael said he was not only a noble, but one of Nature's noblemen, as well as one of God's own gentlemen; Digby said he reminded him of himself; and John, that he was about the most lovable and pathetic thing in human form.

And he had been for fifteen years a private soldier of the Legion!

"Are you gentlemen going anywhere in particular?" asked La Cigale with his pleasant, friendly smile.

"No," replied Michael, "just going to walk abroad, and give the public a treat."

"You were going alone, of course, a single and indivisible trinity."

"We were," admitted Michael, "but we should be delighted if you would care to join us."

"Charmed," murmured Digby and John.

"Thank you so very much," replied La Cigale. "I'm sure that you mean what you say, and that your politeness is not hollow. . . . Had you not invited me, I was going to summon up courage to ask if I might come with you to-night. . . . I am frightened."

The brothers glanced at the old soldier's *Croix de Guerre*, *Médaille Militaire*, and other medals, with incredulous smiles.

"And of what is the *doyen* of the First Battalion of the First Regiment of the Legion afraid?" asked Michael.

"Of loneliness," was the reply, "and of myself. It is terrible to be utterly lonely in the midst of such a crowded life as this, and it is even more terrible to be afraid of oneself—afraid of what one may do. I am haunted by the dread of doing something awful, horrible, disgraceful, and knowing nothing about it until it is too late. And I get these attacks—I can't describe them. I have one coming on now. Every nerve in the body tingles and burns, from the brain to the finger-tips and toes. Every cell in the body shrieks and screams, and I must do something, *do* something—something drastic, and do it instantly. But what that something is, I do not know. It is agony unspeakable. I would sooner have a dozen wounds."

"Come for a walk and a talk," interrupted Michael Geste, as La Cigale paused. It was obvious that the less he thought about himself the better.

"Let's go and find a quiet spot in the Gardens, and perhaps you'll give us the pleasure and benefit of hearing of some of your campaigning experiences? We should like to follow in your footsteps, you know."

"Rather," agreed Digby, "and get as many decorations among the three of us."

"Regard us as your sons, sir, and take us in hand," murmured John.

The quartette set forth, saluted the Sergeant of the Guard, and found themselves safely in the lane that separates the Legion's Barracks from those of the Spahis.

Having induced La Cigale to share a light and not wholly inelegant meal at the *Café de l'Europe*, Michael Geste proposed that they should adjourn and listen to the Legion's band as it played in the public Gardens.

"For myself—I dare not," replied La Cigale. "At times music has a terrible effect upon me. If they were to play a selection from a certain opera that was world-famous when I was a young man, I should go mad. I should completely lose control of . . ."

"Then let's go and sit on a seat in the moonlight, and you shall talk to us. We should enjoy that far more," said Michael quickly. "Come along."

"Not in the moonlight," objected La Cigale, "if you don't mind. Some nice dark place in deep shadow. I think moonlight is terrible—such memories."

*   *   *   *   *   *   *

"I can't tell you how delightful it is to me, to know you," said La Cigale, as they seated themselves on a bench in a dark corner of the Gardens. "Gentlemen and Englishmen. I've always been fond of the English. There was an astonishingly delightful Englishman here, who was a friend of mine for years. Killed trying to escape, with two compatriots—one of them a charming fellow—and a very attractive American.

"Then there was poor young Edwards—yes, he called himself Edwards, I remember."

"And what became of him?" asked Michael, as La Cigale fell into reminiscent silence.

"To young Edwards? Oh, it was a terrible tragedy. I will tell you."

§2

"David Edwards, as he called himself, joined the Legion

some years ago, and was one of the most puzzling of the many people whose presence in the Legion is a puzzle to all who know them.

"He was one of the nicest fellows I've ever known, and it was impossible to suppose that he had left his country for his country's good, or had chosen the Legion as a refuge. It was quite obvious that it was not poverty nor vice, crime, debt, disgrace nor anything of that kind, that had been the cause of his coming here. Nor did he strike one as being of the born soldier type—one of those men who are cut out for a military career, and are fitted for no other. And he wasn't one of the wildly adventurous sort, mad-cap and hare-brained. It was my good fortune to be put in charge of him when he arrived, that I might show him the ropes, and instruct him as to *astiquage, paquetage* and so forth.

"We had much in common, including one or two acquaintances, for I knew the part of England from which he came, and he knew Brussels, where his father, evidently in the Diplomatic Service, had been stationed.

"He was extremely kind and friendly to me, but his *real* friend, pal, and *copain* was, extraordinarily enough, an astounding rascal of the name of Jean Molle.

"It was indeed a case of the attraction of opposites, for this man Molle was all that Edwards was not—the one a gutter-bred rough, the other a public-school man of family and refinement.

"It was really interesting to watch these two, and try to discover what it was in each that interested the other. One would have supposed that Edwards would only have seen in Molle a coarse ignorant ruffian, devoid alike of manners and morals, and that Molle would have seen in Edwards a white-handed, finnicking fine gentleman, full of irritating affectations and superiorities.

"Molle, who had been a Paris market-porter at his best, and a foot-pad *apache* at his worst, was a huge powerful person of most violent temper, and an uncontrollable addiction to drink. But he was droll, I must admit—really very funny when half-sober or half-drunk, and a born mimic, clown, and buffoon. I should think that he must have been attached to a circus in some such capacity, or perhaps was born in one, and he made David

Edwards laugh—laugh until the tears ran down his face, and he had to beg Molle to stop impersonating a *curé*, a *cocotte*, a Colonel, an old market-woman, a Sergeant-Major, or whatever it might be.

"Yes, Molle was very good for Edwards from that point of view, for he kept the Englishman laughing—and laughter is the salt of life, both as savour and a preservative. And, of course, Edwards did not understand the vileness of one half of Molle's remarks, spoken in his almost incomprehensible and wholly untranslatable *argot* of the slums and *halles* of Paris.

"And Edwards was good for Molle in every possible way, and gave the creature ideas such as he had never before dreamed of, standards and ideals hitherto unglimpsed by this sewer-rat.

"Surely a more ill-assorted pair never foregathered, even in the Foreign Legion. I think Edwards grew quite fond of Molle, as the benefactor often does grow fond of the beneficiary, and undoubtedly Molle really loved David Edwards. He would have thrashed anyone who said a word against him, and killed anyone who injured him.

"They quarrelled, of course—as friends must do—generally on the subject of Molle's drunkenness and debauchery. He was one of those *canaille* who simply must, from time to time, give way to the demands of their gross appetites, slink into some horrible hole, and drink themselves insensible.

"Edwards was really wonderful when his friend eluded him and got drunk. He would go from wine-shop to wine-shop in the Spanish quarter, search the houses that are in bounds for troops, ransack *le village Nègre* itself, and when successful, be rewarded by a torrent of oaths and a drunken blow. Time after time he was punished with *salle de police* for coming in late, supporting his drunken friend, whom, for hours, he had been trying to get back to Barracks.

"Never did he desert the drunken brute, even though it meant being out the whole night and returning too late for parade, but not too soon for severe punishment.

"I myself, when on guard, have seen them at the gate in the small hours of the morning—Edwards, who was a teetotaller, by the way, bleeding about the face, and with torn and muddied uniform, supporting and endeavouring to control the singing, shouting, raving Molle, and striving to prevent him from assaulting the Sergeant and resisting the Guard.

"After these disgusting, disgraceful affairs, Molle would be tearfully repentant, grovelling in apology, and loud in self-accusation and promises of reform, and for a time he would behave well, would walk out with Edwards and return quiet, clean, sober and punctual for roll-call.

"Nevertheless he was always extremely dangerous after one of these orgies, for his terrible temper would be in a highly explosive condition—a thing not to be wondered at, in view of the fact that he had consumed gallons of assorted alcohol, and been knocked on the head when fighting like a wild beast to prevent being thrown into the *salle de police*.

"I never ceased to admire the moral and physical courage with which Edwards would come between Molle and his desires when the evil fit was on him, and tackle him when he was in the surly and quarrelsome stages of drunkenness. Undoubtedly, Edwards saved Molle from three times as much imprisonment as he got, and Molle was the cause of practically every punishment awarded to Edwards.

"Can you understand such a friendship between two such men—between a cultured man of breeding and a dissolute brute like Molle? But there it was. And the only explanation I can offer, is that Edwards imagined himself more or less responsible for this creature who had attached himself to him as a stray and homeless mongrel dog will attach himself to a man, and who loved him as such a dog will do.

"Some men will risk their lives to save a dog, and thereafter be very fond of it, and I suppose it was in some such spirit that Edwards risked his life in *le village Nègre*, and his peace, prospects and reputation in the Legion—and became fond of the dog Molle.

"And then one night the tragedy occurred, strangely, suddenly and unexpectedly, as tragedy does occur.

"Molle had been drinking. After evening *soupe* he had evaded Edwards, slipped out by himself, and gone to drink in a low wine-shop. Unfortunately he had not the money to buy enough liquor to make himself drunk, but merely sufficient to see him through the successive stages of hilarity and despondency into that of a quarrelsome moroseness.

"Making his way back to Barracks when his money was gone, and carrying, with the air of a dour teetotaller, enough assorted liquor to intoxicate half a dozen, he strode past the Guard Room across the Parade Ground, and up to his Barrack Room. Here he sat himself down in morose and sulky silence, and sullenly cleaned and polished his kit.

"As he sat, gloomy, heavy and repellent, a dangerous and ugly customer to tackle, Edwards came into the room. He was wearing walking-out kit and overcoat.

"'Oh, there you are,' he cried, on catching sight of Molle. 'I've been looking for you everywhere.'

"'Am I a dog that I should be hunted? And by a thing like you?' growled Molle, glaring angrily at Edwards.

"'Yes,' replied Edwards pleasantly. 'A dirty dog,' and strode across to where Molle sat.

"'Oh! I am a dirty dog, am I?' muttered Molle quietly, without looking up.

"'Regular mongrel,' agreed Edwards, 'but full of clever tricks. . . . Sit up and beg. . . . Up, Fido! Beg, Fido!'

"Molle rose to his feet obedient—and spat in Edwards' face.

"I told you he was a creature of pleasant habits! And I told you Edwards was brave.

"Although Molle was about twice his size, and four times as strong, he let drive instantly with all his strength and landed Molle as fine a smack in the eye as ever I saw a man receive.

"Molle struck back, hitting Edwards with such force that both he and Edwards fell to the ground.

"At that moment there was a cry of '*Fixe!*' and every one sprang to attention, as our Major came into the room. Molle, full of liquor though he was, scrambled to his feet, and stood like a statue at the foot of his bed, steady as a rock.

"Edwards lay where he was—on his face—gasping and coughing.

"'*What's this, then?*' snapped the Major, a man who was always in a terrific hurry. He occasionally made these sudden inspection raids, and indiscriminately dealt out severe punishments to all and sundry.

"Edwards gasped, groaned, and partly raised himself on his

right elbow.

"'I am drunk,' he said clearly, and collapsed.

"'Drunk and fighting in the Barrack Room,' shouted the Major. 'Assaulting your comrades. No one else here is drunk. A drunken, quarrelsome disturber of discipline. . . .'

"And more of the same sort of thing, ending up with an order that the drunkard should be removed immediately and thrown into prison.

"'He is not drunk, *Monsieur le Majeur,*' interrupted Molle, stepping forward and saluting. 'It is I.'

"'Four days' cells for daring to address me, for contradiction and attempted interruption of the course of justice,' roared the incensed officer, as soon as he recovered from his shocked surprise at Molle's temerity.

"I would have spoken up for Edwards myself, but for the absolute certainty that I should also incur a sentence of imprisonment without the slightest possibility of doing him any good. Quite the contrary, in all probability.

"Edwards, really looking the part of a quarrelsome drunkard who had been badly knocked about, was carried off and dumped in a cell, while Molle was led away to the *salle de police.*

"That night I was on guard, and as it happened, it was I who first entered Edwards' cell in the morning, to take him the loaf of bread and drop of water that would be his food for the day. He was lying face downward on the dirty floor, his left arm bent beneath him, and his right extended, the hand touching the wall of the cell. Just above it, I could see, in the dim light, smears and smudges, such as might have been made by a child playing with a house-painter's brush on which still remained a very little half-dried red paint.

"Just so might a little girl, named Susan, have tried to write her name upon the wall—for the first smeared hieroglyphic was a crude but unmistakable *S*, followed by what was almost certainly the letter *U*.

"A finger, dipped in blood, had made the rough double curve that was an S, had twice made a stroke beside it, and, when a little more of the slow and painful medium was available, had joined the bases of the strokes with a curve.

"I saw this much, at a glance, as I knelt to do what I could for

John Edwards. He was quite dead, and had obviously died from loss of blood, after having stabbed himself, or having been stabbed, in the left breast.

"Yes, my friend was dead; I could not be mistaken as to that—I who have seen so many die.

"I looked again at the wall. '*SU*' he had painfully scrawled while still comparatively strong. I think he had then fainted, or perhaps had waited. . . .

"So much of the blood had been absorbed by his clothing, and the pad he had made with his neck-cloth.

"Oh yes, he had done his best, poor boy, but had probably grown too weak to do any more for himself than to staunch the flow of blood.

"Yes, as I read the signs, he had fainted, had revived, and realized that he was dying; had painfully scrawled the first two letters, and had then collapsed—probably through fresh hæmorrhage caused by the effort.

"For there was a space after the *U*, and then a straight stroke, followed by a curved one. Near the top of this was a single finger-print. Evidently, with failing sight and ebbing strength, he had tried to make this curve into the letter *C*, and, ere the heavy hand fell from the wall, he had smeared the beginning of another stroke.

"'*SUICI*' had been accomplished, and he had then either rested from these last labours of his brief life, or had again been overcome by that dreadful sinking faintness that attacks us as the life-stream ebbs from wounds.

"Once again he had recovered. This time he had made a mighty effort, and had been but too well provided with the dreadful medium in which he worked.

"Below the other letters, and a foot to the right of them, shakily but clearly were written the final *D* and *E*.

"*Suicide*!

"*Why*? And with what weapon. And where was it?

"He was not wearing his bayonet, of course. Had he a dagger or clasp-knife which he had returned to its place of concealment, after inflicting upon himself a death-wound? And if so, why?

"And then again, why spend his last minutes of terrible agony—as he lay upon the very brink of the grave, and imminent dissolution was upon him, in such work? Why, I asked myself, should he have been at such pains—such unthinkable pains—to smear this dreadful writing on the wall, in his own life-blood?

"When a *légionnaire* commits suicide, he commits suicide, and there's an end of it. He doesn't trouble to write about it. It is obvious. If he should have anything to record about his death, he would write it before killing himself, wouldn't he?

"Reverently I assured myself of the fact that he had no concealed knife or dagger, and then that there was, in the cell, absolutely nothing of any sort or kind with which he could have inflicted this wound upon himself. A man cannot give himself a neat and clean stab, three quarters of an inch long, a quarter of an inch wide, and deep enough to kill him, without a knife, or something that can be used as a knife blade.

"Men have hanged themselves with their braces, strangled themselves with their bootlaces, opened veins and arteries with a nail, and battered their heads against their cell walls. There is always a way for a determined man to put an end to himself, but he can't fatally stab himself—without at least a piece of glass, or of hard and pointed wood.

"Could David Edwards have had an enemy who had entered his cell and murdered him during the night?

"Absurd nonsense! How could such a man get into the cell, unless it were the Sergeant of the Guard himself? And, if a prisoner were murdered in this way, would he write '*Suicide*' upon the wall as he died?

"It has taken me some time to tell you all this, but I don't suppose it took a second for these thoughts to flash through my mind.

"And then I decided that when a man, at such terrible cost, proclaims the fact that he has committed suicide, he has almost certainly not committed suicide at all, and of course I was confirmed in this belief by my absolute certainty that there was nothing in the cell with which he could have stabbed himself.

"Although I knew that it was perfectly useless to do so, I opened the door of the cell, and examined the floor of the narrow passage outside. As you may not be aware, those beastly cells have no window, grating, nor aperture communicating with the open air. There is nothing but the grating above the door that opens into the passage. It was just conceivably possible that Edwards had stabbed himself with a knife, and had then contrived to throw it between the bars of the grating, so that it fell in the passage without.

"Apart from the fact that this would be an extremely difficult thing to do, and that the sentry would hear the knife fall, why should a suicide do such a thing, particularly when he intended to take the trouble to proclaim the fact that it was suicide?

"Surely it would be obvious enough that he had taken his own life, if the knife were found lying beside him, or gripped in his hand, or sticking in his chest. On what conceivable grounds should a man, after inflicting a mortal wound upon himself, proclaim the fact of suicide and carefully conceal the means whereby it was effected?

"Life has presented me with some sore puzzles, my friends, but I think this was the most insoluble problem with which I had been confronted.

"Well, there it was, in all its stark simplicity of fact. Edwards was dead, with a stab near the heart; there was no knife or other weapon in the place, and he had written the word '*Suicide*' in his own blood.

"And there it was in all its bewildering complexity, its incredibility, its sinister insoluble impossibility. And there I left it.

"I reported to the Sergeant of the Guard that the prisoner in No. 1 had committed suicide.

"The body was carried to the hospital for autopsy, and thence to the mortuary, in the kind of coffin they give the *légionnaire*.

"Next day, David Edwards was buried in the Cemetery of the Legion, and doubtless one can still find his grave—for it became rather famous, and probably the *légionnaire*-pensioner in charge of the Cemetery looks after it. In the past he must have made quite a few sous by exhibiting it.

"No, it was not the mystery attaching to the death of Edwards that made his grave a nine days' wonder. No one takes much notice of the suicide of a *légionnaire*, however interestingly he made contrive his death.

"It was what happened, a week after he had been buried."

§3

"When Molle came out of prison, his first thought was of his friend, and he hurried in search of him. I was in the Barrack Room when he entered, looking all the worse for his term of *cellule* punishment.

"He stared in astonishment at seeing another man sitting on Edwards' cot and obviously occupying his place.

"'*Here, you—where's Edwards?*' he said, approaching the new-comer, a big Alsatian named Gronau.

"'Dead and buried,' growled the fellow, with an ugly laugh.

"Molle planted himself in front of Gronau, his big hands tense, flexed, about to clutch. . . .

"'*Where's Edwards?* I asked you,' he said.

"I got up with some idea of getting Molle away, but Gronau answered again,

"'*Dead*, I tell you! . . . Dead and buried. Dead and damned.'

"And Molle sprang upon him, literally like a wild beast.

"It took half a dozen of us to get him off Gronau before he had choked the life out of him.

"The Alsatian, although a big powerful fellow, was like a child in the hands of Molle.

"We got him down and held him down, and for a time it was more like holding a horse than a man.

"Then suddenly he fell quiet, as though all his strength had gone out of him. And it had.

"His attack on Gronau was his last activity—his last effort, if you understand me.

"He had grasped the fact that David Edwards was dead, and it broke him, mentally and physically. Yes, that is what he was, a broken man—heart-broken and broken in spirit.

"For a few days he moved about, doing things automatically. He reminded me of those stories, that one has heard and read, of the dog that loses its master and straightway loses all interest in life, refuses food and pines and droops. Sometimes such a dog will go and lie upon its master's grave and refuse to be moved.

"Such a dog was Molle.

"He never spoke: he never smiled; scarcely did he raise his

eyes from the ground. He did not sleep; he did not eat, and, marvellously, he did not drink.

"What would one have expected such a creature to do? Obviously to drink himself to death.

"Granted that he were sufficiently human and humane to have been capable of such a love, one would have supposed its effect would have been a plunge into the depths of debauchery, a drowning of sorrow in drink. Surely, nine times out of ten, a man of this type would seek the only anodyne he knows, his accustomed way of escape from reality.

"But no! this astonishing Jonathan took the loss of his David differently, and the debauché became the ascetic, instead of submerging his troubled soul beneath a sea of alcohol.

"I tried to get *en rapport* with him.

"He did not so much repulse me as fail to realize me. I made no impression upon him, and nothing that I said appeared to reach his mind. I think that was wholly unreceptive, as though it had frozen into a solid block of fact—one dreadful fact—*My friend is dead.*

"One day I said to him, 'Look here, Molle. If you don't eat you'll die. Even your strength can't last much longer. Come out with me to-night. We'll have supper together in some nice quiet place.'

"'*Eh?*' he replied.

"And when I had repeated what I had said, he again murmured, '*Eh?*'—and that was as far as I could get with him.

"I completely failed to make him realize that I, more than any man, could understand how he suffered. I, who had lost every one and everything; I, whose mind, like his, had suddenly died.

"With a word of sympathy on my lips, and genuine sorrow in my heart, I turned and left him.

"But I spoke to him once again, and got an answer.

"For my evening walk, I strolled to the cemetery to visit the grave of David Edwards, just to lay a flower and say a word of farewell to a dead comrade.

"A foolish thing, of course, and one I often wonder at—this connecting of the freed and soaring spirit with the poor corrupting clay, and its last resting-place.

"But poor humanity must have its concrete symbols. . . .

"And there was Jean Molle before me lying prone upon the grave.

"I went to raise him up. His left hand was buried quite deeply into the ground, and in his right hand was the knife with which he had stabbed himself.

"As I turned him over, to see if anything could yet be done to save him, I saw that the hand that had been buried clutched an earth-stained letter.

"'What has happened?' I asked, bewildered.

"Molle opened his eyes.

"'I cannot get it down to him,' he moaned. . . . 'Oh, David, my friend, my friend! . . . I did not mean to do it. . . . Can you hear me, David, and will you believe me? . . . I did not even know that *a knife was in my hand*, when you came to me that last night in the barrack-room, and I struck you, David. . . .'

"I tried to stanch the blood that flowed from his bared breast.

"'*Get him the letter*,' he whispered, '*I cannot reach to . . .*' and died.

"I buried the letter. . . . Doubtless Edwards received it. . . ."

THE McSNORRT REMINISCENT

In "The McSnorrt Reminiscent", the Geste brothers meet one of Wren's most recurring characters: The McSnorrt. The tale McSnorrt tells the Gestes is one of two rivals in the ship-building business in Scotland, and how the son of one of them is able to achieve an unknowing revenge. There are thirteen stories either about or narrated by McSnorrt. In addition to this story there are "MacSnorrt" (in volume one of the Collected Short Stories*), "Salvage", "Dead Men's Boots", "Testimonial", "Deceptive", "The Hand of Fate", "The Fires of Hell", "McSnorrt's Love Affair", "Killing No Murder", "Spanish Maine's Little Joke", "The Dust That Was Barren" (all in volume three), and "Jury Rudder" (in volume four). "The McSnorrt Reminiscent" first appeared in* Good Gestes *(1929) and was reprinted in* Stories of the Foreign Legion *(Murray 1947).*

§1

"I say, citizens," quoth Digby Geste, as his brothers entered the barrack-room, "Ludwig'll . . ."

"Ludwiggle?" enquired Michael. "Who's he?"

Digby sighed. "As I was about to say, Ludwig'll . . ."

"You *did* say Ludwiggle," pointed out John.

Digby ignored his younger brother.

Addressing Michael he said firmly, "Ludwig'll . . ."

"He's got this Ludwiggle on the brain," observed Michael. "What's his surname—Hornswoggle?"

"Yes, obviously; what else could it be?" accommodated Digby in a soothing voice, and continued, "Well, Ludwig Hornswoggle'll clean our kit to-night. In fact he's very keen on getting the job, and keener still on the threepence he'll earn by it. Thinking of marrying, I believe, and wants to get a few sticks of furniture for the home."

"Good for Ludwiggle," agreed Michael. "We'll go to Mustapha's and improve the shining hour, and our shining Arabic."

Le légionnaire Ludwig Müller alias Hornswoggle, having

received payment in advance and a promise that it would be recovered if the work were not satisfactorily done, settled down to the evening's labour, as the boys, having brushed each other's coats, took their caps.

"Good-bye, Ludwiggle," observed Michael, as they left the barrack-room. "You speak English, don't you?"

"Yes, yes, I speak it much," replied Müller. "I haf been waiter in London."

"'*Thig or glear?*'" murmured Digby.

"Well then," replied Michael, "you will achieve a just and accurate perception of what I would fain indicate when I say that you have had payment *a priori*, and if we are unable to approve the result of your industry and application, both intensive and extensive, you'll get some *a posteriori* too."

"Yes, and *a forteriori* also, Ludwiggle. Now excogitate the esoteric implications of those few ill-chosen words."

Ludwig Müller grinned and waggled his hands.

§2

"Good heavens, listen," said Michael, suddenly seizing the arms of his brothers, between whom he was walking, as they passed a low café in the Spanish quarter.

"Rough-house," observed Digby, as a man came flying backward through the doorway. "That is what the instructed call being thrown out on your ear," observed John.

"I thought I heard English," said Michael.

"Scotch," said Digby, "or did I smell it?"

"Only the soda," corrected John. . . . "By Jove, it *is* English," he added, as a bull voice roared above the din.

"Is there a man among ye has the Gaelic? . . . Is there a man among ye can speak English even? . . . Is there a man among ye at all? Ye gang o' lasceevious auld de'ils, decked oot like weemin' in spite o' yer hairy long whuskers, full beards and full skirts, ye deceitful besoms. Whuskers and petticoats wi' the vices o' both and the virtues o' neither. *I'*ll sorrt ye."

And there were sounds of alarums and excursions within.

The door opened, and a *légionnaire* came out laughing—a Frenchman called Blanc, once a Captain in his country's

Mercantile Marine.

"Ho, ho, *ce bon* McSnorrt," he chuckled.

"Hullo, there's a compatriot of yours in there," he added, on catching sight of the brothers. "Perhaps you could get him back to Barracks. I can't. He's not coming out of there till some one speaks to him in Gaelic, has danced the sword-dance or sung a *Chanson Ecosse* about Scots who have bled at the same time and place as Monsieur Guillaume Wallace."

Blanc laughed again.

"He's taken a dislike to Arabs, Jews and Spaniards to-night, because they can't talk Gaelic, and he'll kill a few in there unless they kill him first. . . . Well, I've done my best with the old fool."

A few questions elicited the information that *ce bon* McSnorrt was a Scot with a perfectly unpronounceable name—really more a sneeze than a name, explained Blanc,—something between McIlwraith and Colquohoun, who had, long ago, been re-named "McSnorrt" by an English *légionnaire* calling himself Jean Boule. He had taken his discharge three times, and each time had re-enlisted destitute, after a period of peace, retrenchment, and reform, during which he had, according to his own account, been Chief Engineer on great liners.

Apparently he was the pride and joy of his officers in the day of battle, and their despair, disgrace and utter curse, in the piping times of peace. On more than one occasion, nothing but his decorations and glorious fighting record could have saved him from the Zephyrs or a firing-party. According to Blanc, he had been very bad in the days of his friend Jean Boule, and ten times worse since the removal, by the hand of death, of that gentleman's restraining influence.

Followed by his brothers, Beau Geste pushed open the door and entered the wine-shop.

Brandishing an empty bottle, a red man—red of hair, beard, nose and eye—enormous and powerfully built, was threatening an audience of grave and wondering Arabs and grinning, sneering, or scowling Spaniards, Jews, and nondescripts, while he bitterly and passionately harangued them on the shortcomings, impropriety, and general unsuitability of native dress; on their inability to sing the songs that he approved, and their complete ignorance of Gaelic.

Inasmuch as his address concluded with the firm assurance that no man should leave the building until he had cast off his unseemly garb, danced a sword-dance, sung "Annie Laurie," and spoken Gaelic, there appeared to be every probability of serious trouble.

Even as the boys entered, a big, powerful, and truculent-looking Spaniard set down his glass with a loud bang on the zinc bar, lit a cigarette, spat in the direction of the self-constituted censor of local morals, manners and customs, and strode toward the door.

As the McSnorrt gripped him by the arm, he whipped out a knife. Quick as he was, the drunken Scot was quicker. Seizing the upraised hand, the McSnorrt forced the man's arm downward and backward, and then, with a mighty heave and lift, swung round and flung him, like a sack of straw, against the swing-doors—and the subsequent proceedings interested him no more.

There was a general movement and ugly murmurings, as knives were drawn and empty bottles seized, preparatory to a concerted rush.

"Speak Gaelic, ye ignorant and contumeelious spawn of Gehenna, ye dommed dirrty, degraded, derelict descendants o' the Duke of Hell," roared the McSnorrt, in reply to cries of "Stab him," "Get behind him," or "Throw a knife in his ear," and general exhortations of all to sundry that they should do drastic things with promptitude and despatch.

"Hi, comrade, hae ye the Gaelic yersel'?" shouted Michael, as he thrust through the encircling company of murderous blackguards, choice specimens of a cosmopolitan and criminal underworld.

"Not a worrd, laddie, an' I was never further norrth, ye'll ken, than my ain fair city o' Glesgie. Not a worrd, an' I doot if ever I hearrd one. . . . But the soond of yon lovely tongue wad be sweeter in ma ears than that o' the bonnie pibroch itself. . . . Oh, to hear the skirrl o' the bonnie, bonnie bag-pipes, playing 'Lochaber no more,' or the 'Flowers of the Forest' in this meeserable land o' dule and drought. No, I hae na the Gaelic, but I'm goin' to hearr it the nicht. An' no man leaves this den o' thieves until I do, yersel's included."

"Then listen," replied Michael, "listen, my little one, and you shall hear," and in fluent Arabic he continued, "You are a filthy drunken disgrace to the most decent, self-respecting, thrifty and sober people in the world. You are a noisy ruffian, debauched, beastly and detestable, a shame and a reproach to the white race, and to the Foreign Legion."

Michael paused for breath.

"How did you like that?" he inquired. "Pretty good Gaelic, eh?"

"Graand, man! Gie's your hand. Och, the bonnie, bonnie Gaelic. It minds me o' when I was a wee laddie, and paddled i' the burrn. . . . Or the Clyde at Greenock, anyhow."

And the McSnorrt swallowed hard.

"Oh, cheer up, wee Macgreegor," begged Digby. "Listen."

And at the top of his voice he tunefully declared that Maxwellton's braes were bonnie.

Scarcely had he uttered the name of Miss Laurie, and the gift of her promise true, than the McSnorrt burst into tears, and was led weeping away—away back to Barracks, to the strains of "Loch Lomond," and the promptings of a somewhat vituperative-seeming Gaelic.

§3

Every fifth day is "pay-day," the great day when a soldier of the Legion has five *sous* to spend, and can spend it with untrammelled recklessness.

It was a Fifth Day at eventide, and the McSnorrt, established as usual in the Canteen, was rapidly recovering from the drear and dreadful drought of the four previous days, when chill penury failed to repress his noble rage.

Warmed by wine, the McSnorrt was expanding, mellowing and waxing genial, shedding moroseness like a garment, and finding joy, relief, and satisfaction in self-expression. Speech bubbled up within this usually inarticulate man, and he spake with tongues; also he remembered his love of the Gaelic, as he caught sight of the three boys who had come to his rescue in the wine-shop last pay-day.

With a roar and a shout and a wave of one mighty paw, while

the other banged a bottle heavily upon the table, he attracted the attention of the Geste brothers and bade them come, and in return for their Gaelic, hear words of wisdom and delight from a great and good man who had drunk exactly 3,000 gallons of whisky before the three of them had been born.

Nothing loth, the brothers gathered round the veteran reprobate, a man with a vivid imagination, an inexhaustible fund of strange experience, and, on the rare occasions when not possessed of a dumb devil, a copious flow of potent speech.

Ere long, the party was joined by Maris and Cordier, friends of the brothers, and practised users of the English tongue.

Michael, Digby and John, finishing a brief argument as to whether one Robinson, the Carven-Faced Man, should be written down a liar, and if not, should be esteemed something of a knave, were anon aware that the McSnorrt, ancient mariner that he was, had fixed them with a glittering eye and was unfolding a round, if not unvarnished, tale of which they had missed the beginning.

"Aye . . . aye, this Mr. Bute-Arrol was a well-kenned and highly respected man. Last of a great shipping firm he was, and an ornament to Glasgow as he walked aboot it, a fine big upstanding man with the sea in his eyes, and the sun-bronze on his face.

"More like a ship's captain than a shipping-owner, he was, and well he might be, for he had sailed the seven seas, and travelled far and wide. Aye, and Mr. Bute-Arrol, partner in the Bell, Brown, Scott and Bute-Arrol's 'Loch' Line, was a man of parrts and education. . . . Hobbies he had. . . . Nane of yer fule hobbies o' collectin' stamps, or moths, or trouser-buttons, or doin' fret-work or photography, but scienteefic and literary, ye ken.

"And, I say, scienteefic. There was botany and orchids, that cost him a fortune, from South America to New Guinea, and trees and shrubs in his grounds such as ye'd have to go to Kew Gardens to see the like of.

"And then there was zoology and all sorts of weird beasties, snakes and lizards and fishes, chameleons and similar molluscs, and brachycephalous orrnithorhincusses; marvellous-coloured bugs, beetles, salamanders, iguanas and all such-like lepidoptera and hagiologies. He'd got conservatories and an aviary and an insect-house and a reptile-house, all kept as warm as the tropics while Christians went blue-nosed with the Glasgow east wind and whisky.

"Aye, he was a man of interests, this Mr. Bute-Arrol, and three of his greatest were early gold coins, scarce First Editions of bukes, and rare poisons. . . . Yon disreppitable and unneighbourly family of Borrgias. . . . That lassie they ca'ed Madame Brinvilliers, famous poisoners of history—he'd quite a library of them, and the men that hunted him his orchids, humming-birds, butterflies and such *bichus*, had to bring him poisoned arrows o' the heathen, and the little darts they puff through the long blow-pipes. *Sumpitans*, I think they ca' them. And he'd be extra douce wi' any hunter or agent or captain who'd send him, or bring him, specimens o' yon *wourali* stuff fra' South America, or *dhatura* fra' the East, *stropanthus* from Africa, and dozens of other such unwholesome food-stuffs from China to Peru—things ye'd never hear of unless ye went there, and then likely not—and all unknown to the British Pharmacopœia.

"Aye, he was a grraand man, and I'm tellin' ye he had grraand hobbies, and great ideas.

"Aye, and something else he had, and that was a great enemy, a successful rival in love, which was bad, and a successful rival in business which was waur. McRattery his name was, and if ye'd say Bute-Arrol was the finest figure o' a man, a citizen, a gentleman, a pillar o' law, order and property, and ornament o' the Kirk in all Glasgow, ye might perhaps add, 'Unless it's yon Mr. McRattery.'

"A pair they were, but not a pair that would ever run in harness, ye ken, nor side by side, nor in the same direction.

"Rivals and enemies, from their school-days at Fettes, to the prime o' manhood. What the one had, the other must have more of; what the one did, the other must outdo; what the one was, the other must be in higher degree. Aye, what the one wanted, the other must get first.

"And McRattery put the crown on his life's work o' rivalry, thwarting and competition, by cutting in and getting Mary MacDonald just when Bute-Arrol decided that it was time he had a son to follow him, and had marked bonnie Mary down for the high honour and advancement of becoming Mrs. Bute-Arrol.

"Big men they were both, wise and patient and clever, learned and able and dour, ill men to cross, wilful and set in their ways, and neither to haud nor to bind when once started on a course. And perhaps, after all, McRattery was the bigger man, for not only had he beaten Bute-Arrol in love and war, but he had fought fair, and *sans rancune*, as these French havering bletherers say.

"Fight he would, while there was breath in his body, but he bore no malice, and would always fight fair; and ye couldna say the same o' Bute-Arrol.

"*He'd* fight fair wi' the steepulation that a's fair in love and war. An' he *did* bear malice. He was a good hater, and he wasna the man to stultify himself wi' impotent hatred, either. An' McRattery marryin' Mary MacDonald was a turnin'-point in Bute-Arrol's career. Aye, the down-turnin' point, for he grew more and more dour, and then soured and warped.

"And then two things happened which turned bad to worse, and that was very bad indeed.

"The first of these was the death of Mrs. McRattery, that had been his beloved Mary MacDonald; and the second was McRattery beating him over a huge Admiralty contract.

"What made Mary's death more terrible to him, was his firm belief that her life could have been saved. He had a mind like Aberdeen granite, and hard as granite was his belief, his certainty, that if Mary had been Mrs. Bute-Arrol instead of Mrs. McRattery, she'd have lived to four-score.

"'Yon meeserable money-grubbing McRattery simply *let* her die—or else she died wilfully, bein' sick sorry and tired at the sight of her husband's ugly face, and the sound of his croakin' voice. Why; had the creature been a man, he would have defied and fought Death himself—and kept her alive, despite the Devil and all the Imps of Hell. No, she shouldn't have died if she'd been Mary Bute-Arrol, and she wouldn't have wanted to, forbye.'

"That was the way he talked. But when McRattery undercut him with a big contract for the Navy, he didn't talk at all.

"He never said another word against McRattery.

"On the contrary, if anybody at the Club criticized the man, Bute-Arrol wouldna' let it pass, if it were unfair. And, whiles, he would take an opportunity o' publicly speaking worrds o' praise concernin' McRattery; and though he made no overtures nor approaches to his rival, it got aboot that auld Wullie Bute-Arrol's bark was waur than his bite, and that he had naethin' against Eckie McRattery in spite of a'.

"Weel, ye ken hoo things get roond, and in time, McRattery got to hear that Bute-Arrol wouldna hear a worrd against him. And one day, when he said, daffing-like, at his own table, that yon Bute-Arrol was a thrawn diel and an ill cur to turn from his bone, a crony said:

"'Nay, dinna misca' the man, Eckie, for I heard him only yesterday at the Club uphaudin' and defendin' ye like a brither, and sayin' ye were a man that had earrned and desairved every penny o' your fortune, and every step o' your success . . .' and the like.

"An' McRattery, being the man he was, made to out-do Bute-Arrol in generosity, as he had out-done him in business and in love.

"Aye, aye, it's a queer worrld," mused the McSnorrt, gazing pensively into his empty glass and slowly shaking his huge red head.

It was noticeable—that in talking to the Geste brothers—he talked less and less like a Clydeside docker from Glasgow, and more like the educated man he was.

"Aye, a queer worrld," he continued, when his glass was replenished, "an' one o' its queer sights was seen when William Bute-Arrol sat down at a banquet as one of the guests of Alexander Buchanan McRattery—the guest of honour on his host's right hand.

"I can tell ye aboot that banquet at first hand, for I've talked many a time an' oft wi' a man who was there, Sir Andrew Anderson he was, and a great and wealthy marine engineer before he retired. He died at the age of 90, when I was a lad, and many a good turn he did me, had I but had the sense to ha' taken advantage o' them.

"According to his account, it was a richt merry and successfu' dinner, and ye'd have thought that McRattery and Bute-Arrol had been lifelong friends instead o' rivals and enemies.

"For McRattery fairly laid himself out to charm and captivate Bute-Arrol, and Bute-Arrol fairly laid himself out to be pleased and pleasant.

"That dinner-table was a battlefield o' magnanimity. Each o' the two big men strivin' to outdo the other in generosity and great-hearted forgiveness and forgetting o' what there was to forgive and forget.

"They drank each other's health and each made a little speech full o' kindness and compliment to the other, and when they had come to the coffee and liqueurs and big cigar stage, and men leant back in their chairs and unbuttoned their minds socially and right sociably, there was no pair o' cronies that chatted more easily and freely than the generous-hearted Eckie McRattery and his one-time rival and enemy Wullie Bute-Arrol.

"And McRattery must needs strike a match and light Bute-Arrol's cigarette for him, and Bute-Arrol must clip a cigar for McRattery—more like loving brothers than life-long rivals and enemies ye'd believe.

"And as it happened, auld Andrew Anderson was watchin' and wonderin', as McRattery, with his cigar in one hand and a match in the other, laughed long and loud at some sly quip or jest, or mayhap sculduddery, o' Bute-Arrol's.

"And that hearty merry laugh was the last sound poor McRattery made in this worrld, for still shakin' wi' laughter, he put his cigar to his lips, lit it, took one long satisfyin' draught, slowly poured it out fra his smilin' lips, and then gave a start, and, with a terrible expression on his face, gazed around him and died.

"Died there in his chair wi'oot a worrd. His head just fell on to his shoulder, and he sank heavily against his neighbour— William Bute-Arrol.

"O' coorse they all sprang to their feet and dashed water in his face, opened the windows, fanned him, tried to make him drink brandy and did sic-like things, until the doctor came and said he was dead. For dead he was—cut off in the prime of his health and strength, and no healthier heartier stronger man had walked the streets of Glasgae that day.

"An inquest there was, and the two best doctors in the city confessed themselves puzzled and defeated.

"Deceased had a heart as sound as a bell, they said, and not an organ that wasna perfect.

"Naturally, the immediate supposition was that he'd eaten somethin' that had disagreed with him. But how should he have eaten or drunk something that had disagreed with him to the point o' killin' him, when not anither man at the table had felt the slightest qualm o' pain, ill-health or discomfort?

"The contents of the stomach bein' analysed showed absolutely no trace o' anything deeleterious, and the cause o' death was a fair mystery. Apart from the offeecial and scienteefic investigation, the guests themsel's worked it out that he had not tasted a thing from soup to coffee that others had not shared.

"And when some auld fule spoke of suicide, he had but to be asked why Alexander Buchanan McRattery, in boisterous spirits, rude health, and at the height of his success and fortune, should commit suicide, and at such a time and place. And moreover, what of the analyst's report on the absolutely normal and innocuous contents o' the stomach?

"No, it was a mystery, unfathomable and complete.

"It was a nine-day's wonder, too, and the town talked of nothing else, but this awfu' tragedy that cast real gloom over the dead man's wide circle o' freends and acquaintances.

"And none more sorrowfu' and sympathetic than his new friend and old enemy, William Bute-Arrol.

"Aye, an' it was practical sympathy too, for, in order, perhaps, to show how deeply he had been affected by McRattery's death at his very side, nay in his arms, at the very banquet given to celebrate and demonstrate their reconciliation, Bute-Arrol had adopted McRattery's orphan child.

"What were the worrkin's of his mind when he thought o' doin' sic a thing? Who shall presume to fathom the dark mysterious depths of the human mind? Aye, and ye might ask the question anither way, or rather ask a different question a'thgither. Who shall dare presume to fathom and unnerstand the worrkings o' Providence? God moves in a meesterious way His wonders to perforrm.

"Weel, whatever was the man's motive—whether it were a gesture to catch the public eye; whether it were a salve to his conscience; or whether he had some dark design upon the child, and thoughts o' carryin' vengeance against his father even beyond the grave—no-one will ever know.

"But see the result, ponder the ways of the A'mighty, and turrn fra your wickedness. . . ."

The McSnorrt paused and drank deeply.

"Especially drink," he added, wiping his bearded lips with the back of a vast and hairy hand.

"See what happened," he continued.

"Now Alexander Buchanan McRattery's son Uchtred, aged aboot five or six years when Bute-Arrol adopted him—wi' the willing and even thankful agreement o' the executor, a child-hatin' plausible scoundrel, who later defaulted and went to prison—was a healthy and active young limb o' Satan, wi' an enquirin' mind and busy fingers.

"Folk who liked childer said he was an enterprisin' and original laddie; and those who didn't like childer said he was a mischievous and meddlesome young deil.

"But every one thoct it was graand to see the way he and dour Bute-Arrol got on togither, walkin' hand in hand aboot the grounds o' the big hoose, or the boy slippin' awa' doon fra the nursery to get a bit fruit or sweetie or jeelypiece, at dessert.

"Whiles he'd sit curled up in a chair and watch Bute-Arrol with solemn big eyes, and Bute-Arrol'd sit sippin' his porrt and thinkin' his deep thoughts as he stared at the child.

"An' mind ye, the child was fond of him, there's no denyin', and was the only one in that hoose from the butler to the sixth gardener's under-gardener that wasna afeared o' the man.

"No one ever saw Bute-Arrol caress the child, any more than they saw the opposite or heard an unkind worrd; but it was clear enough that the little lad was happy, and had taken no scunner at his dour unsmilin' guardian.

"When the late McRattery's executor absconded to South America and finished what the ruinous strike in the ship-yard had begun, folk wondered if the boy was goin' to become Bute-Arrol's heir—and some of Bute-Arrol's relations had disturrbin' thoughts.

There was other folk—but ye ken what folk are—professed the opeenion that Bute-Arrol deleeberately turrned a very blind eye on the doin's o' the said executor, and had more than a finger in the McRattery strike.

"But what I started to tell ye was this—the boy lived happy and contented with his governess in Bute-Arrol's hoose, and had the free run of it, an' of the grounds too. And while it was a false and maleecious slander to say he was wantonly mischievous, there's nae denyin' he could poke and pry and investigate with the best—an' what normal healthy boy will not?

"An' one day he found something.

"It was in a most attractive and wunnerful box in a big room that opened oot o' his guardian's bedroom—a sort o' combined dressin'-room and study that Bute-Arrol used more than any o' his fine graand rooms doon-stairs. There was a huge great desk in it, and this big old bureau, and a fine safe, and twa-three wardrobes and some big deep arm-chairs, and Bute-Arrol would smoke his ceegar there in his dressing-gown late at night, an' he'd read an' write there more than in his great library.

"Weel, prowlin' round this room, as he loved to do, fingerin' this an' that, the boy spied this fine box.

"Chinese it was, ebony and ivory and mother-o'-pearl, with bands o' brass, brass corners and a brass lock,—and to crown a', a key in the lock. Ye'll imagine it wasna long before the laddie had that box open, and sniffed its lovely scent o' sandal-wood, and pried into every compartment and drawer, amusin' himself, absorbed and happy, for an hoor that went like a meenit.

"He did no harm, and he kept nothing for himself, and the one thing he took oot, he only took that he might do something with it for his guardian—just the little childish ploy that a wee laddie would think of. He guessed that the box had come oot o' the safe or the bureau, had been left out by mistake, and would disappear again when his guardian came home and entered the room.

"That night the boy slippit doon and watched over the banisters o' the stairs until the right moment, and then, in his wee dressin'-gown and bedroom slippers, marched into the big dinin'-room where Bute-Arrol sat all by his lane, the butler havin' set his wine in front o' him and gone for the coffee.

"'Hullo, Uncle,' called the little lad. 'Can I have some grapes?'

"Bute-Arrol, unsmilin', nodded at the child.

"'Help yersel',' he growled, and the boy marched round the table, and then to the big sideboard, spyin' oot the land.

"As the butler came in, carryin' a big silver tray on which were coffee and a box o' ceegars, Bute-Arrol took a ceegar, laid it on the cloth beside his plate, and helped himself to coffee—

which he took with hot milk, cream and sugar. While he did so, the wee laddie came behind his chair, and picked up the ceegar.

"'Can I have some coffee, Uncle?' he asked.

"'Ye canna,' Bute-Arrol replied, 'but ye can hae a sup o' milk.'

"'Pooh! Wha wants milk?' replied the child. 'I'll hae a glass o' wine.'

"'Ye willna,' said Bute-Arrol, and picked up the ceegar that the boy had laid down again, beside his plate.

"The butler put match-box and ash-tray on the table, as usual, and went out.

"Bute-Arrol put the ceegar to his lips, lit it, and took a puff or two.

"He then leant back in his chair, and, wi' an awful look o' fright an' terror on his face, stared at the laughing wee laddie who held out a gold ceegar-piercer in his hand—a thing like a wee pencil-case that ye press at the top, and a sharp hollow steel piercer pushes out of it and into the ceegar.

"'I did the ceegar for ye, Uncle,' laughed the child gleefully.

"Bute-Arrol groaned.

"'*The judgment of God*,' he whispered, and died—poisoned with the instrument he had used to poison the boy's father."

The McSnorrt paused dramatically, and his hearers, who had ceased to smoke and to drink, sat silent.

"How d'you know all this?" asked Beau Geste at last.

"Ma real name's Uchtred Buchanan McRattery," replied the McSnorrt.

MAD MURPHY'S MIRACLE

This story starts out in London with two gentlemen gossiping at a dance during the band's break. The story then switches to the Geste brothers and how Digby is assigned to help a fellow legionnaire, Mad Murphy, cope with his increasing madness. "Mad Murphy's Miracle" first appeared in Good Gestes *(1929) and was reprinted in* Dead Men's Boots *(1949).*

§1

Lord Montaigle, like King Bruce of Scotland, sat himself down in a lonely mood to think—the more lonely because he was in the crowded ball-room of the world-famous Majestic Hotel in the hub of the metropolis which is the hub of the universe.

What was he doing there at his time of life, he asked himself. Rotten new-fangled rubbish—this modern dancing and dance-music. . . . Jazz! . . . Damned row. . . .

Well, at his hostess's earnest request, he had looked in, and now he'd jolly well look out again. . . . Run along to his club and finish the day in peace and quiet and comfort with a book, and a cigar, and a drink—and so to bed.

Hullo, here was dear old Pop, more widely known as Sir Popham Ronceval. Lady Anstruther had dragged *him* here, too, eh!

As the music stopped, Sir Popham Ronceval seated himself in the arm-chair beside that of his old friend, among the palms, near the band.

"Hear oneself speak, now that row's stopped," he observed. "What are you doing here, Monty?"

"Same as you, Pop—going away. . . . Coming?"

"Only just arrived. Let's stick out another dance, and then I'm with you."

Lord Montaigle suppressed a yawn.

"Sad about Tommy Vane," observed his friend, almost casually, though a look of concern shadowed his handsome eyes.

"What about him ?" asked Lord Montaigle, his rubicund and cheery countenance unresponsive as yet to the other's concern.

"Died this morning . . ."

"*No?* Did he? . . . Well, nothing very sad about that—not for him, anyhow. Nor for Long John. Best day's work Tommy Vane ever did, I should say," pondered Lord Montaigle.

"Oh, I dunno. . . . I was rather fond of old Tommy," said Sir Popham Ronceval—"when he wasn't mad, that is."

"When he wasn't!" objected his friend. "But he *was*. . . . Born mad, lived mad, died mad—like his father before him—and his grandfather, too, and his great-grandfather, by all accounts."

"His father shot himself, didn't he?" mused Sir Popham.

"Yes, and *his* father was killed by the man he attacked. Attacked the feller in his own smoking-room, and he knocked Vane out with a bronze figure, or ornament, or something, that stood handy. And Tommy's great-grandfather was hanged—on a silken rope—for unjustifiable homicide."

"Poor old Tommy," repeated the baronet.

"What did he die of?" asked Montaigle.

"Razor-blade," was the short reply. "Just that."

Lord Montaigle nodded his head slowly, and made no further comment than:

"There's a son somewhere, isn't there?"

"*A* son," agreed the other, with meaning emphasis, and added: "Not Tommy's."

Montaigle smiled.

"Long John, eh? . . . The wild Irishman. . . . Aren't we a pair of scandal-mongering old devils?"

"Look here, Claud, I wouldn't talk like this to any other living soul. I'm Long John's *executor*, and I don't mind telling you for a fact what everybody else knows for a guess . . ."

"Guessed it myself," admitted Montaigle. "I saw the boy once at Speech Day—Long John to the very life! . . . Tall, red-haired, blue-eyed, freckled, regular red Celt."

"Yes, I suppose Long John will come home now. . . . Now there's no fear of his murdering Tommy Vane."

"I doubt it. Why should he? He's got a splendid place in East Africa, and it isn't as though Lady Vane were alive," replied Ronceval.

"Died when the boy was born, didn't she?¡? asked Montaigle.

"Yes. . . . Long John nearly went out of his mind. . . . I tell you I had all I could do to get him away. He was all for shooting Tommy Vane first, and himself afterwards. Rotten position for *me*. I was the friend of both of them. Promised Long John I'd keep an eye on the boy. . . . Her boy. . . . *His* boy."

"What became of him?" inquired Lord Montaigle

"Wish I could tell you. . . . He was going up to Oxford for his first term, and never got there. Simply vanished into thin air. Tommy Vane didn't give a damn. But I was frightfully worried. . . . I wish to God I knew what happened to him. . . . I would . . ."

A burst of music from the band cut short the gossip. . . .

§2

Beau Geste strode into the barrack-room at Ain Dula, between Douargala and El Rasa, in search of his brothers Digby and John. In his well-fitting, dark-blue tunic, with its red facings, green-topped, red-fringed epaulettes, his smart white-covered *képi*, brilliantly-polished buttons, belt and bayonet, well-ironed white trousers, and highly-polished boots, he was as smart a figure of a soldier as any in his regiment, famous in the 19th Army Corps for its smartness.

Digby was lying upon his bed, clad in a white shirt and trousers, and engrossed in the study of Arabic, while John sat on the opposite cot writing a letter to Isobel.

Both looked up as Beau Geste approached.

"Ho, pups," quoth he. "Rise up, and stand to attention. Thumbs in a line with the seams of the pyjamas, the weight of the body resting on the chin strap. . . . And listen. . . . My orders to you are '*Keep an eye on "Mad Murphy*," as they call him. The poor chap's up against it badly. I've just had a dose of him. I left him on the bench there by the *entrée de la redoute*.'"

"Poor beggar gets madder every day," observed Digby. "He'll be as mad as John soon."

"Well, two of a kind never agree," observed John, "so you go and play with him, Dig . . . and keep him out of *le village Nègre*. . . . I'm writing to Isobel."

"Righto!" agreed Digby, and, rising from his bed, began to

dress.

"He's got as far as talking to himself aloud," continued Beau, "and, unlike most mad people, he knows he's mad, or very nearly so. His great terror, among a thousand terrors, is that he'll go quite finally insane, and kill somebody—probably his best friend. He's just begged me to drive my bayonet through his throat if he ever so much as raises his fist or snarls at me."

"And you want *me* to go and play with him," observed Digby. "Both of you lend me your rifles—I've only got one."

"What we want is a scrap," observed John. "Poor old Mad Murphy and all the other loonies would soon work their *cafard* off on the Touareg, if they came for us."

"Yes, scrapping is the prescribed cure for *cafard*" agreed Beau. "A bayonet charge must be a wonderful soother. . . . Meantime Mad Murphy is to be kept from using his bayonet on himself or anyone else. . . ."

"We *are* our brother's keeper. We *are*, we *are*, we *are*" chanted Digby, as he buckled on his belt, and straightened his tunic.

§3

Mad Murphy was sitting alone on the bench outside the entrance to the fort, his blazing red head supported upon his clenched fists, his blazing blue eyes glaring at the ground in front of him. His mouth was set in a grim line, and a heavy frown marred his haggard, handsome face.

Digby Geste seated himself on the bench without speaking, leant forward with his elbows on his knees, took his head between his clenched fists, frowned heavily, set his mouth grimly, and stared ferociously at the ground in front of him.

By and by Mad Murphy sat up and stared at his neighbour.

"Go and moult somewhere else," he growled. . . . "I'm dangerous. . . . I'm going mad."

"So am I," replied Digby, "I'm dangerous, too. Please don't let me bite you. . . . Mad as a hatter."

Mad Murphy stared at him, suspicion mingling with anger in his glare.

"Wonder why hatters *are* mad?" continued Digby.

"Go mad making hats for fools like you, perhaps," suggested Murphy.

"Why, of course," agreed Digby. "Who's *your* hatter? . . . Madame la République at the moment, of course. . . . She must be *quite* mad, or she'd make you and me Generals at once. . . . Then there's March hares. Why are *they* mad? March too much, I suppose, like us. I think I'll be a won't-march hare in future, then Lejaune'll get mad. Yes, I can honestly say it was marching made me mad. . . . Lots of times."

Silence.

"La Cigale is a grasshopper, I'm a hare; what are you going to be? A hatter? Depends on what drove you mad, of course. What was it, if one might ask?"

"Are you being funny?" growled Mad Murphy.

"I should think so," replied Digby. "I feel very funny. Mad, you know. Like a hare. By Jove, though, I'm not so sure that I *will* be a hare. La Cigale is a grasshopper, and that makes him hop about on all fours, as you know. It would be a frightful thing if I became a March hare, and simply couldn't stop marching. That would make Lejaune just as mad as if I wouldn't march at all. It's a problem."

Murphy eyed him with less of suspicion and something of concern.

"Any madness in your family?" he asked.

"No," replied Digby. "None apparent, I believe. I'm the first—'hare apparent,' so to speak."

"You are lucky, then," said Murphy. "If you take a grip on yourself, there's some hope for you. My trouble is that I come of diseased, rotten, tainted, filthy, mad stock. . . . Father a mad beast who tortured my mother. . . . Isn't any man mad who ill-treats or hurts a woman in any way?"

"Obviously a criminal lunatic," agreed Digby.

"I've a good mind to go and shoot him before I shoot myself," continued Mad Murphy. "I would, if my mother were alive. She died in giving birth to me. I'm a pretty thing for her to have given her life for, good God!"

"She'd probably think so," observed Digby, and there was now no simulated insanity in his voice.

"Think so?" said Murphy. "She's dead, I tell you."

"Nobody's dead," said Digby.

"No," agreed Murphy, "not *really* dead . . ." and fell into a moody silence, which Digby broke with the remark:

"But, of course, your father may have had a whang on the head, or some illness. I believe some forms of meningitis leave you a bit balmy on the crumpet, and batty in the belfry."

"Illness be damned!" spat Murphy; "he is a *madman*, I tell you. A criminal lunatic. . . . *And*, my lad, so was my grandfather—mad and evil. Best thing he ever did was when he shot himself. . . . And if that's not enough for you, may I mention that my great-grandfather was a homicidal maniac, and was killed by his best friend, whom he murderously assaulted?"

Digby's face grew yet more thoughtful. This was a pretty tale indeed.

"And if you'd like a little more family history, *his* father, after a quiet sojourn in Newgate Gaol, was hanged on Tyburn Tree— and for a very dirty crime. Not even a decent highwayman job. How's that for a family record? And you want to know what drove me mad, do you? Nothing! I was born mad . . . mad for generations. . . . '*Unto the third and fourth generation of them that hate Me.*' . . . Haven't I some cause to hate Him?"

Silence.

"Look here, Murphy. You're evidently not up to date. Don't you know that this heredity business is an absolutely exploded fallacy? Nothing in it at all. A child isn't tuberculous because its parents are, but because it grows up in the same conditions that made them tuberculous. . . . We inherit family likenesses, traits, tastes, and habits sometimes, and *only* sometimes, but we don't inherit microbes, and mental and physical diseases. . . .

"You yourself admit that nothing has driven you mad, and, so far as I can see, you are just a poor weak, feeble ass who is simply, inducing the very thing he fears. . . . *Fears*—that's it. You aren't so much an ass as a coward. . . . A cowardly ass, shall we say."

"Begod, you'd better not," growled Murphy, rising to his feet

"Oh, sit down, man," said Digby. "It's too hot to fight. Besides, an ass, if that's what you're going to be, couldn't fight a hare. It would be all round him. Though, to tell the truth, I think you're more like a broody hen than an ass, really. Yes, you sit here all huddled up, and frightfully concerned with yourself, exactly like a broody hen in a dust-hole, counting her itchings before they are scratched. Yes, a broody hen. We'll be the Hare and Hen. Good name for a public-house! Let's leave the Legion and open one. . . ."

"Isn't there a fable about them? The hare taught us—not to sleep on our posts. Not that one *could* sleep on a post, if you come to think of it."

Murphy sat down again, a very puzzled man.

"Talk sense," he requested.

"I can't," replied Digby. "I'm *mad*."

"You were talking sense enough just now—about heredity," objected Murphy.

"Oh, yes, that was sense all right," admitted Digby. "There is no such thing as hereditary taint."

"And will you then tell me, you damned fool," shouted Murphy, "why I'm the sixth in direct line of homicidal maniacs, of beastly, bloodthirsty madmen; evil, malignant, murderous lunatics? Heredity! Isn't six generations enough for you? It *may* be sixty, for all I know."

"I don't care if it's six hundred," interrupted Digby. "All I know is I wouldn't make the six hundred and first. That's just weak-mindedness, not madness. . . . Just giving way to an *idée fixe,* and deliberately carrying on a family tradition—like that of going into the Army or Navy. Now, *I'm* a proper madman—off my own bat—not a miserable copycat like you want to be. If your people have been madmen, why not start something original, and be a sane person? My people have all been sane for six generations—or sixty—or six hundred perhaps, but *I'm* going to be mad. Would you mind addressing me as Monsieur M. Hare, in future?"

"I say, old chap, do you *really* think you're doing dotty?" asked Murphy, with anxious concern.

"Well, it's like this," replied Digby. "I've been watching you a lot lately, you know, ever since your detachment joined ours at Douargala, and I fluctuate with *you*. When you give way to this madness, I do, and when you pull yourself together, I buck up like anything. I wish you'd help me. Can't you drop this heredity idea ?"

"Look here, Jones," said Murphy, laying his hand upon Digby's knee, "you're sane enough—if you don't give way. You must pull yourself together, and keep a tight hold on things. Now, listen—you're all right—tell me . . . what would *you* have done in a case like this? Just when I left school, I realized I was in love with the most glorious, wonderful girl in the whole world. The best, and loveliest, and dearest, and sweetest woman that ever lived . . ."

"Her name's Isobel," observed Digby.

"No, *Mary*—Mary Ronceval, daughter of Sir Popham Ronceval, my guardian. . . . I was up in town getting some kit . . . on my way to Oxford . . . and went to a dance at their house. . . . And do you know what devilish thing I did? Could you imagine it; guess it; dream it? I lost my head in the moonlit garden, and told her that she was all the world—and all heaven—to me, and that I had loved her for years. . . . And I kissed her, and heard her say that she had always loved *me* . . . !

"How's that, for the last of a line of malignant maniacs—foul, homicidal madmen? . . . Oh, God, *Mary! Mary!*" . . .

And Mad Murphy bowed his head, and covered his face.

Digby Geste swallowed. . . . Had it been he and Isobel! . . .

"And so you bolted to the Legion!" he said, and, rising, laid his hand on Murphy's shaking shoulder.

"Keep sane, for her sake, old chap," continued Digby. "You *can*, you *can*! Of course you can; and go back to her when you've conquered. . . . I and my brothers will help you, and you can help me to . . ."

"*Sixth* of the line," groaned Murphy. "*Sixth* to my certain knowledge. . . . Homicidal maniacs . . ."

§4

Lieutenant Debussy was *au fond* a kindly person, though a strict disciplinarian, and very popular with his men, especially when on active service. They then saw far more of him than they did in barracks.

As he stepped, that evening, from his lighted room, mud-walled, mud-floored, and furnished with nothing but a table, a chair, a bag, and a radio set, he saw three of his *légionnaires*—

three brothers, Englishmen, of whom he approved.

"*Ah, mes enfants*," said he, as they sprang to attention. "I've just been listening to something which would interest you—a band playing in one of your London hotels. . . . Would you like to hear it for a few minutes? I shall be gone for about half an hour. Have it for ten minutes each. . . . All most irregular, improper, and contrary to discipline, so don't get caught."

And, with a laugh, the gay and debonair young man descended the steps into the courtyard of this outpost that he commanded.

"*Quick!* Fetch Mad Murphy," whispered Beau Geste, as their hands dropped from the salute. "Do him a world of good. 'His need is greater than ours.'"

"Rather," agreed John. "Let him have the whole half-hour. We three can 'keep *cave*.' . . ."

§5

But Mad Murphy did not have his full half-hour.

For a few minutes he listened with a tortured smile on his face, as his foot unconsciously beat time to the music.

The music stopped, and with its stopping the chatter and applause of the crowd on the *Majestic's* dance-floor came through the headphones with a distinctness which to the listening exile painfully bridged the gulf between London and the desert around him.

"Rotten position for *me*," said a voice above the murmur of the ballroom. "I was the friend of both of them. Promised Long John I'd keep an eye on the boy. . . . Her boy . . . *His* boy."

"What became of him?"

"Wish I could tell you. . . . He was going up to Oxford for his first term, and never got there. Simply vanished into thin air. Tommy Vane didn't——"

And then he started up.

The smile left his face, and a look of astounded wonder and bewilderment took its place. Soon his face wore the expression of a man gazing at the foreman of a jury, whose "*Guilty*" or "*Not Guilty*, my Lord," means life or death to him. He paled beneath his tan, gasped, and suddenly cried:

"God in Heaven! . . . Long John . . . *Sir John Fitzgerald* . . . the great sportsman and big-game shot. *My father! . . . Mary! . . .*"

He swayed, staggered, sagged at the knees, and, to the consternation of the watching Digby Geste, burst into tears.

BURIED TREASURE

"Buried Treasure" is a story in which the Geste brothers help La Cigale cope with his seeming madness.   But is he really seeing and conversing with the ghost of a Roman legionnaire?   La Cigale and the brothers also have to cope with The Treasure; a legionnaire who is a particularly bad lot. "Buried Treasure" first appeared in Good Gestes *(1929), and was reprinted in the Murray (1947) and Macrae-Smith (1948) editions of* Stories of the Foreign Legion.

§1

"Poor old Cigale's pretty bad these days," said John Geste to his brothers Michael and Digby as he stepped into a tent of the standing camp some ninety kilometres south of Douargala.

"Yes," replied Digby, as he rose to help his brother remove and stow his kit in the tiny space which was allotted to each of the twelve men who lived in the little tent that could uncomfortably accommodate eight.

"Moon getting to the full," observed Michael. "We shall have to keep an eye on the poor old chap. What's his latest?"

"Seeing ghosts," replied John. "He's just been telling me all about it in the Guard Tent. When he was on sentry last night, he saw somebody approaching him. Such a very remarkable and extraordinary somebody that, instead of challenging, he rubbed his eyes and stared again. He told me all this in the most rational and convincing manner. It was really almost impossible to do anything but believe. He said:

"'When I looked again I hardly knew what to do.   There undoubtedly was a man coming towards me out of the desert, from the direction of the ruins. Nothing strange in that, you may say, but the man was a soldier in uniform. And the uniform was not of this regiment, nor of this army, nor of this country—nor of this century—no, nor of this thousand years. His helmet was of shining metal, with ear-pieces and neck-shield, but no visor— rather like a pompier's helmet, but with a horsehair crest and plume, and he had a gleaming cuirass of the same metal. In fact, I thought, for a moment, that he was a trooper of the Dragoon Guards until I saw that he carried a spear, at the slope, across his right shoulder, and for side-arms had a short sword—broad, but not much longer than a dagger. Under his cuirass he wore a sort of tunic that came down to his knees, and over this hung a fringe of broad strips of metal on leather. He wore metal greaves on his shins and sandals on his feet.

"'In fact, he was a Roman soldier marching on patrol or doing sentry-go on his beat. For one foolish moment I thought of enemy tricks and stratagems and also of practical jokes, but then I realized that not only could I see him as plainly as I see you now, but that I could see *through* him. No, he was not nebulous and misty like a cloud of steam; his outline was perfectly clear-cut, but, as he approached me, he came between me and one of the pillars of the ruins, and though I could see him perfectly clearly and distinctly, I could also see the pillar.

"'I was in something of a quandary. As you know, I try to do my duty to the very best of my poor ability, and aim at being the perfect private soldier. But there is nothing laid down in regulations on the subject of the conduct of a sentry when approached by a ghost.

"'In the Regulations it says, "Anyone approaching," and at once the question arises as to whether a ghost is anyone. You see, it is the ghost *of* someone, and therefore cannot *be* someone, can it? . . .'

"Thus spake the good Cigale," continued John, "and I assured him that personally I should not turn out the Guard nor rouse the camp to repel ghosts."

"No," agreed Digby. "I don't think I should, either. Sure to be a catch in it somewhere. The moment the Sergeant of the Guard came, the dirty dog would disappear—the ghost, I mean—and then you'd be for it.

"On the other hand," he continued, "if you didn't challenge him, he might go straight into the General's tent and give the old dear the fright of his life—and then you'd be for it again."

"Very rightly," agreed Michael. "What good would the General be at running a scrap next day, if he'd had a Roman soldier tickling him in the tummy with the butt-end of a spear all night?"

"True," mused John. "It's a problem. There ought to be a section in the Regulations. They certainly provide for most other things."

"And supposing it were the ghost of a most lovely *houri* approaching the General's tent?" asked Digby. "Should it be left to the sentry's indiscretion? And suppose the General came out and caught him turning her away—or turning unto her the other cheek also—"

"It's weird, though," Michael broke in upon these musings. "You can be absolutely certain that La Cigale thought he saw a Roman soldier, and if you think you see a thing, you *do* see it."

"What's that?" inquired Digby incredulously. "If I think I see a pimple on the end of your nose, I *do* see one?"

"Yes, you do, if you really think it. There is an image of it on the retina of your eye—and what is that but seeing?"

"He did more than see him, too," put in John. "He had a long conversation with him. They compared notes as to their respective regiments—the Third Legion, and the French Foreign Legion."

"By Jove, that's interesting!" observed Beau Geste. "I should have liked to hear them."

"I wonder if you'd have heard the ghost?" said Digby. "Of course, if you *thought* you heard him, you *would* have heard him, eh?

"I say," he added. "I just thought I heard you ask me to have a cigarette. Therefore I *did* hear it."

"Yes," agreed Michael. "And you thought you saw me give you one. Therefore I did give you one. Smoke it."

The tent-flap was pulled aside, and La Cigale entered.

"Come along, old chap! Splendid! We were just talking about you and your interesting experience with the Roman legionary," Beau continued.

"Yes, yes," replied Cigale. "A charming fellow. We had a most interesting conversation. His depôt was here, and he'd served everywhere from Egypt to Britain, had sun-stroke twice in Africa, and frost-bite twice when stationed on The Wall, as he called it—Hadrian's Wall, that would be, between England and Scotland.

"He actually spoke of the Belgæ, and must have been stationed quite near my home at one time. A most intelligent chap, and with that education which comes from travel and experience. A little rocky on Roman history, I found, but who would expect a private soldier to be an authority on history—even that of his own country?"

§2

La Cigale fell silent and mused awhile, breaking thereafter into mutterings, disjointed and fragmentary.

"Most interesting fellow. Rome in Africa, five centuries; France in Africa, one century; the sun the unconquerable enemy of both. Rome did not assimilate although she conquered. Will France assimilate, or be herself assimilated?"

And turning to Michael Geste, said:

"He was stationed at Cæsarea once. They called it 'The Athens of the West.' We talked of Masinissa, the Berber King of Cæsarea and all Numidia. You will remember he fought against Rome, and then against Carthage in alliance with Rome. He was the grandfather of the great Jugurtha.

"We chatted also of his son Juba, who fought for Pompey in the civil war and committed suicide after Cæsar defeated him at Thapsus.

"*Most* interesting fellow. He told me that Antony's wife Octavia adopted Juba's little son and brought him up with Antony's own little daughter by Cleopatra—young Silene Cleopatra he called her. Quite a charming little romance he made of it, for the two kiddies grew up together at the Roman Court and fell in love with each other—married and lived happy ever after. They went back to Cæsarea and he ruled in the house of his fathers. Rather nice to think about when one considers those cruel times—"

§3

"Oh, for God's sake, shut your jabbering row," growled The Treasure, from where he was lying on his blanket. "Enough to make a dog sick to listen to you."

"Then suppose the dog goes and is sick outside, and doesn't listen," suggested Digby.

"Yes, a charming little story," agreed Michael. "What else did your visitor talk about?"

"Oh, places where he was stationed," replied La Cigale, "and about his Legion. He was frightfully proud of that—like we are of ours. He was in the Third African Legion. 'The Augustine,' he called it. He says it was three centuries in Africa. They only kept one legion in Africa, he tells me, though there were three in Britain. Great fellows, those Romans, for system and organization. What do you think? In this Third Legion of his, the recruiting was almost purely hereditary. Think of that— hereditary drafts. When a man had served his time in the Legion they gave him land on the understanding that he married and settled down there, and sent his sons into the Legion. No wonder there was *esprit de corps* in the Augustine Legion. By the way, they built that place over there in A.D. 100, called it Sagunta Diana, and built it on the ground plan of a Roman camp.

"By Jove, he did a march that I envy him. First they marched right across North Africa, from here to Alexandria. There they embarked in triremes for Italy, and marched to Rome. Thence north, right up Italy, and all across France to a place whence they could see Britain. Then by transports again to Dover, whence they marched to London, and from there through the length of England to Hadrian's Wall. Twenty times 2,000 paces was their day's march—all marked off by regular camping-places.

"He tells me they had a frightful row in camp outside Alexandria with the Sixth Legion from Judea—the Ferrata Legion they called it. It seems the Third Legion hated the others coming into Africa to relieve them while they did their tour of foreign service; they looked upon Africa as their own, and didn't want interlopers in their stations, such as Timgad, Lambæsis, Mascula, Verecundia and Sitifis. He called Timgad *Thamugadi*. I didn't recognize the word at first, as he pronounced it. He was awfully interested to hear that I'd been there and could identify some of the temples in which he had worshipped. It is still in a wonderful state of preservation, as you know. Lambæsis was his favourite camp, for some reason. He was delighted when I told him that the Arch of Septimus Severus is almost as perfect to-day as when he saw it last. That led us to speak of the Arch of Caracalla. That's at Theveste—about 200 miles from Carthage, you know. I'm afraid he began to think I was pulling his leg when I told him I knew it, as well as his beloved Temple of Minerva. He got quite excited."

The Treasure growled, cursed, and spat.

"Told you all that, did he?" he said. "Damn fine ghost! Pity he couldn't have told you something useful. Where he'd buried a few bottles of wine, for example. D'you know what there was when you and your ghost was jabberin'? Two village idiots together—that's what there was."

"If you interrupt again I'll put your face in the sand, and sit on your head till you die," murmured John Geste.

"But there wasn't two *crétins*," continued The Treasure. "There was only one barmy lunatic, and he was talkin' to hisself. 'E's talkin' to three others, 'e is, now."

John Geste rose to his feet, and The Treasure scrambled from the tent in haste.

"And this is a *most* interesting thing," continued La Cigale, still staring at the ground between his feet, as was his habit when not on duty or employed. "Very curious, too. He told me about a deserter from the Roman army—the Legionary Tacfrineas he called him, who went over to the enemy, and organized the Berber tribes against Rome. The Third Legion was frightfully sick about it. Of course, it was just as though one of us deserted and joined the Senussi or the Touareg or the Riffs, and taught them our drill and tactics, trained their artillerymen, gave them our plans and passwords and generally made them about ten times as dangerous as they are.

"I'd certainly never heard of this Tacfrineas before, so I couldn't have *imagined* all this, could I?"

And he gazed appealingly at the faces of the three brothers.

"Of course not," said Beau Geste. "Extraordinarily interesting experience. It must give you great pleasure to think that, out of all the Battalion, it was you whom the Roman soldier chose to visit."

"Oh, yes. Indeed yes," agreed La Cigale, smiling. "I feel quite happy to-day, and can even bear the sight—and smell—of The Treasure. And the Roman soldier has promised to come and visit me again when I am on sentry, and he's going to tell me a great secret. I don't know what it is, but it's something about some gold."

La Cigale fell silent, pondering, and gradually the light of intelligence faded from his eyes, his mouth fell open, and he looked stupid, dull and miserable.

Digby Geste leant over and shook him by the knee.

"Splendid, old chap," he said. "You're a very remarkable man, you know. I envy you. What else did you and the other old *légionnaire* yarn about?"

"Oh, we compared pay, rations, drill, marches and all that sort of thing, you know," replied La Cigale, brightening like a re-lighted lamp. "They had the same infernal road-making fatigues that we do.

"Why, he tells me they built one hundred and ninety miles of solid stone road from Thevesti to Carthage. Think of that— *stone!*

"Oh, yes, we exchanged grumbles. They had the same god-forsaken little outposts down in the South and much the same sort of tyranny from 'foreign' N.C.O.'s, of whom they were more afraid than they were of the Centurions themselves. Yes, they had an iron discipline and even severer punishments. In a case where a man here might get *crapaudine*, because there were no cells in which to give him thirty days' solitary confinement, he would have been flogged to death in the Third Legion, or perhaps crucified.

"I say, I *do* hope he comes again. Do you think he will? He gave me the happiest night I've had since I went—went—went—"

La Cigale groaned, and gazed stupidly around.

"Eh?" he asked. "What's this?" and lay down upon his blanket to sleep.

§4

La Cigale's *bête noir* was a person who, in full possession of his faculties, had less understanding and intelligence than La Cigale at his maddest.

He was that curious product of the Paris slums, that seems to be less like a human being than are the criminal denizens of the underworld of any other city—Eastern or Western, civilized or savage. He was not so much a typical Paris apache, as an apache too bestial, degraded, evil and brutish to be typical even of the Parisian apache. Even the Geste brothers, who could find "tongues in trees, books in the running brooks, sermons in stones, and good in everything," could find no good in "The Treasure"— as Sergeant-Major Lejaune, with grim irony, had christened him. They had, individually and collectively, done their best, and had completely failed. That such a creature, personally filthy (inside his uniform), with foulest tongue and foulest habits, degraded and disgusting, a walking pollution and corruption, should be one's intimate companion at bed and board, was one of the many things that made life in the Legion difficult. One had to sleep, eat, march, and take one's ease (!) cheek by jowl with The Treasure, and could not escape him.

§5

And the Treasure, by nature indescribably objectionable, deliberately made himself as personally and peculiarly objectionable to La Cigale as he possibly could. From the store of his vile, foul manners, he gave the sensitive ex-officer constant experience of the vilest and foulest of his filthy and revolting speech. Of his mean, low, injurious tricks, he reserved the worst for La Cigale. When accused by a non-commissioned officer of some offence, he invariably laid the blame upon La Cigale, in the reasoned belief and reasonable hope that the poor madman would have either too little wit or too much chivalry to defend himself and arraign his lying accuser.

On one occasion, at Ain Sefra, Beau Geste had seen The Treasure, just before kit inspection, direct the attention of La Cigale, by a sudden shout and pointing hand, to something else, while he snatched a belt from La Cigale's kit and placed it with his own. This saved him from eight days' prison and transferred the punishment to the bewildered La Cigale, who could only stammer to the roaring Sergeant-Major Lejaune that his show-down of kit had been complete a few seconds before. But it had earned The Treasure a worse punishment, for the indignant Beau Geste had soundly and scientifically hammered him, until he wept and begged for mercy, with profuse protestations that he had not done it, but would never do it again.

He never did, but he redoubled his efforts to render La Cigale's life insupportable, and showed something almost approaching intelligence in ascertaining which of his foul habits and fouller words most annoyed, shocked disgusted and upset his unhappy victim.

For Beau Geste, The Treasure entertained a deep respect, a great fear and a sharp knife, the last-named to be taken as prescribed (in the back), and when opportunity and occasion should arise. These would have arisen long ago but that his enemy had two brothers and two horrible American friends who rendered an otherwise perfectly simple job not only difficult but extremely dangerous . . . (Remember poor Bolidar!)

Like almost all of his kind, The Treasure was a drunkard, and there was nothing he would not do for money, inasmuch as money to him was synonymous with liquor. Having been, in private life, a professional pickpocket and sneak-thief, he was able to keep himself modestly supplied with cash while avoiding the terrible retribution which overtakes the *légionnaire* who robs his comrades.

§6

"Do you know, young gentlemen," said John Geste, one afternoon, to his two brothers as they strolled from the parade ground whence they had just been dismissed to the tent where they would now settle down to the cleaning of their kit, "I've had an idea?"

Digby seized John's wrist that he might feel his pulse, and observed:

"An idea, Beau! He's had an idea. Hold him while I fetch some water."

"He's got plenty already," replied Michael unperturbed, "on the brain. Idea's probably drowned by now."

"No, no," said John. "It's still swimming around. It's this: La Cigale is for guard again to-night and simply bubbling with excitement at the thought of seeing his Roman soldier again."

"What! Do you want to go and pal up with him?" interrupted

Digby. "Butt in and make up to La Cigale's old pal—severing two loving hearts—green-eyed jealousy—"

"No, the pup only wants to see a ghost," said Michael.

"Well, of course, I would," admitted John. "But what I was going to say, when you two—er—gentlemen began to bray, was this. Poor old Cigale may do anything under the disturbing influences of full moon and a private visit from this Shade."

"Shady business," murmured Digby. "He may go clean off the deep end in his excitement—start showing him round the camp, take him in to gaze upon the slumbering features of Lejaune, or even toddle off with him to visit a two-thousand-years-closed wine-shop in the forum at Sagunta Diana. It occurred to me that a few of us three might exchange with fellows who are for guard, and keep an eye on the poor old chap."

"Quite so," agreed Beau Geste. "Good lad. I fancy Lejaune would be only too glad of the chance to smash La Cigale for being a gentleman and an ex-officer. And if the doctor or the colonel or a court-martial officially pronounced him mad he might be put in a lunatic asylum. And that would be about the cruellest and most dreadful thing one could imagine, for he's half sane half the time, and as sane as we are occasionally."

"Oh, yes," agreed Digby. "Far saner than some people—John, for example."

§7

In the early moonlit hours of the following morning, John Geste patrolled the beat which adjoined that of La Cigale, while Michael and Digby took turns to sit outside the guard tent to watch.

For an hour or so of his tour of sentry go, La Cigale behaved quite normally.

Suddenly John, marching on his beat towards where La Cigale stood staring in the direction of the ruins of Sagunta Diana, saw him spring to attention, present arms, hold himself erect and rigid as a statue, relax and stand at ease, change his rifle from his right hand to his left and then, bowing, warmly shake hands with some person invisible.

"I am so glad you've come again, my friend," John heard La

Cigale say. "Most kind and charming of you. I'm awfully sorry I can't show myself as hospitable as I should like to be—but you know what it is. No, we shan't be disturbed until I'm relieved. Grand Rounds passed some time ago."

John Geste shivered slightly.

A most uncanny experience. It was perfectly obvious that La Cigale was talking to somebody whom he could see and hear and touch.

Could it be that ghosts really exist, and are visible to those who are what is called psychic?

He stared and stared at the place where anyone would be standing who was talking, face to face, with La Cigale. Nothing, of course.

He rubbed his eyes and, clasping the blade of the long bayonet in his hands, leant upon his rifle while he concentrated his gaze as though peering through a fog.

Nothing, of course.

But *was* there nothing? Was there a shadow confronting La Cigale? The shadow of a medium-sized thick-set man leaning upon his spear in the very attitude in which John was leaning upon his bayonet and rifle.

Or was it pure illusion? All moonshine—a curious optical delusion enormously strengthened by La Cigale's conduct and the fact that he was talking so naturally.

Yes, a clear case of hetero-suggestion. Curious, though, that one's ears could so affect one's eyes that one could imagine one saw what one imagined one heard.

Would he hear the Roman soldier's voice in a moment? If so, he would be perfectly certain that he *could* see the figure of a Roman soldier wearing a helmet like that of a fireman; a moulded breast-plate from which depended heavy hangings; metal greaves; and high-laced sandals—a man who bore a longish shield curved at the sides and straight at the top and bottom, on which was painted an eagle, a capital A, and the figure III.

He only *thought* he saw him now, of course, and in a moment he would think he heard his voice. At present there was but one, and hearing it was like listening to a person who is using the telephone in the room in which one is.

*   *   *   *   *   *   *

"Were you really? No! How very interesting!"

*   *   *   *   *   *   *

"Oh, yes; I've been there several times. To think that we have trodden the same streets, entered the very same shops and dwelling-houses, temples and theatres, actually drunk from the same faucet and washed our hands in the same stone trough! I think that one of the most interesting—the most *human* and real—things in all the wonderful Pompeii are those grooves worn in the edges of the troughs where thousands of people for hundreds of years all laid their right hands on the same spot to support themselves as they bent over the trough to put their lips to the faucet from which the water trickled."

*   *   *   *   *   *   *

"Yes, of course you have, many and many a time, and so did I once—just to be one with all those departed Romans."

*   *   *   *   *   *   *

"Yes, that's what makes it so wonderful. Not merely a case of my having been in a place which is only on the site of a place in which you have been. Yes, exactly. The very same actual and identical houses. You and I, my friend, have trodden on the same actual paving-blocks, and have sat upon the same stone seats. I have walked in the very ruts in which the wheels of your chariot rolled as you drove it down the stone-paved High Street of Pompeii, and I have stood in the wine-shops in which you have drunk."

*   *   *   *   *   *   *

"Yes, a very funny picture, indeed. It is still there, the colours as perfect as when you saw it last. They've got glass, and a sort of blind over it now, and a custodian to guard it. To think you actually saw it being painted and remember roaring with laughter when Balbus drew your attention to it."

*   *   *   *   *   *   *

"Oh, didn't you? A pity. History says that he was living there about that time."

*   *   *   *   *   *   *

"Yes, you must have hated returning from furlough just then even to the Third Legion."

*   *   *   *   *   *   *

"Well, no, we aren't supposed to do it—and there'd be precious little to be had if we were. One hears tales, of course. There's a place we call Fez where one or two are supposed to have got hold of a little."

*   *   *   *   *   *   *

"Really? By Jove, that would be an interesting find for anybody who unearthed it now. . . ."

*   *   *   *   *   *   *

"*I* could? I'm afraid it wouldn't be of much use to me— though it would be most awfully interesting to see it. There would probably be coins of which no known specimen exists at the present day. Priceless. Oh, yes, they would fetch any sum. . . ."

*   *   *   *   *   *   *

"By Jove, that was hard luck! They don't seem to have changed much, from your day to ours. We call them Bedouin and Touareg. Attack us in much the same way. Stamp us flat occasionally, but discipline always tells. . . ."

*　　*　　*　　*　　*　　*　　*

"Could you really? The very spot? Very kind of you—most charming. I should love to see the coins."

*　　*　　*　　*　　*　　*　　*

"Oh, no, I shouldn't wish to remove it, but if you could spare one or two specimens that are unknown to-day, I should love to have them as souvenirs. I should not part with them of course. One or two early Greek gold ones."

*　　*　　*　　*　　*　　*　　*

"Now at once? Really most kind of you. A very great honour. Oh, no, I wouldn't dream of showing anybody else. I never betray a confidence. . . ."

*　　*　　*　　*　　*　　*　　*

And then John Geste rushed forward as La Cigale, throwing his rifle up on his right shoulder, marched off in the direction of Sagunta Diana. Digby Geste came hurrying from the direction of the Guard Tent.

Seizing La Cigale's arm, John swung him about.

"What are you doing, man?" he expostulated. "You can't leave your post like this. You're a pretty sentry! You don't want to be shot, do you?—not at dawn by a firing party of your own comrades, at any rate!"

Digby arrived and seized La Cigale's other arm.

"Come home, Bill Bailey," quoth he. "Setting us all a nice example, aren't you? And I thought you were the model *légionnaire*."

"Good God, what am I doing!" stammered La Cigale and passed his hand across his eyes as the brothers released him.

"Thank you so much, gentlemen. This absent-mindedness is terrible. Do you know, a friend of mine, a most interesting chap, strolled over from his lines and we fell into conversation. I actually forgot that I was on sentry. I am getting *so* absent-minded. When he invited me to come over and—er—look at something, I was just going to walk across with him. Thank you *so* much."

"All right now?" asked Digby.

"Oh quite, thank you!" replied La Cigale. "It was only a momentary aberration. I'd sooner die than leave my post, of course."

"What became of him?" asked John.

"Oh, he went off without me," replied La Cigale. "There he goes, look. I hope he's not offended."

§8

The brothers stared and stared in the direction of La Cigale's extended hand.

"See anything, John?" whispered Digby.

"Well, do you know?" answered John, "I couldn't absolutely swear that I didn't see a nebulous figure. And the astounding thing is that I saw or thought I saw something that La Cigale never mentioned."

"The shield?" whispered Digby. "With a capital A and the Roman III, and something at the top?"

"Did you see it, too?" inquired a voice from behind. Michael had joined them.

"Clearly," replied Digby. "Did you, Beau?"

"Absolutely distinctly," replied Michael. "I saw a Roman soldier. I could describe every detail of his kit; I could sketch him exactly as he was."

"I, too," affirmed Digby.

"You, John?" asked Michael.

"Couldn't swear to it," replied John. "Cigale was chatting away so naturally with *somebody*—that I couldn't help fancying that I saw the man to whom he was talking. I certainly didn't see anything clearly and definitely like you two seem to have done. And yet I fancied I dimly saw the III A shield. If nobody else had mentioned it I should have thought that I'd dreamed the whole thing."

"Rum business," murmured Digby.

"Not an 'absinthe' business, anyhow," replied Michael, as John and La Cigale turned about and began to pace their respective beats.

"You and I are fey, Digby Geste," smiled Michael, linking his arm through that of his brother as they turned back to the guard-tent.

§9

The Treasure lay hid in the black shadow of a crumbling arch watching with wolfish eyes a man who laboured to remove the light, loose sand that had collected at the base of a wall at a point twenty-five paces from a pillar—the fourth of a row that had once supported and adorned the front of a Temple of Diana. Something approaching excitement stirred the sluggish depths of his evil and avaricious soul as he once more assured himself that he was on the track of something good.

Yesterday—with his back turned to his comrades and an appearance of great absorption in his work—he had listened with close attention as this bloomin' lunatic told his blasted friends, those bestial Englishmen, about how he was going to sneak over to these ruddy ruins and dig out a *cache* of gold coins of which he had got wind. Some poor legionary had hid his little bit of loot there one night and the place had been rushed and sacked at dawn, the next morning. Gold coins, too! Nice, handy, portable form of loot, too! And the dirty double-crosser was only going to take one or two to look at, was he? The sacred liar! Not so *fou* as he pretended, that Cigale. Oh, very tricky. Well, other people might know a few tricks, too! What about letting the swindling silly hound sweat for the stuff, and a better man scoop it when the fool had got it?

§10

An hour or so later, La Cigale straightened himself up, gazed around the moonlit ruins in a dazed manner, climbed out of the hole that he had excavated, and made his way towards the camp.

The Treasure crouched back, motionless, in the darkest shadow, until his comrade had passed, and then, rising, followed him—a large stone in his right hand.

The Treasure was a workman skilled in all branches of his trade—one of which was the throwing of knives and other weapons of offence. The heavy stone, flung at a range of six feet or so, struck the unfortunate Cigale at the base of the skull, and by the time he had recovered consciousness The Treasure had come reluctantly to the conclusion that the accursed lying swindling *crétin* had only got a single old coin of some sort, gold, and curiously shaped, about his person. One ancient gold coin, the size of a two-franc piece.

By the time La Cigale had painfully raised himself upon his hands and knees, The Treasure was working feverishly in the excavation that his comrade had recently left.

By the time La Cigale had recovered sufficiently to rise to his feet and gaze uncertainly toward the ruins whence he had come, a dull rumbling, followed by an earth-shaking crash had startled the watchful sentries of the camp. An undermined pillar had fallen.

The Treasure was seen no more by his unsorrowing comrades.

Buried Treasure.

THE DEVIL AND DIGBY GESTE

The main human characters in this story are Digby Geste and another recurring character, Tant de Soif. This story is one of several experiences Digby had while separated from his brothers: he is stationed at Tokotu and the brothers are at Fort Zinderneuf. While on patrol Digby and Tant de Soif spend the night in a tomb at an oasis, and they encounter . . . the devil? "The Devil and Digby Geste" was first published in Good Gestes *(1929) and was reprinted in* Stories of the Foreign Legion *(1947).*

§1

"Look here," said Digby Geste, known locally as *légionnaire* Thomas Jones No. 18896, "will you kindly endeavour to get into your magnificent brain, Monsieur Tant de Soif, once and for all, the fact that I will *not* drink absinthe with you? . . . Very kind of you, and all that; but I don't like it, and I don't want it, and I'm not going to drink it."

"And would you have me *faire Suisse*?" asked the *légionnaire* Tant de Soif, as, with trembling hands, he poured an evil-looking fluid from his water-bottle into a tin mug.

"I don't care what you *faire*, you old marvel, so long as you don't *faire* yourself a nuisance. If you do I'll pour that muck out on the sand."

Tant de Soif shuddered.

"Hush!" he begged. "Do not utter such horrible words—even in jest! . . . It is a kind of blasphemy," and he drank deeply from his mug.

"*Horrible* language," he grumbled, wiping his bearded lips with the back of his hand. "Never heard anything like it in all my forty years of soldiering—and I've heard some awful language, too, in the *Marsouins*[2] and the Legion. . . . And so I must *faire Suisse* at last—after fifty years of soldiering! . . ."

---

[2] Colonial Infantry.

"Once again, *faire* what you like, only don't *faire* nuisance. That's just what you are when you're drunk—'a fair nuisance.'"

"Eh? . . . *Mon Dieu!* . . . *To me!* . . . After sixty years of soldiering! . . . What did you say? A *nuisance?* . . . Say it again. . . ."

And, with drunken gravity, old Tant de Soif rose to his feet, drew his sword-bayonet, and advanced upon the admired comrade whom he loved as a son.

"Say it—*hic*—again if you please," he requested.

"*Vous êtes une peste pour tout le monde*," repeated Digby slowly. "Understand? A nuisance to everybody, when you're drunk."

And, seizing the bayonet with his left hand, he gave the aged gentleman a shove with his right. The bayonet and its owner parted company.

"A nuisance when I'm drunk?" murmured Tant de Soif incredulously, as he sat suddenly down. "And am I to hear *that* said of me, after seventy years of soldiering? . . . Why, I was born drunk—I've lived drunk, and shall *die* drunk! And be a loved and respected centenarian soldier. . . . Yes. . . . The Government will give me a tomb like that of Fräulein Eberhardt, the Spahi Sergeant, at Figuig. . . . On it they will write the dignified and simple epitaph, '*One hundred years a soldier*.'"

A tear trickled from the eye of Tant de Soif as he contemplated his apotheosis.

"More likely '*One hundred years drunk*,' you old lunatic," laughed Digby Geste. "That's what you are—the original and authentic Lunatic among the Tombs."

"Undeniably we are in a tomb," replied Tant de Soif, nodding his head thoughtfully, "but it is not *I* who am the lunatic. . . . It is not *I* who am refusing good liquor. . . . No, indeed! . . . Nor have I, in eighty years of soldiering, met a man who *did*. . . . No, not until this night. . . . And now I am in a tomb with him. *I*, Tant de Soif, with a lunatic in the Tomb."

In a tomb they undoubtedly were, and in a place of tombs, built none knew how many centuries before—perhaps on the site of some battlefield, where great men had fallen and received princely sepulture. Or possibly some holy and far-famed *marabout* had dwelt at this tiny oasis, had been buried here by the sorrowing devout; and around his tomb had been laid those of the pious who had wished to sleep near him in death, as they had dwelt near him in life.

In the largest of these tombs the two *légionnaires* had taken up a strategic position for the night. Fastening the still practicable heavy door, and using the two horizontal tombstones as beds, they had converted the mosque-like *taj* into a barrack-room and a fort.

The two graves were extraordinarily reminiscent of a pair of crusader, princely, or episcopal tombs in a European cathedral— save that no recumbent effigy adorned the large, flat, oblong stone that formed the top of each. Ideal beds—if a little hard— roomy, level three feet from the ground, and thus well above the sphere of operations of scorpion, serpent, and objectionable insect left by pariah dog or wandering beggar.

As though in their heat-warped and horrible caserne at Tokotu, whence they had come on this patrol, the two soldiers made ready for the night, and, having cleaned their accoutrements and folded the clothing they had removed, laid themselves down upon their cold and silent tombs—their temporary graves, as Digby Geste described them. The "night attire" of the latter consisted of white canvas shoes, belted canvas trousers, and a short-sleeved white shirt. Tant de Soif, for reasons best known to himself, wore only his *képi* and his boots. He explained, with convincing clarity, that, in the case of emergency, he was thus protected against the sun (or moon) at the one end and against sharp stones and thorns at the other; while, if no emergency arose, all was still well, as it was obvious to the meanest intelligence that if the head and the feet were kept hot, the intervening and adjacent tracts must inevitably be benefited and remain in a satisfactory condition.

"So you always sleep in your *képi* to keep your tummy warm, eh?" observed Digby, as he settled his head upon his knapsack.

"And my boots to keep the lumbar regions protected," was the reply. "I have suffered from lumbago, and one cannot be too careful . . . especially when one has no blood in one's veins. . . . I have no blood at all, and, when wounded, I bleed absinthe."

"Valuable gift," murmured his companion sleepily. "Good

idea. Every man his own canteen. Like the pelican in the wilderness, or the camel feeding on its own hump. . . . G'night, Gran'pa, and don't you dare speak another word till daylight doth appear. . . ."

Ere he fell asleep the thoughts of Digby Geste wandered. First, to Brandon Abbas, where dwelt the girl who had been his life's sunshine, the sound of whose voice had been his life's music, for a brief sight of whose face he would now have given almost anything—certainly a year of his life.

"Darling Isobel," he murmured. "Darling, Faithful Hound," and smiled. Next he thought of his brothers, Michael and John, at the Fort of Zinderneuf.

"Dear old Beau. . . . Dear old John. . . . Hope all's well with them. . . . Wish to God I could get transferred there. They must be having a thin time with Lejaune. . . . Wonder if de Beaujolais would listen to me if I asked to be sent there. . . .

"Glad old St. André and Maris, and Cordier are there too. Decent chaps. . . . Wish Hank and Buddy were—much as I should miss them at Tokotu.

"Wonder if I and old Tant de Soif ought to keep watch and watch? . . . No point in doing so, really. If a raiding-party come, they come—and they get us, anyhow. . . . And it wouldn't be till dawn. . . . I shall be awake by then. . . ."

But Digby Geste was awakened before dawn.

Silence. . . .

Outside the tomb a world of silence—a Universe of Silence, broken only by the occasional sound of a soft, light footstep, almost inaudible.

Silence and stillness, upon which the great full moon looked down . . . upon the illimitable desert, all patined with fine silver, over which the shadows thrown by the few scattered palms and by the ancient domed and minareted mosques lay black as ink.

Into one of these mosques the great moon peeped, and by the light of her own rays beheld, through a narrow unglazed window, two faces—the one innocent, calm, peacefully happy, the other debased, scarred, haunted, contorted in the agony of some miserable nightmare.

The moon watched. . . .

Suddenly at the opposite aperture, appeared the face of another watcher—a horrible face, a terrible face—long, gaunt, bearded, with the shallow, soulless eyes of a beast.

Within the tomb, silence, broken only by the sound of breathing, and an occasional sigh from Digby; from Tant de Soif a groan.

§2

An unusually loud groan from the restless veteran awoke his young comrade from a deep dream of peace. The latter raised his head from the knapsack on which it rested.

"What's up, Daddy?" he said, and yawned.

The old man murmured something concerning a *courant d'air*, and the extreme unwholesomeness of ventilation.

With a laugh the boy sat up, stretched and yawned hugely, and, with a remark to the effect that, in his own callow and uninstructed mind, he regarded absinthe as even more unwholesome than fresh air, he spread Tant de Soif's *capote* over him and bade him be of good cheer, for he couldn't much longer survive the troubles of this vale of woe.

Returning to his stony couch, Digby gazed around the moonlit chamber, so chapel-like with its high, narrow "windows," its pair of tombs, high, vaulted roof, and stone-flagged floor. In the moonlight the figure of old Tant de Soif might well have been a stone effigy, as he lay like a warrior taking his rest, with his martial cloak around him.

The boy closed his eyes.

Darling Isobel. . . .

What was she doing now? . . .

Sleeping, of course. . . . Sleeping in her moonlit, panelled room at Brandon Abbas. . . .

Same jolly old moon that was looking into this mosque was peeping through the leaded panes of her casement. Funny if she were awake, too, and wondering whether he were looking at the moon at that moment. . . .

Darling Isobel! When would he see her again? Not till his five years were up, anyhow; unless, of course, they were sent back to Sidi-bel-Abbés and she came there. . . . Even when their time had expired they couldn't go back to Brandon Abbas until that astounding business was cleared up. . . . Beau running off in that extraordinary way. . . .

And young John, the silly young ass! . . . Daring to run away from home, too, like his elders and betters—a child like that. . . . A good year junior to the twins. . . . Frightful little ass. . . . That's what happens when the young are released from proper, repressive discipline. . . . Very 'cute of him, though, to guess that they had joined the Legion. . . . Pretty mess he'd have found himself in if he'd been wrong. . . . Dear old Johnny. . . . How ghastly if anything happened to him. . . . Thank God he was with Beau. . . . Beau would look after him all right. . . . Yes, Beau would look after him.

Yawns. . . .

Digby Geste slept.

And was awakened later by a blood-curdling yell—a terrible scream, like that of a wounded horse. In almost one movement he was on his feet, crouching between the tombs, his rifle in his hands, his head turning swiftly from window to window at the opposite sides of the chamber—the one idea on his mind being of an Arab raid.

Nothing at either window.

No rifles thrust through the ten-inch aperture, between the stone sides of the high, narrow openings. No heavy blows upon the door. . . .

And then he was aware that Tant de Soif was pointing with trembling hand to the window nearest to him—the one through which the moon did not shed her soft light. Bringing his rifle swiftly round, he "covered" the aperture and waited.

Strange! . . . Why hadn't the devils shot at them from both windows as they slept? And why hadn't old Tant de Soif made one jump for his gun? Why had he screamed like a tortured woman, and why was he still lying there, trembling from head to foot? Old Tant de Soif, with his *Médaille Militaire*, brave as a lion?

"Arabs?" whispered Digby.

"No, no," groaned the old soldier. "Oh, my God! . . . God forgive me . . . forgive me all my wickedness. . . . Oh, *mon Général le bon Dieu*, have mercy on an old soldier . . . *première classe . . .*"

"What is it, you old fool?" urged Digby, breaking upon the prayer. "God helps those who help themselves. What *is* it, if it isn't Arabs? A lion, or a . . . rabbit, or what?"

"*Hush*! Don't blaspheme," whispered Tant de Soif, turning from the window, flinging his arms about Digby, and crushing his bearded face against the boy's breast.

There was no doubt that the old man had had a terrible fright, and, indeed, a terrible shock. He was sober enough now, and in a state of absolute, utter terror.

There is nothing more infectious than panic, terror, fear—and particularly fear of the utterly unknown.

Perfect love casteth out fear. So doth perfect anger—and a good deal more quickly. Digby's anger was certainly perfect—at being awakened; at being made to jump and take cover; at being—well—frightened or at any rate threatened with fright— by this old drunkard.

"What *is* it?" he repeated. "What did you see—or think you saw?" And his free hand was upon Tant de Soif heavily laid, though not in the way of kindness.

But Tant de Soif could say nothing. His teeth were chattering with fright.

It was useless to be angry with the old man. He was most obviously terrified almost to death.

"What *is* it, old chap? What did you see?" Digby asked again, without taking his eyes from the narrow aperture, of which the base or window-sill was some three feet from the ground. "What did you see?"

"*The Devil himself*!" whispered Tant de Soif, and, with a hollow groan, let his head fall heavily back upon the stone.

"Oh—*the Devil*?" replied the incensed Digby. "Is *that* all! . . . I'll show you something worse than the Devil if you wake me up again with your nightmares—you walking whisky-flask; you woolly-witted wine-cask; you bibulous brandy-bottle, you . . ."

"Oh, God!" moaned the old soldier. "Oh, Jesus Christ! Oh, Holy Virgin! Guard me this night. It was *the Devil himself*. The Devil has come for me—at last! . . ."

"Well, he hasn't *got* you yet, has he?" expostulated Digby. "And he won't. . . . But *I* will. *I'll* get you all right, old son, if you wake me up again."

"The Devil has come for me, and I am dying," groaned the old soldier as he turned his face again toward the window. "We were mad to come in here. . . . It is a sepulchre. . . . This tomb is my bed, and this bed will be my tomb."

"It'll be all *that*," replied Digby, "if you don't shut up. Go to sleep, you silly old ass. Do you think the Devil's a fool, that he should want *you* in. . . ."

An awful scream interrupted the speaker as the lower part of the unglazed "window" was filled by a truly appalling face.

Tant de Soif again flung himself upon his comrade, effectually pinning his arms to his sides.

Digby Geste was a brave man—young, strong, healthy, and devoid of nerves. He felt his blood run cold, his knees weaken, his heart pound furiously, and the cold perspiration start forth upon his skin.

Not one of these symptoms would have been evoked by the sight of the most evil face of any human being, Negro or Arab, looking at him from behind a levelled gun. Rather would Digby Geste's pulse have tingled with the joy of battle as he jerked his rifle forward, and tried to shoot ere he was shot.

But this was face neither of Arab nor of Negro. . . . Nor of any human being.

Tant de Soif looked again, and shrieked again—the dreadful, agonized shriek of a madman.

It was *not* a human face. It was the face of a . . . the face of a *devil*. . . . The face of *the* Devil!

Yes . . . merciful God . . . from the forehead that overhung the glowing luminescent eyes—the dreadful, shallow, bestial, devilish eyes—to the bearded chin, the face was fiendish. . . .

The hideous mouth, with its great strong white teeth, opened to speak, and closed again in silence. The hideous lips twitched in a sneering smile, and the whole awful face, long, gaunt, and hairy, leered with a hellish malignity, triumphant, terrible, cruel beyond expression.

But Digby Geste was more afraid of fear than of the Devil. Wrenching himself free from the frenzied clutch of Tant de Soif, he threw his rifle to his shoulder—only to find it torn almost from his hands as Tant de Soif seized it, and scrambling to his knees, fell upon him.

"*Don't! Don't!*" he screamed. "*It is the Devil.* . . . You cannot shoot the Devil."

"Watch me," laughed Digby, his own man again, and with a strong thrust sent Tant de Soif sprawling on the ground, instantly raising his rifle as he did so.

But the Devil had gone.

Nothing was to be seen, but the silvered sandhills, and some distant palms.

Digby lowered his rifle and stared aghast. Was this a nightmare? No, he was awake, and here was Tant de Soif clasping him round the knees, and praying to God and to the Devil impartially.

Was it hypnotism . . . auto-suggestion . . . hetero-suggestion? Was he, for some reason, seeing with his own eyes what this poor drunken old sot, in an attack of delirium tremens, thought he saw with his? Was there something in the physical or psychic atmosphere of this ancient mausoleum that was supernatural or, at any rate, super-normal? *Were* there djinns in these lone desert places?

"*Kneel down and pray! . . . Kneel down and pray!*" gabbled Tant de Soif.

"Stand up and watch, more sense," replied Digby. "There's a time for everything. . . . Get up and get your rifle."

"You can't fight *the Devil*," groaned Tant de Soif.

"There isn't any devil," affirmed Digby.

"Haven't we just *seen* him, you fool?" replied the drunkard.

"And if we can see him we can shoot him. . . . Pull yourself together, you old coward," growled Digby.

"I'm not a coward. I fear nothing human, nothing solid. . . ."

"Pity you don't fear nothing liquid, too. . . . Absinthe, for example. . . ."

Yes, that was all very well, but he, Digby Geste, had never tasted absinthe in his life, and most undoubtedly he had seen what Tant de Soif saw. . . . Seen it clearly and unmistakably, and for at least a minute. . . . Had seen the dreadful eyes move, the ghastly mouth smile horribly.

Stooping, he pulled Tant de Soif to his feet.

"Now, then," he said. "Pull yourself together, you wretched old woman. Put on your overcoat, and pick up your rifle. Cover that other window, while I cover this one. . . . If nothing happens I'm going outside for a scout round. . . . If it's the Devil, I want to see a bit more of him. . . . Cloven hoof, and all that. . . ."

But Tant de Soif was past self-help.

"For the love of *God* don't open that door," he stuttered. "Don't leave me. . . . For the love of *Christ* don't leave me. I . . ."

"Look!" he shrieked, and collapsed. The Face had reappeared at the window. . . . Terrible, gleaming, yellow eyes. . . . Inhuman, sub-human, devilish, shallow eyes. . . . Terrible, inhuman mouth with twitching lips and gleaming teeth. . . . A gargoyle face, the face of the Devil as portrayed in ancient books, wood-carvings and gargoyles.

Digby Geste raised his rifle, and the lips parted in a brutish smile.

Digby Geste stood firm and steady, the foresight of his weapon pointing between the gleaming eyes—eyes that shone as though each contained a glowing core of fire—his forefinger curled about the trigger—and did not fire.

Undoubtedly he had been frightened. He was not frightened now, and he refused to panic. He was not going to blow a hole in the middle of a face simply because he didn't like the look of it. That was not the sort of thing that Beau would do. To shoot first and ask after was to exhibit the fear of which he was afraid. . . .

Stalemate. . . .

The devilish Face watched him, and he covered the devilish Face.

Stalemate. . . .

His arms were growing tired. . . .

Why didn't the Thing do something? Did it calmly await his futile shot, secure in the knowledge of its immunity? . . . *Was* it a devil? . . . *The* devil?

That dreadful, impish, evil face . . . that hairy, bearded mask of evil . . .

Mask! . . . Mask? . . . Was this some Arab trick to frighten them? . . . To drive them, screaming in terror, from their stronghold?

Absurd! The man could have shot them sleeping. . . . Perhaps he had no gun.

The great mouth opened.

No, that was a face, and not a mask. Should he fire? No. One does not shoot an "unarmed," unarmoured Face.

Digby Geste lowered his rifle and backed slowly to the door, his eyes fixed upon those other terrible eyes that followed his every movement.

"Tant de Soif!" he called. "Get up and open this door. Tant de Soif—you coward—get up!"

Tant de Soif stirred, struggled to his feet, glanced at the Face, howled, rushed to his comrade, not to obey him, but to get behind him.

Turning his back upon the Face, Digby thrust Tant de Soif aside, knocked up the heavy bar with the butt of his rifle, glanced across the tomb at the motionless, basilisk head, dashed through the doorway, his rifle at the ready, crept round the building, turning the second corner, and there beheld, up-reared upon the cloven hooves of its hind legs, a large billy-goat.

THE MULE

"The Mule" is another story of Digby Geste while he was with the mule company at Tokotu. The story is primarily about Digby and the problems he has with the mules and a legionnaire named Xarro. Buddy, Hank, and de Beaujolais also have small parts in the tale. There is also an interesting sub-story about when Digby is on sentry duty one evening when the company is out on patrol. Interesting in the light of Wren's comment about being on sentry duty in "Twenty-Four Hours in the Foreign Legion" (in this volume of The Collected Short Stories*). "The Mule" appeared in* Good Gestes, *which was published in February 1929. It was also published in the* Pall Mall Magazine *in September 1929, and reprinted in the British* Argosy *six months later in March 1930. "The Mule" was reprinted in* Stories of the Foreign Legion *(Murray 1947) and the British edition (but not the American edition) of* The Best War Stories *(1985).*

§1

It is said that there is good in everyone, and that though the whitest sheep has a black or a grey hair somewhere, there is no black sheep so black that he has not one grey lock, if he cannot boast a white one.

Be that as it may, *le légionnaire* Xarro, blackest of black sheep, did marvellously conceal the fact if he possessed the faintest redeeming shade of lighter colour.

Although admittedly a black sheep, *le légionnaire* Xarro was known as "The Mule." This name had been bestowed upon him only partly in tribute to the fact that he was astonishingly mulish, surly, cross-grained, stupid, malevolent and dangerous. For the other part, the name was esteemed appropriate by reason of the fact that the company mules apparently accepted him as a friend and a brother. He was one with them, and they were at one with him. No mule ever kicked, bit, thwarted or disobeyed *le légionnaire* Xarro. Mules were his friends, if not, as his comrades averred, his relations. A fiendishly cruel man, who delighted to torture other animals, and to devise tortures which he hoped some day to inflict upon Arab men, women and children, he was never cruel to a mule.

Nor was this merely one of those beautiful instances of virtue being its own reward, and kindness begetting kindness. Digby Geste was just as kind to his mule as Xarro was to his, but this did not induce the beast to lose any opportunity of kicking or biting Digby; of slipping his heel-rope and absenting himself without leave; of throwing his load whenever he could; of instigating his fellows to stampede, and generally of being as ungrateful, obnoxious and exasperating as only a mule can be.

Digby Geste loved animals, and hated this mule as he had never hated anything before—with good reason—and the more he hated it, the more kindly he treated it. The more kindly he treated it, the more evil it seemed to grow—*seemed*—because no one would care to state categorically that there was room for it to grow more evil. . . .

Yet when this same mule was in the hands of *le légionnaire* Xarro, it was the Perfect Mule—an animal without moral spot or blemish, wearing in its head-stall the white flower of a blameless life.

It pleased the good Xarro enormously that any peculiarly intractable and unmanageable mule should be handed over to him with the sure and certain knowledge that, while in his hands, it would be entirely docile.

Had *le légionnaire* Xarro been any other than *le légionnaire* Xarro, he would have been promoted, and made one of the non-commissioned personnel at a Mounted Infantry depôt where men and mules are trained. He might have become Sergeant-Major or even *Adjudant*, and had a glorious opportunity of exercising his markedly developed traits of cruelty, malevolence, brutality and spite, upon *les légionnaires*, whom he hated collectively and individually.

But, in spite of these qualities, it was quite impossible to promote *ce bon* Xarro. He was too utterly unreliable and untrustworthy; too debauched, depraved and slovenly; too mean, ineffectual and stupid; too bad a soldier, and too good a liar, thief and drunkard.

Nor can it be urged in his favour that he was fond of his mules.

Love is a lovely thing—if it be only love for a mule; but Xarro loved them no more than he did pariah dogs of the *Village Nègre*, wild cats of the rocks, and vultures of the air.

When a mule was hit by a bullet, fell down a precipice, or suffered a broken leg and was butchered to become steaks and cutlets for hungry soldiers, he was inordinately amused, and apparently very pleased.

No, he certainly did not love them, but he understood them, and they understood him, and were perfectly *en rapport*.

It was said—and probably truly—that he had been a muleteer "in real life" (that is to say before he joined the Legion), and had been bred and born among mules, thinking their thoughts, feeling their sensations, needs, desires and sufferings, and, moreover, speaking their language—this last because he uttered words, if such sounds could be called words, which the mules understood.

Digby Geste, watching him, was reminded of what Uncle Hector had told him about *mahouts* in India, who undeniably had an elephant-language which their charges understood and obeyed.

Seated on his mule, Xarro, without movement of hand or heel, could cause his mount to sidle a few paces to the right or to the left, to advance a few steps or to rein back—merely by the use of a single word for each movement. His mule would halt, about-turn, or wheel to the right or left, at a word. More, it would lift a left or right hoof, come to its fore-knees, or lie upon the ground, at Xarro's command.

His particular beast, known as "Satan," was a rare black animal, big beyond the size of large mules, and, save in the hands of Xarro himself, a fitter inmate of a cage in a Zoological Gardens than a place in a mule-line. Among mules, Satan was as objectionable and detestable as Xarro was among men.

§2

We have it on excellent authority that we needs must love the highest when we see it. *Le légionnaire* Xarro must have been an exception to this golden rule. Definitely he did not love the highest when he saw it. Hating all his officers, non-commissioned officers and comrades, he hated the best most. For scoundrels like Bolidar, Boldini, Guantaio and Vogué (all now away at Zinderneuf) he had quite a mild detestation.

The three English brothers, who called themselves Brown, Jones and Smith respectively, he loathed peculiarly, and of these the one named Jones, who was here at Tokotu, he abhorred most of all. Was he not always merry and bright, laughing and smiling—curse him! As if there were anything whatever to laugh or smile about, in this devilish world! Was he not always pleasant and friendly—damn him!—in contrast to one's own morose ill-humoured surliness? Was he not open and frank and generous—blast him! Was he not popular and cool and unafraid? Was he not rich, a gentleman, an aristocrat? Yes, and after all, what was he, with all his airs and graces, but a damned jewel-thief, hiding from the English police? Who was *he* to give himself airs, and walk in pride?

Pride goeth before a fall. Aha, yes, *a fall!* . . . A bright idea! . . . And *le légionnaire* Xarro showed a mouthful of blackened and broken teeth, in an artful and evil grin.

§3

"Sunday pants of Holy Moses! What in Hell's that guy Xarro up to *now*?" exclaimed Buddy to his friend Hank one evening, as, having strolled beyond the rough and dirty camp known as *le Village Nègre*, they seated themselves upon the summit of a sand-dune and gazed across the stretch of level country, an unbroken plain of rock, sand, and gravel, which stretched before them.

Unaware of their presence, Xarro and Satan, a couple of hundred metres distant, were engaged upon some mutually diverting exercise. It soon became apparent to the interested watchers that Satan was learning a new trick, or rather was learning to do, instantly and methodically, at the word of command, what he sometimes did at the prompting of idle errant fancy. He was learning to roll—on his back, over and over, to and fro, bent legs waving in the air—as, and when, ordered to do so.

Hank and Buddy who, in their time, had played many parts and been many things to many men, were intrigued.

"Say, that guy and his burro ought to be in vaudeville," quoth

Hank.

"Sure thing," agreed Buddy, "Xarro and his Performing Mule."

"And a prize to be given for the first member of the audience as correctly guesses which is the mule."

Their usual laconic silence then descended upon them, and they watched.

Satan stood at attention, Xarro three paces in front of him, both motionless.

Suddenly Xarro uttered a single word of command, and down went Satan as though shot.

Thrice he rolled from left to right and right to left, arose to his feet, and stood like a graven image—of wickedness.

Xarro strolled away, and, from a few yards distance, threw a word over his shoulder. Instantly the mule rolled, and arose again. Xarro returned, patted the animal's neck, and gave it something from his pocket. Proceeding to the rear of the imaginary rank which Satan adorned, Xarro wheeled about, and again at a few yards distance uttered a word of command from behind the mule, and again Satan rolled.

Xarro now varied the proceedings. Placing his hands on Satan's back he lightly vaulted astride him, and sitting with folded arms bade the mule rein back, right close, left close, advance, about turn, walk march, right wheel, left wheel and halt. He then, once again, uttered the sharp short word of command, and sprang clear as the beast instantly obeyed, threw itself down and rolled thrice upon its back.

"Say, Hank, what d'you know about *that*," murmured Buddy, as the last manœuvre was again repeated. "He surely is the World's Champion Mule-Tamer. What's the idee?"

"Got me guessing, Bud," was the reply. "P'raps he plans to get a job lion-taming in a circus, when he's through with the Legion."

"He surely does understand mules," said Buddy. "I've known guys make horses act that way, but I allow he's the first man ever taught a mule to sit up and beg. Wonder how he does it?"

"Power of the human eye over the savage beast," opined Hank.

"Pity he don't try it on the Sergeant-Major then," observed

Buddy, rising to his feet, and the two sauntered back to the *poste*.

§4

The mule-*peloton* out on a recognizance patrol was taking an "easy" in the shadow of a great rock, or small cliff, that marked the turning point of their journey, and weary men stood easing weary limbs, each at the head of what one would have supposed to be a weary mule.

Not so, however, the four-legged fiend in mule-skin in charge of Digby Geste. The phrase is ambiguous, and so was the situation, inasmuch as the mule appeared at times to be in Digby's charge, and the mule at times to be in charge of Digby.

Suddenly the devil entered into the beast, or else the devil that never left it awoke, and with an energy rarely displayed in a legitimate cause, the perverse animal began to back, to kick, to buck, rear and plunge, as though its soul's salvation depended upon creating the maximum of confusion in the ranks, wrath in the Commandant, and despair in the unfortunate Digby. A torrent of abuse from the Sergeant-Major did nothing to help the matter, though it seemed to amuse and exhilarate the mule who, with a neigh of laughter, bounded the more vigorously and struggled the more violently to be free, free to roam the wide desert o'er, untrammelled and untied.

Genuine hearty mule laughter!

'*He saith among the trumpets ha, ha! and he smelleth the battle afar off, the thunder of the captains and the shouting,*' quoted Digby from the book of Job.

"There will certainly be some thunder from the Captain in a minute, and the Sergeant-Major is undoubtedly shouting," he added, as he clung to the equine-asinine rebel.

The mule, rearing and lashing out with his forefeet, made a noble effort for liberty and self-determination.

But Digby Geste had a word to say to that, and the struggle continued.

Giving his rein to his right-hand man, *le légionnaire* Xarro stepped up to the kicking, struggling mule and quieted it with a word.

"That's the way to handle a mule," he said. "You take mine,

and I'll ride this one back. But remember this. You mustn't hit it or touch it with your heel. If you want to steady it, you must just say *'Brrrtsch'*—like that. Understand? Just *'Brrrtsch'*—and especially when we are on that narrow path with a precipice on one side, and a cliff on the other be sure to say *'Brrrtsch'* and it'll prick up its ears, and know you for a friend. See?"

"Thanks very much," replied Digby. "But I'll stick to this Father of Vice."

"Don't be a fool," urged Xarro. "You'll find my mule like a lady's hack."

"Thanks again, very much," replied Digby. "It's very good of you, but I mustn't let this beast get the better of me. I must make it quite clear that it is out with me, and not I with it."

"It'll get away," persisted Xarro, "and you'll do fifty-two days' solitary confinement for a start, if it's lost. You go and take old Satan. He's more like an Arab horse than a mule. And don't forget to say *'Brrrtsch,'* when you want to steady him."

"It's most kind of you, Xarro," said Digby again, "but I really mustn't let this beast defeat me."

"More afraid of Satan, I suppose," jeered Xarro. "Afraid he'll play some trick on you, eh?"

"Put it like that if you wish," replied Digby. "Anyhow, I'll stick to this moke. Thanks all the same."

And with a sneering laugh, Xarro shrugged his shoulders and turned to Satan.

However, although *le légionnaire* Xarro had not done all that he intended to do, he had done something, for Digby's mule gave no further trouble, either on the narrow and dangerous mountain path or upon the open plain.

§5

Digby Geste, alias *le légionnaire* Thomas Jones, was puzzled. An unsavoury comrade of the name of Xarro whom he particularly disliked was making repeated overtures of friendship, and equally often-repeated suggestions that Digby should ride his mule Satan. It seemed an obsession with the man, and he was particularly urgent when the *peloton* was at a maximum distance from Tokotu, or about to pass through difficult and dangerous mountain country.

But *le légionnaire* Xarro had made a great mistake. He had dared *le légionnaire* Jones to ride the mule! He had foolishly said:

"Jones, I'm willing to bet any amount that you are afraid to ride Satan. You would like to do so, but you refuse because you haven't the pluck."

To which Digby had replied:

"Obviously that must be the reason. It needs a hero like you to ride the old black moke," and neither jeers nor cajolings could induce Digby to do so.

What he did do was frequently and lengthily to wonder what the man's object could be. Doubtless Satan would give anyone but Xarro a great deal of trouble, but he couldn't give Digby more trouble than did the malevolent Son of Sin and Sorrow with whom he was at present afflicted.

One thing was very certain. Xarro—the surly, quarrelsome, insolent Xarro; the malignant, sly, dangerous Xarro; full of ill-will, ill-nature and ill-breeding—was not offering the mule to Digby for Digby's good. It was very puzzling. . . .

But one tragic day the puzzle was solved—quite horribly.

The Mule-Company to which Digby was attached rode out from Tokotu one red-hot morning, on a forty-eight hours' patrol and tactical exercise as Mounted Infantry. On this occasion they were given admirable exercise, for they were followed at a most respectful distance by a Targui scout, and when at night they halted and made their desert bivouac, he rode off with the glad news that rifles were to be had for the snatching; mules to be captured, and Roumis to be hunted down, shot and tortured.

*   *   *   *   *   *   *

A little camp was pitched in the form of a square, the mule-lines in the centre, each man sleeping in his own *tente d'abri* which, being only one foot high, two feet wide, and three feet long, sounds rather more than it is, particularly on occasions of heavy rain, snow, sand-storm or blasting sunshine.

When a unit of the Legion bivouacs, its Commandant's first thought is to choose a place close to water, so that if the force is pinned to the spot, thirst, the greatest enemy of all, shall not fight on the side of the foe.

Each quarter of the force forms one side of a square; mounts all its tents in a line; and then, at the order, *aux murailles*, builds a stone wall some eighteen inches high, parallel to that line. Should that part of the country be devoid of stones, suitable to dry-wall building, a trench is dug instead, and the earth thrown up to form a parapet. By the time each of the four divisions of the force has done this, the bivouac is a square perimeter camp, surrounded by four defensible walls or trenches.

This temporary fortress having been constructed, fatigue parties are told off to fetch in a sufficient supply of fuel and water.

When, as upon this occasion, neither is likely to be procurable, each man carries his own supply of both, and unless he wants to go hungry, supplies his personal quota to the cook.

At sunset, the guard is mounted for each of the faces of the camp, to the extent of four to a Company, and each sentry does two hours on guard and four hours off.

In theory, these sentries patrol continually, in a smart and soldier-like manner, and meet other sentries at each end of their respective beats.

Digby Geste, being for guard that night, found himself posted at a corner of the Square, and, had he been less utterly weary, saddle-galled and knee-sore, after a long day's wrestling with a most uncomfortable and refractory mount, he would have enjoyed his two hours of peaceful solitude beneath the glorious moon and incredibly great stars, as he gazed out over the silent and illimitable space. . . .

All was very still and very silent. Not even the sound of marching feet disturbed the perfect peace—for no feet marched. Every sentry about the camp was apparently lost in admiration of the wondrous desert night—or more probably in sleep.

Not so Digby Geste. He was on duty, and he had a habit of doing his duty and a little more. He was there to watch, and he was watching—so carefully and so conscientiously, in fact, that he almost thought for a moment that a distant bush moved! Bushes frequently do move, but not when there is no wind blowing, and the air is still as death. Nor in the night-time, when no bird alights nor flies away, causing a branch to quiver and sway.

But then again, moonlight is notoriously deceptive and treacherous, making hovels look like palaces, witches look like fairies and—stationary bushes to look like moving bushes.

But the thing *was* moving. . . . Surely . . .

Digby rubbed his eyes.

It must be a trick of moonlight. A bush might conceivably shake when there was no wind blowing, and no big bird alighting nor flying away; for some small nocturnal animal or snake might possibly cause its branches to move. He stared so hard and so long that his eyes watered, and he closed them for a moment. When he opened them again he was instantly convinced that the bush was moving, and moreover, that it was *moving along!*

Now, bushes that move in this manner are really interesting phenomena, and Digby was duly interested. Placing the butt of his rifle on a stone, he crossed his arms upon its muzzle, pushed back his *képi*, yawned loudly, and leant his head upon his arms. With one eye open the sentry slept at his post—or apparently the bush thought he did, for it moved several yards nearer—or perhaps the sentry, in turn, thought it did, because he had only one eye open.

Again yawning, he drew his body erect, struck the attitude of "Stand-at ease," and contemplated infinity. He also contemplated the bush, and, before very long was absolutely certain that the bush was approaching him. He was about to raise his rifle when he was overwhelmed with the thought that, by firing a shot, he would arouse the whole company, officers, non-commissioned officers and men, all weary to death and almost preferring death to a needless awakening.

If he roused them from their sleep without the best of good reasons, he would become an object of universal execration, the focus and target of their ferocious wrath, hatred and contempt.

"*I thought I saw a bush move,*" would be a fine excuse when brought before the Commandant to offer any explanation he could find for rousing the camp and wasting ammunition. They would say he had been asleep and had fired off his rifle in a nightmare.

No, the bush was not moving. . . . Not moving now, perhaps,

but it certainly *had* moved, for it was undoubtedly nearer than when he had first noticed it. . . . Or was it all moonshine?

An idea! . . . There was an almost white stone shining in the moonlight a few yards from the bush.

Digby Geste deliberately turned his back toward the bush, slowly patrolled his allotted distance and returned. . . . The bush had moved.

It was nearer to the stone by a distance about equal to the length of his beat. While he had been patrolling from his post, the bush had moved forward, and when he had turned about to come back, the bush had halted.

How many other bushes were approaching the camp in similar fashion? Or was this a solitary rifle-thief, intending to crawl into the camp, silently slit the throat of a sleeping man, and crawl away richer by a good Lebel rifle? More likely the idea, since he was making a straight line for him, was to get sufficiently close to a somnolent Digby Geste, to rush him and stab him to the heart before he could make a sound.

Nasty man! . . . Whole company asleep. . . . Mustn't make a mistake. . . . Plenty of time for one more patrol—to make sure. . .
.

No, a better notion. Digby Geste yawned, stretched himself, sloped his rifle, turned his back upon the mystery bush and marched off. But, at the end of half-a-dozen paces, he swiftly wheeled about—and saw the bush progressing quite quickly in the direction of his post. Raising his rifle Digby fired at the lower part of the bush, and with all the strength of his lungs called:

"*Aux armes! Aux armes!*"

Immediately each one of the chain of sentries fired his rifle at nothing in particular to show that he too was a keen, wakeful and watchful warrior, and bawled "*Aux armes!*" in evidence that he had seen something suspicious, and probably saved the life of every soul in camp.

In less time than it takes to tell the men were under arms and lining the perimeter of the camp, each man at his own *créneau* loop-hole.

From each of its four sides levelled rifles were ready to pour forth a hail of death upon a charging enemy.

But no enemy charged.

Nothing happened.

In a very few minutes, lightly clad men were grumbling angrily as they shivered in the bitter cold, and demanding the blood of the nervous fool who had brought them from their warm blankets and snug bivouacs.

Making his rounds, the Sergeant of the Guard found that no sentry had fired first until he reached Digby Geste, who promptly confessed to being the offender, or, if the Sergeant liked to put it that way, the saviour of the situation.

"What did you fire at, you half-witted *salo*? You trembling, squint-eyed, frog-faced Afraid-of-the-Dark?"

"At that bush," replied Digby, pointing.

"Oh you did, did you, *salo*? . . . Is *that* what you are afraid of? Did you think it was going to bite you?"

"I didn't know *what* it might do—when it got here, Sergeant," replied Digby, standing stiffly at attention.

"When it *got* here? What do you mean, you sodden lunatic?" roared the Sergeant, and, before Digby could reply, an incisive voice cut in sharply with:

"What's all this about?" and the Sergeant and his satellites sprang to attention.

"This is the man who caused all the trouble, *mon Commandant*," answered the Sergeant, saluting. "He confesses that he deliberately fired at a bush."

Major de Beaujolais turned to Digby Geste, little thinking that this Soldier of the Legion was one of the three boys to whom he had told stories of just such nights in the desert, years before, at beautiful Brandon Abbas in England.

"And why did you fire at a bush, might one ask?" he inquired coldly.

"Because it was moving toward me, Monsieur le Majeur," replied Digby.

"Or because you dreamed that it was?" asked de Beaujolais sternly.

"No, Monsieur le Majeur," replied Digby, firmly but respectfully. "The bush moved toward me. I measured its progress by that stone."

"Then go and fetch it," ordered de Beaujolais. "Quickly, *au pas gymnastique.*"

With his rifle at the ready, and his heart beating rapidly, Digby doubled out toward the bush. Arrived near it, he changed his pace to a slow walk and covered the bush with his rifle.

He reached it.

Nothing happened.

But when, seizing a branch in his left hand, he pulled, the bush yielded instantly, and with complete ease he dragged it to where the little group awaited him.

"Show a light here," ordered Major de Beaujolais, and it was immediately seen that the bush had been cut off at ground level.

"You have done well, *mon enfant*," he said kindly, and turning to the Sergeant, added:

"A good thing if all your men were as ready to shoot at bushes that move at night! This was a spy. Probably there's a Touareg band somewhere near. Quite possibly we are surrounded, and shall be attacked at dawn. Double your sentries, and see if any more of them can spot moving bushes. Bring this man to me in the morning."

And the Major strode away to give orders for the doubling of sentries on the other sides of the camp, and for "Stand-to" an hour before dawn.

But at dawn no attack materialized, and the company struck camp and moved off as though surrounded by enemies from whom an attack was imminent.

The retreat from the position was made a useful tactical exercise, and proved to be particularly so when, from distant rocks and sandhills, came a sudden outburst of irregular firing.

Major de Beaujolais appeared quite pleased, and a look of boredom promptly departed from his handsome face as he stood up in his stirrups, and gazed coolly around in all directions and indicated that the company would proceed at its best pace to a not far distant *ravin* which appeared to offer excellent shelter for mules, while an adjacent knoll provided an eligible site for riflemen. From there he would give his force a lesson in attack as infantry, and mobile rearguard tactics as rifle-armed cavalry.

*　　*　　*　　*　　*　　*　　*

In the rear of the company rode Digby Geste, his happiness faintly clouded by anxiety as to the conduct or misconduct of Mildred, his mule. It would be quite the wrong time for her to have a fit of self-determination, to demonstrate, and to try to make the Sahara a country fit for mules to live in. What would she do if she were hit without being seriously wounded? Probably bolt and take an undeserved place at the head of the column. Just as likely to bolt in the opposite direction.

Crash! . . . Hullo, someone was down. A few yards to his right a *légionnaire* had fallen from his saddle. He had clung to his rein, and the mule had come to a standstill beside him. Digby pulled up, as he realized that the man's efforts to get to his feet were in vain.

Riding across, while bullets knocked up puffs of dust and sand around him, he saw that the man was Xarro, and that he was hit in the right knee. He was obviously in the greatest agony, and quite helpless. Springing to the ground, and putting his rein over his shoulder, Digby lifted Xarro in his arms, sat him sideways on Satan, who stood steady as a rock, and then lifted Xarro's left foot and leg across the mule so that he was seated astride and firmly in the saddle.

As Digby thrust Xarro's left foot into the stirrup the wounded man, who appeared about to faint from pain, shock and loss of blood, drooped forward on Satan's neck and groaned:

"I can't! . . . *I can't!* . . . Tie me on. . . . For God's sake. . . ."

Easier said than done, with bullets smacking around, and the enemy drawing nearer and nearer, as they dodged from rock to rock and bush to bush.

"Cross your wrists under the mule's neck, quick," cried Digby, and, snatching a weary-looking handkerchief from his pocket, he swiftly and firmly bound Xarro's hands together. Then, slipping the off stirrup-leather from its fastening beneath the saddle-flap, he unbuckled the strap, thrust the end through the girth, through the buckle, and pulled the thick strap tightly across Xarro's left thigh.

He could not now possibly fall from the mule, even if he fainted, and, provided Satan would canter after the Company, there was no reason why Xarro should not get safely to hospital.

Smack! A bullet had struck Xarro, and another hit Digby's

water-bottle. Seizing Satan's rein, he swiftly scrambled on to the back of Mildred, who, with all the incalculable perversity of the mule had behaved like a perfect lady at a moment when a little misconduct on her part would have been literally fatal.

As he urged the two mules into a canter, he realized that some of the nearest Arabs had ceased firing, and were actually rushing forward to capture them and their mules alive. Live men can be tortured, and live mules can be ridden or sold.

"First catch your hare," quoth Digby as Mildred and Satan surpassed themselves. Never had he known mules to go so fast. Pity there wasn't a mules' Derby. Was it because Xarro was present?

Hullo! . . . What was this? . . . Two men galloping back from the main body.

Hank and Buddy! . . . Silly asses; they couldn't do any good, and were merely risking their lives for nothing.

The two reined up, dismounted, and, with reins looped over arms, knelt and opened rapid fire on the running Arabs. These having magically disappeared behind bushes, stones, mounds, boulders or such sufficient cover (for an Arab) as a dead leaf, Hank and Buddy again jumped on their mules and cantered after Digby and Xarro.

A few minutes later, still holding Satan's rein, Digby galloped into the mouth of the nullah, wadi or *ravin*, in which the other mules stood in groups of four, the reins of each group being held by the No. 3 man of the group. A few wounded men sat or lay on the shady side of the nullah, in the charge of a medical-orderly or dresser.

The remainder of the Company, strongly and invisibly posted, was waiting to give the advancing Arabs a warm reception.

Leading Satan to where the wounded lay, Digby called out to the *infirmier*, the medical subordinate:

"This man's wounded in the knee and chest," and then, reining in, endeavoured to bring Satan to a standstill.

But Satan seemed agitated. Perhaps he missed his master's voice. Perhaps he thought that in his master's best interests he had better make straight for Tokotu, and his comfortable mule-lines.

He declined to stop.

145

Xarro opened a sickly eye and groaned. He was not as good at bearing pain as he had been at inflicting it.

"Whoa, whoa, Satan!" cried Digby, and, as he took his right foot from the stirrup, to dismount from his own mule, he remembered the word, or sound, that Xarro himself had told him to use, when he wanted to steady Satan.

"Whoa, Satan! . . . *Brrrtsch!* . . ." cried Digby. . . . "*Brrrtsch! . . .*"

Satan pricked his ears, and instantly flung himself down and rolled—as he had been trained to do, at that word of command.

With his last breath Xarro shrieked in agony, as the huge mule rolled upon him thrice.

LOW FINANCE

"Low Finance" is a story of how Hank and Buddy financed a visit to Monte Carlo. "Low Finance" was first published in February 1929 in the Pall Mall Magazine *and* Good Gestes, *and was reprinted in* Dead Men's Boots *(1949).*

Seated on his bed in the barrack-room, and doubtfully assisted by the comments of his brothers, Beau Geste was making up his accounts for the month.

Gradually and unintentionally, he had drifted into the trade, business or profession of money-lender. In so doing, he had incurred the most bitter animosity of Monsieur Veidhaas, a gentleman remarkable by reason of the fact that he was at once a Jew, a *légionnaire,* and a financier; and that he could reap a harvest in so poor a soil.

Of the two financiers, Beau Geste had by far the bigger business, and the more rapidly it grew, the more swiftly did that of Monsieur Veidhaas decline; and yet the latter was undoubtedly the better business man.

The explanation of the phenomenon probably lies in the fact that Beau Geste charged no interest whatsoever, whereas Monsieur Veidhaas charged exactly 5,200 per cent, per annum. That is to say, he would lend you a *sou* to-day, provided you handed him two *sous* to-day week.

Beau Geste's method of business was to lend any reasonable amount to any friend who wanted it; his only reservations being that he didn't lend money to assist and encourage drunkenness, nor did he lend a second sum until the first had been returned.

As Monsieur Veidhaas pointed out to him, with gesticulatory hands and screaming voice, this not only wasn't business, but wasn't common honesty and fair play to Monsieur Veidhaas. In fact it was just the low, mean, dirty, silly sort of trick that an Englishman *would* play.

In point of fact, things were even worse than has been stated, for not only did this blackleg financier charge no interest, but he took no security!

The very thought of such conduct sickened Monsieur Veidhaas to the depths of his soul, and indeed, almost to those of his body. He felt physically nauseated when he saw men casually borrowing good copper *sous*, without bond or receipt, and as casually returning them. For, curiously enough, return them they did, in spite of the lack of documentary evidence against them, their own cruel poverty, the absence of security, and the fact that return was never demanded.

Nevertheless, Beau Geste kept account of these loans, varying from a *sou* to a whole franc, because, though he had an unquenchable desire to help and oblige, he had no desire, nor intention either, to be robbed or to encourage cadging.

"Bloated bloodsucker!" accused Digby, sitting beside him, and watching him cross off the names of men who had paid their debts that day, fifth-day—pay-day—when every man received the sum of 2½d. for five days' labour, whether he deserved it or not.

Hank and Buddy approached, and John Geste moved up, and made room for them on his bed.

"Bank still open for the transaction of business, Bo?" inquired Hank.

"To a valued and respected client, yes," replied Beau Geste. "How much do you want to pay in?"

Hank patted his pockets.

"Say now, that's too bad," he said with heavy concern. "I've come without it. I must have left it where I left me youth and innocence. No matter, I'll draw a bit, instead. I'll draw myself a cheque for fifty centimes."

"Me too, Bo," added Buddy. "If it ain't making what you might call a run on the Bank, like. I'll cover the overdraft next pay-day, and if I'm caught short, I'll sell something of Hank's and make it up."

"Same here, Son," assured Hank. "I can always sell something of Bud's, if it's only his scalp for a pen-wiper, or to Lejaune for a sooveneer to hang at his belt."

"Or we could go hotel-borrowing again," mused Buddy.

"What *is* hotel-borrowing?" inquired Digby Geste. "I've borrowed various things in my life, but I don't remember ever borrowing an hotel."

"No, Son, you ain't got it right," replied Buddy. "Hotel-borrowing ain't borrowing hotels, it's borrowing *from* hotels, like."

"Shouldn't have thought they were prompt and ready lenders," observed Beau Geste.

"No," replied John. "In fact I've always rather loved the expression 'hotel *guest*.' A gentle irony about it!"

"Oh, that's all right," affirmed Digby. "The hotel guessed it could make a bit out of you—and it was right—so what's wrong?"

"Peace, pups," quoth their brother. "How does one induce hotels to lend anything, Bud?"

"Well, they don't, rightly know they're doing it, Son," was the answer, "and it's one of them cases of money making money, and 'unto him that hath shall be given. . . .' But if you've got 150 francs, you can borrow quite a lot from hotels."

"At what rate of interest?" asked John.

"None," replied Buddy.

"For what period?" inquired Digby.

"Long as you like," was the answer.

"But why *hotels*?" asked Beau.

"Oh, reasons," answered Buddy. "I'll tell you . . . give you an example, like. Shall I, Hank?"

"Wel-l-l," mused Hank. "Yes-s. . . . You might tell it to *these* boys. They got high principles and are above temptation. It wouldn't be likely to deterioralize them."

And fixing each of the brothers in turn with a calm, ingenuous eye, he added:

"Nobody oughtn't never to indulge in the sport and pursuit called hotel-borrowing unless they are strictly honest, particular and high-principled, and with strong firm character. . . . Oncorruptible."

The three Gestes slowly nodded their heads in understanding and agreement.

"We was in Monte Carlo," observed Buddy. "Also we had one hundred and fifty francs, and there was lots of hotels. . . ."

"Some lovely place, Monte Carlo . . ." remarked Hank. "Nothing wrong with Monte Carlo . . . 'cept the people in it."

"That's so," agreed Buddy. "There's a lot there that ain't so simple-minded as they oughta be. Sets their hearts on things of this world—dross and filthy looker. . . . And the one hundred and fifty francs didn't seem to us a right and sensible sum of money, somehow. . . . If it had been a hundred and fifty thousand, we could have made ourselves comfortable. . . . We could have gone to the *Imperial Splendide Continental* and been two of them eccentric and amusin' American millionaires what nobody minds what they does—as long as they hands it out in wads. . . . Or if it had been one hundred and fifty centimes, we could have tramped along to Marseilles and enlisted in the Legion. . . . As it was, it was a foolish sum of money."

"Not so foolish either—in a way," mused Hank.

"No," agreed Buddy. "In a manner of speaking it weren't. . . . You see, it happened, by the kind and loving mercy of Heaven, to be in two notes. Being the financiers you are, you'll grasp the fact that it was thus a hundred-franc note and a fifty-franc note. . . . Well, we was sitting on a seat on that sorter River-Front Drive what looks over the sea, and listenin' to them heroes down below, blowing the back-ends off lame tame pigeons, when Hank has an idee . . ."

"That's a lie," interrupted Hank, "you miserable back-bitin', evil-speaking', character-takin', foul-mouthed little runt. It was *you*."

"Oh *me*, was it?" replied Bud. "Very well . . . *I* had the idee then, that we oughta give the bigger note to the Society for the Protection of Cruelty to Animals and use the other fifty to rush us a growler of beer and then git up and git, and go on walking."

Hank snorted, as Digby murmured:

"Quite so."

And Beau gravely observed:

"I'm sure you did."

"And then Hank had the idee," continued Buddy, gazing mildly at Hank, who remained watchfully silent, "of using the money otherwise, so to speak.

"*His* notion was for him to take the hundred-franc note and me to take the fifty-franc note. . . ."

"It was *your* notion, you anæmic Ananias," shouted Hank, seizing Buddy by the scruff of the neck.

"Very well! . . . *Very* well! . . . It *were* then," agreed Buddy .
. . "for us to take the notes and invest them in real estate and
begin to lead a higher and a better life as solid citizens. Hanks
says he wants to turn honest and live respectable—after watching
me."

The three Gestes contrived to separate the two Americans and
to keep them apart while Buddy developed his exposition of the
art of hotel-borrowing.

"Well, as I was saying," he continued, straightening his
disarranged clothing.

"Hank says:

"'You march into the *Hotel Imperial Splendide Continental* as
though you owned it, and wasn't proud of it. When the head
waiter comes to throw you out or show you to a seat, you gaze
upon him as though he was mud and you didn't want to tread in
it. . . . Then you order a good blow-out and have eggs-and-bacon
in it, or pork-and-beans, or something else they haven't got. And
then call 'em a ten-cent hash-joint, not fit for a salmon-canning,
corned-beef-packing, lumber-king to sit down in. Drink water
because you're a rich eccentric millionaire and can afford to, and
don't spend more than ten francs. . . . When the waiter brings the
bill, pay with the fifty-franc note, and then set and chew a tooth-
pick cheerful, until poor Alphonso comes back with the change.

"'When he does—*don't take it*. . . . Let it lie on the plate
while you smiles a kinda sad sooperior amused smile, and gently
shakes your head from side to side. Then you says, still amused,
but dignified and kinda ironic:

"'"What's the game, Alphonso—you poor, feeble, flat-footed
fish! What do you take me for? A half-witted Wop, or the
monkey off the organ?"

"'Then you tells him to fetch the Head Waiter or the Manager
or the Owner if he likes, and sits back calm and sooperior while
he does it. . . . When the Head Waiter or the Manager or the
Owner arrives, look him up and down slow-like—take a good
stare at any cracks in his shoes and then admire where his pants
goes baggy at the knees. Then take a interest in any grease-spots
on his weskit. Then sorta brace yourself for a stare at his face;
give a shudder at the sight of it, and then work downwards again.
. . . In course of time, when you've looked him all over, say

quiet, in a pompshus and contempshus voice:

""How often d'you get away with *this* frame-up, Son?"

"'And when he replies that he *nong comprongs*, you say:

""Cut it *right* out, Bo! . . . Can it! . . . Fergit it—and listen an earful. . . . I just give Mr. Alphonso Alonzo Fandango Lorenzo a hundred-franc note, and he's brought me change for a fifty-franc note, and if you think you can pull that bunk on me, you got another think coming. . . . See? . . . So cut out the funny stuff, and get busy with another fifty francs."

"'When you said all that, the Head Waiter or Manager or Owner or whatever It may be, he'll give you the soft and saucy answer that turneth on wrath. He'll tell you that your sort of poor bone-headed hoodlum tries that silly old stale trick in that hotel about seven times a day and fourteen on Sundays. And right there, you rises to your feet, Bud, and with all the weight and dignity of an American Citizen, with Old Glory flying over him, and the Band playing "Yankee Doodle," you says in a crool, cold and cutting voice:

""Before I bring in the Police, will you have the goodness to go to your cashier's desk *and see whether she has, or has not, a hundred-franc note* (and right here you draws out your pocketbook) *numbered 624 in the top left-hand corner and E11373 in the right-hand corner—and reverse as usual at the bottom.*"

" 'Nacherally the guy, whether he's Head Waiter, Manager or Owner, will look foolish in the face and make a quick hike to the cash-desk. . . . You'll foller him too, lookin' haughty, but cold and crool. And right there among the hundred-franc notes, on the very top or near it, *there will be our old pal E11373.*"

"'How will there, you old fool?' says I to Hank.

""*Cos I shall have paid it in meself, in another part of the room, ten minutes before,*' replies Hank. . . ."

"An' lo! it was so," added Buddy.

Silence.

"And you got away with it?" inquired Beau.

"Sure thing," replied Buddy. . . . "Hank walks into that *Imperial Splendide Continental* and turneth unto the right hand. . . . A quarter of an hour later, I walks in and turns unto the left hand and we has our eats. . . . Soon as I seen him go out again, I calls for my bill, and pays—and behold Francesco Gorgonzola only brings me change for the fifty-franc note which I had give him! . . .

"When the Manager comes, I says:

"'I have not the slightest wish to get Giuseppe Spaghetti into trouble, nor yet the cashier, so if you'll be good enough to give me my proper change for my lill' ole E11373' (consultin' my notebook) 'we'll say no more about it.'

"Off goes the Manager, while I gazes idly round, and comes back in a minute, most apologetic.

"Me, I'm quite affable and pleasant and we parts the best of friends. . . .

"Well, not being too bad at games of skill and chance—so called becos we has all the skill and the mugs hasn't a chance, we makes that fifty into five hundred and sends fifty of it back to the *Hotel Imperial Splendide Continental* with our love and no explanations.

"Yes, we has quite a good time at Monte Carlo, hotel-borrowing and hotel-repaying; winning at poker and losing at roulette. Quite a good time, we has, and we leaves Monte Carlo owing nobody a *sou*, and not owning one ourselves."

Silence.

"Gee," murmured Hank. "He oughta married that dame Sapphira, but I wouldn't have liked to be the off-spring."

"Me?" replied Buddy in hurt surprise. "My second name is George Washington. It was you thought of it, and you what paid in the hundred-franc note that caused all the trouble and dishonesty! . . . If it hadn't been there, there wouldn't been fifty francs profit every time. . . . *You!* . . . Why, you'll prob'ly pinch angels' wing-feathers on Judgment Day and sell 'em in Hell as sooveneers. . . . No, you ain't what *I* call a good, simple, honest man."

And Buddy walked away, as one too full for further speech.

PRESENTIMENTS

This story is a tale that a legionnaire tells the Geste brothers on the eve of a battle. He has a premonition that he is going to be killed on the morrow and wants to tell the tragic story of his drunken father and the death of his mother. "Presentiments" first appeared in Good Gestes *(1929), and was reprinted in* The Mammoth Book of Thrillers, Ghosts and Mysteries *(1936), and in the Murray (1947) and Macrae-Smith (1948) editions of* Stories of the Foreign Legion.

§1

When a dam bursts, a mighty flood follows; when a notably silent man talks, he is apt to say a good deal.

Wine sometimes loosens the tongue, particularly if the drinker be habitually abstemious. There are men who talk when they have fever; others when the moon is full, and the desert and night sky a vision of loveliness and a dream of peace; some when the nerves are frayed, so that they must do something or go mad, and talking is the easiest thing to do; others, again, when they are fey, and are well aware that to-morrow's battle will be their last.

Le légionnaire Max Linden, a forbidding person, so taciturn, so inarticulate, as to be known as the Dumb Devil, was talking to the Geste brothers—and to some purpose. It was the eve of the battle of El Rasa, and Linden affected to be perfectly certain that he would be killed on the morrow.

"Oh, rubbish, man," said Michael Geste; "not one in a hundred of these presentiments is justified."

". . . Begun in blood . . . ended in blood," growled Linden, raising himself on his elbow, and staring out into the moonlit night. . . . "But that her blood oozed and spread and trickled in the direction of the door, reached it, and slowly, slowly crept underneath it and out on to the white doorstep, I should not be here now . . . here now, awaiting my death from an Arab bullet."

"Cheer up, old bird," said Digby. "Have a cigarette," he

added, offering a packet of *Caporal*. "I bet you I'll give you another, this time to-morrow, and that you'll smoke it."

"You may stick it in my dead mouth if you like," replied Linden, "before they shovel me under the sand.

"No," he continued, "if her blood had never reached the door, I shouldn't be here now. . . . On the other hand, my father would not have been executed, which would have been a pity. Executed for the murder of my mother."

The brothers eyed each other uncomfortably. No wonder Max Linden was a bitter and tragic-looking desperado, whose rare speech was either a snarl or a growl.

"Your father murdered your mother before your eyes, and was hanged?" murmured Michael Geste, as Linden turned to him and apparently awaited a reply.

"He was hanged for it, anyhow," replied Linden, and he laughed horribly as he added:

"Death on the scaffold was the terror of his life, too. Yes, an absolute obsession, this fear of the rope. And the executioner got him all right. . . . What about that for a presentiment coming true? *And I could have saved him.*"

"What about a spot of sleep?" suggested Digby.

"It was all clear enough to the police, when they burst in," continued Linden, ignoring the hint. "It didn't need a Lecoq, nor your Sherlock Holmes, to see what had happened. It leapt to the eye.

"Picture it.

"Old Franz Muller, nosing about the dust-pails and gutters in the early morning, sees a pool of blood on the doorstep of the little house where lives the drunken *mauvais sujet*, Marc Linden. He knocks at the door, tries the handle, peers through the keyhole, kicks heavily, runs round to the window. No sound nor sign from within; and, full of importance, off he goes to the police.

"All in their own good time, they send a man along to see whether there's a word of truth in old Franz Muller's story; or whether there is a spot of red paint on our doorstep, and we peacefully asleep in our beds.

"The man reports that blood has oozed under the front door, spread across the step, trickled down the sides and soaked into the dust.

"The police come, burst open the door and find—what?

"A woman lies at full length upon the floor, dead. So great a quantity of blood has flowed from her head and neck that, if she was not killed outright at the time, she has bled to death.

"Seated in a wooden arm-chair, and half sprawling across the table, is a man. He is still in a drunken slumber, his head pillowed upon his bent left arm, the hand of which clutches an empty bottle. His right arm, outstretched before him, and resting on the table, points in the direction of the body of the woman. In the man's right hand is a pistol, its muzzle resting on the table. One chamber has been discharged. In a corner of the room, a boy—a stunted undersized boy—lies on the bare floor.

"They thought he was dead, too, until the Police Surgeon discovered that he was only suffering from a severe blow on the head, a dislocated leg and various minor injuries. He was very emaciated, and had a number of old bruises, weals, abrasions and contusions. It was noticed, too, that the eyes of the woman were blackened and that her face showed evidence of brutal injury.

"'Aha!' said the police, 'a wife-beater; a scoundrelly brute that assaults children in his drunken frenzy; and now he has gone too far. He has deliberately murdered his wife, and perhaps has fatally injured his son!'

"They reconstructed the crime.

"The man had come home drunk, as usual, bringing with him a bottle of cheap and fiery spirit. He had savagely assaulted the woman, beating her insensible, and had then struck and kicked the boy, finally hurling him across the room, where he had lain unconscious and half-dead

"The ruffian had then seated himself at the table to drink. Unfortunately, before he had fallen into this drunken slumber the unhappy woman had recovered consciousness and, clutching at the table, had raised herself to her knees and reproached or defied him, or perhaps had begged him to get help for the injured child. His drunken fury blazing forth again, he had snatched the pistol from his pocket and shot her dead. He had then emptied the bottle at a draught, and fallen forthwith into the sottish, swinish slumber in which they had found him.

"Thus the police. And thus was the accusation of wilful

murder framed against my father.

"Nor could a shadow of doubt remain in the mind of any reasonable and unbiased person who heard the impassioned speech of the prosecuting Counsel, the Advocate-General, who demanded a life for a life, the heaviest of punishments for the foulest of crimes.

"Certainly there was no doubt in the mind of the Judge. How should there be? What would you three have concluded if you had been the three policemen who burst into the room, and saw the body of a slaughtered woman lying in a pool of blood that had flowed from a wound caused by a bullet that had severed jugular vein and carotid artery? What would you have concluded if, facing the murdered woman, there sat a man, a noted brute and wife-beater, whose hand clutched the pistol from which the bullet had been fired?

"What, I ask you?" insisted Linden, seizing the wrist of Michael Geste in his hot and shaking hand. "Tell me; what?"

"I should have said that things looked black against the man," replied Michael Geste, "very black."

"Would you have sent him to the scaffold if you had been his Judge?" asked Linden.

"Don't know, I'm sure," was the reply. "Probably. . . . Possibly not. Evidence all circumstantial. . . . We have a different system, you know. If a jury brought him in guilty of wilful murder . . .

"Yes, but it wasn't England, you see," interrupted Linden, "and we don't assume that every villainous criminal is innocent. We leave him to prove that he is—if he can.

"What would *you* have done if you had been the Judge?" he added, turning to Digby Geste.

"What the Judge did do, I suppose," replied Digby.

"And you?" continued Linden, turning to John Geste.

"Oh, I don't know," replied John. "Benefit of the doubt, if there were any doubt; and I suppose there always is a possibility of doubt when there are no witnesses."

"There *was* a witness," said Linden. "Myself . . . I witnessed the whole affair from beginning to end."

"And you could have saved your father," remarked Michael softly. "What a terrible position for you! Poor chap. . . . You'd have had to perjure yourself to have saved him, I suppose? What a ghastly predicament! Did you give evidence against him, or did you refuse to speak?"

"*Aha!*" replied Max Linden, and grinned unpleasantly.

Silence fell on the little group, and three of the four settled themselves for slumber. But Max Linden, sick-souled and devil-driven, had more to say.

"It is pretty generally true," he went on, "that bullies are cowards, and that those who are readiest in inflicting torture are the worst and feeblest in bearing pain.

"When they reconstructed the crime, my father made me, if possible, still more ashamed to be his son.

"As soon as I had recovered sufficiently, they took me back again from the hospital to the house, and put me on a mattress in the corner of the room, just as the police had found me. The body of my poor mother was arranged exactly as it had lain when the police entered the room. My father was seated in his chair, and made to assume the position in which he had been found. The pistol, clutched in his right hand, was laid on the exact spot—marked by a pencil—where it had rested.

"A police agent then enacted my mother's supposed part in the tragedy. First he lay upon the floor as though stunned by a blow. He then seized the edge of the table opposite to my father, dragged himself to his knees, and showed how a bullet, fired from the pistol as it rested on the table, would penetrate the side of his neck while he was in the act of rising from the floor.

"My father shuddered, shrieked, covered his eyes, and then struggled to escape. Alternately he screamed his protestations of innocence and grovelled for mercy. Weeping, he would point out that he could not possibly have done such a thing and know nothing about it; and he called God and all His saints to witness that he did know nothing about it.

"Then, tearful and voluble, he would point out that he was drunk when the police found him, and that if he *had* done it, he had been too drunk to know what he was doing. Surely they would not punish him for a thing done in ignorance and innocence? His only fault was that he had got drunk.

"Then he would call upon the world to witness that no man, so drunk as he had been, could possibly aim and fire a pistol. But the *Juge d'Instruction* coldly asked him what evidence there was that he had not deliberately murdered his wife and thereafter drunk himself insensible?

"And that was where I came in.

"Sobbing, groaning, weeping, and sweating with fear for his own miserable skin, this creature, this man, this Noblest Work of God, suddenly caught a glimpse of salvation.

"A bright ray of hope shone into the black darkness of his soul.

"'My son!' he cried, 'my son! He was in the room throughout the night! He can tell you what happened, *Monsieur le Juge.*'

"They took my evidence, and I gave it freely up to a certain point. I said:

"'For as long as I can remember, my father has been a drunkard and a brute, living God knows how, and by any means but honest work. Times without number, I have seen him thrash my mother unmercifully, with a stick, with the buckle-end of a heavy belt, with a whip, and with his fist. Times without number, I have seen him knock her senseless with a single blow, and then kick her as she lay. More times than I can tell, he has flogged me, either for no reason whatsoever, or because he had sent me out to steal and I had brought back nothing. It has been his habit, when in funds, to bring in good food—fish and meat and vegetables—and to stand over my mother while she cooked it. He would then eat the meal himself, while we had nothing but stale bread, and not enough of that. Frequently the rich food and bottle of wine would put him into such high good humour that he would observe that we had no need to eat dry bread, for we could wet it; and that there was no necessity for us to drink cold water, since there was no reason why we should not warm it. . . .

"'On the night of my mother's death, he came home neither more nor less drunk than usual, bringing with him a bottle of liquor, but no food.

"'He demanded *soupe* and bread.

"'When my mother told him that there was no food of any sort in the house, and that we had that day tasted nothing whatsoever but a cup of re-boiled coffee-grounds, he knocked her down, and then kicked her until she managed to pull herself together and rise to her feet. He then announced that he would "feed me to rights." Since I wanted food, he'd feed me with a stick.

"'As I tried to dodge past him and escape from the house, he kicked me with all his strength, and then, picking me up from the floor, flung me across the room, so that I struck the wall and fell in a corner. He then got the stick, and, as my mother threw herself between him and me, he struck her repeatedly with all his strength, until she fell to the ground near the table. Having kicked her several times, he seated himself at the table and drank from the bottle.

"'I think I then became unconscious for a time. When I recovered consciousness, my father was drinking from the bottle, and my mother was making feeble efforts to lift her head from the ground and raise herself upon her elbow.

"'What I saw after that I will never tell. Not though I am *tortured* will I say one word; not though I spend the rest of my life in prison will I add another syllable.'

"Naturally the police thought that I was reluctant to give testimony which would instantly destroy any chance my father would have of escaping the scaffold; and, while respecting the filial feelings of an unhappy boy, most miserably situated, they drew their own conclusions. Naturally, too, it was perfectly clear to them that my mother could not have committed suicide, inasmuch as the pistol was in my father's hand. Moreover, had it been a case of suicide, I, of course should have testified to the manner of her death, and removed all suspicion from my father.

"Still protesting his innocence, weeping, shrieking and struggling, my father was taken back to prison, charged with the wilful murder of his wife."

§2

Linden bowed his head upon his hands and fell silent.

"Look here, you've talked enough for to-night, old chap," said Michael. "Lie down, and try and get to sleep."

"Oh, let me talk, let me talk, now I have started," groaned Linden. "Let me finish, anyhow. I shall be under the sand this time to-morrow—shot, as my mother was shot, through the face and neck. I want to tell the truth about my father. . . . Let me get it off my chest. . . . I must tell somebody. . . . Let me go on."

"Why, of course," agreed Michael, "talk as much as you like."

"Yes, rather," added Digby; "if it will do you any good, we'll listen all night. But you've really told us everything, you know. . . . Poor old chap! . . . Rough luck. . . ."

"Awful hard lines," murmured John. "Some people *do* have frightful tragedies in their lives. . . . But doesn't it make it worse for you, to rake it all up again? . . . And as my brother says, you've really told us all about it."

"Oh, have I?" replied Linden, again grinning unpleasantly. "Listen.

"Between the Examining Magistrate's preliminary investigations and the Court trial, I begged and prayed and implored that I might be allowed to have an interview with my father in his prison cell.

"And one day I found myself alone with the man who had made my life, and that of my mother, a hell upon earth.

"In the most revolting manner, he fawned upon me, kissing me repeatedly, and straining me to his breast.

"'My son! My son!' he snivelled, 'my saviour! You'll be famous throughout Europe as the boy who saved his innocent father's life. . . . How wonderful are the ways of God! Wonderful and yet terrible—for I have always had this awful fear of the scaffold, and now I have stood within its very shadow. The thought has been my nightmare and presentiment from childhood, and here I sit within a dozen yards of the dreadful thing itself. But my own beloved son has come to save me! . . . My little Max has come to tell me all that happened on that dreadful night when his poor dear mother took her life.'

"And again he thrust his beastly and tear-bedewed face against mine.

"'Yes, father,' I replied, 'that is just what I have come to do. Listen:

"'You nearly committed two murders that night. It was not your fault that you did not first kick your own beloved little Max to death, and then his poor dear mother. As a matter of fact, you beat them both insensible. The mother recovered first, thought her child was dead—as he lay there, white and still, where his loving father had flung him.'

"'And thinking so, she took her life. . . . She took her own life. . . . *She committed suicide,*' gabbled my father.

"'Listen,' I repeated. 'The half-murdered woman, regaining consciousness, despairing, dazed, beside herself with agony and grief, stared at what she thought to be the body of her murdered child, and then at the sodden brutal face of the bestial ruffianly sot whom she supported by her unceasing labours, and who repaid her love and generosity as a wild animal would not have done. . . . It was a terrible look, and would to God that the eyes of the swinish drunkard could have encountered it.'

"'But they could not! But they could not!' yelped my father. 'He was drunk, he was insensible; the poor fellow was helpless in a state of stupor, dead to the world . . . innocent, *unconscious.*'

"'Quite unconscious,' I agreed, 'drunk and incapable. Entirely unable to see that terrible stare from the woman who had loved him. Nor could he see her, after many failures and superhuman effort, rise to her hands and knees and drag herself to her feet.'

"'But *you* saw, *you* saw!' cried my father.

"'Oh yes, I saw everything,' I reassured him. 'I saw her drag herself to the cupboard where you hide your pistol. I saw her stagger from the cupboard with the pistol in her hand, and I saw her crawl into a chair, fainting, and apparently about to die.'

"'Yes, yes, yes,' urged my father, 'and then *she shot herself,* eh? Thank God! Praise God that my own precious boy saw it all, and can save his innocent father from this horrible false charge!'

"'Listen,' I said a third time. 'How long my mother sat there, I do not know, but, after a time, she got to her feet once more, went and drank water, and then, with one hand holding the pistol and the other supporting her against the wall, she stood and peered at me.

"'*Dead!*' she whispered. '*My little Max, dead!*' and turned again and looked at you, dear father. . . . I would willingly have died if I could have made you meet that look. It would have haunted you, sleeping and waking, to your grave.'

"'But you were *not* dead,' interrupted my father. 'Why did you not speak to her? Why did you pretend?'

"'Because I thought she was going to shoot you, dear father,' I replied. 'Going to shoot you, in the belief that you had killed me. Not for worlds would I have let her see that I was alive. I was dazed and half-delirious, but I had my wits sufficiently about me to realize that mother was (thank God!) about to shoot you, and that I could swear that I had seen you commit suicide! So I lay still as the dead, in that dark corner, my eyes half-closed, and looking like the corpse I almost was.

"'And *then*? And *then*?' begged my father.

"'And then my mother made her maimed and broken way across to where you sat and snored, your head upon your left arm, your left hand clutching the bottle, your right hand and arm extended across the narrow table. . . . And, to my astonishment, what did she do but carefully, painfully, gently, slowly, open your right hand and clasp it about the handle of the revolver, your forefinger through the trigger-guard, and resting on the trigger.

"'And then my brain cleared somewhat, and my heart beat fast with joy, for I realized that my brave and clever mother was going to make you commit suicide! You were going to be found with your pistol in your hand and such brains as you have scattered about the room! . . . I almost moved and spoke. I nearly cried "*Bravo*, mother!" and blessed her name.

"'And, wide-eyed, I watched as she went round to the opposite side of the table and knelt facing you . . . watched to see her take your right hand in hers and bend it round so that the pistol touched your loathsome face . . . watched to see her press your forefinger when the muzzle of the pistol was against your temple, or your eye, or thrust into your open slavering mouth. . . .

"'She took your right hand in both of hers, and, to my puzzled amazement, presented the pistol—the butt of which rested on the table as you gripped it—*straight at her own neck*.

"'Even as my amazement turned to horror and I screamed aloud "*Don't mother! Don't!*" she must have pressed your forefinger with her two thumbs.

"'There was a deafening report, and she fell back.

"'Even as she died, she seemed to be trying to get farther from the table. . . .

"'And then, too late, I understood. Thinking me dead, she had come to join me, leaving you, the murderer of her child, to explain as best you could the corpses, the blood, the discharged revolver clutched in your hand.'

"'*Devilish! Devilish!*' whispered my father. 'The vile hag. . . .

But God looks after the innocent; and my child was there and saw it all—to testify truly that his dear father was the victim of a horrible plot.'

"'Yes, dear father,' I replied. 'Your child was there, and saw it all, and has truly testified.'"

"My father was now anxious to be rid of me, and could scarcely contain himself until he could communicate with the lawyer charged with his defence. From this gentleman I soon received a visit in hospital.

"'Well, well,' quoth he, standing beside my bed and rubbing his hands. 'What is this, what is this, my silent young gentleman? You've found your tongue with a vengeance! . . . Now tell me again very carefully all that you told your father,' he continued as he opened his bag, took out a large notebook, and seated himself on my bed.

"'Now, my little man,' he smiled, smug and self-satisfied, 'let us have it.'

"I gazed with blank incomprehension upon the smug face of the lawyer. *Found* my tongue with a vengeance had I? On the contrary, I had lost it with a very real vengeance.

"'Sir?' I stammered.

"'Come on,' he encouraged, 'and be very careful and exact, especially about your mother putting the pistol in your father's hand and pressing the trigger.'

"'About my mother doing *what,* sir?' I faltered.

"'You heard what I said,' he snapped.

"'Yes, sir,' I agreed. 'I heard what you said, but I don't know what you are talking about.'

"'Your father has just told me,' was the reply, slow and patient, clear and impressive, 'that you have admitted to him that you witnessed the whole affair, and did not, as you previously stated, lie unconscious until you awoke to find your mother dead. He says you told him how you saw your mother put the pistol in his hand, and then deliberately shoot herself.'

"I smiled with pale amusement.

"'My father seems to have been dreaming, sir,' I said.

"The lawyer stared at me in amazement.

"'*Dreaming? . . . Dreaming? . . .*' he said, at length. 'What do you mean? Are you implying that the whole story is a tissue of lies?'

"'*I* called it a dream, sir,' I answered meekly.

"The lawyer stared the harder.

"'A wonderfully coherent and circumstantial *dream*,' he said. . . . 'Astonishing amount of detail . . . don't you think so?'

"'My father didn't tell it to me, sir,' I said simply.

"'Well, I'll tell it you now, my young friend.' . . . And he proceeded to give a very full and accurate repetition of what I had told my father.

"'A really marvellous dream, sir,' I remarked, when he had finished.

"'And haven't you dreamed the same dream yourself?' he asked.

"'I *never* dream, sir,' I replied.

"'Couldn't you dream that dream to-night?' he suggested, with a subtle smile and a would-be hypnotic gaze.

"'I *never* dream, sir,' I repeated, and matched his subtle smile."

The three brothers stared incredulous at *le légionnaire* Max Linden, their young faces expressing a variety of emotions—wonderment, contempt, pity.

"But did they confront you with your father?"

"Oh yes," replied Linden, "and he, having faithfully repeated the story I had told him, flung himself at my feet, and implored me to corroborate it; begged me to speak the truth; besought me to save him; shrieked to me that he was innocent, *and I alone could prove it.*"

"And what did you do?" asked Michael Geste, as Linden fell silent.

"I saw the wraith of my mother standing behind him, and turning to the Advocate-General, who was present, I tapped my forehead and smiled."

"'Dreaming again, eh?'" growled the great man.

"'Yes, sir,' I agreed, 'he is still dreaming.'

"And so my father's presentiment came true."

"Excuse me," asked Michael Geste, as *le légionnaire* Max

Linden lay back and prepared to sleep, "but was the tale you told your father *true*, or did you actually invent it with the object of torturing him?"

"*Aha*," grinned *le légionnaire* Linden, and composed himself to slumber.

On the following day his own presentiment came true, and he died on the battlefield of El Rasa. A bullet struck him in the neck, and, as no one had any time to attend to him, he bled to death.

DREAMS COME TRUE

In "Dreams Come True", the fourth longest of Wren's short stories, an incident from Beau Geste *(1924) is given its backstory. The incident is one of those unfortunate series of events that allowed Lejaune to become the leader at Fort Zinderneuf: the murder of a Sergeant, and the subsequent suicide of the Corporal who was the murderer. "Dreams Come True" first appeared in* Good Gestes *(1929) and was reprinted in* Stories of the Foreign Legion *(Murray 1947).*

I

"Have you come across an extraordinary bird whom they call The Apostle?" asked Digby suddenly, as the three brothers sat in the *Jardin Publique*, and rested their weary bones, after a week of murderous manœuvres, marching, counter-marching, skirmishing, attacking and trench-digging, during each day of which they had been burnt almost unbearably by the sun, and, during each night, soaked and chilled by a cold relentless rain.

"What's he like?" asked Michael.

"An Apostle," replied Digby.

"What's an Apostle like?" inquired John.

"Don't pretend an ignorance and innocence beyond your years," requested Digby. "It is perfectly well known to any student of German oleographs that an Apostle has a mild and beautiful face, enriched by limpid and liquid eyes like those of a camel; a longish, curly but well-trimmed, golden beard; long hair, curling in ringlets about his shoulders; and an expression of relentless benignity."

"And a halo," added Michael.

"Well, this chap has to make a *képi* do for a halo," said Digby, "but I really think that, back in the old Home Town, he must have been a professional sitter."

"What d'you mean—a sitter?" inquired John.

"It's the opposite of professional stander," replied Digby. "A person who makes a business of standing drinks. . . . There is no such person; but a professional sitter is a person who makes a practice of sitting for a photograph. Surely you've seen the Beach Bathing Girl, laughing like two tickled hyenas, waving a hand in the air; the Brother-in-Law of the Murdered Man, marked with a cross, who had nothing to do with it; the Mother of Nineteen, who might have reared twenty only he swallowed a very bad penny; the Channel Aspirant, who had to give up toward the evening of the third day, owing to currents in the bun they gave her; the Very-Respectable Man in Shirt Sleeves who won the Football Forecast Competition at the 297th attempt, and is going to buy his wife (inset) a mangle, because they've never had a cross word competition in their lives . . ."

"Shut up," growled Michael.

"Certainly, sir," agreed Digby. "And the Apostle must have made his living sitting for the pictures that adorn the books on which Good Children are brought up."

"Nearly finished?" inquired Michael, "because if so, I believe I know the chap you mean, only he was pointed out to me as the Dreamer. He's a friend of Cordier, who, as a doctor and a psychologist, is deeply interested in him."

"Oh yes," said John. "I know the Dreamer. Most extraordinary creature. Preaches, dreams and sees visions."

"Yes, by Jove, I remember now. Some one called him *Le Reveur*."

"Well, what do you think of him?"

"I *don't* think of him," said Michael. "I prefer not to. He gives me the creeps."

"That's interesting," put in John.

"Why?" inquired his brothers.

"Well, I was on a fatigue with him, and after some hours, and quite a long talk, I really didn't know whether I liked or loathed him; nor whether he was quite charming or—not quite charming; almost sinister in fact."

"That's the word," observed Digby. "Sinister. . . . You feel he's a most interesting and delightful chap, and then suddenly you come up against something which is, as you say, almost sinister."

"Unwholesome, what?" suggested Michael. "Bizarre, abnormal, got a mad streak in him."

"Streak is a good word, too," agreed Digby. "You may

conceivably have encountered the expression Streaky Bacon. He's like that. A nice expanse of fat white piety and virtue, and then a hard red streak of something lurid."

"A wretched and vulgar simile," commented Michael. "But I know what you mean. He's certainly of less homogeneous structure, more conglomerate, of more diverse elements compact. . . ."

"Yes, Papa," agreed Digby hastily. "In short, a weird bloke. Let's cultivate him for our collection."

"Or collect him for our cultivation," added John, as they arose to return to Barracks.

§2

Le légionnaire Maximilien Gontran, as he called himself, seated at a table in the Canteen, held a circle of his admirers spell-bound by his eloquence—a thing he loved to do, and which he could do at will. He was describing one of those astoundingly vivid and circumstantial dreams that had won him the sobriquet of "The Dreamer," while his unusual appearance, manner and conduct had won him that of "The Apostle."

As the three brothers approached, warmly welcomed by their friends Maris, Cordier and St. André, Gontran paused to bow courteously and suggest refreshment. He then resumed his well-told and realistic account of his latest dream.

"No, I couldn't tell you what place it was," he said, "save that I got the impression of a kind of Cathedral Chapter-House, or some such place; nor could I say for certain whether it was part of a Catholic or a Protestant foundation. It might have been the Vatican, Canterbury Cathedral, Notre-Dame, St. Paul's or St. Mark's. It may have been in Seville, St. Petersburg, New York, Athens or Bruges, but it was a magnificently ornate interior of lace-like ancient stone carving, lace-like old wooden carving, jewel-like mediæval stained-glass, all mellowed and harmonized with the patina of Time.

"In this great room with its marble pavement, from which grew great pillars branching and exfoliating in the dim recesses of the groined and lofty roof, was a great old table from the refectory of some monastery. It was surrounded by great old

169

carven chairs, each worthy to be a Bishop's throne. And in these chairs, about this table, sat a great company of Princes of the Church, over whom presided the most wonderful and venerable figure of that most wonderful and venerable Ecclesiastical Court. A Prince Bishop, Cardinal, Archbishop or Pope. I can see his face now, old ivory, aquiline, austere, beautiful, beneath the silver hair and golden mitre.

"His vestments, stiff with brocade, precious metals and more precious stones, were the most wonderful that I have ever seen; even more costly, ornate and marvellous than those of the constellation of lesser lights that shone around him.

"I can see the faces of those others, too. One was that of a strong—perhaps headstrong and violent—man; a face that could flush to dull purple with anger; a face of heavy brows, heavy jaw and heavy looks. When opposed by one of his colleagues, he bared strong even teeth and covered them again reluctantly.

"Next him, in purple and gold and finest lawn, with a great jewel upon his white fore-finger, sat a gentle, quiet creature who, in silken tones, angered and goaded the strong and violent man, with honeyed words and mocking smiles. A subtle wily man, a very fox of Æsop.

"And on the other side, a pompous dullard, diseased with egoism and conceit, a man who thought, if he did not actually say, 'God and I in our wisdom have decided and ordained . . .'

"And others there were of the great and good—and successful. And they talked about it and about, while the High Priest in the high chair slowly nodded his august head in agreement, or pursed his thin lips in even more august disapproval.

"What they discussed with such intensity of feeling, such veiled acrimony and bitterness, I do not know; but I rather fancy that some liturgical practice was in process of revision; the proposal of some modification of ritual was being defended and attacked; some alteration in the long-established forms of ancient prayers. I know not what—but it was abundantly clear that while some evidently thought the proposals would afford the Almighty considerable satisfaction, others were of an adamantine certainty that Almighty God would be frightfully put out about it. One man—if one may use the mere word 'man' without irreverence—

arrayed in clothing more beautiful and costly than that of a great Queen at a State Ball, spoke most eloquently of Progress, of the necessity of the Church's parallel growth and development with that of the development of the mentality and education of the nation. A good and learned man, he said that when the nation was a child, it thought and prayed as a child, but that now it was attaining to lusty youth and incipient manhood, it would no longer think and pray as a child, and the Church must realize the fact.

"As he resumed his seat, after a most moving peroration, the beautiful and saintly figure at the head of the table slowly nodded its noble and most venerable head. And even as it did so, another Prelate sprang to his feet, and with clenched fist and blazing eye called down the curse of God, the rebuke of the High Priest, and in culmination, the disapproval of the Prime Minister, on the impious head of him who would dare to lay defiling, desecrating and sacrilegious hands upon the most treasured, the most beloved, the most sacred heritage and possession of the People. If such a dreadful thing were done, they would not believe their very eyes when they opened that book which so rarely left their hands. They would not believe their ears when they detected a change in the service of those churches which they daily thronged. And when the awful truth at last dawned clearly on their shocked and shattered souls, they would swarm forth into the streets and market-places in their millions, and with tongues of men and angels, they would—er—do all sorts of things.

"And as this impassioned Defender of the Faith sank back exhausted upon the velvet cushions of his Throne, and wiped the foam from his lips with an embroidered handkerchief of finest lawn, a little wicket opened in the vast oaken double doors of this great Chapter-House. The little wicket, not five feet high, not three feet wide, opened, and through it stooped the figure of a man—a common coatless working man, wearing overalls and an apron, and carrying, slung over his shoulder, one of those flat straw baskets in which carpenters carry their tools. From its ends protruded saws, hammers, and the handles of other such implements used by those who work in wood.

"Humbly, quietly, treading as softly and silently as the contact of his hobnailed boots with that wonderful marble pavement permitted, the workman, with averted eyes and meekest mien, made his unobtrusive way toward a piece of unfinished work in the far distant corner of the Hall. There, in silence, absorption, and obscurity, he went about his business of measurement and then of boring into some rotten wood. In fact, he had settled to his work of restoration before the Lords Spiritual had properly recovered from the shock of his intrusion.

The High Priest at the head of the table, as became a Leader, was the first to give voice to the indignant astonishment of the august assembly. But it was the headstrong and violent Prelate who first took action. Even as the High Priest cried with a stern note in his beautiful silvern voice:

"'Go hence! Depart! . . . You intrude. . . . This is not the time for you to enter here,' . . . the strong-faced Prelate, rising from his throne, strode across to where the carpenter worked engrossed, his back turned upon that judicial Court of Princes of the Church.

"Seizing the intrusive workman by the arm, he swung him about, and with an angry glare and display of strong white teeth, shouted,

"'Here, what's the meaning of this? Who are you, that you should come into the presence of the Lords Spiritual themselves, even while they deliberate on high matters of the Church— actually while they debate changes in the Form of Worship of Almighty God! . . . Who are you, sir?'

"A sweet and gentle smile wreathed the lips of the carpenter.

"'I am Jesus Christ,' he said softly. . . ."

Le légionnaire Maximilien Gontran, known as the Apostle, and also as the Dreamer, laughed, and then emptied his glass, while the Geste boys eyed him critically.

§3

The patrol under Corporal Heintz, twenty-four hours out from Douargala, sprawled wearily about that great man's feet, as they rested in the providential shadow of a great rock in that thirsty land.

There were present, the Geste brothers and most of their

escouade, Maris, Cordier, St. André, Hank, Buddy, Boldini, Brandt, Haff, Delarey and a few others, including La Cigale, old Tant de Soif and Gontran—who distinguished himself next day and was soon afterwards promoted Corporal.

To become the equal and even the superior of Corporal Heintz was the dream of Gontran's life, for he hated Heintz with an unspeakable, unappeasable, almost unbearable hatred. If there were, in the whole world, another hatred that equalled it, it was the hatred of Corporal Heintz for Gontran.

"Well, Apostle," growled Heintz with a bitter vicious sneer, as he looked down, from where he was seated on a big stone, at the prostrate form of Gontran. "Had any more dreams lately?"

"Not lately, Corporal Heintz," replied *le légionnaire* Maximilien Gontran, softly, as he turned his large mild eyes toward the hard, handsome face of his enemy.

"Not lately, eh?" mocked the other. "Then I must see if I can't give you something to dream about. I wonder if you'd dream better in the cells or *en crapaudine*. . . . Tell us one that you *haven't* dreamed lately. . . ."

"I'll tell you one I once dreamed about a bully," replied Gontran, sitting up suddenly, and looking Heintz squarely in the face. "Two, in fact, if you'd care to hear them. I do not know whether you ever went to school, Corporal Heintz. . . . Yes? . . . Indeed! . . . So did I, and they sent me when I was very young— far too young, in fact. I first went to school on my third birthday, and I went in fear and trembling unbelievable, for the Schoolmaster was a known bully and brute, who ruled his unhappy charges with a rod of iron, or rather with a rod of pliant cane, that left blue weals and bruises on their tender bodies. He did not spare the rod, but he spoiled the child, by making him a trembling little coward, an arrant little liar. What child, who thinks he can escape torture by means of deception, will not deceive? This brutal bully, this cruel sadistic savage, enjoyed beating children and thrashed them, not 'for their own good,' but for his own enjoyment, and made them furtive, treacherous, cowardly and untruthful. He also made their days a misery, their nights a terror, and their lives a burden. I can see him now, with his flaming red beard, red hair, red nose and cold greenish eye, a great powerful, vindictive ruffian of whom our parents were as

173

much afraid as we were.

"It was no Academy for the Sons of Gentlemen, our school, but a log hut in a forest, a mile or so from our village, and there can be but few buildings in this world from which more screams of agony had rung out. One reads of tortures, tortures of the Chinese and of the Holy Inquisition; one has seen photographs of the bodies of our poor fellows tortured and mutilated by the Arabs; but, you know, I doubt if any tortured person suffers more from steel, or cord, or red-hot iron, than does a tender child from the stinging, biting cuts of a swishy cane applied by a master hand.

"To me, at any rate, it was a refinement of agony ineffable, and I suffered it daily for years, dreamed of it nightly for centuries, and tried to find the courage to commit suicide. But *tout lasse, tout casse, tout passe*, and at length I was free, and went out into the great world where I grew big and strong.

"Oh yes, I'm very strong, Corporal Heintz, and most patiently I developed and trained my strength, as the earnest pupil of a great and famous professional Strong Man.

"And then came this dream of which I started to tell you.

"I dreamed that one fine morning I revisited the village of my birth, spent a delightful hour with my dear old parents, and then took a stroll through the forest to the scene of my happy school-days—those days which we are told are the very happiest of our lives. Nothing had changed in the five or six years of my absence; not even the sound of agonized shrieks as I drew near the building; not even the sound of the cutting blows upon bare flesh as I drew near the open windows of the school-house; not even the savage grin of enjoyment upon the vile face of my erstwhile preceptor. . . .

"With my blood boiling, my nerves tingling and my fists clenching and unclenching, I flung open the door, and strode into the room, smelt the old familiar smell, saw the rows of strained white faces, heard the stifled sobbing of a cruelly-beaten child.

"'You dog,' I said quietly. 'You brutal, savage, snarling cur.'

"And as he whirled upon me, I struck with all my strength, and he went down, down across the whipping-bench, over which he had held me a thousand times. And I saw fear in that brute's eyes as he rose to his feet, and again I smashed my fist between them, with all my strength.

"When he could stagger to his feet no more, I flung him across that whipping-bench on which my young life and soul and nature had been warped, and taking his own cane, I flogged him until I was too weary to raise my hand again.

"And as I resumed my coat, I told him that I would keep in closest touch with certain of his pupils, and that if ever I heard of his striking one of his pupils a single blow, I would visit him again and give him a punishment compared with which this would be as nothing.

"Wasn't that a fine dream, Corporal Heintz? Oh! *I am a good hater and I always repay! I always repay!*"

"I suppose it was a true dream," observed Michael Geste.

"Yes," replied Gontran. "A day dream—and quite true."

"You spoke of two," observed La Cigale, who had shuddered and covered his face with his hands during Gontran's description of the sufferings of the children. "What was the other, might one ask? Did you dream that some scoundrelly ruffian was punished in that one also?"

"Ah, a curious dream," murmured Gontran, eyeing Corporal Heintz. "Very curious. . . . '*Wage du zu irren und zu träumen*,' as Schiller says. . . . 'Dare to err and to dream.' . . . Yes, there was a scoundrel in this one also, and I think one may say he was punished. . . . A woman too. . . ."

"Do you never have beautiful dreams of drink?" inquired Tant de Soif. "I once dreamed that I was swimming in a river of wine. Lovely. . . . Wonderful. Every night I go to sleep hoping that I may dream it again."

"I suppose you drank while you swam?" inquired Boldini.

"No, I swam while I drank," replied Tant de Soif, "and I drank so much and so fast that I choked and woke up, to find that it had come on to rain, and that a stream of dirty water was pouring from a roof-gutter into my open mouth. Fancy dreaming of wine, and waking to water."

"That is life in epitome, my friend," observed La Cigale, "to find your wine is water. Tell us your other dream," he added, turning to Gontran.

"Oh, it was nothing . . . nothing much. There are really only a few varieties of dream. They all belong to one or other of about half a dozen kinds. This was quite a stock one—the old triangular dream, you know; two men and a woman. She was a remarkable girl. Of course, all women are remarkable, I know. But she was doubly so, for the simple reason that she was two women."

"So you had two wives, bigamist?" growled the Corporal.

"I did not say that she was my wife—and after all, I'm only telling a *dream*, am I not, Corporal Heintz?

"Yes, she was a gentle, timid, soft little thing, meek and nervous and humble, full of gratitude for your smile, fearful and anxious and cringing at your scowl."

"Proper sort for a wife," smiled Boldini, and licked his lips.

"And yet there was a core of granite at the heart of this soft clay; there was steel somewhere beneath the silk."

"Perhaps she had a heart of gold," sneered Boldini. "Gold's hard enough, and hard to come by."

"Excellent," smiled Gontran. "What a very clever man you are! It must have been her heart of gold that one occasionally came upon beneath that tender softness. Quite so; for she was good. Oh, unutterably good and sweet—the sweetest nature, the sweetest disposition, the sweetest temper—oh, incurably sweet. How would you like to eat honey all day long? And think of the flies such honey attracts. There was one fly in particular. . . . To pursue the simile a little further, he got honey on his wings and couldn't fly away. . . . Sticky stuff, honey. . . . And he got it in his heart, and certainly in his voice. Oh, honeyed words, I assure you. The husband listened secretly.

"He was a gentle soul, this Lover . . . made for love. . . . Undoubtedly in a previous incarnation he had been a Provencal *jongleur*, a wandering minstrel of love, going from castle to castle, and from Court to Court; singing of love; making love; a very warrior in the lists of love; right welcome at King René's Court of Love; slender, willowy, white-handed, large-eyed, long-haired, golden-bearded—oh, a great lover.

"And she, pleased and smiling, always pleased and smiling, but discreet. . . . Oh, yes, always discreet. . . . And virtuous. . . . Or so the Husband hoped. And believed—sometimes. And sometimes he did not. When he was with them he believed, as he gazed upon that lovely Madonna face, and looked into the soulful, gentle eyes of his sweet-mouthed friend; but when his affairs took him away, as periodically they did, and he must leave his Mountain Forest châlet for days at a time, he did *not* believe; and a dark cloud of jealousy gradually overspread the heaven of his soul.

"Jealousy, to change the metaphor, that purest poison, that deadliest and most damnable distillation of the Devil. . . . And the poison spread and spread until his mind was rotted and corrupted, his conscience paralysed, his better nature dead.

"And as poisoned love was metamorphosed into hideous hate, he watched and schemed and plotted and laid traps. And worse—he made opportunities for them. He would say to his friend:

"'This time to-morrow night I shall be on the Rhine again, gazing on moonlit schloss and vineyard, and thinking of my girl, lonely at home here. Pass the cottage on your night round, comrade, and try the door and window. She is young and careless, and thinks no evil. She does not believe the world holds thieves and robbers and evil men.'

"And the young forester would eagerly agree. What had he to guard one-millionth part as precious as little love-faced Heart-of-Gold?

"And the Husband would take an impassioned farewell of his Dutiful Beautiful, and bid her not to mope in loneliness during his week of absence. Why should she not go and visit Frau Englehardt, and take some dainty for her invalid and aged husband? Young Fritz would see her safely home if she lingered after nightfall.

"And departing, he would swiftly return—and watch.

"And one night he was rewarded—or punished, for he saw her sauntering beneath the trees with her Lover, strolling hand-in-hand in the moonlight, and lingering in the black patches of darkest shadow.

"At the door of the cottage they stood and spoke awhile, and then she drew him in and closed the door. Would a light appear, and if so in which room? With teeth embedded in the knuckle which he gnawed, the Husband waited . . . waited . . . waited. And a light appeared. They had lit the lamp in the sitting-room downstairs.

"Cautiously he crept to the window. Blind and curtain were drawn and he could see nothing. Later, the Lover emerged and strode off into the forest, whistling, his gun upon his shoulder. Scarcely could the Husband refrain from rushing to the house, taking down his own gun from where it hung upon the wall, and stealing off to waylay him on his round. But that would be crude—and dangerous; and it was just possible that he was wrong, his suspicions unfounded. He would make absolutely sure—and then his vengeance should be dreadful.

"But it would be a poor game to alienate his wife, lose his friend, and put a noose about his own neck, for nothing at all— put himself within the shadow of the prison—of the gallows— because of a suspicion that might be as baseless as the airy fabric of a dream.

"*Prison! Gallows!* Unpleasant words, and conjuring up unpleasant thoughts in the mind of one who already had a guilty secret—one who already knew what it was to feel uncomfortable at the approach of a *gendarme*, to feel a certain apprehension whenever there came a sudden and heavy knock upon the door. Such a sinister and sullen sound, ominous and foreboding.

"So he waited . . . waited . . . waited through that night, seated with his back against a tree, his eyes upon his moonlit silent house, wherein the light had disappeared from the sitting-room, appeared in the bedroom, and suddenly gone out. And later, the Lover returned from his round, whistling merrily until he was near the house, when he fell silent and walked delicately, making no noise with his iron-shod boots.

"The Husband rose to his feet and stiffened like a hunting-dog that sees its prey. The forester entered by the little garden gate, and crept silently to the door. The Husband, in the shadow of his tree, took a step forward, and the faint sound of the intake of his breath was audible.

"The door did not open. Nor did the window. No light appeared within the house, and the Lover strolled silently away.

"At a short distance from the house, he turned, bared his head, extended both arms in the direction of the upstairs window, and stood as though in adjuration and in prayer. Then, wafting a kiss in the direction in which he gazed, he suddenly turned and strode swiftly away.

"Nothing much in all that, you will say. And so the Husband said—for a time. But, being of a jealous nature, he could neither let well alone nor ill, if ill it were—until, one night, returning two days before he was expected, he found his house silent, empty and deserted.

"Stunned and incredulous, he seized his gun, and strode out of that unbearable and mocking house, and, with murder in his heart, rushed through the forest, bareheaded and distraught. He realized that his feet were carrying him in the direction of the cottage where dwelt the *garde-champêtre*, and his aged parents.

"Why? She would not be there. They would have fled.

"But she *was* there, serene and calm, sitting with her lover in the porch, while, in the room above, the old mother ministered to her sick husband, the invalid for whom the girl had brought some delicacy. Coolly she greeted her husband, and told him that he was just in time to take her home, instead of Fritz, who had kindly offered to do so.

"'But why the gun?' jeered the Lover. 'Going rabbit-shooting in the dark?'

"'Yes, I'm going to shoot a rabbit,' replied the Husband, in a deadly quiet voice, 'and quite probably in the dark.'

"Thereafter his mind dwelt much on shooting, but he feared the law. He feared what his wife might suspect, and say, and do, if suddenly her lover disappeared. For he knew in his heart, though never a word had been spoken, that his wife was but too well aware of his jealousy and his hatred; and he suspected that the forester knew of it, too.

"With amusement? With contempt? Would they laugh at him together behind his back, adding vilest insult to foulest injury? The thought was unbearable, and his soured suspicious mind was all but unhinged.

"One day, the dark recesses of his mind were brilliantly illuminated by a lurid idea, and he could scarcely await the hour for translating thought into action—the action that would give completest proof and every excuse and right for committing a *crime passionel*. The law would pardon the deed, and public opinion condone it. Proof, confession, punishment. Punishment for them both. The utmost penalty of the law—the unwritten law.

"Having made his usual preparations for a journey, and requested his wife to put a change of clothing and a parcel of food in his rucksack, he announced his departure for Cologne, and his intention of returning on the fifth day at earliest.

"'There is no time earlier than the earliest, is there?' observed his wife, with her enigmatic smile; and bade him a sufficiently fond farewell.

"He returned the next night, and once again watched and waited for the passing of Fritz, the *garde-champêtre*. This time he waylaid and accosted him, a quarter of a mile from the house; and, as though even more in sorrow than in anger, in wounded misery than in savage and vengeful wrath—accused him of being the Lover of his wife.

"It was the young forester who was angry, and angry that the woman should be accused, that a single word should be uttered against her, a single breath of suspicion tarnish her good name. Of himself he said nothing—this sole reply was to condemn the unbelievable baseness and villainy of the mind that could think such thoughts, the man who could speak such words of his innocent wife—and such a wife.

"Oh, it was well acted, clever and very plausible, and when the Husband bade him cease to speak of the woman, and to answer the charge brought against himself, he replied:

"'Why waste my time and trouble, madman? But take note that I am merely *suspected* of a vile thing, and that by only one man—if you are a man. Whereas you have done—actually *done*—a most vile and awful thing.'

"The Husband recoiled in alarm.

"'*What have I done?*' he cried.

"'Fouled your own nest, bird of ill-omen,' was the reply. 'Falsely and filthily accused the sweetest and most innocent of women. Spat your stinking poison at a star of Heaven, immeasurably above you. Yes, and it falls back upon your own most beastly face.'

"The Husband laughed.

"'Why all this heat,' he asked softly, 'since you are not her lover?'

"'Because she is an innocent woman, you diseased hound, and I will not hear her name befouled, not even by you. Nay, *especially* by you, who should be her sure shield and strong protection. You, the very man who should strike dead the lying scoundrel who spoke evil. . . .'

"'Or did evil, eh?' interrupted the Husband. 'Strike him dead, you said.'

"'I did, and I repeat it,' replied the forester. *'Evil* in connection with that true, sweet, innocent woman!'

"'She is innocent, eh?' interrupted the Husband again.

"'You know it.'

"'And you? Are you innocent?'

"'You know it.'

"'Good. Then you shall prove it. Refuse to do what I now order you to do, and I shall know, *know*, once and for all, that you are a liar, a coward, and a thief, and that she is a . . .'

"The forester raised his clenched fist, and the Husband sprang back.

"'Blows prove nothing,' he cried. 'Fists are not arguments. Come with me, and we shall see what we shall see—or hear . . . *Innocent*, is she!'

"And with a bitter laugh he strode in the direction of his house, followed by the forester.

"Silently opening the little garden gate, he laid a finger on his lips and whispered:

"'Make a sound, and it is a certain proof of guilt. Come.'

"And taking the key from his pocket, he crept to the door, and silently unlocked it.

"'Follow me,' he whispered almost inaudibly, and drew the Lover into the house.

"There, in the darkness, behind the closed door, they stood. The Husband, shaking with jealous rage, and scarcely able to keep his twitching hands from the throat of the man whom he hated beyond telling or belief; the Lover, sorely bewildered and disturbed, but strong to protect and defend the woman whom he loved.

"Thus they stood, silent in the noiseless darkness, till suddenly the Husband, in low, tense whisper, bade the Lover mount the stairs and open the door of the room where the woman slept.

"'Go up, you dog,' he whispered, 'softly open the door, and

say, "*Lisette, it is I. I am here, Lisette, it is I, Fritz*"—and we shall hear what she replies! Innocent, is she! We shall see.'

"'I do not know the door,' answered the Lover. 'I have never set foot upon those stairs.'

"'Liar!' whispered the Husband. 'Coward! Liar again! You dare not. You are afraid of what she will say. You dare not stand there in the dark, knowing that I am behind you with my hunting-knife against your back, and say, "*Lisette, it is I, Fritz. I have come to you.*" No, you know too well what she will answer. "*You are late, my beloved*" . . . or "*And I am waiting, my sweetheart Fritz,*" . . . Eh? That's about what we should hear, isn't it? Very awkward with the point of this between your shoulder-blades, eh? . . . No, you don't know the way to the door, do you?'

"'No,' replied the Lover. 'Show me the way. Creep softly, and open the door yourself. Then stand behind me, place the point of your knife just where you will, and I will call, "*Lisette, it is I, Fritz. I have come to you,*" and abide the result. Lead on.'

"'Bluff and bravado,' growled the Husband, softly. 'We shall see.'

"'Lead on,' whispered the Lover, and slowly, stealthily, silently the two went up the stair. At the top, the Husband, seizing the Lover's wrist, crossed a little landing at the end of which a small window, vaguely outlined by starshine and the feeble fleeting light of a lean cloud-haunted moon, was visible.

"'This is the door,' he breathed, then directed the Lover's hand toward the latch, swiftly stepped behind him and drew his knife.

"After a brief fumbling at the latch, the Lover opened the door, and with low insistent voice called, '*Lisette, Lisette.*'

"And again:

"'*Lisette, Lisette.*'

"There was a faint sound of movement from the bed, and the Lover felt a pressure on the left side of his broad back.

"'*Lisette,*' he called urgently.

"'*What? Who's that?*' came a woman's voice from the pitchy darkness of the room.

"The pressure increased behind the forester's heart and he fancied he felt the knife-point against his skin.

"'*It is I, Lisette,*' he said. '*It is I, Fritz. I have come to you,*

Lisette.'

"Dead silence in the blank black darkness.

"No reply. No movement. No sound—even of breathing.

"The pressure increased, and no doubt remained as to whether the knife-point pricked the Lover's skin.

"'*Lisette,*' he said again. '*Speak to me, Lisette . . . Say something. It is I, Fritz. Standing here in the doorway of your room. Speak, Lisette.'*

"Silence.

"Aching, unbearable silence and suspense.

"'*Say something, Lisette. Speak to me.'*

"Silence.

"And then suddenly, at what seemed to be the very end of Time itself, a voice came out of the darkness.

"'*You, is it, Fritz?'* spoke the woman. '*And you have opened the door of my room, and are standing there. Ah! . . . Then listen, Fritz. And when I have spoken, you will know what to do.'*

"The voice ceased, but not the increasing pressure behind the young man's heart.

"'*I am listening, Lisette,*' he said.

"And Lisette spoke again.

"'*On the 25th day of June of last year, at about 9 o'clock in the evening . . .'*

"The pressure suddenly relaxed—the knife was no longer touching the young man's back.

"'*. . . a man was sitting on a log in the forest near the waterfall. He had sold his winter's wood-carving that day, and returning homeward had sat him down to rest and to gloat upon the money he had got for it.*

"*By a curious chance two people saw him—one of them from some distance, but not from so far away that there could be any possibility of mistake as to who sat there with the last rays of the setting sun shining full upon him—nor any possibility of mistake as to who was the other person who saw him, and who crept stealthily upon him from behind. THAT man was . . .'*

"'That's enough,' roared a bull voice in the darkness, and almost in Fritz's ear.

"Dead silence.

"And then the voice of the Husband, a little shaky, false and falsetto, gabbled unconvincingly,

"'Ha, ha, ha! What do you think of this for a joke, my love? Fritz and I thought we'd play a little trick on you. I met him in the forest on my way home. He said, "*Let's go and give little Lisette a fright.*"'

"'*Oh, you are there too, are you, Karl?*' replied a cool voice from the darkness. And I swear there was a smile in the voice.

"'*I think it was a splendid joke . . . a wonderful little trick for Fritz, of all people, to suggest. And now the little Lisette has had her fright, eh? Or IS it the little Lisette who has had the fright?*'

"'Get out of this, you, quick,' growled the Husband, and gave the Lover a thrust that sent him headlong down the stairs.

"Rising to his feet, the young forester debated for a moment as to whether he should return in triumph and demand an apology, in the name of Lisette, from that evil-thinking, unworthy animal above. But natural delicacy joined with instinct and with wisdom to forbid. Rarely are peacemakers really blessed who come between husband and wife. . . . And the young man, bewildered, indignant, angry and sore at heart, quietly went his way.

"And then for the Husband there followed a period of hell upon earth that made the recent months of misery seem like halcyon days of peace and joy. He had shown his hand, and Lisette had shown her knowledge—her knowledge of a deed which he had hitherto supposed no human eye had witnessed. He had shown his hand, insulting and alienating his friend, insulting and alienating his wife, and had proved nothing, gained nothing. Gained nothing, save a dreadful Fear, a Fear that dogged him by day and gripped him by night.

"How much did Lisette know?

"Everything, of course.

"How otherwise did she know the very hour at which old Caspar Knutzen met his death. Had she followed and watched as he dragged the frail old body to the mouth of the old disused mine and thrust it over the edge? It mattered not, since she had witnessed the crime.

"What a woman—to live with that secret in her heart and to say nothing! But had she said nothing? Had she told her lover?

And if she had not told him, would she tell him now, in revenge for his unpardonable offence, the insult of the unforgivable accusation he had made against her and Fritz?

"In what a morass of fear, horror and suspense had he to walk? If she had not told Fritz up to that very day, she might tell him on the morrow. After any quarrel she might run to him with this story of the murder.

"Did Fritz eye him queerly nowadays?

"Was there special meaning and triumph, as well as contempt and scorn, in the glance which he gave him?

"And if she did tell Fritz, what was there to prevent their getting him sent to the scaffold that they might be free to marry? Or, for fear that that might look like interested collusion, why should not Lisette denounce him to the world, go to the Police and, after his execution, marry Fritz quietly, in due course?

"And if she had not yet breathed a word about it to any living soul, might she not still use this awful secret for her own ends? Use it to secure his acquiescence and compliance? Perhaps use it to make him agree to her divorcing him?

"Ah, divorce! Could he not divorce *her*, with the help of perjured witnesses?

"The Husband was well aware that there are base scoundrels who rid themselves of women from whom they wish to be free, by taking action against them in the Divorce Court, and putting them in the position of having either to defend their good name and remain tied to the foul beast, who has accused them; or of gaining their freedom at the cost of leaving the perjured liar's filthy accusations unrefuted.

"But what would he gain, even if she and Fritz were willing to remain undefended, and he succeeded in divorcing her? They would marry and she would surely tell Fritz the husband what she might not have told Fritz the lover. And Fritz, of course, would use the knowledge to punish him for the lies and insults of the divorce.

"And meanwhile, how much longer could he go on living in the same house with this woman whom he dared not look in the face? This woman whom he had so injured and insulted, even while she knew this dreadful thing, and had said no word. And how could he continue to meet this Fritz daily, this Fritz whom he had insulted and accused, and who might, at any moment, learn that he was a murderer, might indeed know it already? How much longer could he go on living here, awaiting the heavy hand that would one day fall upon his shoulder; awaiting the heavy knock that would one day fall upon his door; fearing every stranger who approached him; fearing the sound of every foot that followed him in the forest or the town.

"Flight?

"And if he fled? Whither? And where would he be secure? For the arm of the law is long, and the voice of the murdered dead is loud, as it crieth for vengeance from the unconsecrated grave.

"What to do? How many people knew? Almost certainly no more than Lisette and Fritz. Quite probably Lisette alone. And if Lisette alone knew, and anything—happened to—Lisette, then *no one* would know, and all would be well, and the Husband could struggle out of this fearful morass, shake its mud from his feet, and walk forth a free man.

"But then again, how could one live without Lisette, the beautiful, the sweet, the charming—and maddening—Lisette?

"Well, better to live without her, a free man, than live without her in prison, or die without her, on the scaffold. Lisette was dear, but life was dearer, and self-preservation is man's first law.

"Yes, it looked as though the dear Lisette might have to die, but clearly the first thing was to find out whether the good Fritz had been told of the fatal secret. . . . And if he had, why then it might prove a fatal secret indeed—for Fritz.

"How one's mind did run on! And how one thing led to another—two more murders to cover one!

"Meanwhile Fritz, the *garde-champêtre*, lived in a state of unhappiness far removed indeed from the guilty misery of Karl, but almost as far from his former condition of light-hearted contentment and *joie-de-vivre*. Why had that ill-conditioned cur behaved so, and spoilt everything between him and Lisette; made them self-conscious and uncomfortable? Nothing could ever be the same again, now that this hog had wallowed in the dainty dream-garden of their delight.

"Life was spoilt and defiled, and instead of rising in the

morning with a song in his heart and thoughts of a glimpse of
Lisette, a word with Lisette, perhaps a walk with Lisette, he must
now avoid her, and slink shamefacedly past the cottage that had
been the lodestone of his thoughts, the haven of his dreams, the
shrine of his dear love.

"And what was the meaning of that astounding bedroom
scene, that drama played in darkness? What had Lisette meant,
and why had her reference to a man seated on a log so suddenly
changed a blustering and menacing bully into a frightened fool?

"How had Lisette known that Karl was standing there?
Woman's quick wit and intuition telling her that her friend Fritz
would not have come to her thus? . . . Had she guessed; and
instantly realized the plot and trap? Possibly she had heard them
whispering below. Anyhow, the cunning blackguard had had his
lesson; the evil-minded dog come whimpering to heel.

"But everything was spoilt and a heavy dirty hand had
roughly and rudely brushed the bloom from life's fairest and
sweetest fruit. Why was it that women such as Lisette married
such men as this Karl the Miller?

"What a man, what an animal, to be the husband and owner
of Lisette! How could she possibly tolerate him, much less love
him?

"No, if truth were told, the man whom Lisette loved was . . ."

"*That's enough*," suddenly roared Corporal Heintz. "Fall in.
Stir yourselves, *salauds*. . . ."

And the weary squad dragged itself to its feet, and painfully
heaved its *sacs* to its shoulders.

§4

On the following night, as the squad sat about the camp fire,
digesting the indigestible and smoking the unsmokeable, Michael
Geste requested *le légionnaire* Gontran to continue the story of
his remarkable dream concerning the miller and the forester.

"It certainly was some dream," observed Hank to his friend.

"You've said something," replied Buddy. "If I could dream
like that, I'd dream you was a lovely girl, old Hoss; or else that
you was rich and had a generous nature. Nothing ain't impossible
in dreams."

"Which is the true dream, and which the true reality—that of the sleeping night, or this of the waking day?" asked La Cigale.

"How did the dream go on?" replied *le légionnaire* Gontran to Michael Geste. "Oh, I dreamed that the woman died. . . . Yes, in my dream I saw that unhappy lover, Fritz, receive a letter. It was handed to him by a neighbour's half-witted son, who, on being asked later whether a woman gave it to him said 'Yes,' and on being asked again if a man gave it to him, also said 'Yes.'

"The letter was in the handwriting of Lisette. It seemed to have been written in a state of some agitation and in great haste, and it bade him come to her at ten o'clock that night, for speak to him she must—and in the absence of her husband. The latter had again gone away that day, saying he would be absent for three nights at least. She relied on Fritz to come to her; she knew that he would come, for she needed his help, and there was something that must be done and done quickly.

"Beneath the signature of Lisette was an urgent appeal. It seemed that she had started to write with discretion and restraint, and at the last moment her feelings had overcome her. Terror, anxiety and the very fear of death had broken the bonds of prudence. She had written:

"*Come and advise me and help me. He is so strange and terrible, and I feel that I am in the greatest danger. I truly believe that I'm being poisoned. What shall I do? Where can I go? Help me, Fritz.*'

"You may imagine the state of mind in which the Lover spent the hours which intervened. They were the longest through which he had ever lived.

"At ten o'clock that night, he approached the dark and silent house, opened the little garden gate, crept to the door, and tapped softly.

"No answer. No movement within.

"Again he tapped, and again without response.

"In conjunction with the fact that no light burned in the sitting-room, this was vaguely disquieting, though not alarming.

"He tried the latch of the door, and found that the door was not fastened. Should he walk in? She had bidden him come at ten o'clock and the hour had struck.

"He entered warily, closed the door behind him, and softly

called, '*Lisette, Lisette.*'

"He struck a match, and entered the living-room. It was, as he had expected, empty, though he had half hoped to see her sitting there in the dark, awaiting him.

"Similarly deserted was the kitchen at the back of the sitting-room.

"With swiftly-beating heart, he went to the foot of the well-remembered stairs on which he had set foot but once, and called her name. Again he called, more loudly; and yet again, receiving no reply.

"What could be the meaning of this? Was it a trap, some new and devilish ingenuity of her husband? Should he go up? No. How explain his presence there, if Karl sprang out upon him, or were lurking, awaiting him in the bedroom?

"But she had sent for him. She had implored him to be there at ten o'clock, and time was passing. Should he not go up? Yes. Lisette would not send for him and then go out of the cottage.

"And if it were a trap, let the good Karl see what he had got in his trap! He would not be the first setter of traps that had caught a Tartar—not the first spider whose net had caught a wasp.

"Yes, he would go up, and if the worst happened, things could be no worse, apparently, for Lisette, and might, indeed, be made very much better.

"The Lover climbed the stairs, and was confronted by a closed door. Upon this he knocked again and again, receiving no answer.

"He then tried the door, and found that this also was unfastened. Opening it, he whispered, '*Lisette!*' and louder and louder said, '*Lisette! Lisette!*' She could not have gone to bed and be sleeping so heavily that his voice failed to wake her.

"Of course she would not have gone to bed after having begged him to come to her at ten o'clock. Could she possibly have gone out into the forest to meet him, and have missed him in the darkness? Almost impossible.

"With fear clutching at his heart, he struck a match. A terrible cry burst from his lips, and dropping the match, he covered his stricken eyes with shaking hands. On the bed lay Lisette—dead. Murdered. Most violently and brutally murdered.

"The reactions of the human mind to sudden emergency or shock are strange and unaccountable, and are not to be foretold. His first impulse was to flee from that dreadful spot. The next thing was to fling himself upon the bed and shield in his embrace that dear defiled and injured body; coax it back to life and movement with his caresses.

"What he *did* do, was to strike a match and fumble at the lamp with trembling fingers, the while waves of nausea, grief, and rage shook him from head to foot. Having succeeded in lighting the lamp, he took a grip upon his courage, and then, turning to the bed, repressed his shuddering horror and strove to do what might be done.

"Hopeless and useless. A hunting-knife had done its dreadful work too well, in heart and throat; and all that the stunned, incredulous and broken-hearted man could do, was to pray that he might be vouchsafed sufficient length of life and health and strength to become the instrument of vengeance.

"It was thus the police found him—the police who, it appeared, had been anonymously warned to surround and enter the house at the hour of ten-thirty, if they wished to prevent the perpetration of a terrible crime, involving robbery and murder, in the absence of the miller—a crime arranged for the hour of eleven.

"There they found him, his hands stained with blood—a picture, at any rate to the Police, of guilt as well as of horror at the deed he had committed. Nor was the Sergeant of Gendarmes disposed to change his opinion when he noticed that every drawer in the room was opened and ransacked; and that a box, evidently dragged from beneath the bed, had been burst open.

"To the fierce questions and demands of the Police, Fritz could give no satisfactory reply. He could but protest his innocence and swear that he had *happened* to enter the house, had *happened* to go upstairs. . . .

"'Oh, quite so . . .' the Police had observed, nodding its collective head. 'And had *happened* to go into the poor woman's bedroom, and had *happened* to find her robbed and murdered. A likely story.'

"And why, pray, had he gone to the house at all, at that time of night?

"And in reply to that awkward question, the prisoner had preserved a dogged silence.

"But the case proved to be far less simple than had, at first sight, appeared, and the Police were mystified. Though they had caught him in the very act—in the ransacked room itself, where was the loot? Where were the money and poor jewellery that had undoubtedly been taken from drawer and box? Though he had been caught red-handed indeed, his hands red with the murdered woman's blood, where was the weapon, and what the motive?

"And another most extraordinary feature of the case—where was the husband? He had absolutely disappeared—vanished from off the face of the earth.

"And was it literally from off the face of the earth, and was he now under the earth in some secret grave dug for him by this monster?

"And then again Fritz the forester was most certainly not a monster, but a most worthy young man of excellent education, known good character and unimpeachable virtue. Hitherto, at any rate. But you never knew, you never knew. And the Police shook its head darkly. Nevertheless the Police was mystified.

"But heart-broken Fritz the forester, in his dank dark cell, was not mystified. He knew, with absolute certainty, as if he had seen it all, that Karl had murdered Lisette, and with superhuman devilish cunning had contrived to divert suspicion, blame, and accusation upon the friend of whom he was jealous.

"Karl had never been the same man since that night of mad accusation and infamous attempt at proof. He had gone from bad to worse, and quite obviously had rendered Lisette's life unbearable, until at length she had been driven, in fear of her life, to write Fritz the letter that had brought him to the house that terrible night.

"Obviously her husband, having told her that he was going away from home again, had spied upon her and had either caught her in the act of getting the letter to the half-witted go-between, or had intercepted it *en route*. He had then waited as long as he dared, had most foully and brutally murdered the poor girl, and had taken all the money and jewellery that was in the house, leaving the bedroom in calculated disorder.

"He had then gone off in the darkness, sent his anonymous

message to the police and escaped.

"A neat plot, and worthy of the Devil himself. But not quite successful, for the four absent elements saved Fritz's life— probably because he valued it so little—absence of motive, absence of stolen property, absence of weapon, and absence of the husband whom it was decided could not have been murdered and disposed of—at any rate by the prisoner—between the time he was last seen alive and the time of the arrest. Fortunately for Fritz, his movements and whereabouts were known throughout the earlier part of that evening.

"So, finally, Fritz was discharged with a stain upon his character—a stain indelible; and in despair he left his home, his beloved forest and his native land, and joined the Legion of the Self-condemned. . . ."

The Dreamer fell silent.

"And is he in the Legion still?" asked Michael Geste.

"He dreams that he is," was the reply.

"And do you dream that he is?" asked John.

"I dream that I dream that he is," replied Gontran, turning his curious pale, unsmiling eyes upon the boy.

II

Life at Zinderneuf was life in death, and not infrequently death in life. As *le légionnaire* Gontran observed, it was like nothing on earth, but was indeed most remarkably like something in Hell—one of Hell's punishment cells, where the Devil sends defaulting fiends from his Penal Battalions when other means have failed to repress them. But *le légionnaire* Gontran had great compensations, for he had been promoted Corporal.

On the day on which he stood forth, a Corporal revealed, with two chevrons upon his cuff, he had gone in search of Corporal Heintz. And tapping the two red chevrons upon his sleeve had said:

"Ha, ha, my friend, now we shall see what we shall see."

But the triumph of Corporal Gontran had been brief, his grim and menacing complacence short-lived, for the last official act of the Commandant, Captain Renouf, on the very day that he shot himself, was to promote Corporal Heintz to Sergeant. So a

Sergeant, pending confirmation in orders, Heintz became. And a Sergeant can make himself quite as painfully unpleasant to a Corporal as a Corporal can to a *légionnaire*. He can get him reduced to the ranks, for example. Meanwhile he can punish him with confinement to Barracks, or with *salle de police* and he can get him sent to prison. Without punishing him at all, he can make his life a burden, a misery and a shame, by undermining his authority and making him ridiculous before the men of his *escouade*. And he can legally and officially hold him responsible for every fault committed by every man of the room of which he is in charge.

It is probable that, on the whole, Sergeant Heintz made life even more unbearable for Corporal Gontran than had Corporal Heintz for *le légionnaire* Gontran. He quickly succeeded in turning the unfavourable attention of *l'adjudant* Lejaune upon the unfortunate man. To show forth their proper zeal beneath the watchful eye of l'adjudant Lejaune, Sergeant Dupré and Corporal Boldini, friends of Sergeant Heintz, joined enthusiastically with him in discovering cause for dissatisfaction with the work of Corporal Gontran.

One fortunate result of this state of affairs was that neither Heintz nor Gontran had much time for bullying other people and became almost popular.

But Sergeant Heintz overdid it, and, one night, Corporal Gontran dreamed another dream, and when on the following day, according to his wont, Sergeant Heintz jeeringly inquired as to whether he had dreamed anything of interest lately, Corporal Gontran replied that he had indeed. And something, moreover, of personal interest to the good Sergeant himself.

It was a curious dream, and in two parts.

In the first of these, the Dreamer had dreamed of a most regrettable and deplorable event, which was nothing less than the premature demise of Sergeant Heintz himself.

Yes, he had seen him die.

"And how, might one inquire?" sneered Sergeant Heintz, moistening dry lips.

"Well, in this curious dream of mine, Sergeant, you were stabbed, just here and just here," and Corporal Gontran indicated his heart and his throat. "Yes, you were stabbed in the heart and in the throat, and you bled to death. When the murder was discovered it was too late to do anything for you. You were dead—oh, quite dead."

"And the second part of this interesting dream?" asked Sergeant Heintz, as listening men, lounging outside the Guard Room, edged nearer and nearer.

"Oh, very vague—you know what dreams are, Sergeant Heintz—but somehow mixed up with the first one. As far as I can remember, it was mainly about a *légionnaire* who had a mission in life."

"What, to shirk work, and give trouble to his superiors?" inquired Heintz.

"No, no. So far as I can remember, it was something more difficult than that. It was to inflict punishment rather than to get it. In fact, to inflict punishment without getting it. Yes, that was it. I remember it quite clearly now, that part of it. Yes, this *légionnaire* had to kill a man."

"Murder, eh?" sneered Sergeant Heintz. "Sort of thing you would dream about."

"Well—not so much murder him as execute him. Take the law into his own hands, or, one might say, assist the law—do what the law had failed to do. Carry out the death sentence which the law would most certainly and most righteously have passed upon him had not the bestial and cowardly Judas fled beyond the reach of its arm.

"Oh yes, an execution. That was his mission. And he not unnaturally wanted to live awhile, to enjoy the satisfaction that his good deed would bring him. . . . But in my dream—and I remember this part most clearly—it seemed that he had come to the conclusion that it really did not matter whether he lived or not once he had fulfilled his task, done his duty by the community and mankind in general, punished an unspeakable villain, and avenged the best and sweetest soul that ever graced this world. . . ."

"Quite a dream, in effect," interrupted Sergeant Heintz, his livid face twitching.

"Yes, Sergeant Heintz," continued Corporal Gontran. "Quite a dream. And making it perfectly clear that this *légionnaire* had most finally and firmly decided that he had done wrong and acted foolishly, in waiting for an opportunity to execute justice without himself falling beneath the sword of justice. . . . Yes, he saw the error of his ways, in that he had not immediately done his duty and carried out his mission most cheerfully—as soon as he found the man—and willingly offered his life as the price of that privilege. Why, man, he had prayed—prayed most fervently—that he might live to be the instrument of vengeance upon that foul savage beast, that treacherous base brutal . . ."

As he spoke Corporal Gontran thrust his suffused face close to that of Sergeant Heintz, raised his clenched fists, and slavered at the mouth.

Clearly a case of *cafard*—the man was going mad—and Corporal Boldini, seizing his arm, pulled him roughly away.

"I'll give you something to dream about," growled Sergeant Heintz, "and before long, I'll put you where you'll stop dreaming altogether."

§2

That night, a night so unbearably and dangerously hot that but few could sleep, Beau Geste and his brother John sat side by side beneath the desert stars, and talked of Digby, away at Tokotu, of Brandon Abbas, and of old, happy, far-off things.

After a time they fell silent, and from the darkness of the black shadow in which they sat against the wall, idly watched the occasional comings and goings of their comrades, commenting from time to time upon their more salient characteristics.

"Who's that with Boldini?" murmured Beau as two men passed in the moonlight, their heads together in whispered converse.

"That weed Bolidar. They're very thick these days," replied John.

As he spoke, Sergeant Heintz approached, and Bolidar slunk away into the shadows. Heintz gave Bolidar a sharp order, and as he hurried off to fulfil it, another man, descending steps that led down from the roof, approached.

"The Lover and the Husband," murmured John. "Which is which?"

"Neither of them really knows much of love, I think," replied

Beau.

Corporal Gontran and Sergeant Heintz met in front of the brothers, and a few yards from where they were sitting.

"Get to your room and dream, you dog," growled Sergeant Heintz. "Dream while you have yet time. Dream you're on the scaffold and . . ."

"I'm dreaming now, Sergeant Heintz. I'm dreaming *now*, you cesspool of sin," and, drawing his sword-bayonet, he stabbed Sergeant Heintz in the left breast.

"*Lisette!*" he shouted, and as the stricken man staggered back, sagged at the knees and fell to the ground, Corporal Gontran struck again, driving the bayonet through the Sergeant's throat.

"*Lisette!*" he cried a second time, and as the astonished brothers sprang forward, he whipped out an automatic pistol.

"Stand still," he shouted, "or I'll shoot you both. Stand to attention until I tell you to move," and he covered them alternately with the automatic.

"Keep still, John," murmured Beau, in English. "He's quite mad and won't care whom he shoots. Wait till I say 'Now,' and then jump to the right as I jump to the left. . . . *Wait*, though."

"Good," whispered John. "You duck and collar him low, and I'll jump for his pistol."

Corporal Gontran kicked Sergeant Heintz heavily.

"Can you hear, you dog?" he shouted. "Or are you dead? '*Quite a dream in effect*,' eh?"

And then, with an incredible change of voice, he said, softly, as he placed the muzzle of the pistol to his temple and gazed upward at the stars:

"*Je viens, ma Lisette.*"

THE ROMANTIC REGIMENT:
THE STORY OF THE FRENCH FOREIGN
LEGION

In this non-fiction article about the French Foreign Legion, Wren provides a history of the Legion as well as what it would be like to be in the Legion. He does not present a very flattering picture of the Legion. The real question, that almost anybody who reads Wren asks, is, did he actually serve in the Legion? Wren was always in the affirmative when questioned about this, and his stepson, Richard Alan Graham-Smith, always "strongly maintained that Wren had indeed served in the French Foreign Legion and was always quick to refute those who said otherwise."[3] Based on the documented events in his life it is difficult to see when he could have actually served in the Legion. "The Romantic Regiment" was first published in the second issue of the pulp magazine, Soldiers of Fortune *(December 1931). This is the first reprinting since that time.*

A hundred years ago, in March, 1831, the French Foreign Legion was reorganized in the form which it has retained until the present time. Previous to that, the regiment had existed for many centuries and had been known under various names, and with different nationalities and personnel, such as the Scottish Archers, the Irish Brigade, the German Regiment and the Swiss Guard.

The French kings, from Crusading times to those of Louis XVI, always believed in having a foreign bodyguard of highly trained, well paid, mercenary troops on whom they could rely. The French emperors and the French Republic have held the same view and maintained foreign mercenaries, also highly trained if not so well paid, to fight their battles.

To-day the French Legion of Foreigners is perhaps the best trained and worst paid fighting force in the world.

A hundred years ago the military fame of France, thanks to

---

[3] http://en.wikipedia.org/wiki/P._C._Wren

Napoleon, was very great indeed, and after the Revolution of 1830 it was realized that there was an enormous number of foreigners living in France, a very great majority of whom were trained soldiers.

The Government of the day had the brilliant idea of turning this horde of foreigners from a potential danger into a valuable asset, and at the same time removing it from France.

They were enrolled as a Foreign Legion to be employed abroad, and were at once sent to Algeria to take a leading part in the conquest of that country.

The men of the force that landed at Algiers in 1831 were the forerunners and military forefathers of the French Foreign Legion as it is today, and the force was the first authentic French Foreign Legion under that name.

Then, as now, it was more than a regiment; it was a small army, for it consisted of seven battalions, each of eight companies, and each company quite elastic as to size. There were three battalions of Germans, one of Spanish, one of Italians, one of Belgians, one of Dutch, and one of Poles.

Before very long, however, it was found that it was a mistake to have complete and separate battalions of the separate nationalities. They fought each other instead of fighting the enemy, and soon the légionnaires were all mixed together irrespective of nationality, so that in a single company there might be Swiss, Croats, Greeks, Belgians, Dutch, Italians, Irish, Spaniards, Turks, Russians, Corsicans, Poles, Portuguese, Albanians, Americans, English, Serbians, Austrians, Swedes, Bulgarians and Danes.

After the conquest of Algeria the French Foreign Legion consisted for a time of two regiments, the first stationed at Sidi-bel-Abbès and the second at Saida. At present there are four regiments, the depot of the first being still at Sidi-bel-Abbès; that of the second at Meknez; that of the third at Fez; and that of the fourth at Marakeesh, the last three towns being in Morocco.

In all, there are probably somewhere about 20,000 men in the Legion, and the majority of them are scattered about the country in camps and outposts; working on road, bridge, and building construction; on punitive expeditions against unsubdued or insurrectionary tribes; and in the "peaceful" penetration and occupation of the Riff country and elsewhere.

Who joins the Foreign Legion to-day?

Is it a romantic army of adventurers, or is it, as is sometimes said, a collection of the criminal scum of Europe?

What are the conditions of life in the Legion at the present time?

A very large proportion indeed of the French Foreign Legion of to-day are men who served in the Great War, and who, in November, 1918, were unable to find employment in their own countries. Their need was France's opportunity, and France was fortunate to be able to obtain the services of thousands and thousands of the best troops of Europe, allied and enemy; soldiers made, to her hand, trained and taught and experienced—metal forged on the anvil of War itself.

To-day such men are still joining the Legion. But a great proportion of the 1931 recruits are, and will be, out-of-work unskilled laborers who join for food, a roof, a bed, and clothing.

Out of every hundred recruits seventy-five or so will be men of this type, men accustomed to manual labor, willing and able to live a rough, hard life of toil, privation, monotony, and occasional danger.

Among the other twenty-five will be a few "gentlemen," ex-officers, professional men who have come to grief, and youths in search of adventure and romance, eager for change, travel, foreign countries, and active service.

Of these, one is inclined to say "Heaven help them," for they may find nothing more than five years of manual labor with pick and shovel in wholly uncongenial company.

Among the few that remain to make up the hundred will be perhaps a few who are wanted by the police of their own country, and possibly a very small sediment of professional criminals— but probably the genuine criminal element is no larger in the French Foreign Legion than in any other army.

The French Foreign Legion must not be confused with the Bat d'Af (the Bataillon d'Infanterie Légère d'Afrique) which consists entirely of criminals—men who have been sentenced to penal servitude before they have done their ordinary military service as conscripts in the French citizen army.

It is a mistake to suppose that once a man gets into the French Foreign Legion he is absolutely safe, whatever crime he has committed. A known murderer, for example, will be handed over to his country's police if his extradition be demanded.

On the other hand, there is undoubtedly a very small proportion of what may be called refugees, men who have fled from their family and their social circle for some reason best known to themselves, and men who, though they have not committed a very serious crime (bad enough for their extradition), would be arrested by the police of their own country if they remained in it.

Undeniably there is a very large class of men in the Legion who maintain strict secrecy as to their reason for coming there, but that does not necessarily mean that they are criminals, or that they have committed any act of which they need be ashamed.

When a man joins the Legion, no question is asked as to his reason for doing so, and no inquiries are made with regard to his past life. It is, however, the humor of a certain type of N.C.O. and old soldier to presume, or pretend to presume, that every recruit comes to the Legion to escape an even worse fate in his own country.

A certain number of Frenchmen in the Legion (and there are not many Frenchmen there) have been given a light sentence of imprisonment in their own country with the option of serving for five years in the Foreign Legion instead. Some prefer the prison sentence.

A rather bad type of Frenchman to be found in the Legion is the one who has joined as a Belgian, in order to avoid having to produce his papers, and to account for French being his mother tongue.

Attached to the military infirmary at Sidi-bel-Abbès is an Army Medical Corps N.C.O., who is something more than he appears to be. In point of fact, he is a detective from the Paris Sûreté (the Scotland Yard of France). Should any "wanted" French criminal come and endeavor to "lose himself" in the Legion, this official would notify the police authorities at once.

If he were not immediately "wanted" in connection with some recent unsolved crime, he would probably be allowed to serve his country for five years and be arrested on the day he took his discharge.

Thus, though a French first offender who is unknown to the police may lose himself in the Foreign Legion, it would be extremely difficult for a previously convicted criminal to do so.

Conditions of life in the French Foreign Legion are undeniably hard—very hard indeed. As I have said, it is only the man accustomed to hard outdoor manual labor, or inured to the hardship of active service campaigning, who is suited to them. This applies to mental and spiritual as well as physical conditions.

A public school and university man, for example, who was a powerful athlete, would be physically equal to marching, stone-carrying, road-making, and other hard-labor fatigues, but he might not be mentally and spiritually equal to the terrible monotony, the utter absence of all intelligent and intellectual companionship and conversation; the lack of that mental and moral environment to which he has been accustomed; and the want of a great many of those things that mark the difference between *homo sapiens* and the animal.

Nor is there any hope of a career for a man of whatever degree of education, courage, ability, and physical strength. His highest hopes and possibilities are bounded by non-commissioned ranks. It is extremely difficult and rare for a foreigner to rise from the ranks to a commission in the French Army.

The very rare exceptions are men of distinguished birth and military rank in their own armies (such as Prince Aage of Denmark, who was a captain in the French Foreign Legion).

So a man who, acting under no stress of fear and desire for escape, deliberately enlists in the French Foreign Legion, has got to reckon with the fact that he is in a blind alley, and that at the end of five years—if he survives—he has got to face life afresh or else re-enlist and postpone the evil day for another five years. It is, of course, extremely likely that he will not survive, for the wastage in the French Foreign Legion, even in peace-time, is enormous.

During this time he will find that—unless he is one of those born romantics who can make their own romance and see it wherever they go—life is apt to be terrible in its dullness, monotony, unvaried, unrelieved work and hard living.

If he be a naturally keen soldier, and lucky enough to be on active service, he will accept hardship and danger as all in the day's work. But if, as is quite probable, he spends his life in the terrible monotony of garrison duty and drill, varied only by the heaviest, unskilled manual labor as a navvy, he will at times, if not all the time, wish he were dead.

So to any who ask the question: "Shall I join the French Foreign Legion?" I would answer:

Yes, if you are willing to work for five years for a penny a day, under what is perhaps the most rigid military discipline in the world; if you are willing to receive what you will consider injustice at the hands of foreigners whose language you do not understand, and who neither understand yours, nor wish to do so; if you wish to risk spending five of the best years of your life in a little desert outpost where there is sufficient of nothing but heat and sand; if you wish to have to associate by night and by day with a very mixed collection of foreigners, some of them men of the very lowest type, without hearing your own language from year's end to year's end.

At the same time, to be perfectly just, one has to admit that Englishmen and Americans who have served in the French Foreign Legion have spoken well of the years they spent in its ranks and as N.C.O.'s. Some of these, moreover, have been officers in the British and American armies before enlisting in the Legion. It is also true that a good many men re-enlist for a second, and even a third period of five years, though some of these were probably driven back to the Legion by hunger and the impossibility of finding work.

The military-minded young Englishman or American who contemplates joining the French Foreign Legion with the object of getting to romantic Algeria and Morocco, of seeing the world and satisfying his craving for change, excitement, and broader horizons, should remember that the British and American armies serve in equally romantic and wonderful countries.

He will see quite as much of life in his own army as he will in the French; he will receive far better pay and treatment, have far greater opportunity of advancement; and, when fighting comes, will have the satisfaction of knowing that he is fighting and suffering for his own country.

TWENTY-FOUR HOURS IN THE FOREIGN LEGION

This is the second of the two non-fiction articles included in this volume of The Collected Short Stories. *In this article Wren describes several of his comrades from his escouade and an exciting twenty-four hours experience. Of note is the mention of a Spaniard, Ramon Diego, who may have served as the inspiration for the character of Spanish Maine. "Twenty-Four Hours in the Foreign Legion" originated as a broadcast from the BBC radio in the summer of 1932 in a series titled "The Hazard Series." After a print version, under the title "Hazard X. Twenty-four Hours in the Foreign Legion by Major P. C. Wren", appeared in the BBC magazine,* The Listener *(July 27, 1932), the BBC series was published by John Lane—The Bodley Head in book form in* Tales of Hazard, Being the Personal Narratives of Ten Men Who Have Hazarded Their Lives in the Carrying Out of Some Important Work or in Some Notable Adventure *(1932). The version included in* Tales of Hazard *(and here) is slightly longer than the version that appeared in* The Listener. *The article was also reprinted in* Fifty True Stories, Stranger Than Fiction *(Odhams Press, 1936) and in the American magazine,* Living Age *(October 1932) under the title "With the Foreign Legion."*

In recent years a good many books have been published concerning that amazing military organization, the French Foreign Legion.

As a result, or perhaps a cause of this, a good deal of public interest has been aroused in the Legion, the more so, doubtless, by reason of the titles of these books, the majority of which call the Legion, "*Hell*," and allude to its members as damned.

Probably the hand of the journalist rather than that of the genuine ex-légionnaire is responsible for the more lurid touches and purple patches. Anyhow, there has been a vast amount of nonsense, a great deal of rubbish, and much absolute untruth written on the subject.

It is noteworthy that three British officers who saw service in the Legion wrote books that were far from being sweeping condemnations of the famous Regiment. On the other hand, an officer who served with distinction throughout the Great War in a Royal Fusilier Regiment, and then throughout the Riff Campaign in the French Foreign Legion, concluded an account of his experiences with the words:

"Home at last after five years of Hell. . . ."

*   *   *   *   *

But I am not concerned with the general subject of Life in the French Foreign Legion so much as with one particular Hazard.

I went to the *Bureau de Recrutement* in the Rue St. Dominique for enlistment in the Legion, and, to be quite fair and honest, I fully admit that the recruiting officer there made no secret of the fact that he thought I was a fool. I thought it was very decent of him. He didn't actually try to deter me from joining; but he mentioned casually that the Foreign Legion was, rather the Spiritual Home of the labourer, the long-service professional soldier, and the man who had really roughed it in earnest. He added that he would be very glad to enlist me, in view of my inches and enthusiasm, but I must go away and sleep on it, think it over in the light of what he had said, and return next day if I were still of the same foolish mind.

I returned. I was vetted *bon pour le service* by the Medical Corps doctor, and enlisted. I had contracted to serve France for five years in any part of her colonial possessions for the sum of a halfpenny a day, without deductions or income tax.

Purely in the spirit of romance and make-believe—for I was not fleeing from Justice—I took a name that was not my own. Most légionnaires do this. A few, because they are fugitive criminals and the vast majority for the same reason that small boys wear black masks or feather head-dresses when playing robbers or Red Indians.

*   *   *   *   *

I travelled that night to Fort St. Jean at Marseilles, the bureau depôt and clearing-house of the XIX Army Corps, which is the Army of Africa. Here, it is true, I found dirt, discomfort, fatigues, nasty menial, manual labour, and somewhat rough contemptuous treatment; but what did these things matter? My barracks was a moated, mediæval castle, within sight, of Monte Cristo's Chateau d'If, and my companions were wearing the most romantic and attractive uniforms in the world!

Every branch and service of the French Army was represented, and if the noise were reminiscent of a parrot house, so were the colourfulness and the exotic sights and sounds. There were Spahis, in incredibly gorgeous dress, Zouaves, Turcos, Tirailleurs, Chasseurs d'Afrique, Colonial Infantry, Gunners, Sappers and Légionnaires: and undoubtedly the parrots could swear—as well as eat, drink and flutter gay plumage.

I was thrilled, and couldn't see or hear enough of these men who brought a breath of so strange and different a life from across the sea—men who had marched and served and fought in such strange places—men from Africa! And I thought of a Latin tag from schoolboy days: "There's always something new from Africa."

I made no friends among the recruits on our way to join the Legion. Frankly, I didn't like the look of them. Nor did I gather that they particularly liked the look of me. They were mostly unshaven, unwashed, collarless men, rather rough, rather dirty, and with ways that differed widely from those to which I had been accustomed. They were entirely foreign to me in speech and habits, and some of them reminded me of the sea-captain's terse official report on the manners and customs of the Cannibal Islanders: "Manners none and customs nasty!"

After a few days at Fort St. Jean we were shipped across to Oran in Algeria, and taken thence by train eighty miles inland, to Sidi bel Abbès, the depôt of the 1st Battalion.

Here things were different. We had our uniforms now, and uniform was a great leveller. We were all soon shaved and clean and shining bright. Everyone understood French, which was the *lingua franca*, and one quickly found one's own level, and companions of one's own sort and kind. That is one of the marvels of the Legion. Every nation is represented: and not only every class, but every sort and kind, every rank and trade and profession. I was most enthusiastic, and derived endless interest from observing my comrades—the most incredibly mixed assemblage of men on the face of the earth. They included not only people of all the nations of Europe, but even Chinese, Japanese, Arabs and assorted Africans.

I was glad when I completed a selection of representatives of all five continents by meeting an Australian and more than one American.

*   *   *   *   *

I have to tell you about one particular day of glorious life in the Legion, and will first describe some of the men of my own *escouade*, my comrades of the day in question.

First of all, there was Pierre. You would have liked Pierre—one of the merriest souls I ever met. Nothing could damp his joyous cheerfulness, except wine, and that in sufficient quantity to quench him altogether. Pierre only ceased to be amusing when he could speak no more. Only at one stage of his long and happy journeys from sobriety to speechlessness was he ever a bore, and that was the moment—the inevitable moment—when he would tell you all about his murder. I am afraid the story must have been true, for he always told it in the same way and never varied a detail. And nothing could stop him.

"And to think how kind I always was to her," he would expostulate. "I hardly ever beat her when she didn't deserve it. She always had plenty to eat—when there was plenty; and she frequently tasted wine—when I was asleep. . . . Why, I actually married the woman. And what did she do when my back was turned—and my stomach was being badly turned—while I was doing six months in The Box for borrowing money from a bourgeois, without telling him, one night, in the Place Pigalle? She went off with Tou-Tou-Boil-the-Cat, the lieutenant of our band. Fact. She did. She won't again, though. I went after her when I came out.

"'Your heart's in the right place, my love,' I said. 'It's your head that leads you astray.' Then I cut it off. *Qui, Monsieur.* I, Pierre Pompom, held her up by her hair with my right hand—so—and cut her head off. . . . . *Psstt!* Yes. With this very knife."

And at this point Pierre would produce a knife from the back of his belt.

Yes, I believe Pierre was a murderer. But he was a very nice one to meet, and only made these *faux pas*—or talked about them—when not quite himself. I never met a braver man in my life. He was true as steel, a splendid comrade, and faithful unto death.

In curious contrast to him was Müller, a German—an aristocrat, an ex-officer and a typical Junker. He was as self-controlled and unemotional as Pierre was vivacious and flamboyant.

"Hans Müller," he called himself (though he was certainly *von* and *zu* and probably *Graf* or *Baron*, and possibly Hohenzollern or Hohenlohe). He was a man who simply hated to laugh with joy, or swear with rage, or to express any emotion whatsoever. His exceedingly handsome face, with its cold blue eyes, high-bridged nose, golden moustache, hard mouth and fine chin, was a face that never changed—never smiled or frowned. And this wasn't by any means because he was stupid, stolid or phlegmatic: not a bit of it. He was an extremely, clever man—musical, widely read, highly cultured, travelled, and, in the best sense of the word, a gentleman. I knew nothing of his life, but only of his death. Why he joined the Legion I don't know. But there was certainly a woman in his story. For in a quiet voice and with an expressionless face, he would speak most bitterly of women. And it was his intention to remain in the Foreign Legion until he died.

There was Ramon Diego, a very tough Spaniard from the Pyrénées, smuggler or smuggler's muleteer, known as "The Devil." And he was a devil—to fight, though unfortunately he would only fight with a knife. As he explained, it was the weapon he had been taught to use in childhood, and since then he had used no other. He was a big, dark, saturnine, smouldering sort of volcano, always about to erupt. Much, respected by those who didn't care for knife fighting.

I was very fond of Ramon, a simple forthright soul.

Then there was "Ivan the Terrible"—six foot seven: I am not sure it wasn't six foot eight—weight unknown, as he always broke the machine. He had been a subaltern of the famous Preobrazhenski Regiment of the Imperial Guard (alas! no more, I fear), and made no secret of how he came to the Legion. He went on leave, and followed a lady, of whose appearance he approved, the length of the Siberian Railway from Port Arthur to St. Petersburg, thence to Paris, on to Marseilles and across to Algiers.

There the dream had ended, probably with Ivan's money. And finding the French Legion nearer than his Russian Regiment, and probably much more likely to extend a welcome, Ivan had turned in with them, instead of going back. He was a great lad with a heart of gold, a tongue of silver, a hand of iron, and a front of brass.

Torvaldsen the Dane was another fine fellow: so clean-looking and clean-living. A seeker of adventure.

Cortlandt, the Dutchman, unlike nearly all Dutchmen, was a bad lot, though he had had a lot to make him bad. And once he was up against a sergeant, his stubborn Dutch spirit kept him there. He used, to drink a vile rice-spirit called *tchum-tchum*, which was, I suppose, the nearest thing he could get to *Schnapps*, and when he had had a drink or two of this poison, he would seek me out and remind me that the Dutch once sailed up the Medway. I invariably replied: "Never mind, Fatty. Nobody noticed them." And he would go away and think this over, with the help of more *tchum-tchum*, until he fell asleep.

What makes the particular day I am going to tell you about an outstanding one for me, is the fact that on it I lost these friends of mine, and though I hadn't known them long I missed them badly; also because I got an interesting, little souvenir scar on my head and an interesting little souvenir dagger which now decorates my study wall, having failed to decorate my stomach.

We were on the march, and in a hurry. We slept where we dined, and we dined where we fell down, after marching the whole of a terrible day, over sand. Although I had done some gruelling marches during training days and after, I thought of the warning of the recruiting officer in Paris. There *was*, as he had ironically said, "lots of sand; blue sky; no rain; no snow; no fog; sunshine—sunshine all the time." Camels (glimpsed far off—with scouts on them), mirages, palms and oases (in the mirages). I thought not only of the recruiting officer, but of Coleridge's *Ancient Mariner* and his bitter complaint. You may know the verse beginning:

> *"And all in a hot and copper sky*
> *The bloody sun at noon*
> *Stood right above . . ."*

the whole beastly show. And at 4 a.m. next morning the buglers blew reveille, and this particular, slightly hazardous day in the Legion began.

I rolled over and dressed—by putting on my *képi.* I then slipped on my equipment, and was ready. I was particularly ready for my share of the contents of the pail brought from the company cooking-fire by Ivan the Terrible. It was hot, liquid, sweet, and had an unmistakable flavour of coffee. I dipped out a mugful of this heartening brew, and produced the remainder of my breakfast from my haversack. If I remember rightly, it was a hard, dry biscuit and some soft, wet macaroni.

We fell in by sections, each section in three ranks, so that when we got the order to right-turn and march, we marched in threes, and not in columns of fours as the British Army does. One long march is very like another, but this was more so than most, by reason of the record length, the record heat, the soft looseness of sand, and the fact that we were marching, by compass, across sand-dunes, and were perpetually climbing up one side and down the other, instead of marching on the flat.

We were literally crossing an uncharted ocean—of sand; and its billows were as regular, numerous and monotonous as those of any of the great ocean wastes of waters. However, we realized that it was necessary to avoid the usual road or caravan route, for we were hastening to the relief of a suddenly beleaguered fort; and the Arabs would no doubt be on the watch for us on the road. We were a surprise-packet, posted to arrive when and where least expected.

Nor did we march as the British soldier does under a tropical sun, in pith helmets, half-sleeved open-necked shirts, shorts and puttees. We wore cloth Caps with a peak in front and a white or khaki curtain hanging round the neck behind; thick, long, heavy overcoats buttoned right up to the throat; baggy trousers tucked into leggings; thick heavy boots and no socks. We were pretty well loaded, too, with long rifles, long bayonets in steel sheaths, very big water-bottles, two hundred rounds of ammunition, stuffed *musettes* or knapsacks, containing spare kit, laden haversacks, canteens, and spare pairs of boots. But besides these things each man had some such extra load as part of a tent, firewood, or a cooking vessel; so that the top of the load on one's back rose as high, as the top of one's head—or higher, and bumped against it. It took me a long time to get used to this.

No. We weren't a bit smart to look at, and there was no march-discipline. We didn't march. We shuffled, shambled, staggered, tottered, strolled, rolled, bowled and pitched along anyhow. The one thing we didn't do was to straggle. The pace was set and the pace kept, and the slogan was "*Marchez ou crevez!*" ("March or die"), for if you didn't march you would most certainly die—of thirst and starvation if you were lucky, or of Arabs if you weren't.

At the end of each hour the whistle blew and the little column halted for "the cigarette-space," just time to smoke a cigarette. In theory it was ten minutes in each hour.

During one longer halt, the cooks prepared a meal of a sort of stew.

In time the strain began to tell, and it was just about when people were beginning to grumble that I realized that the recruiting officer had been premature in his sarcastic praises of desert life as regards the absence of fog. For, to the appalling heat and electrical atmospheric conditions, fog was added. A beastly oppressive choking fog—of dust, that diminished the circle of our horizon and rendered the almost unbearable conditions of marching even more unbearable.

"Sand storm," said the less experienced soldiers, but the old, long-service men growled that a sand storm wasn't a sand storm while you could see and breathe and march and weren't buried alive—or dead. This was nothing but a little dust!

It was truly awful anyway, and I plodded along, bent nearly double, not caring what particular name they gave it.

There was one thing to be thankful for, however. We were off the soft, shifting sand-dunes, and now marching across a level plain of hard, sand-covered ground. Between us and the sky was a veil of dust through which the sun did not so much shine as loom like a great ball of brass in the hot and coppery sky. And from time to time, great blinding clouds of sand enveloped us.

*   *   *   *   *

I suppose it was owing to these conditions that the Arabs caught us as they did.

We had out a "point" and flankers, of course, but presumably the flankers were ridden down when plodding along, bent double, seeing nothing but the ground, and not caring if it snowed Arabs.

They seemed to come down the wind like the dust itself. There were a few shots, a whistle, one or two orders, and thanks to Legion drill and Legion discipline, the Arab charge was met in the right way, and just in time.

My own *escouade* was unlucky in happening to be opposite to the thickest part of the Arab line, and, in spite of the number of men and horses that our fire brought down, the remainder charged home with lance and sword, and long gun fired at short range from the hip—with a weird and wild war-cry of "*Lah illa il Allah! Allahu Akbar!*" It sounded rather like a pack of jackals.

Just behind me the excellent Sergeant Krantz, a cool veteran, shouted his orders.

"Steady, now, steady! Aim low. Shoot at the horses! Aim low!" until suddenly, for the best of reasons, he stopped.

I don't really remember very much of this particular scrap. But I do remember the incredulity and the thrill at finding that I was actually taking part in a real good old-fashioned fight; just the sort of thing one had read about.

"This is what I came for," I said to myself. "The genuine thing! What splendid luck! A real fight with real Arabs in a real desert! It doesn't seem real."

But it was, and we got what is known to the vulgar as a "bellyful." Since the first shots and shouts it was only a matter of seconds, I suppose, when, with an earth-shaking thunder of hoofs, the leaders of the charge were upon us.

Suddenly I realized that a big bearded man in flowing, fluttering, dirty-white garments, with a nasty long lance was coming straight at me—me personally. I fired at him point-blank, and apparently missed him. Also his spear missed me, due

212

to the fact that Pierre shot either him or his horse

Quite unwounded, I was knocked head over heels, either by this horse or another, and got to my feet as an Arab, who had reined up, or whose horse had been wounded, made a cut at me with a sword. More by luck than judgment I parried the cut, the sword striking the curved cross-hilt of my bayonet. As I drew my rifle back to lunge, the Arab whirled up his sword and cut again; and either my bayonet went in under his ribs below his raised sword-arm just before the blow fell, or else Ivan shot him from behind, just in time. Anyhow, the sword-cut which should have split my skull, only gave me a cut on the head.

As I staggered back, a bit dazed, a man on the ground grabbed my leg, tripped me up, and slashed at me with a dagger. He meant well—but was presumably a bit shaken by the fall that had sent his lance, rifle or gun flying from his hand—and only struck my cartridge pouch.

After an intimate minute with him I got the dagger.

Once more I rose to my feet and saw that the Arabs were in full flight—not in defeat, but according to their tip-and-run plan.

"Salvo" or rather "Volley fire" continued while they were in sight. It was not until the "Cease fire!" sounded that I realized what this little fight had cost me personally.

Pierre, was dead. The front of his coat was sodden with blood. Hans Müller was dead, with a hideous spear-wound in his throat. Ivan, was dead, and, ironically in the case of so tigerishly brave a man, had his wound in his back. Torvaldsen was dead; demonstrating in death what we had known of him in life—that he had a brain. Cortlandt, though not dead, was unconscious and dying, kicked on the head by a horse. Ramon was all right, and showed me the body of an Arab whom he had killed. The bayonet in Ramon's empty rifle had been bent double, and whipping out his knife, Ramon had done the Arab's business.

Kneeling beside this man, Ramon patted his face in a friendly manner.

"*A carne de lobo, diente de perra,*" he grinned, as he felt the point of his knife. "For the flesh of a wolf, the tooth of a dog."

There was undoubtedly a good deal of the Arab in Ramon, for the Moors owned his part of Spain for five hundred years.

*   *   *   *   *

I think that, for a little while at least, this violent interlude in our monotony of misery did us good.

And after a brief rest, and the somewhat sketchy burial of our dead, we marched on again, talking of our miraculous escapes and wonderful deeds, until the heat and choking dust defeated us.

*   *   *   *   *

At sunset the scorching wind dropped and the fog of dust slowly turned to a mere mist. When we could go no further we camped for the night, or rather for a small, part of it, on a sandy plateau, scratching out a hasty square of trenches in the sand, posting sentries, and then just falling down and sleeping where we fell; many too weary even to eat.

*   *   *   *   *

My own personal cup was not yet quite full, as I was chosen for guard, and had to do two hours sentry-go forthwith.

Long before dawn we marched again, and when we reached the Fort it was to learn that its attackers had raised the siege and departed, probably at receiving news of the approach of the main body of the relieving force.

It was probably a tribe belonging to the besieging force who, on their way home to bed, had encountered us.

So ended, very tamely, a nevertheless sufficiently strenuous twenty-four hours in the Legion—strenuous, but not, in the eyes of survivors of the Great War, particularly hazardous.

No. 187017

"No. 187017" was the first story in the collection, Flawed Blades *(1933). It was one of three stories in Part I, which was entitled "Tant de Soif", the narrator of the stories. "No. 187017" is the story of a French officer who used a certain rifle during the 1870 Franco-German war, and found the same rifle in the hands of the enemy during the 1891 Dahomey campaign. The story is probably based on an incident related in* Life in the Legion, *by Frederic Martyn.[4] "No. 187017" also appeared in the Murray (1947) and Macrae-Smith (1948) editions of* Stories of the Foreign Legion.

Except when, with solemn countenance and serious voice, old Tant de Soif was deliberately pulling the leg of a *bleu*, or ragging Père Poussin, he was, for an old soldier, a remarkably truthful man.

Undeniably, some of his stories were almost incredible, but then old Tant de Soif had undoubtedly had some almost incredible experiences in the course of his long and varied military service in Cochin China, Madagascar, the Sahara, Morocco and Dahomey.

The most astounding story of all, concerned the last-named country, for Tant de Soif had served in the horrible Dahomeyan campaign.

So strange and so interesting was the story, and such was Tant de Soif's warmth of asseveration as to its truth and his own personal friendship with Captain Battreau, that I was at pains to verify it.

Tant de Soif's amazing story is not fiction, but unadorned recorded fact which can be verified by reference to French newspaper files of 1891.

It is one of the most astounding examples of the aptness of the old saw, *Truth is stranger than fiction.*

Any writer of fiction who had the courage to use this incident

---

[4] Martyn, Frederic. *Life in the Legion.* London, G. Bell, 1911. p. 208-209

in a novel, would inevitably be laughed to scorn by the wise and learned men who reviewed his book.

The story begins in the year 1870, when the Hun was ravaging France, Paris was besieged, and its inhabitants thankful to be able to buy the flesh of cats, rats and mice at fabulous prices.

As in 1914, every Frenchman who could bear arms was fighting to save his beloved country and to drive the loathed invader from its sacred soil. Young boys and old men marched and fought beside those of military age. Among the first was a boy named Battreau, a burning patriot and a keen and ardent soldier, who quickly rose to the rank of Sergeant.

Battreau was the Happy Warrior

"that every man in arms should wish to be",

for his profession was his hobby, he loved his work, and this campaign was to him a Crusade and a Holy War. Unlike the majority of soldiers, especially those of a conscript army, he positively enjoyed drill, and regarded his Chassepôt rifle rather as a pet or a beloved comrade than as a heavy encumbrance and a beastly thing that he had to sweat over, and keep speckless.

If ever young Battreau got a punishment, which is improbable, it was certainly not for having a dirty gun. To him indeed was applicable the saying that "A soldier's best friend is his rifle."

Curiously enough, the number of Battreau's gun was 1870, and 17 his own age—187017, a number easily remembered and one that he never forgot. And Private Battreau did more than love and polish and treasure his beautiful new gun; he used it to some purpose, for he proved, even from his recruit days, to be an exceptionally fine shot.

According to those who knew him, Battreau, although a keen soldier, was anything but bloodthirsty, and it was not in a revengeful spirit of murderous triumph that he recorded on the butt of 187017 the number of Germans who, to his certain knowledge, he killed with it.

No doubt he shot many more than his tally showed, but whenever, in single combat or when sniping, he killed his man, he drove a tiny tack or shoe "brad" a little way into the butt of his rifle, and then pulled it out again.

What with its number, composed of the date of the year and his own age, and the neat row of tiny holes in the stock, it was not likely that Private Battreau, Corporal Battreau, Sergeant Battreau, would have any difficulty in identifying his rifle among a number of others, or in recovering it from any comrade who "scrounged", "found" or "won" it when its owner's back was turned.

And at St. Privat, during the terrible battle of Gravelotte, the gun received an honourable scar, a decoration that would have enabled its owner to identify it among a thousand others, even had he been blind.

For when the famous and magnificent Prussian Guard charged the French position and was repulsed with tremendous slaughter, Battreau, suddenly feeling a jarring shock and a blow that nearly knocked him down, found that a German bullet had passed clean through the stock of his rifle.

As neatly as though the work had been done by a cabinet-maker or a highly skilled carpenter, a smooth, clean hole had been drilled through the butt of 187017.

His beloved gun, that had killed so many of the enemies of his adored country, had saved his life, for the bullet, in passing through the thick wood, had lost so much of its velocity that when it struck Battreau's heavy leather pouch and belt, it failed to penetrate to his body, and merely knocked him backward, with no greater injury than a severe bruise.

Is it to be wondered at, that Battreau's affection for his rifle was increased immeasurably, and that he would scarcely have parted with it for its weight in gold?

Throughout the remainder of the Franco-Prussian War, Sergeant Battreau served and suffered, starved, frozen, ragged, often sick and weary unto death, but with 187017 still upon his shoulder, as he marched the long, long roads of France.

At the end of the campaign he was alive, unwounded, and determined to remain in the army as a professional soldier. One can imagine the pride he took in his curiously decorated rifle, and the number of times that he told the story of how it got the hole in its butt and saved its owner's life.

One can also imagine the regret with which Sergeant Battreau parted with this "best friend" when the French Army discarded the Chassepôt gun and was re-armed with the Gras rifle.

Poor Battreau made application to be permitted to keep 187017 as his personal property, but his request was refused. Red tape is red tape, and is nowhere ruddier that in the French Army.

How could the French Republic be expected to lose the few francs, or even sous, that an old discarded gun might yet be worth, and give it to the man who had carried it so long, fought with it so bravely, and killed so many of the Republic's enemies?

Could not Sergeant Battreau be permitted to buy it from Madame la République at its original cost, or more?

Certainly not, replied the Red-Tape-Worms of the War Office. Whoever heard of such a thing as Madame la République trafficking in old iron? The rifle must be returned to store at once, and with no more idiotic applications from presumptuous and half-witted sergeants.

* * * * *

But traffic in old iron Madame la République undoubtedly did, and sold the whole discarded consignment to a syndicate of those Christian patriots who supply the ignorant, barbarous and comparatively harmless savage with weapons of precision wherewith he may fight the fellow-countrymen of the said Christian patriots, or slay his brother with greater facility and despatch.

§2

The scene is changed—also the date.

It is now the year 1891, and a small French force, headed as usual by a detachment of the French Foreign Legion, is making its way from Porto Novo, in the Bight of Benin on the West Coast of Africa, up the left bank of the river Oueme, with the high hope, firm intention, and moderate chance, of reaching Abomey, the capital of Behanzin, King of Dahomey.

With this detachment of the French Foreign Legion was one

Captain Battreau, formerly a Sergeant of the Line and now a distinguished officer of the Legion.

Of all Captain Battreau's military experience, this campaign was the worst.

As frequently happens in war, *the* enemy was almost the least of the enemies to be fought: and whenever the Dahomeyans attacked the little expeditionary force on the march, or in the perimeter camps of their halting-places, they were regarded rather as an added nuisance than as the dangerous and murderous enemy that they were.

Far worse than these savages were the terrible heat; the vitiated, steam-laden air; the stifling gloom of the dense impenetrable jungle; virulent malignant fever; the agonizing labour of hacking their way through dense pathless jungle at the rate of three miles a day; and almost unbearable thirst.

The torture of thirst was not rendered easier to bear by the knowledge that the force was advancing parallel to the bank of a great river. Although this was only a few miles away, it was as inaccessible, owing to impenetrable jungle, as if it had been in another continent.

On many a day the force would struggle for hours to cross a mangrove swamp so water-logged and swollen that it was almost impassable, and yet as devoid of visible water as any desert. Here water was an enemy, and, turning the ground beneath their feet into slimy mud, but added to their sufferings.

Nor was the force allowed, as Captain Battreau humorously remarked, to fight in peace—to fight its way through the terrible swamps and jungle where the overhead foliage was so dense that the rays of the sun never penetrated it.

Without the faintest warning, and at any place or moment, thousands of silent shadows would suddenly materialize from the surrounding jungle, and swoop like hawks upon their prey, each shadow a tall savage armed with slashing *coupe-coupe* (or *machête*), sword and spear. Or the heavy boding silence of the jungle would be shattered by sudden volleys, and from both flanks a heavy fire would be poured in, at short range, upon the struggling men hacking their way in the thick bush or stifling elephant grass in which they worked blindfold, swallowed up like dogs in a cornfield.

At night, too, when the weary force sank to the ground, too exhausted to eat, there was little rest, for, in addition to constant heavy sniping, most determined attacks were made by innumerable hordes of spearmen, outnumbering the French by thousands.

As usual, whatever the sufferings of the other units, those of the Legion were greater; for they were in the van; they blazed the trail, they bore the brunt of the frontal attacks, and to them fell the lion's share of camp and water fatigues, and picket and outpost duty.

Always to the fore, leading, encouraging and heartening his splendid *légionnaires*, was Captain Battreau, admired, beloved and trusted by his Company, every man of whom knew him to be a better soldier than himself, a man whose word was "Come on" rather than "Go on", first in the fight and last to lie down in camp, as careless of his own life as he was careful of those of his men.

*　　*　　*　　*　　*

And one day happened the incredible thing, the impossible event, the fact far stranger than any fancy.

The Legion advance-guard, debouching suddenly from the terrible, gloomy jungle, entered an open glade or savannah, and simultaneously came under a tremendously heavy fire from a force completely concealed in the thick bush opposite.

"Come on, boys!" yelled Captain Battreau. "Into them with the bayonet!" and, drawing his revolver, he led the charge of his weary, thirsty, half-starved men, across the open.

The Dahomeyans stood fast, and in a few moments spear clashed on bayonet, and a fierce hand-to-hand struggle took place.

As Captain Battreau, leading, rushed at a tall Dahomeyan, who had just re-loaded his rifle, the savage threw it forward and fired at Battreau point-blank. As he did so, Battreau pulled the trigger of his revolver, and both men fell to the ground, the Dahomeyan with the revolver bullet through his heart, Battreau untouched.

As he himself afterwards said, he had not the faintest idea as to whether he flung himself down when he saw the muzzle of a rifle pointing straight at his face, or whether he tripped over a tussock of grass, or some such obstacle.

What he did know was that, as he arose, slightly stunned by the explosion, so close to his face, of the heavy rifle, he saw with no small surprise, that the rifle lying at his feet was a French Chassepôt, complete with bayonet.

Snatching it up as an excellent weapon for use in the hand-to-hand rough-and-tumble into which he was about to dash, his eye fell upon something the sight of which gave him pause, even in that moment of strenuous excitement.

There was a hole through the butt of the rifle!

Swiftly turning it over, Captain Battreau read the number. It was 187017. In the stock was a neat row of tiny holes.

In Captain Battreau's hand was his own rifle—the rifle with which he had fought throughout the Franco-Prussian War of 1870.

For a moment the noise of battle all about him was that of Gravelotte, and the fall from which he had just risen was that caused by the blow of a Prussian bullet that had passed through the stock of his rifle before striking him.

"I am fey . . . I am mad . . . I am dreaming," said Captain Battreau, and rushed into the fight, wielding once more, with deadly effect, the weapon that he had used more than twenty years before.

There was nothing dream-like, from the Dahomeyan point of view, about this terrible white man, and, before long, the savages broke and fled, leaving their dead upon the ground; and the survivors of the Company triumphed with the feeling of satisfaction that follows a hand-to-hand and man-to-man fight on equal terms, with no advantage from superior weapons.

For though disciplined troops armed with a rifle should, and almost always do, defeat a savage enemy, it is quite a different matter when bayonet meets spear, and the better man wins.

Captain Battreau sat himself down and stared at 187017, still unable to believe the evidence of his senses. But there was no room for doubt.

There could not possibly be in the whole world two Chassepôt rifles, each bearing that number, each marked with that record of slain Germans, and each with a bullet-hole drilled through the butt in exactly that spot.

*   *   *   *   *

Captain Battreau again made application for permission to keep the rifle, and this time, as it was no longer the property of Madame la République, this was graciously accorded, and 187017 returned to France in his possession.

This story, as Tant de Soif told it to me, is absolutely true.

BOMBS

"Bombs" is a story related by Tant de Soif to several characters from Wren's novels, Soldiers of Misfortune *(1929) and* Valiant Dust *(1932). It is the first story told about Odo Klemens, a real-life person from the 1920s and 1930s. The other "Odo Klemens" stories, "The Return of Odo Klemens", "The Betrayal of Odo Klemens", and "The Life of Odo Klemens" can be found in volume four of* The Collected Short Stories. *"Bombs" is the story of how Tant de Soif was able to solve the mystery of missing (stolen) bombs, which is another name for hand grenades. "Bombs" was the second story in Part I, "Tant de Soif", of* Flawed Blades *(1933), and was reprinted in* Stories of the Foreign Legion *(Murray 1947).*

Old Tant De Soif, Father of the Battalion, was inevitably a walking encyclopædia of Legion lore, and it was to him that one applied for historical and other information.

If not exactly *arbiter elegantiarum*, he was undeniably arbiter on disputes and questions concerning matters of fact and fiction relating to the Battalion and the Regiment.

"*Did* I know Odo Klemens? Why, it was through Odo that I came near to losing my own identity. I, Tant de Soif, almost came to be known merely as The Friend of Odo Klemens," he would say when questioned on the subject.

One had to believe Tant de Soif's oft-told biography of Odo Klemens because it rang true, and contained those little touches that no one would think of inventing.

Moreover, I discovered as an indisputable fact, that Tant de Soif was at one time a comrade, if not the *copain*, of Odo Klemens.

Nevertheless, I have not yet made up my mind as to whether he was embroidering the story and varnishing the tale when he told us the amazing yarn about Odo Klemens' dog.

§2

"That was another thing about Odo Klemens," quoth Tant de Soif, after reminiscing about some of his hero's doings when scouring Morocco and combing her cities in disguise, searching for secret-service information, and spying upon spies.

"Another of the many strange qualities that made him so different from ordinary men—the amazing power he had over animals—including women. . . . Talk about old Bombelli taming his lions! Klemens would have tamed them and the Strong Woman too. . . . Why, he could tame army mules; tame mad camels; tame wild goats, wild sheep, any wild bird. . . . I tell you he would make a vulture alight near him and eat out of his hand. . .."

"Could he tame Sergeants and make them eat out of his hand?" inquired Bombelli.

"He did better than that, Funny-Face. He became a Sergeant himself and had other people eating out of *his* hand. . . . He'd have broken a thing like you and thrown the bits to his dog. . . . You keep your head shut when I'm talking about a man whose buttons you aren't fit to polish. . . .

"Where was I when the hole in that thing's face fell open? . . . Yes. . . . I said he'd have fed his dog on bits of Bombelli— though I don't say the dog would have eaten them—though he was only a village pariah cur when Odo Klemens adopted him.

"Just that. We were going through a *ksar* with our bayonets, in style. . . . I dashed into a house and saw Klemens, who had just pinned a man to the wall. Such a funny sight. The Arab, who'd got a knife, couldn't reach Odo with it, and Odo couldn't withdraw his bayonet, and there they were, *planté là*. . . . Stuck. . . . Odo was laughing—as he held on to the butt of his rifle at arm's length (and the Arab looked just like a big dirty beetle on a pin)—because a pariah pup was biting away, like the devil, at Odo's gaiters and trying to hang on to his trousers.

"He could have kicked it half a mile, stove its ribs in, but he only laughed and encouraged it.

"When I finished off the Arab and we got Odo's bayonet out of the beam he'd driven it into—and it took the two of us to shift it—Odo grabbed the dog, held it still, and stared into its eyes.

"Then he flattened it, belly down, on the floor, and kept

drawing his finger down its head, between the ears, to the nose, and prolonging the line on the ground while he talked to it in Arabic, repeating the same two words over and over again. . . .

"All this only took a minute or so, yet when we bolted out of the house, the dog followed us as though Klemens had owned it for years.

"Wherever we went that day, the dog went too—and it must have seen some funny sights. . . . Me, I had something else than village curs to attend to, but when we made camp that night, there was the dog all right; and Odo told me it had stuck to him all day, and hadn't tried to help any more Arabs again. Quite the other way round.

"Well, that dog became like Odo's shadow, and he taught it all manner of amazing tricks—really astounding when you remember it wasn't a civilized poodle from a Paris flat, but practically a wild and savage animal.

"Odo called him Abd-el-Kader because he was a good fighter. Perhaps the most remarkable thing about it all was the fact that the dog would go and do something Odo told him to do, when he spoke in an ordinary conversational way, using quite a long sentence.

"It's one thing to shout '*Beg, Fido!*' or '*Jump, Fido!*' at a dog, and make some appropriate gesture which the dog understands and connects with the order and the trick that is expected of it.

"But it's quite another thing to say quietly,

"'Go into the barrack-room and bring me my *képi* off my bed'; or to pick up a stone, spit on it, show it to the dog, and say,

"'If I throw this stone, be good enough to leave it alone, will you?'—and to have correct obedience every time.

"You don't believe it, Bombelli? No? Of course you don't. You haven't the intelligence, nor the imagination. You think that everybody is a Bombelli, I suppose—and that what you can't do, nobody can do. Why, man, Odo Klemens could do much more than that—he could have taught *you* tricks. Made you quite useful. Useful to him, anyhow. . . .

"Well, as I was saying, when poor Bombelli's face leaked again, it was really wonderful. . . . Why, I've heard Odo say to that village pariah cur,

"'If I throw this stone over my right shoulder, you'll stand as you are. But if I throw it over my left shoulder, you'll lie down at once. If, however, I do neither, but just drop it, you will bark twice . . .' and the dog would do accordingly, and be right every time."

"What language did he talk?" asked Bombelli.

"The dog, do you mean, Fish-face? He generally barked in Arabic."

"No. . . . Odo Klemens, of course," replied Bombelli angrily.

"Oh, Klemens. . . . He began by talking Arabic, but when the dog was well trained, he would speak German to it. Sometimes French, for the public benefit, when he was showing-off, so that everyone would know what he had told the dog to do.

"He got very fond of the beast—we all did, in point of fact— and I think he would have killed anyone who mistook it for a tender spring-chicken when we were on short rations. Any stranger passing through, I mean, for anyone of our Section would as soon have thought of eating a comrade as of eating Abd-el-Kader. Cannibalism, eh, Poussin?"

"Certainly—if *you* ate a dog," replied Père Poussin.

"I don't know what we should have done without that dog— especially when things were very difficult and there was a lot of *cafard* about. We had a bad time in that *poste*, just about then, because on top of the usual troubles of life in the Legion, we were haunted by an extraordinarily clever thief, or else by a *djinn*—an evil spirit, as invisible as it was malevolent.

"When I say a thief, I mean one from outside, of course, an Arab; and the fact that someone was stealing things was connected with another undeniable fact—that someone, or something, not in uniform, was seen flitting or slinking or dodging about.

"Seen by more than one person, more than once.

"About half of us had had some queer experience or other, with this visitant; and those who hadn't had one, invented one— so that there was plenty of mystery and unrest in that damned *poste*.

"Then, one evening, my turn came for a bit of a surprise and a little shock. . . .

"No, I didn't see anything—that was the uncanny part of it. I wished I had seen something.

"I was on sentry, and as we were liable to be attacked at any hour of the day or night, each sentry was given a couple of bombs—and instructions to use them, pretty dam' quick, if he saw, or heard, occasion to do so. . . .

"As you know, Arabs like bombs even less than they do bayonets. They dislike Rosalie for her own sweet sake; but for Arabs, bombs have a nasty effect both here and Hereafter, since a good Mussulman can't go to Heaven if he is blown to pieces on earth. . . . How could Mahommet recognize him for a True Believer if he arrived at the gates of Paradise in a thousand bits? It might be some damned dog of an Infidel, trying it on. . . .

"Well, there I was, doing sentry, with my two bombs at my feet, nice and handy; and, for the sake of my own hide, I was keeping a sharp look-out, I can tell you.

"By-and-by, I turned and glanced round the *poste*, for a change, and, as I moved, I half-unconsciously glanced down to see that I did not kick or tread on my bombs.

"Well—there wasn't much fear of my doing that—for they weren't there . . . !

"Those two little flat iron 'pine-apples' simply weren't there. . . .

"They had vanished—and they had been there less than two minutes earlier.

"And, another thing, not a living soul had been anywhere near me for a good half-hour.

"What d'you make of that, Bombelli? Any funny remarks or clever theories? . . . No? . . . You surprise me; I should have thought you could explain it instantly. . . .

"I don't mind telling you, *mes amis*, that I was in a perishing blue funk, and for two reasons. I'd got to explain the disappearance of those bombs to Sergeant-Major Essad—a damned old Turk, if ever there was one; and I'd got to explain it to myself too.

"One doesn't like it when solid heavy things—such as bombs—vanish into thin air. . . . Bombs aren't feathers to be blown away by the wind, are they? No, bombs do their own blowing—and it's you who go away.

"Oh, I was frightened all right. . . .

"I was afraid of Sergeant-Major Essad; I was afraid of

whatever invisible Thing or Power had pinched the bombs; and I was also damned well afraid that they'd come flying back—over the wall or out of the blue or somewhere.

"I stood and sweated; stood and gaped like a . . . like a Bombelli . . . and wondered what the devil to do.

"I felt I ought to do something and do it quick—but I couldn't very well give the alarm, and then say it was because my two bombs had evaporated or lost themselves or something.

"I tell you I had *un mauvais quart d'heure* then, and a worse one when I was up before Sergeant Essad. He was a terror—that one.

"They called him 'The Red Devil'.

"Been an officer in Albania or somewhere, and had had to bolt for his life from Abdul the Damned.

"A huge chap he was, with red hair and a perfectly red face, not brown at all; blue eyes; and the biggest moustache I have ever seen. He had to turn sideways to get it through a gateway.

"He had a voice to match it, too, and could drill a battalion a mile away.

"But he never roared at individuals. Not even at defaulters. No, his voice was very soft and gentle and quiet for them. The sweeter and softer it was, the worse for the defaulter, and the bigger the trouble that was coming.

"And he never said what he'd do to you—he merely did it. No threats—but a punishment worse than the sentence. Yes, Essad Bey's bite was a lot worse than his bark; and his performance worse than his promise.

"Was his voice sweet and low when I was brought up before him?

"Like silk. Like the voice of a girl talking love.

"'Ah! They disappeared, did they, *Légionnaire* Soif,' he whispered, smiling.

"'Disappeared when you weren't looking, eh? Vanished— *pouf!*—just like that, eh? . . . When you weren't looking. . . . Exactly. . . . When your eyes were shut, in fact. . . . Not looking. . . . Precisely. . . . You have told the truth. . . . Not looking. . . . And sentries are not posted for the purpose of looking, one observes. . . . No, no! . . . They are not there to look. . . . They are there for ornament.'

"I respectfully swore that I had never relaxed my vigilance for a second; that I had borne myself in a smart and soldierly manner; and that no human being had approached within a hundred feet of me, from the moment when I was posted to the moment when I was relieved.

"Essad smiled pleasantly.

"'Any private theories of your own to explain this remarkable phenomenon?' he purred.

"Absolutely none.

"Sergeant-Major Essad had a theory though.

"'I believe your story, *mon brave*,' he murmured, 'and I have a theory. . . . You will find it proves to be correct, I am certain,' and his blazing cold eyes smiled into mine.

"'It is this. You had, perhaps—in fact, you had, without doubt—just a moment or two of, shall we say, absence of mind—for you have a mind, I verily believe. . . . And at the end of this brief period of absence (of mind) you—shall we say?—awoke. . . . That is to say awoke, not from sleep, but to the more immediate realities of existence. You have told me you did not sleep on your post, and of course that settles the matter. But you brought your bright intelligence back to earth and mundane matters again—and as you did so, you yawned and stretched and violently shook yourself. . . . One does, you know. . . . And as you violently shook yourself, a number of strong hearty healthy insects fell from your clothing and person to the ground—near the bombs. . . . These the insects immediately shouldered and bore away. . . . Doubtless they took them to your bed, where they will surely be found.

"'Sergeant, put *Légionnaire* Soif, who "wasn't looking", where he will have no occasion—or indeed opportunity—to look.

"'Let there be neither water nor food nor blanket to look at, and let the little place be so perfectly dark that he couldn't look at them if they were there. . . . For how long? . . . Oh—I don't know—you mustn't be too red-tape-bound, Sergeant. Say about as long as Jacob's Ladder put end-to-end with the Prophet's Beard . . . or until we want him again . . . whichever is the mercifully shorter period. . . .'"

Old Tant de Soif took a pull at the contents of my mug, bowed to me, and wiped his beard with his sleeve.

"That's how Sergeant-Major Essad, the 'Red Devil', talked," he continued.

"It was how he acted too; for I was in solitary confinement in the dark until The Red Devil wanted the cell for somebody else.

"And it didn't do me any good. Nor Sergeant-Major Essad either. . . . No. . . . For he died bravely, leading his men, with his face to the foe—and a Lebel bullet through the back of his neck. . . ."

"Who fired it?" asked Otho Bellême. "You?"

"Huh! Who fired it? Who knows? Some good friend of Sergeant Essad, anyway. Why?"

"Only that—if you did it—I was going to say that you are a filthy cowardly cur whose corpse a starving hyena would be ashamed to eat," replied Bellême.

"Sure thing," agreed Joe Mummery, and Sailor Harris nodded emphatic agreement.

"I didn't say that I did it," replied Tant de Soif, after an appraising stare at Bellême.

"No," said Bellême.

"Well—go on," I urged, in the rôle of peace-maker.

"So there I sat in the dark—and a heat like the ground-floor of Hell—wondering, day and night, what the devil had become of those two bombs, until I got bombs on the brain, and could see them floating about in the pitch darkness.

"And I got a bit of a shock one day or night,—for night and day were exactly the same in that Black Hole—when I came to myself, so to speak, and found I was crawling round and round the floor of the cell looking for—bombs.

"Meanwhile things were happening outside.

"Sentries kept getting glimpses of the thief, at nighttime— apparently an Arab in a white *burnous* or sheet or something— and no less than four men lost their bombs.

"I heard all about it when I came out from my little hell one evening, just before Retreat.

"This happened when Sergeant-Major Essad wanted the cell for someone else.

"I was brought up before him, yellow, filthy, bearded, half mad, and with my bones sticking through my scaly hide.

"'Look here, *Légionnaire* Soif,' he purred, 'I really can't let you have that room, Number Four, any longer. You have had your turn and must make way for others. I'm sorry, but you'll have to clear out at once. And you've no cause to grumble at being turned out, for you have had it all to yourself and had a nice rest too. Not to mention a special diet. . . . Quite a "cure", as the doctors call it. . . . At least, I hope it has been a cure—for your sake, *Légionnaire* Soif. . . .

"'Now go and cleanse, beautify, and perfume yourself, and report for guard in an hour. You'll be on sentry, with two bombs, and I don't really advise any of that "not looking" this time. . . . Good evening, Légionnaire Soif.'

"That was how The Red Devil talked.

"Well, I got cleaned up somehow, and reported for duty at guard-mounting, though I could scarcely stand, and kept turning giddy; and the light hurt my eyes so badly, after those days and nights of utter blackness, that I could hardly see.

"And there I was again, on sentry-go once more, and with two bombs at my feet. . . .

"Bombs! They fascinated me. I'd fairly got bombs on the brain, I tell you. I leant against the wall and stared at them till the tears ran down my cheeks. I wasn't going to take my eyes off those damned bombs for the whole two hours of my tour of duty. Not once.

"Or so I thought.

"But it wasn't very long before I discovered that such a thing can't be done. Especially by a man in a very weak condition. He falls down if he tries it.

"I soon found that my eyes wandered.

"And, suddenly, they had good cause to wander, for I heard a sound, and instantly glancing in the direction whence it came, I distinctly saw someone—or something—move.

"It might have been a man dressed up in a white sheet, or it might have been an Arab in a white *burnous*, or again it might have been a ghost.

"Anyhow, whoever it was, or whatever it was, I wasn't going to give it a chance to get my bombs.

"In the same second that I saw the Thing, I glanced down at the bombs to be sure they were there all right, and threw up my rifle.

"If this was what had got me a solitary confinement sentence, I was going to shoot it first, challenge it second, kick it third, and talk to it afterwards.

". . . It was moving across my front stealthily. The light—or rather the darkness—was very patchy, and the Thing progressed in a curious manner. Not exactly undulating like a snake, but rising and falling as it went along, so that at one moment it looked about six feet high, and the next moment about three feet low.

"Pausing for a moment so as to get it at its biggest, I fired. And it wasn't a case of,

"'*Halt! Who goes there? . . . No answer. . . . Bang!*', so much as a case of,

"'*Bang! . . . Halt! Who goes there? . . . . No answer.*'

"And over I rushed to where the Thing had fallen to get the answer.

"The answer was the Company cook, groaning and moaning and calling me a sacred assassin.

"Luckily for me, the silly fool, who was dressed up to look more or less like a ghost, was on his way back from his little raid on the store-room, and laden up with bottles of wine and other stuff that he'd stolen.

"It was thus easy enough for me to pose as the eagle-eyed ever-watchful hero who had laid the ghost, solved the mystery, and obviously caught the thief who, for some strange reason, had been stealing hand-grenades from the sentries.

"It had only taken me a few seconds to shoot Cookie (and he was the type of cook that deserves to be shot daily), to identify him, and get back to my post: and as I reached the spot where my bombs were—I saw that they weren't.

"No, *mes amis*. Those two good solid little iron pine-apples were not.

"They weren't there.

"They'd gone.

"I gazed at the spot whence they had gone.

"I tapped my forehead hard with my knuckles.

"'Good evening, Tant de Soif,' said I to myself.

"'Good evening,' said myself to me.

"'The bombs *were* there when you fired your rifle, Tant de

Soif, were they not?' asked I.

"'They were, my dear friend,' replied myself. 'I glanced down at them as I brought my rifle up from the "*Order*" to the "*Present*".'

"'And you shot the wine-stealing, bomb-throwing rascal in his tracks, didn't you?'

"'I did,' I replied.

"'So *he* couldn't have pinched them, could he?' I asked myself.

"'Of course he couldn't,' was the reply. 'Don't ask such silly questions.'

"'Then who did take them?' I asked.

"'How the devil do I know, you silly old fool?' I replied.

"And so brief a time had elapsed since I fired my rifle, that it was only at this moment that the guard turned out, the hue and cry was raised, and the hullaballoo began.

"Well, somehow the Sergeant of the Guard got the impression, from my prompt and intelligent answers to his foolish questions, that Cookie was the bomb-thief, and had stolen my two bombs and had been shot by me, in the execution of my duty, as he had attempted to get away with them.

"I don't know how it was, but he certainly seemed to get that impression.

"'Then where the devil are they now? What's he done with 'em, *salaud*?' roared the Sergeant.

"To which I could but shrug my shoulders and answer,

"'Where indeed? . . . What indeed, *mon Sergent*?'

"And really, you know, it wasn't my business, was it? I could do no more than shoot the treacherous scoundrel, the villainous robber, who came to steal my bombs, could I? Surely it was for him to explain what he'd done with them, not me.

"But unfortunately—or fortunately—Cookie couldn't explain.

"He was dead . . . and gone to his own place—apparently taking my bombs with him.

"At least, that was how I tried to explain it to The Red Devil when he had me up and put me through it.

"And at the end of our long and unpleasant interview, I don't know whether The Red Devil or I was the more puzzled man.

"From his point of view, and knowledge, there had been a

thief about, at night. Several sentries had seen someone dressed up in white, dodging about inside the *poste*: and ten bombs had been stolen, and every time from a sentry.

"It was quite impossible for the men to steal them, as there was daily kit-inspection, and no possible hole or corner in the *poste* that could be used as a place of concealment.

"And now a sentry had seen this strange, lurking, stealthy figure, white-clad, mysterious and suspicious-looking, and had, according to his own account, challenged it three times.

"Instead of replying, it had rushed at him, ducked beneath his fixed bayonet, snatched up his bombs and fled.

"Naturally thinking it to be an Arab rifle-thief turned bomb-thief, the sentry had again challenged the figure, called upon it to halt, and then, as it neither replied nor halted, had very properly shot it dead.

"But the supposed Arab raider had turned out to be the Company cook, and his loot, bottles of wine instead of bombs.

"But the sentry's bombs had been taken.

"Where were they?

"Yes, The Red Devil was a puzzled man.

"And in addition to the major problem of the bombs was the minor problem of the sentry.

"If he were an abominable liar—and of course he was an abominable liar, like all *légionnaires* (until they are promoted to be N.C.O.s)—what had he done with the bombs? He certainly hadn't got them, any more than the dead man had, and whether he were a liar or not, he had undoubtedly killed a man in defence of his bombs.

"Why should the sentry have shot the fellow, if he had not been behaving in the way that the sentry said he had?

"And undoubtedly, the dead man had been engaged in some villainy or other, or why was he got up in that fantastic fashion—dressed as a ghost?

"And, anyway, if he hadn't been stealing bombs, he'd been stealing stores.

"And once again, where were the stolen bombs?

"Yes, The Red Devil was puzzled.

"But he wasn't as puzzled as I, who knew that neither Cookie nor anybody else had been within twenty yards of those two bombs.

"The Red Devil sat at his table and stared me in the eyes until I began to feel that he could read every thought that was in my mind, and a good many that weren't.

"'I'll see you again later,' he whispered, at length, 'when I have made further inquiries, and if I find you've told me a word of untruth, you shall have some cause to share your mother's favourite wish.'

"He didn't say what that was, but I imagined the fellow intended to suggest that my mother wished I'd never been born.

"However, that very night something occurred to turn The Red Devil's attention elsewhere.

"Another sentry lost his bombs!

"That really put Sergeant-Major Essad on his mettle.

"He swore by Allah and a number of other remarkable phenomena that he would do the next bomb-loser to death in a curious manner.

"And that he would raze the *poste* to the ground, tear it to fragments piecemeal, and sift the scraps through a sieve, but that he'd find those bombs—if they were in the Fort.

"You can imagine the state we were all in by that time, and, had it not been for the fact that Essad stopped the issue of bombs pending the solution of the mystery, I don't know what would have happened. We should have all shot each other, I think, we were so jumpy and nervous.

"The day that The Red Devil cancelled the order for issuing bombs, I was sitting talking to Odo Klemens.

"'And thank *le bon Dieu* for that,' said I. 'If I'd gone on sentry one more time, with a couple of hand-grenades, I should have thrown them at myself.'

"Odo Klemens laughed.

"'Wonderful mystery, wasn't it?' he said,

"'A bit too wonderful for me,' I agreed. 'Thank God we shan't have any more of it.'

"'No, we shan't have any more of it,' grinned Odo, and laughed again.

"'Something seems to be amusing you,' I growled.

"'Something certainly is amusing me,' he laughed afresh.

"I didn't like Odo's laugh. It was always more or less

unpleasant, and when it did not give the impression that he was laughing at you, it quite distinctly gave the impression that he was laughing at something you were too stupid to understand.

"I quite distinctly remember feeling, on that occasion, that he was enjoying a joke that, though far too subtle for me, was fully shared by Abd-el-Kader.

"He patted the dog's head and pulled its ears as he spoke, and the dog rolled over on its back, its bent legs in the air, and laughed aloud.

"Odo Klemens laughed again.

"And the dog laughed again.

It rolled over on its side, helpless with laughter.

"I was quite annoyed at the way they shared the joke while excluding me, so I got up and went to the cookhouse.

". . . Did I mention that The Red Devil had appointed me Company cook—solely on the grounds that I'd shot the official incumbent? . . .

"However, as you know, *mes amis*, I am of a gentle and forgiving nature, and when Abd-el-Kader called round, a little later, I gave him a big bone that had already seen its best days— and a good many of them.

"With a word of thanks and a nod, the dog took the bone, and did not gnaw it.

"On the contrary, he marched away with it and a great air of purpose.

"'Well, damn it all,' said I. 'Is the dog going to sell it, or frame it, or what?'

"I followed him to see what he did do with it.

"He did nothing with it—except use it to keep me following him. So long as I followed, he did nothing; and as long as he did nothing, I followed.

"And I got tired first.

"'Well,' thought I, 'Abd-el-Kader is as clever as the devil, as artful as the devil's daughter, and as cunning as her mother. But surely I, Tant de Soif, a man, am as intelligent as Abd-el-Kader, the dog?'

"So when I saw old Père Poussin, I seized him by the arm, turned my back on Abd-el-Kader, and pointed up to the sky.

"'Look, *petit* Poussin,' said I.

"'What at?' asked he.

"'Nothing,' said I. . . . 'But listen. Follow Abd-el-Kader, your cousin, without appearing to follow him, and see what he does with that damned great bone that he's carrying about like a cornet-player. Go on, my clever Poussin. Follow him. . . . Watch him. . . . Secret Service. . . .'

"'Follow him yourself,' replied Père Poussin, who, as you all know, is a mannerless and foolish old man.

"'I've been doing so for some hours,' I replied. 'Now you take up the trail, and I'll give you my wine-ration to-morrow if you—deserve it.'

"By-and-bye, Poussin came and told me that, from a coign of vantage, he had looked down upon Abd-el-Kader, and watched his doings unseen.

"The dog had merely buried the bone.

"Nothing much in that! . . . Quite so.

"*But*, that evening, being on sentry, I noticed Abd-el-Kader leave the fort.

"'You'd better do your business quickly, my lad,' I admonished him as he passed, 'or take your latchkey with you.'

"And, as I spoke, I noticed that, whether Abd-el-Kader had got his latch-key with him or not, he'd certainly got the big bone.

"'Well, now,' thought I, 'where's he taking that? Does he think he'll get a better price for if in the Arab market?'

"It struck me as queer that Abd-el-Kader should bury the bone in the *poste* and then, just before the gates were shut, exhume it and take it outside. Very curious; for Abd-el-Kader always had a good reason for anything he did.

"So I watched him, thinking I'd see which way he went, and note whether he came back before Retreat. . . . The thought did cross my mind that he might be going to treat himself to a night out, and that the bone was intended to be in the nature of a—what shall we say? . . . A love-token; a bribe; a *pourboire* . . . ? But I put the thought away.

"'*Honi soit qui mal y pense*,' said I. 'What reason have I to doubt the moral character of Abd-el-Kader?'

"But, somewhat to my surprise, he didn't go very far, nor had he any assignation.

"He merely went to our only tree, some four hundred metres

away, and there, so far as I could see, he again buried the bone.

"Having done so, he deliberately made a detour, approached the *poste* from a different direction, and, just as the gates were being shut, came in with a rather smug look on his face, as of one who says,

"*Something attempted, something done, to earn a night's repose.*"

Tant de Soif stopped and eyed his audience.

Bellême passed him a mug, and Tant de Soif bowed and drank.

"Next afternoon," he resumed, "finding myself passing our only tree, I remembered Abd-el-Kader, and thought I'd play a little trick on that self-sufficient dog. Since he had refused to let me see what he did with that bone, I wouldn't let him see what *I* did with it. I'd remove his bone, and then watch him scratch his puzzled head when he came to look for it.

"I kicked away some sand, and delved a little with my hands, and, sure enough, discovered the bone.

"Also, some other bones.

"Likewise, some things that were not bones.

"Not bones at all. Nothing like bones.

"And what were they?

"The missing bombs!

"I nearly fainted. . . . And I nearly swore.

"I saw it all.

"Odo Klemens!

"Yes; my friend Odo Klemens. He had trained that infernal dog to steal and bury bones in the *poste*—secretly. Then, to dig them up and take them out of the *poste*—also secretly. When no one was looking.

"When Abd-el-Kader was word-perfect in his part, and as clever as Houdini, Cinqvalli—or *ce bon* Bombelli himself—Odo had led him on, from stealing bones to stealing bombs, and following the same procedure with them.

"Doubtless he deceived the dog, or at any rate interested him, by rubbing the bombs with mutton-fat.

"I don't know.

"But I do know that, in one blinding flash of revelation, I saw the whole thing.

"I saw those bombs disappearing, one after the other, from the very feet of the nervous, worried sentries who gazed anxiously and watchfully around, looking for the approach of a man, an Arab, a ghost, a devil, a *djinn*—while Odo Klemens' faithful doggie, Abd-el-Kader, sat at their feet or played around and helped beguile the tedium of their watch.

"'I see it all,' said I.

"'And I'll see some more,' I added.

"'*Mon Dieu*, yes. I'll bide my time and catch *ce bon Monsieur* Odo Klemens out. I'll watch, and I'll wait, and I'll see some more.'

"But I didn't see any more—for Odo Klemens and Abd-el-Kader deserted that night.

"And in the morning, full of importance, honest indignation, and vindicated righteousness, I obtained an interview with The Red Devil himself.

"I told him the whole story.

"I led him to the *cache* of bombs.

"There were no bombs.

"There was only me . . . and The Red Devil."

MASTIC—AND DRASTIC

"Mastic—and Drastic" is the final story in Part I, "Tant de Soif", of Flawed Blades *(1933). Captain Le Sage assigns Tant de Soif to discover what is driving legionnaires crazy (even killing one of them). Again, certain characters in this story are featured in the novels* Soldiers of Misfortune *(1929) and* Valiant Dust *(1932). "Mastic— and Drastic" was reprinted in* Stories of the Foreign Legion *(Murray 1947).*

Old Tant De Soif, incurable *laudator temporis acti*, was reminiscent on the subject of his admired and beloved Captain Le Sage, of whom our Lieutenant Desalles reminds him. Tant de Soif can pay no man a higher compliment than to permit him to remind Tant de Soif of this legendary officer, his *beau idéal* of a leader and a fighting man.

"Lieutenant Desalles will do," said he, as we lolled and lounged through *siesta*-time after our sumptuous lunch.

"He has the makings of a Legion officer of the old school and the right stamp. . . . But yes, he will grow up into something very like a man. . . . He may even become another Le Sage—of whom he already begins to remind me, young as he is.

"'What was Le Sage like?' . . . Oh, like a soldier. Like a man and a leader and an officer worthy to command *légionnaires*—by which I mean *légionnaires* also of the old school, of the type that has vanished, or is rapidly vanishing. . . . Men like myself, *par exemple*. He was quiet . . . almost gentle . . . and grim; low-voiced, easy; very clever; with the determination of a bull-dog. He had no courage because he had no fear and did not know what danger was.

"He neither wanted to live nor to die; to be wounded nor remain unwounded; to be promoted nor to be passed over; to be decorated nor to be left in obscurity.

"He cared for none of these things. No—but he cared for us. . . . And he cared for his job.

"What he did want, was to be the perfect soldier and officer, rendering absolute obedience—even unto Death—and exacting

240

it.

"He lived for his work—and we lived for him.

"'What was he like?' . . . Oh, tall, splendid physique, well set up, strong, lithe, and agile.

"'In face?' . . . Oh, rather narrow and long, with grey-green eyes; straight mouth beneath small clipped moustache; a twinkle of humour about both mouth and eyes—when they were not grim and hard with determination, pain or anger.

"For he was quick to anger as he was slow to forgive.

"Ah, I shall not look upon his like again, unless I live to see Lieutenant Desalles grow into such another . . .

"My Captain . . .

"Did I tell you about him and the enterprising citizen who proposed to turn an honest penny by poisoning, maddening and actually killing us, Le Sage's silly *légionnaires*, in his foul *bouge*?

"No? . . . Oh, that was good. Really good. And so typical of our quiet, clever and ruthless Captain Le Sage. . . . A neat little sample of his methods, and an epitome of his logical thought, character, actions and ways.

"Le Sage, you must know, considered no man as being drunk so long as he could perform his duty when on duty, and behave quietly and properly when not on duty.

"He did not punish for drunkenness, but he severely punished the wrong-doing due to drunkenness. I mean that drunkenness was absolutely no excuse whatsoever for any misconduct whatsoever.

"Also he tried to see that we got nothing but good wine— when we got anything at all. And he was as blind as any blind man to those things which a good officer knows that it is better for him not to see. . . . On a feast day, or some good occasion and opportunity for proper rejoicings. . . .

"But a real breach of discipline—Heaven help him who committed it.

"And when he marched us into Fort Bugeaud, away down in the South, there was not a finer Company, commanded by a finer officer, in the French Army—and that is to say in the whole world.

"There was nothing to do at Fort Bugeaud—except work . . . nothing to see but sand and sky . . . nothing to drink but some poor wine in the little shops of the bazaar—miserable huts and holes-in-the-wall mostly kept by Arabs . . . and nothing to eat but army rations.

"However, we being the men we were, and Le Sage being the commandant that he was, we didn't fare too badly. He found us plenty to do, and saw that we did it; and there was no harassing for the sake of harassing, no overdriving, no bullying, and very little punishment indeed. Fort Bugeaud was the model poste, for efficiency, smartness and discipline.

"And then, suddenly, trouble began—quite remarkable, inexplicable, and ugly trouble.

"It began by Maartens and Burgher, two very good Dutchmen, being brought back from the bazaar one night, drunk and very much more than drunk. . . .   Mad, in fact. . . . Absolutely raving mad, fighting mad . . . amok . . . dangerous. . . .

"Now Maartens and Burgher were two of those proper *légionnaires* who never get drunk in any circumstances, or under any temptation, inducement, or compulsion.   Those two had never been drunk once in all their years of service, for nothing could make them drunk.

"Nor—if any conceivable mixture and variety of good liquor could have been poured into them in such quantities as to intoxicate those two Dutchmen—would it ever have had the effect of making them fighting-drunk.

"For they were stolid, sensible men, who, being paid to fight, fought when they had to, for their pay and nothing else.

"When they had to fight, they fought like tigers, but they did not fight for amusement—any more than a navvy digs up a road for amusement, after he has done his day's work at digging up a road.

"And here were Maartens and Burgher dragged back from the village into the *poste*, like the most savage of wild beasts just captured in the jungle.

"Their uniforms were shameful—and shameless—rags; they were covered in blood and dirt; and they had made the picket that brought them in nearly as bad as themselves.

"And, safe inside, they were like a pair of panthers in a trap.

"Maartens sprang on Sergeant Meredal, knocked him out, and nearly killed him before we tore the raving maniac from the prostrate form of his superior officer. Not that we tore too hard, for we weren't very fond of Sergeant Meredal, whereas we had the greatest liking for Maartens, and admired him the more for putting up this wonderful drunk—Maartens who had always been as sober as a judge, when full as an egg and tight as a tick. . . .

"And while I was trying to get Maartens' hands from around Sergeant Meredal's neck just in time for that competent N.C.O. to recover (and no sooner), I saw Burgher shake off the three or four men who were holding him, and make a swift dash in the direction of Captain Le Sage, who was approaching to see what all the row was about.

"I stuck out a leg and luckily brought him down, for he had murder in his eye, and absolute madness in the hole where his mind should have been. Just sheer blind, maniacal lunacy, for both he and Maartens loved Le Sage as a father, and a fine one at that. . . .

"Well—it was a job of work to get those two madmen in cells, and then we had to go in to them again, for Le Sage said they were to be bound, hand and foot, for their own good, and gagged for his. He'd have had no sleep otherwise, and he never lost his proper sleep unless he were fighting overtime, or doing a forced march. He used to say that it was a soldier's duty to sleep, when it wasn't his duty not to sleep. . . .

"He gave orders for Maartens and Burgher to be brought up before him next morning. But it wasn't next morning for the Dutchmen. They were deaf, dumb, blind and silly; and we only knew that they were still alive because they still breathed.

"Not that one should really call the disgusting noise 'breathing' . . . worse than old Père Poussin sleeping on his back. . . . Snorting, snoring, what you will.

"Anyhow, they were making sounds indicative of life—and suggestive of early death.

"I never in all my days saw two such utter complete and perfect drunks—until a day or two later . . . and then I saw three of them.

"One of them was Père Poussin here, and as you know, Père Poussin is no drunkard. . . . He does his best, I admit, but there is no man alive—except myself and the survivors of the garrison of Fort Bugeaud, if there be any—who ever saw Père Poussin drunk. But he was as drunk as seven owls that night, all right. And the other two were Petrovitch and an ex-Prussian Grenadier named Krafft.

"Now Petrovitch was a former Sergeant of the Russian Guard—the famous Preobrazhenski Regiment, a man weaned on vodka, and who could drink vodka or any other neat spirit just as freely as the modern soldier can drink cold water after a dry march, and with as little effect on his brain, if he had any.

"And Krafft was a man of iron, a real Prussian, who could look a nine-gallon barrel of beer in the face at sunrise, and defeat it ere the sun went down upon his thirst that day.

"Now what, I ask you (and Captain Le Sage asked himself), could have happened to three such men as these, that they also should be brought in—not so much intoxicated as poisoned—not so much drunk as mad.

"For they had gone mad as dogs do when they get rabies and develop hydrophobia.

"In a sense, they had always suffered from hydrophobia, of course, as they hated water, whether inside them or outside them, whether falling upon them from Heaven as they marched, or splashing beneath their feet as they forded streams.

"The scene they made in the village, on the road coming back, and inside the *poste*, was similar to that staged by Maartens and Burgher, but conceived and executed on a grander scale, because they were grander men—bigger and stronger, both as men and as drinkers.

"Also, there were three of them.

"And I can inform you, *mes amis*, authoritatively, that there was considerable wear and tear, especially tear, and much disharmony and friction, before those three heroes were safely trussed-up in the cells.

"When I looked in, later on, to see that Père Poussin was comfortable, I could only distinguish him from the Russian and the Prussian by the fact that his right hand still clutched a good fistful of beard. Not his own, for he shaved regularly every Saturday night so as to start the week well, and look smart and soldierly all the time.

"Well, while these three poor fellows were still unconscious, and breathing like stranded whales, Burgher and Maartens recovered sufficiently to attend a reception held in their honour, and in the orderly-room, by Captain Le Sage.

"The charge was one of resisting the guard, damaging Government property, over-staying leave, and using language prejudicial to good discipline. . . . No mention of drunkenness. . . . Nothing about striking a superior officer—which would have been somewhat more than serious for Messieurs Burgher and Maartens, with a prison and Penal Battalion sentence as the least they could hope for.

"The two Dutchmen, still as drunk as newts and sick as salamanders, pleaded absence of mind, recent bereavements, some bad tinned fish, birthdays, senility, moon-stroke and a bottle of flat beer between them, taken upon empty stomachs and a foolish impulse.

"Captain Le Sage sentenced them to twenty-one years' solitary confinement—with remission of twenty years and fifty-one weeks, provided they told him exactly what they had drunk, and where they had got it.

"But that was the trouble. . . .

"Anxious as they were to shorten their sentence by even twenty years and fifty-one weeks, they simply could not tell Le Sage anything about it. . . .

"Not a word. . . .

"They could not even tell us, their admiring comrades, who longed to emulate their really fine feat and, if possible, to lower their record—until that night the record drunk of the Foreign Legion. They could not even tell each other—for they did not know. . . .

"All they did know was that they had marched out of Fort Bugeaud one evening, sober soldiers of blameless life and spotless record, and had more-or-less awakened two or three days later more-or-less alive, to find themselves bound and gagged comfortably at home in their old familiar prison-cells.

"As to the intervening period, their minds were blank, and blank they remained.

"Le Sage sent them back to *la boîte*, and there applied various stimulants—to the memory. . . . But you can't stimulate what is dead. . . . You can't get something out of nothing—and their minds were nothing. . . . They were vacant. . . .

"Then came the turn of Père Poussin, Krafft and Petrovitch, who, as I have told you, had set up a fresh record so soon after the new one established by Maartens and Burgher.

"Just the same with them.

"Not even the wiliness or the ruthlessness, not even the cajolery or the leniency of Captain Le Sage could get out of these three any account of what had happened to cause their downfall, from the position of soldiers who can carry their liquor, to the level of pimply *pékins* who cannot.

"Nor is it for one moment to be supposed that these five were stoutly guarding a sacred secret—the whereabouts of a hidden shrine in which Bacchus could be invoked with a liquor so potent that even a seasoned *légionnaire* could not get away with it. . . .

"Old Père Poussin would have told me at once, and if he had not, I'd have wrung his soul from his miserable body and his secret from his more miserable soul.

"No—they simply did not know.

"Whatever they had drunk was like one of those poisons that injure the mind more than the body, and destroy the memory completely.

"In this case, of course, it was only the destruction of memories and not of the memory itself—and of memories, curiously enough, connected with the drink itself, prior and posthumous . . . I mean posterior. . . . What are you laughing at, Poussin, my gentle jackal? Yes, I said 'posterior' . . . .

"Speaking to the more intelligent of my audience, I remark that, curiously enough, they remembered everything up to the time of going in search of a drink. . . . They clearly remembered what they said and did when dressing for walking-out, and when going along the road to the village . . . things like that . . . but nothing about the place to which they went, nor of what they did there. "Not one of the five could remember that. A queer business. . . ."

Tant de Soif fell silent in reminiscence for a minute, and I tried to recall the name of a drug (dhatura) of which I had heard a good deal in India—a horrible poison used by the *thugs*—of which a certain dose would infallibly kill a man, a lesser dose render him insane for life, and a yet smaller one cause complete loss of memory and general vacuity of mind.

"Well," continued Tant de Soif, "Le Sage dealt faithfully with the five of them, and promised that what they got was nothing to what they would get if it happened again, and less than nothing to what anybody else would get if it happened to him.

"Naturally this rendered us all very anxious.

"No, my excellent Harris, not anxious lest we should inadvertently drink of this new and strange potion, and innocently come upon trouble.

"Not at all.

"Our anxiety was lest Le Sage should discover the source of it before we did.

"Then, while the five heroes were still *gareeb* and *miskeen*, still shaky and quiet, sick and sorry, distrustful of life and of alcohol itself, D'Alvers, a nice French boy, who had come to the Legion because his Mistress had married his Papa—a distinguished General—followed in their footsteps. . . .

"Only he did not follow them far enough. . . . Only into the cells—and not out again. . . .

"He died there.

"A joke's a joke, as Bellême frequently observes, but this was carrying a joke too far—carrying it to the Gates of Hell and through them.

"True, he was only a child of three years' Cavalry service and four years' Legion, and he had been trying to drink himself to death ever since he joined us, but it was not right that one evening's fun should kill him.

"Yes, he behaved exactly as the others had done—like a cross between a wild beast and a raving lunatic. No—he did not die of the treatment he got, because he was not gagged nor unduly trussed up . . . nothing like *crapaudine*, only just hands and feet for his own good.

"Why wasn't he gagged? Because he wasn't howling. He was dumb and frothing at the mouth.

"Either he had had a bigger dose than the others, which is likely—as he only drank in order to forget and to hasten his end—or else he was of poorer drinking-physique than the others, which is also likely.

"Probably both.

"Anyhow, he died.

"No, my dear Cigale, it was not a lovely death. . . . Not at all.
. . . Not the peaceful and pleasant passing of one who sinks
beneath the strong Waters of Lethe after having bathed in them
for a life-time.

"Le Sage was really troubled about it—for he knew *le bon
papa Général*, and he was fond of the boy, a real soldier who, but
for the unfortunate love-affair, would undoubtedly have grown
up to be a distinguished General himself.

"Yes, Le Sage was troubled, angry, and on his mettle.

"As usual, when in trouble, he sent for me.

"'Tant de Soif,' he said, 'you damned drunken old scoundrelly
grognard'—that was only his way of showing his affection for
me, just a term of endearment—'Tant de Soif, *mon vieux*, I want
your help . . . I rely on you. . . . You have got to find out what
this high-explosive poison is, and where these half-witted, half-
human idiots are getting it.

"So far, I am defeated. I have been to every filthy *bouge* and
casse-croûte, every hut and hole and shed that sells anything at
all, and have found—nothing. Nothing but the usual muck with
which you peripatetic barrels—no, you walking dust-bins, you
wandering garbage-boxes, you perpendicular sewers—poison
your foul and worthless selves. . . .

"'You are a Frenchman, Tant de Soif. You have been
decorated twice. You are a soldier and a patriot, a man of
honour, a real . . .'"

"'Liar,' interrupted Père Poussin. 'A real liar.' That's what Le
Sage said. He also said, 'Tant de Soif, if that great red nose of
yours can't smell out this stuff, what good is it and what good are
you? None—for you certainly are no good for anything else, you
drunken disreputable ration-robber.' That's what he said. . . ."

And having delivered himself thus, Père Poussin closed his
eyes and his mouth and began to snore.

"The poor ancient is failing—rapidly," observed Tant de Soif
with apparent concern. "Poor old soul. . . . Drink. . . . Drink. . . .
Alas!

"However, as I was saying, Le Sage turned to me in his
trouble, and when such a man as My Captain wants my help, he
gets it.

"'I want your help,' he repeated. 'I rely on you. You've got to solve this mystery. Find out what they're getting, and find out where they're getting it.'

"'Consider it done, *mon Capitaine*,' replied I, in a prompt and soldierly manner, as I saluted, turned about, and marched from the orderly-room.

"'Hi!' he called, as I reached the door. 'I can consider it done, can I? . . . Well, don't you keep me considering too long.

"'You are excused from duty until you've solved the problem, or until somebody else gets drunk,' he added, and as I again saluted he added some more.

"'And if that happens before you track it down—I'll put you into cells for thrice that period. . . .'

"Once more I saluted and turned to go.

"'Hi!' called Captain Le Sage again, as he saw my back. 'Here's a franc. Lay it out wisely and well in the wine-shops, for I'll have it—and another—out of you, if you discover nothing. So don't go and sit down and drink it, and come back with a *conte borgne*.'

"Well, off I went to the wine-shops of the *village nègre*, with a roving commission, and thoroughly and copiously, albeit discreetly, I sampled their goods—or rather their bads.

"Alleged wine I drank in each; near beer, problematical *pernod*, reputed rum, villainous vermouth, ambiguous absinthe, synthetic syrops, concocted cognac, supposititious slivoviche, absolute alcohol and pure genuine, unadulterated, methylated spirit. Also *tchum-tchum*, a very beautiful rice-spirit.

"All these things I drank, severally and separately, as well as in every conceivable permutation and combination. Did they make me drunk? Not in the slightest degree, much less raving mad.

"Also I tried a very good combination of *tchum-tchum*, methylated spirit, *pernod* and *rogomme* on old Poussin here. Did it make him raving mad? No. . . . Make him drunk? No. . . . On the contrary. Our Poussin demanded that I add cognac to the mixture to give it a kick.

"By the time I had worked through the whole lot—every single place in the bazaar where one could get a drink of any sort—I had to confess that I was puzzled.

"Foiled, defeated, despairing? No. But puzzled, decidedly.

"I followed all our distinguished drinkers about, tracked them to their lairs, spied upon them—in their own best interests, *bien entendu*—but discovered nothing.

"For each one merely emerged on his feet, or on his ear, at closing time, or at such time as, having spent his *sous*, he could no longer maintain his position against the assaults of mine host and his myrmidons.

"But whether he came out on his own feet or on a comrade's back; whether he came out on his own back or beneath his comrades' feet, dragged along by his own, he was no more drunk than a good soldier should be.

"Every man of them was able to hit—or miss—a comrade, to embrace him or to kick him, and if some weakling were not equal to these feats, he was at least ordinarily peaceful, could easily be dragged along the road, and be quietly, comfortably, thrown into cells.

"Yes, I was puzzled, and by the time a week had passed, I was worried as well as puzzled, for Le Sage was always a man of his word, and I knew that if we had another such *delirium tremens* case that Saturday night, I should get three weeks' *cellule* punishment.

"Then Luck, Chance, Fate, or the Guardian Angel of all Good Soldiers, or my own private Patron Saint, took a hand and came to my help.

"There was a queer chap in the Company then, a Finn. I don't know whether Finns are really Swedes, Russians, Eskimos, or a kind of Red Indian, but they have very fine heads.

"Manly beauty? No, I don't mean that. Great brains and intellect? No, that's not what I mean. When I say fine heads, I mean very strong heads.

"They're rightly called Finns, for fins suggest fishes and they can drink like fishes. In a manner of speaking, you might say that all Finns are teetotallers, inasmuch as no Finn has ever been seen the worse for liquor. No Finn ever gets drunk. He can't.

"Well, one night, when I was sadly returning to Fort Bugeaud very late—I had a permanent late pass, of course—I suddenly almost stumbled over the body of one of our men.

"The corpse was lying with its feet in the gutter and its head against the doorstep of a house.

"'*Mon Dieu!*' thought I. 'Murder! Stabbed in the back for a handful of copper coins.'

"Stooping, I turned the body over, so that the moonlight fell upon its face. It was Idensalmisen—the Finn whom I mentioned.

"No need to close his eyes, as they were already shut. No need to staunch his wound, as there wasn't one. No need to fetch a stretcher-party for the body, as it suddenly heaved a sigh and emitted a gentle snore.

"In my relief, and to show my pleasure, I fetched Idensalmisen a good kick in the ribs. When I say a good kick, I mean one calculated to rouse the dead—or the drunk.

"It did not rouse Idensalmisen, and as he was not dead, obviously he must be drunk.

"Idensalmisen had broken the Finnish national record. He had achieved the impossible. He had got drunk.

"But what, *what* could possibly have made Idensalmisen drunk?

"And then my Patron Saint or the Guardian Angel of all Good Soldiers opened the door of his guard-lantern and let in a great light upon my brain.

"Of course! Of course! Ten Thousand Thundering Tin Devils Capering Convulsively on a Corrugated Iron Roof! That which had put Idensalmisen gently to sleep must be the Identical Drink that had driven Maartens, Burgher, Père Poussin, Petrovitch and Krafft raving mad, and had killed the French boy.

"It leapt to the eye. I felt certain that I was seeing daylight— as well as moonlight—at last.

"And assuming that I was right, where had Idensalmisen got it? Would he remember, when he recovered? And would he tell me if he did remember?

"Both were possible, if not probable. Seeing that a poison, which had sent five men mad and killed another, merely put the good Idensalmisen peacefully to sleep, it seemed quite likely that the same poison might have no effect upon the memory of the granite-headed Finn.

"Another idea occurred to me—for, as you have noticed, I am a man of ideas—and that was the notion that the house outside which Idensalmisen was lying might very well be the one in which he had been defeated. Defeated by the bottle, I mean.

"Judging from the way in which he was lying, his appearance, and the cleanness and general condition of his uniform, Idensalmisen had not been in trouble. He had not been fighting; he had not been violently thrown out of a wine-shop; and he had not been rolling about in the gutter.

"In fact, it seemed to me probable that he had stepped out of the house, thought to himself, 'I feel very sleepy. I think I'll have a nap,' had promptly lain down, and with the low door-step for a pillow, peacefully composed himself to slumber.

"I looked up at the house.

"It was one of the best, or should I say, one of the least bad, of the shops in the bazaar, a place kept by a camp-follower, a sutler, who called himself a Greek because he was as much that as anything, or perhaps because he was neither wholly Arab, Negro, nor Mussulman.

"Anyhow, he dressed more or less like a European, wore a *fez* cap and called himself Papadopoulos.

"*Les légionnaires* called him Papa Something-else in recognition of the fact that, even for a half-caste Greek sutler, he was something quite special.

"Yes, he was a bad one, that Monsieur Papadopoulos. And my comrade Idensalmisen was lying outside his house.

"Well, as soon as the bright light, which I told you about, illuminated my brain, I stopped kicking Idensalmisen and kicked the door of Monsieur Papadopoulos instead.

"Getting no more result from kicking the door of Papadopoulos than I had from kicking the ribs of Idensalmisen, I rested awhile.

"Then for a time I kicked alternately at the door and the Finn.

"When this again became monotonous, I desisted, sought for a stone, found what I wanted, and threw it at the window which opened on to the rickety verandah that overhung the ramshackle shop of Monsieur Papadopoulos.

"Noises followed. A satisfactory crash, a tinkle of falling glass, squeals, squeaks and squawks from frightened or delighted or hopeful females, and a loud roar from Monsieur Papadopoulos.

"'Thieves!   Robbers!   Assassins!   Murder!' he bawled. 'What's that?'

"'It was the Archangel Gabriel's slipper,' said I.

"'What?' shouted Papadopoulos, bounding out on to the verandah in the shirt and trousers which evidently he wore in bed, as well as out of bed. '*What?* . . . The Archangel Gabriel?'

"'Yes,' said I, 'and worse—the picket. Come down and open the door at once.'

"I think Papa had gone to bed a little drunker than usual, or perhaps had been awakened too suddenly, and was somewhat confused in his mind. Anyhow, a minute later, bolts and bars were withdrawn, the door unlocked and opened, and there stood Papa, full of wrath, fear, bluster and liquor.

"'What's this?' he bawled.

"'A corpse,' said I. 'A murdered man. A *légionnaire*. Killed in your house . . . assassinated by . . .'

"'Nonsense! Rubbish! He's . . .' spluttered Papa. 'Why, he walked out of my shop as . . .'

"'*Oho!*' said I. '*Aha!*' said I. 'Walked out of *your* shop, did he? I thought so. Well, I'm going to walk into it.'

"'You're not,' contradicted Papa, as he suddenly sat down, and I stepped over him into the dark interior.

"'Assault!' shouted Papa. 'Battery! Robbery with violence! Burglary!'

"'Murder too,' I agreed. 'If you don't light the lamp.' And I drew my bayonet as noisily as I could.

"I was not going to stick Papa, of course. It was only for what they call moral effect. Or immoral effect. Anyhow, Papa lit the lamp as quickly as could reasonably be expected.

"'Now then,' said I. 'First of all, we'll bring the corpse inside, and then we'll reconstruct the crime. Then I'll fetch the picket to arrest you, so be careful—for anything you may say will be twisted into evidence against you.'

"'I tell you I'm innocent,' shouted Papa.

"'Don't tell me,' I replied coldly. 'Tell Captain Le Sage. But don't tell him more than once, unless you want to make him angry. Come and fetch the body in before somebody else robs it. You take the feet . . . so . . .'

"Reverently we laid the body of Idensalmisen on the floor

beneath the lamp, and I closed and locked the door.

"'Now then,' said I. 'Tell me exactly what happened.'

"Papadopoulos had been pulling himself together, and what brain he had was beginning to work.

"'Happened?' he blustered. 'How do I know what happened? I never saw him before in my life. Is it my fault that somebody knocked the drunken dog on the head, outside my shop? . . . Are you such a fool as not to know that when they murder a man in one of the dives, they always lay his body outside somebody *else's* house?'

"'Oh, that's your habit and custom, is it, Monsieur Papadopoulos?' I replied. 'Well, we'll use that piece of evidence against you. Now then, stop lying, and tell the truth. Directly you saw, by the pure cold light of the moon, the poor dead face of my murdered comrade, the first words you uttered were,

"'"He walked out of my shop."

"'Those were your very words, your voluntary free confession. And to that I'll take my solemn oath before the drum-head court-martial that to-morrow will sentence you to be shot.'

"I spoke like Justice Incarnate, cold, incorruptible, remorseless, inexorable, inevitable—and Papadopoulos was badly shaken.

"He began to wilt, to tremble, to pale beneath his dirt.

"'Soldiers of France are not murdered,' I began.

"Idensalmisen emitted a loud snore.

"'No,' agreed Papadopoulos quickly. 'They get drunk.'

"He perked up visibly, shrugged his shoulders and laughed loudly. Papadopoulos was himself again.

"But I had been myself the whole time.

"'Soldiers of France are not murdered with impunity, I was about to say,' I resumed, 'and soldiers of France are being poisoned, assassinated, murdered, destroyed in this foul den, this sewer, this sink of iniquity.'

"'That one, for example?' sneered Papadopoulos, as Idensalmisen snored again.

"'Yes, that one, *par exemple*. That one, now dying at your feet. That one who will soon be as dead as poor young D'Alvers, the son of a General. Yes, *Monsieur l'Assassin*, what of D'Alvers, now lying stiff beneath the sand? . . . Poisoned by you.

... What of him and of my other comrades, Maartens, Burgher, Poussin, Petrovitch, Krafft? All dead; all murdered; all poisoned. ... And who all died accusing you.'

"'What?' cried Papadopoulos, aghast.

"'Yes,' said I. 'All dead . . . and this one dying. . . . All poisoned here.'

"I knew he could not have seen any of the five, for those who weren't in the holes labelled *Cells*, were in the similar hole labelled *Hospital*.

"'Now will you tell me the truth? Or must . . . ?'

"And I pointed the question—with the tip of my bayonet, to which Papa's paunch seemed to act as a powerful magnet.

"'What?' cried Papadopoulos again. 'Dead? Died accusing *me*?'

"'Yes, *Monsieur l'Assassin*,' I replied. 'Poisoned by you, Mr. Retail-Grocer-and-Wholesale-Murderer.

"'Your infamous name will live. Live to be spat upon by all decent men, and coupled with those of the most notorious and infamous criminals, the scum of the earth.

"'Now then, once again and for the last time, how did you poison them? What dreadful drink did you give to these splendid men, these distinguished drinkers, these men who could drink anything without turning a hair, much less without turning the whole place upside-down? What did you give them, I say?'

"'What did I give them?' snarled Papadopoulos. 'What should I give them but a bottle of good honest *pinard*? If I ever gave them anything at all, that is to say. I doubt if I ever set eyes on one of them. What do I know of your silly Burghers and cunning Kraffts and Spring Poussins? What *you* want . . .'

"And suddenly he stopped, and a look of slyness, an artful smile, and the light of an idea illuminated his dull and greasy countenance.

"'Yes?' I drawled sneeringly.

"'What *you* want, I say, is a drink,' continued Papadopoulos.

"And, even as he spoke, I saw his game, I got his idea, I followed his train of thought! A very nice train, too, *mes amis*, and going in the right direction; in fact, straight to the very point at which I wanted to arrive.

"They are curious, these sudden premonitions, revelations,

illuminations; these *je ne sais quoi*—whereby one knows, with absolute certainty, what is about to happen, what is about to be said, what is about to be done . . . perhaps some trivial, inconsequent thing . . . perhaps something of the first magnitude and highest importance.

"Before he said another word, I knew with absolute certainty that *ce bon* Papa was going to pour me out a bottle of the identical high-explosive that had shattered my five comrades, blown poor young D'Alvers to Hell, and put Idensalmisen gently to sleep.

"I was right.

"'You wait one moment,' said Papa, 'and I'll give you a bottle of the best wine you ever tasted. None of your Algerian slops. Some real Greek wine that's travelled thousands of miles and cost me an incredible amount for carriage alone. And if I give you a bottle of this priceless stuff, you've got to carry this dog's-body out again, and get him along the road. . . . Get him back to the Fort. You wouldn't abandon a comrade in distress, would you? . . . Leave him for the picket to find? . . .'

"I could have laughed aloud. Instead, I smiled pleasantly.

"This was good. This marched indeed. Papa was going to put me to sleep, too—or to death; or else send me raving mad like Messieurs Burgher, Maartens, Poussin, Krafft and Petrovitch. He was going to produce a bottle of the very stuff, the poison— stronger than a cocktail of arsenic, strychnine and prussic acid— of which I was in search.

"*Bon.* I had deserved well of My Captain. I, Tant de Soif, had done as he had bidden. I had discovered the man, the place and the potion.

"My smile must have grown wolfish, for, without another word, Papa waddled off, leaving me alone with the body of my comrade and the stock-in-trade of Monsieur Papadopoulos.

"Promptly I 'decorated myself' with a few useful and profitable articles, until, hearing the clip-clop of the returning slippers of Papa, I again kicked Idensalmisen in the ribs, and then bending tenderly over him, held his hand and soothed his brow.

"'Yes, he is dying,' I said, as Papa entered the shop from the door at the back, behind the counter. 'Dying here in a foreign land so far from home and . . .'

"'Well, drown sorrow then, *légionnaire*,' interrupted Papa brutally, as with a loud pop he drew a cork and poured a yellowish liquid, heavy and oily-looking, into a mug.

"'There,' he said, 'drink that, and you'll feel better. . . . Then you help your dying comrade home.'

"I picked the mug up and smelt the stuff.

"Now of what did it remind me? I wonder if you've noticed—but of course you must have done—how smells evoke memories. Yes, much more than sounds or sights. I never smell a tannery without seeing a certain town in France where I had happy days. . . . I can never smell a certain flower without immediately seeing a girl who—But we're talking of the poison of Papadopoulos. . . .

"Directly I smelt this 'wine ', I had a vision of my Section at work on a ground-clearing fatigue. I was hacking-down and grubbing-up *lentisk* bushes.

"I beheld the scene as distinctly as I now smelt resin. . . . 'Greek wine!' We got some once, I remembered, on the way to Saigon—or was it Beyrout? Anyhow, we got it at Alexandria. They called it Greek wine, and we called it stewed pine-bark, boiled resin, and extract of fir-cone.

"'Drink it, man, drink it. Drink it down,' urged Papa. 'You a *légionnaire*, and afraid of a half-litre of fine wine!'

"Cautiously I tasted it, just a sip.

"Name of a name! But it was fiery stuff. It was real drink. It made *tchum-tchum*—a sip of which will knock a mule down—seem like milk, seem like a bland and gentle beverage for the weaning of tender infants.

"Tilting back my head I filled my mouth. It burnt it. My friends, that distilled brimstone burnt the mouth of Tant de Soif. The mere fumes of it affected my brain.

"Staggering to the door of the shop, mug in hand, I lurched out into the street, emptied my mouth into the gutter—and smacked my lips.

"I could taste nothing, feel nothing.

"*Mon Dieu!* What marvellous stuff! What a temptation! Bottled Satan!

"Did I fall? Did I falter? Did I fail? Did I show myself unworthy of My Captain's trust? No. A thousand times no!

"I thought of Le Sage and said, 'Get thee behind me, bottled Satan.'

"I thought of three weeks in a black but red-hot cell . . . and I was true to my trust, faithful to my master, loyal to my officer.

"'Get thee behind me, Papadopoulos,' I bawled; dashed the contents of the mug upon the ground; and stormed back into the shop.

"'I'm drunk,' I roared. 'I'm mad. I'm the Archangel Gabriel. . .
.'

"Papadopoulos sniggered.

"'That's so, *légionnaire*,' he said. 'You are, and you'll be in Heaven in a minute. That way to Heaven, through the door, and turn to your left. Take your copain with you. Come on, catch hold. . . .'

"And a minute later, Idensalmisen and I were out in the street and Papa's door was banged, barred and bolted behind us.

§2

"'*Bon, mon enfant*,' said Captain Le Sage next morning when I told him of the adventure of the night.

"'And *le légionnaire* Idensalmisen is still asleep, is he? . . . H'm. . . . While ideas were flowing so freely into your otherwise empty skull, you didn't get the bright idea of bringing the bottle along with you, I suppose? . . . No? . . . You wouldn't. Would you know it again, or a similar one?'

"'But yes, *mon Capitaine*. Half-litre size, with sloping shoulders, rather like a hock-bottle; indentation in the base and a thickened rim round the neck."

"'Most observant. First-class scout—among bottles,' said Le Sage. 'Good. You are excused—cells. I'll think about that franc. Return to duty. Tell Sergeant Salzburger that I shall accompany the picket to-night, and that he's to take you.'

"Oh yes, *mes amis*, Le Sage was like that.

"Sure enough, out he marched with the picket that evening, and went into every wine-shop in the place.

"Oh, but it was amusing!

"Salzburger would kick open the door, call out, '*Garde à vous*,' and everyone would jump up and spring to attention.

"Then Le Sage would stalk in and look round, and there would be some funny sights as a drunken man would be wedged upright between two faithful comrades, or a more drunken one shoved under a divan. . . .

"One splendid fellow, all present and correct, stood magnificently to attention—with a basin on his head. . . .

"The procedure in each place was the same.

"Having satisfied himself that all things were in order, and that every *légionnaire* who should have a pass had got it, Le Sage smiled in a fatherly manner, and then, in his most brutal voice, ordered everyone to clear out immediately and to report at the poste as soon as possible or a good deal sooner. Back to barracks at the *pas gymnastique.* . . .

"You'd have thought there was a road-Marathon in progress.

"And, last of all, we came to the shop of Monsieur Papadopoulos. The same there.

"'*Garde à vous!* . . . Fixe! . . . Show all passes. . . . Excellent.'

"And then,

"'Sergeant Salzburger, take names. Every man, drunk or sober, dead or alive, to be inside Fort Bugeaud within five minutes.'

"You should have seen them jump to it—and run for it. Believe me, My Captain was a disciplinarian.

"'Carry on, Sergeant Salzburger,' says he, as soon as the shop was empty.

"'Close the door and guard it, Tant de Soif,' he added, as the picket tramped off.

"And you can bet that having closed the door, I mounted guard on the *in*side.

"Then Le Sage turned to Papadopoulos, who was looking mighty uncomfortable, and a bit yellower than usual.

"'Now, my friend,' said Le Sage, and seated himself at a little table by the counter. 'I must apologize for—er—disturbing harmony and—er—possibly interfering with business and—er— curtailing profits and—er—spoiling sport, and all that. However, we'll have a little harmony all to ourselves, you and I, shall we . . . and perhaps a little—er—profit, eh?'

Papadopoulos spread his big hands abroad and raised his

shoulders above his ears.

"'*M-Monsieur le C-Commandant* . . .' he stammered.

"'Yes, a little harmony and a little profit. You and I are going to crack a bottle together, Monsieur Papadopoulos. Or better still, we'll have a bottle each. More profit, eh, Monsieur Papadopoulos, if not more harmony!

"'Yes, a bottle each. Now, first of all, you fetch me a bottle of your very best. The very best you've got, Monsieur Papadopoulos.'

"'*Monsieur le Commandant*, it is too much honour for my poor wine-shop. *Hélas!* I have nothing worthy; nothing better than the wine of Algérie, only poor *pinard*!'

"'And it's half water, eh? And dirty water at that. Well, it has to be good enough for my brave fellows, so it has to be good enough for me. Bring me a bottle.'

"With more waggles of his great hands and shrugs of his fat shoulders, Papadopoulos began another apology: but as Le Sage eyed him with the tigerish glare—that could make even us *légionnaires* tremble—and picked up his riding-whip, Papadopoulos leapt about and seized a bottle from the scores arrayed on the shelf behind him.

"With this and a glass and a corkscrew in his hands, he galloped round the counter, placed the glass on the table before Le Sage, drew the cork and poured out the wine.'

"Picking up the glass, Le Sage smelt the wine, tasted it, and replaced the glass upon the table.

"'Like a kind of wine,' he said. 'There's a smell and a flavour about it that suggests a sort of . . . almost . . . should one say? . . . a species of bad claret, *hein*? . . . H'm. Now a bottle for Monsieur Papadopoulos. Yes, a bottle for Monsieur Papadopoulos, and he and I will sit down and drink together—in harmony . . . and with profit.'

"'Oh, *M'sieu le Commandant*. It is too great an honour . . . far, far too great an honour,' gabbled Papadopoulos.

"'I agree,' assented Le Sage. 'But get your bottle.'

"With a somewhat shaky hand, Papadopoulos returned behind the counter and took another bottle from the same shelf—a bottle exactly like the one he had given Le Sage.

"'Oh dear me, no,' protested Le Sage, as Papadopoulos turned round with the bottle in his hand. 'Surely *Monsieur le Propriétaire* doesn't propose to drink the same poor stuff as he gives his customers. Most unfitting! We're not driven to that yet, I think. No, no, put that back, Monsieur Papadopoulos, and get yourself a bottle of your best, your rarest, your ripest.'

"'But *M'sieu le Commandant*, I assure you, with my hand on my heart,' began Papadopoulos.

"'And I'll assure you with my hand on your throat,' replied Le Sage, 'if you don't do what I tell you. You go and get a bottle of that rare old Greek wine, the fine grand wine that has travelled thousands of miles and cost you an incredible amount for carriage alone. Leave me the Algerian slops, and get *Monsieur le Propriétaire*—as is only fitting—a bottle of that priceless stuff, that "best wine he ever tasted".'

"'*M'sieu le Commandant*,' whimpered Papadopoulos, 'I do not understand. . . .'

"'No? Well, get a bottle of the wine you gave my rascals, Burgher and Maartens and Krafft and Poussin and Petrovitch. Yes, and poor young D'Alvers. Get a bottle of the wonderful wine you opened last night for that scoundrel over there.'

"And swinging his great body round, Le Sage pointed at me.

"I thought he'd forgotten all about me, or supposed that I had mounted guard outside the door—and I knew that, in the confusion and his general fear and perturbation, Papadopoulos had not noticed me.

"'Come here, *salaud*,' shouted Le Sage. And in a smart and soldierly manner I marched forward and stood to attention in the light of the lamp.

"'Recognize him?' he growled at Papadopoulos. 'He's the man you didn't poison last night. The one you did poison is still asleep.'

"Papadopoulos stared at me and his loose mouth fell open.

"'Wonderful feller, isn't he?' jeered Le Sage. 'All merry and bright, smart and smiling—after drinking a bottle of your rare Greek wine—perhaps.

"'*Rare Greek wine!*' he growled. 'Well, it's going to be rarer.

"'Go and get a bottle, quick,' he snapped.

"'It's finished, *M'sieu le Commandant*. I swear to God that was the last bottle. It's finished.'

"'What's finished?' asked Le Sage quietly.

"Papadopoulos bit his knuckle.

"'The wine, Excellency.'

"What wine?'

"'The . . . the . . . the . . . the wine you were talking about.'

"'Ah? Yes? The wine that killed my *légionnaire*. So you did sell it to them, did you? Until it was finished, eh?'

"Le Sage rose to his feet and I thought Papadopoulos was going to fall down.

"'Listen, my good Papadopoulos,' said Le Sage in his softest, silkiest voice. 'Be wise. Be advised. Go and find just one more bottle of the rare old Greek wine.'

"'Excellency, there isn't one. There's not one left. Before God, I swear . . .'

"'Last chance, Monsieur Papadopoulos. Go and get a bottle of the rare old Greek wine. I don't swear anything at all, but I do most faithfully promise that it will be worse for you if I have to get it myself.

"'And mind you,' he added, 'I'll find it all right, if I have to bring my men here and pull the place to pieces. . . . Now I'll give you one minute in which to go and get a bottle—half-litre size, sloping shoulders, like a hock-bottle, base indented, and rim round the neck, eh?'

"And Le Sage glanced at the watch on his left wrist, as he took up his riding-whip in his right hand.

"With the sweat running down his fat face, Papadopoulos threw his hands downward, outward and apart, as though he were pulling open a concertina, shrugged his shoulders, shook his head, cast up his eyes, and turned to the door behind him.

"'Go with him, you,' snapped Le Sage.

"Nothing loth, I saluted, dashed round the counter and through the doorway, in pursuit of Papa.

"Down a short flight of steps he waddled into a sort of cellar or *silo*, dimly lighted by a native lamp.

"'*Sh!*' whispered Papa, glancing apprehensively over his shoulder. 'What about a ten-franc note—and the wrong bottle, *hein*? Ten francs. . . . A thousand centimes. A clean, new ten-franc note. . . .'

"I felt that if I were exceeding my duty and going beyond my instructions in fetching Papa a kick, I could plead excess of zeal.

"It was a good kick.

"I exceeded again.

"Papa, with a groan, and what I think was a wicked word in Greek, scurried to the corner of the cellar and picked out one of a mound of bottles, lying on their sides, piled one upon the other.

"It was of the right size and shape, anyhow, whatever it might contain.

"'Ah!' smiled Le Sage, as we re-entered the shop. 'Found one, have you, Monsieur Papadopoulos? Good. Now, open it and come and sit down.'

"'*M'sieu le Commandant*, it is too much honour. I . . .'

"'Open that bottle, pour out a glass, and sit down on that chair.'

"Trembling, with shaking hands, Papa obeyed as best he might.

"'Ah, a golden wine,' observed Le Sage. 'Wine of Chios? . . . Allow me.'

"And picking up the glass, Le Sage smelt the liquor.

"'H'm. Curious. Also resinous. D'you know, my friend, anyone who did not know that this was rare old Greek wine might be forgiven for thinking it was *raki* or *arrak* or medicine . . . or furniture polish . . . or *mastic*?

"'D'you know, Monsieur Papadopoulos, that that's what I should have called it—*mastic*? Just nasty, dangerous, deadly poisonous mastic. However, I'm glad I'm wrong. I'm glad it's rare old Greek wine—for your sake. Drink it up.'

"'But *M'sieu le Commandant*, your Excellency, I never drink. I'm a man of the most abstemious . . . the most teetotal . . .'

"Le Sage laughed.

"'Come, come, Monsieur Papadopoulos. Abstemious of truth,' he said. 'A teetotaller there, all right.'

"Papadopoulos spread piteous, appealing hands.

"'In fact, you're a damned liar,' continued Le Sage. 'You go to bed drunk, or as drunk as you can get, every night of your life.'

"And then his voice changed suddenly and sharply.

"'Drink that up,' he ordered, and unfastened the flap of his pistol holster.

"Really pale by this time, and with a hand that shook till the 'wine' spilt, Papadopoulos obeyed.

"'Ah!' smiled Le Sage, and sipped at his own drink. 'A glass of wine with Monsieur Papadopoulos!

"'Fill up again,' he said in his orderly-room voice, a minute later, 'and don't spill any.'

"'*M'sieu le Commandant*, I beseech . . .'

"Le Sage put his hand on the butt of his revolver.

"'At once,' he said, and with a quick look round like that of a trapped beast, a glance that came to rest on Le Sage's half-drawn automatic, Papadopoulos again obeyed.

"'Ah!' smiled Le Sage, 'we'll call that Burgher's bottle, eh? Now we'll have Maartens'. Then Krafft's. Then, after that, Poussin's and Petrovitch's. Then one for Idensalmisen—who is still asleep. And so we shall arrive at D'Alvers' bottle. Eh, Monsieur Papadopoulos? D'Alvers' bottle. I hope we get as far as D'Alvers' bottle.

"Papa hiccupped.

"'Oh, but a monumental, a colossal hiccup.

"'You should put your hand up when you do that,' rebuked Le Sage.

"'Go and get Burgher's bottle,' he continued.

"'*M'sieu le Comma . . . Comma . . .* hic . . .'

"Le Sage made a threatening movement, and Papadopoulos lurched to his feet.

"'Go with him, you,' ordered Le Sage.

"And again we went to the cellar.

"'Twenty fr . . . fr . . . *hic* . . . ancs,' hiccupped Papadopoulos, and made toward a different heap of bottles.

"I kicked him twice.

"I could not lose twenty francs for less.

"For a teetotaller, Papa had a good head and a good stomach.

"He opened the second bottle himself, poured out the two big glasses one after the other, at Le Sage's word of command, and drank them both.

"'Now, I think, a bottle for Krafft, eh?' suggested Le Sage.

"Papa's reply was really inaudible, incoherent, and incomprehensible; and it was quite obvious that the third bottle would have to be brought for him.

"I fetched it and opened it, but Papadopoulos drank it.

"I imagined that the last of his powers to fail would be the power of lifting a glass to his lips.

"They say, my friends, that there is good in everyone; something to admire in the worst of us.

"By the time Le Sage had made Papadopoulos drink to the living men, whom he had nearly killed, I began quite to admire him. Papadopoulos was a really eminent drinker.

"Yes, I found myself admiring him.

"He couldn't talk, he couldn't walk, and I doubt if he could see.

"But he could drink. He could drink, and he could understand what was said to him.

"And so it went on.

"Then suddenly Le Sage said,

"'We will now drink to the *memory* of a man, a fine man, a soldier who called himself D'Alvers. Open the bottle, Tant de Soif, and fill the glass of Monsieur Papadopoulos.'

"I did so.

"Le Sage raised his glass.

"'To the memory of *le légionnaire* D'Alvers,' he said. 'Drink, Monsieur Papadopoulos.'

"For the last time, Papadopoulos obeyed. Lowering his head to the glass, he drank suckingly . . . clutched the glass in his two hands, drank from it, dropped it with a crash, and sprawled across the table.

"'Hi! Wake up! . . . Manners, manners! . . . Sit up, man,' cried Le Sage.

"But Papa could not sit up. In fact, he couldn't sit at all, for suddenly he slumped, lurched from his chair, fell, and lay sprawling on the floor.

"'Wake him up,' ordered Le Sage. 'Revive the gentleman. Bring him round.'

"I rendered First Aid. . . . And Second. . . . And Third.

"I did things to Papa that should have raised the dead, let alone the drunk. Things that should have galvanized a mummy into life.

"Le Sage stood tapping the leg of his boot with his whip.

"'Well, you certainly found the stuff, my lad,' he said at

length. 'That was the genuine article, all right.'

"'*Oui, mon Capitaine*,' said I. 'I'm afraid I shan't be able to bring him round—for some more. He's dead drunk.'

"Le Sage laughed.

"'He's drunk dead, too, *mon enfant*,' he said. 'Quite dead.'

"And, as always, My Captain was right.

"Papadopoulos was dead . . . dead as poor D'Alvers."

A LITTLE TRUE TALE

*"A Little True Tale" is the story a legionnaire tells about why he joined
the Legion. He was happily married, though not in love with his wife,
when he had a mid-life crisis and fell in love with another woman.
There is the slight, but now unknowable, chance that there are some
autobiographical parts to this story. In May 1927 Wren was named as
the co-respondent in a divorce suit, and in December 1927 he married
the woman, Isabel Graham-Smith. According to family tradition,
Isabel and Wren had known each other in India, but the attraction
between them strengthen while Isabel was nursing Wren after his
injuries/sickness from his participation in the East African campaign of
World War I. "A Little True Tale" was first published in Part IV,
"Nous Autres", of* Flawed Blades *(1933) and has not been reprinted
until now. It is one of the two stories that were not reprinted in the
omnibus collections of* Stories of the Foreign Legion *(1947) and* Dead
Men's Boots *(1949) taken from the Foreign Legion collections*
Stepsons of France *(1925),* Good Gestes *(1929),* Flawed Blades *(1933),
and* Port o' Missing Men *(1934).*

I find myself liking a man named (or called) Nemo, very
well.

I don't know his nationality, but he is a Northerner and speaks
quite perfect English—but as he also, so far as I can tell, speaks
perfect French and German, he may be a Norman, Alsatian,
German or Briton.

He is tall, strong and soldierly; middle-aged, quiet, patient
and obviously of good birth, breeding and education.

He told me his story, this evening—a very simple though
interesting little tale, so lacking in violence and apparent tragedy,
a drama that is scarcely tragic at all, though Nemo's position is.

"Did a woman bring you to the Legion?" he asked suddenly,
as we sat doing 'spit and polish'.

I laughed.

"Yes," I replied. "In a way, a woman undoubtedly brought
me here. . . . Also a man."

"Ah, I thought a woman must have been in it. It's so often

cherchez la femme in the case of good-looking boys—who could not possibly be criminals . . ." mused Nemo.

"And you?" I said—for I wasn't going to miss the chance of getting a story for the want of asking.

"I? Oh, yes—a woman brought me to the Legion, though she doesn't know it. . . . Also a man. . . . Shall I tell you? I haven't talked to anyone for years. Not about myself, I mean. . . .

"I had one of the best wives in the world. No man ever had a better. I was ever so fond of her; and she loved me. We used to travel a good deal, after I left the sea, and we did everything together. . . . Friends. . . . Real understanding friends and companions. . . . We could sit reading for hours, and never speak to each other—and the whole time there was a deep abiding sense of companionship.

"And we liked the same books, plays, music, people, games and pastimes. A wonderful wise woman of good-will—and wholly incapable of pettiness, jealousy, shrewishness, or any spite or meanness. . . . A 'good sort' in every possible way. . . . And knew when to talk and when to stop. . . . Never jarred in the slightest degree whatever.

"I pitied other men when I saw and heard them with their wives, in their homes and in hotels, trains, country-houses where we visited, and such places.

"For years and years we went on without a wry word, awfully fond of each other, never separated for more than a few hours, and never wishing to be. . . .

"Am I boring you?

"And one day—one awful, glorious day—I fell in love.

"I fell in love, like a boy of eighteen! . . . I who had never been in love in my life—as I now realized—grey-haired, experienced, a little cynical, and very world-battered (for I had lived really hard before I met my wife), fell in love, absolutely, completely and finally.

"Although I realized it almost from the day I first saw her (this Dear Disturbance of my life), I did not realize its implication. I did not realize that something fundamental, cosmic, had happened to me, and that while my inner life was utterly transformed, my outer life remained the same, and flowed on as calmly and peacefully as before.

"It is an astounding thing, this 'falling in love', as it is called. . . .

"She was a fellow-guest of ours at a house-party, and my wife and she made friends, and this resulted in her visiting us three or four times a year.

"We also encountered each other on various social occasions, but I made no effort deliberately to meet my Dear Disturbance, overwhelming as the temptation was to do so.

"And this 'love at first sight' grew and grew and became a burning and devastating love, the obsession of my life.

"What was I to do?

"I heard her voice in all music and sweet sounds of Nature. I saw her face everywhere. I held imaginary conversations with her, by the hour. I lay awake at night in order to think of her in peace, and without distractions and interruptions.

"I fought against this love, though. . . . I mean that I swore to myself that neither my wife nor my Dear Disturbance should ever know. . . .

"When reading or hearing of this love-business, I had always been more than a little contemptuous, and had regarded men who 'fell in love' as weaklings, effeminate, self-indulgent and feeble.

"Love was right and proper for Golden Lads, and perhaps for those strange creatures who foster an Artistic Temperament—but what had mature men to do with it? How should a grey soldier be a mooning love-struck calf, a moping day-dreaming lover, sighing like a furnace?

"Well, I was punished for my blasphemy against Love, for the savour of life slowly turned to dust and ashes in my mouth, and I could neither work nor play, sleep nor eat, nor do any of those things that make the world worth while.

"But, as I say, I put up a good fight.

"For how long? . . . For years.

"Actually for several years, I held on. And then, one day, when she was paying one of those visits to us—which were such an unbearable agony of joy to me—I lowered my guard in a moment of carelessness, forget-fulness, or weakness, and slipping my arm through hers as we strolled on the terrace in the moonlight, I called her 'Dear Disturbance' . . .

"'Do you find me a disturbing person?' she smiled.

"'You are Disturbance Incarnate—to me,' I replied, 'a Walking Temptation, although unintentionally. . . .'

"And then she knew, and we fell silent—and there was a little rift in the great dam of strong-willed opposition that I had built across the torrent of my love for her.

"The dam was weakening and the power of the torrent was growing.

"I fought on. I dragged my wife abroad, and fled from Love. Fled, pursued by the Hound of Heaven, of Paradise itself. . . .

"I must be boring you? . . . No?

"She came to see us, on our return—and the sight of her was too much for the will-power on which I had always prided myself.

"What is the will of a man against the power of Love?

"I was beaten. Defeated.

"Suddenly the dam burst and the deluge followed."

"And I told her everything."

"No, I don't mean I made love to her, proposed to her, asked her to run away with me, or anything of that sort. And, of course, such a thing as a clandestine love-affair with her never entered my head.

"I am not a religious man and I am no moralist—but I draw a line at base and beastly actions, and I could conceive of no baser and beastlier action than my desertion of my wife would have been. Absolutely the blackest, vilest treachery, ingratitude and villainy. Like kicking a little child that came to kiss you. . . .

"Why did I tell this woman that I loved her, then?

"I don't know. . . . I had to. . . .

"It was in the nature of Confession without hope of Absolution. I had an idea that it might ease my mind and my conscience, and perhaps help me to find peace, or a little measure of peace. . . ."

"Did the woman love you?" I asked Nemo.

"Er—no . . . No . . . But I'll swear I could have made her love me, had I been free to do so. She had never thought of me in that way, of course, and had not seen very much of me.

"I don't suggest, for one moment, that her seeing very much of me would have meant that she would have loved me, at all— but I do know that I could have made her love me, had I met her in time. . . .

"Well—I told her.

"How did she take it? Oh, she was kind and understanding beyond words. Surprised and incredulous; a little pleased, as any human woman is when a man worships her; very sorry for me, and sympathetic—and left it at that. . . .

"Do you know what the real test of love is?"

"I do, Nemo," I replied. "It is the power and will to put giving before taking. I think unselfishness is the acid test. Real and true Love says, 'Let me make you happy' rather than 'Make me happy" . . . That's my idea, anyhow. . . ."

"You've been in love, my son," replied Nemo. "You know what love is.

"Well. Life went on. Somehow. And I think that, on the whole, it was easier now. Confession is good for the soul.

"But life wasn't easy, and I had an unconquerable yearning to see her, an unquenchable thirst for sight and sound of her. And I weakened. The released torrent flowed ever stronger, roared ever louder in my ears, drowning the voice of conscience.

"Then I fell from grace, and wrote her mad letters. Mad. Only love letters, quite hopeless and harmless, proposing— nothing. Quite mad.

"Shall I go on?"

"Yes."

"I don't know how I lived through the days—still less the nights. For I could not work.

"What is a man without work?

"Work—'the curse of Adam'? . . . What utter rubbish! . . . Work—the blessing and salvation of Adam and all the sons of Adam. I was very sick—mind, body and soul.

"'And no medicine for my sickness,' thought I, one day; almost, I fear, verging on that foul destructive thing—self-pity.

"No medicine? Perhaps not—but there may be surgery.

"'There may be surgery,' I said aloud—and found I had said it to my brother who was visiting us. Home from his job in one of our Colonies—a fine chap doing some fine work.

"'One *has* heard of surgery,' he murmured, eyeing me critically.

"We were sitting in the smoking-room, on either side of the

fire, in deep arm-chairs, with our pipes alight, talking desultorily between long silences.

"'Look here,' he went on, 'is there anything wrong with you? . . . Or is there anything right with you, one might ask?'

"Surgery!

"'I'll tell you what's wrong with *you*, Bean-stalk,' I replied. 'You want a wife. You ought to marry and settle down.'

"'Really what I came home for,' he yawned. 'I want a missus. Getting on. Getting bachelorish. Someone to hold my thumb when I'm lonely. Tired of living in clubs. . . .'

"'We've got the girl for you, Bean-stalk,' I managed to say. 'Ideal wife for you. . . . Beautiful; well-bred; sportsman; splendid type; soft, low voice; gentle. . . .'

"Bean-stalk yawned again.

"'Garn,' he said. 'What's the game? What's *your* rake-off? Tired of her?'

"He little knew how he hurt."

Nemo fell silent and rubbed hard at his bayonet.

"I'm sorry," he went on. "Must have bored you frightfully.

"Long and short of it is—

"Bean-stalk fell in love with her and they were married. A fortnight after the wedding, my wife came home from a dance, sat down, said,

"'I do feel funny,' and died in the arm-chair.

"Heart. . . .

"And left the loneliest, saddest man in two hemispheres. . . . A man quite dead, though alive. . . .

"And I know my Dear Disturbance would have loved me. . . .

"So I lost them both.

"Silly little tale, isn't it?"

"No."

"And wasn't I a fool to come here?"

"Yes."

AN UNFLAWED BLADE

"An Unflawed Blade" is a story told by Nemo about his experience in being torpedoed by a German submarine during World War I. "An Unflawed Blade" was first published in Flawed Blades *(February 1933) and was reprinted in the newspaper* The Evening News *on August 5, 1933. It was also reprinted in* Dead Men's Boots *(1949).*

"Coming for a walk?" asked Nemo.

"Yes, delighted, if you'll just wait till I've polished this," I replied.

It was the first time that Nemo had honoured me with a request for my company, and I at once began to hope that he would tell me something more about himself.

All that I knew about him, so far, in addition to what he had told me of his love-affair, was that he was an Englishman, and had served in the Navy during the War.

§2

"Let's sit down for a bit, before we turn back, shall we?" suggested Nemo, as we reached the cluster of palms for which we had been making.

I agreed, and sitting down on the still-warm sand and leaning against the trunk of a palm, produced my pipe.

This was a fortunate move on my part, for had I not done so, Nemo would not, for his part, have produced the following story.

"Got a knitting-needle, or a crochet-hook, or a hair-pin, or a bayonet, or anything?" I asked facetiously. "The bottom of the bowl of this damned pipe is bunged up."

"I've got a knife with a long thin blade," replied Nemo, producing a pocket-knife.

"Thanks," said I, and began vigorously to scrape and pick my pipe.

"Don't break it!" suddenly said Nemo, as I finally got the point of the blade into the hole at the bottom of the bowl, and

273

bent it against the edge, trying to work the orifice clear.

"What—the pipe?" I asked.

"No, my knife," replied Nemo.

"Give you two new ones if I do," I laughed.

"Rather have that one than the price of two hundred new ones," said Nemo very seriously.

"Heirloom?" I asked. "It looks well worth ninepence for itself alone."

"Saved my life," said Nemo, adding, a moment later, "And six others too."

"By Jove!" I observed. "You must have done a lot of stabbing with it—or did you cut bread for a starving family?"

"Cut a rope," said Nemo.

"Gallows?" I murmured.

"No—three-inch painter," was the reply.

"Peter the Painter," I observed rather pointlessly, as I blew down the pipe, and continued,

"How? Expound, ancient mariner."

"Pushed off once, during the War, in the *Aquamarine* from Tilbury. Wasn't an H.M. Transport ship, that trip. We were off to Philadelphia, only partly loaded.

"Big ship? No, three thousand three hundred and fifty register, and carried about seven thousand five hundred tons cargo. Forty-two hands all told.

"Happy ship, and a nice Old Man.

"Well, there happened to be a nail driven into the bulkhead by my berth, and somehow that old knife hung itself on it.

"I used to smoke in my berth a lot, and was always wanting a knife for a scrape out, or to ease up the baccy or something. Don't know now how it came into my possession. I certainly never bought or stole it; I expect it took to me, like a stray dog takes to one, you know.

"Anyhow, I hung it up on that nail.

"One evening, I relieved the Chief Officer for his tea at six-thirty.

"Hazy weather and moderate swell; pretty well clear of the English Channel. By the time I'd taken a couple of turns up and down the bridge, my pipe 'stuck', and the harder I sucked the tighter it got.

"I put my hand to my coat pocket as the thought flashed through my mind,

"'Did I catch up the old knife from the nail in the bulkhead as I hurried from my cabin, or did I dream it? Queer thing if I did take it, for I've never done so before.'

"It was not in my left-hand pocket, and as my right hand touched the flap of my right-hand pocket, I was blown clean across the bridge from one side to the other.

"It was a most tremendous explosion. Some funny dogs will tell you that a torpedo makes a 'dull thud', or something of that sort. As I was fetched up by the rail at the other end of the bridge, my back against it, I saw that the man at the wheel wasn't at the wheel at all, but lying up in a corner like a bundle of rags, and that the compass was blown clean out of the binnacle on to the deck below.

"When I pulled myself up on to my feet, I realized that I was white from head to foot—as white as if I had been dipped in a vat of white paint—boots and all.

"Then I remembered that the enormous volume of water that had risen up to the sky as I flew across the bridge was not water at all, really, but Devonshire cream."

"Were you drunk or dreaming, or knocked silly?" I interrupted.

"No," continued Nemo. "I wasn't drunk, dreaming, or knocked silly. I was particularly clear-headed, with all my senses unusually alert and receptive. I never felt better, more competent, or more capable in my life. The only drawback was that I couldn't move."

"Mere trifle!" observed I. "But what about this Devonshire cream—or was it Bristol Cream,[5] by any chance?"

"Chalk!" replied Nemo. "As I landed with a crash against the rails at the other end of the bridge, and entered this state of extreme clearness of mental perception and extreme physical incapacity, I tasted chalk.

"Did you ever, as a school-boy, put a stick of chalk in your mouth, pretending it was a cigarette? I did so, more than once. And while that great mountain of Devonshire cream seemed to

---

[5]A very fine sherry.

hang, for a second, in the air, I saw the interior of an old school-room, and myself with the master's chalk between my teeth, striking a fancy smoking-attitude behind his back.

"Yes, we were ballasted with chalk, and the great column of water, thrown up by the explosion to an incredible height, was, as I say, white and thick with it.

"As I lay and looked, for some fraction of a second that seemed like minutes, it was as though I could not only taste and see and feel chalk, but also smell and hear it too. Life, and space, and time seemed to be made of chalk.

"And then I was aware of planks, rails, debris, and portions of the ship's cargo flying high in the air; and solemnly remarked aloud,

"'This means that three iron decks and two wooden ones have been penetrated.'

"And as I said it, I saw a great plank, or log, with jagged iron projections, hurtling like an arrow, fall smack upon a little knot of men as they rushed out on deck from below.

"Only one of them continued on his way, and he crawled, dragging a leg—of which the foot pointed to the sky instead of downwards.

"I sprang up, shocked, to go and help him, and was surprised to find that I could spring up.

"I wondered how long I had lain there, and found afterwards that it could not have been for more than a second or so.

"Then I saw that the Captain had put the engine-room telegraph at '*Stop*', and realized that he was ordering me to go and read the log at the after end of the ship, and to note our position (by her run) on the chart.

"As I ran down from the bridge, I noticed, with wonder, that my trousers were torn and blood-stained, and that both my legs were very painful.

"Coming back from reading the log, I ran into the Marconi operator. He was blundering and fumbling about like a blind man—because he was blind.

"His poor face was a shocking sight.

"'Chalk,' he said. 'I'm full of chalk. My eyes have turned to chalk.' (One of them was gone, and the other looked like a bladder of blood.) 'God! Remember the Kaiser and his crew.'

"I grabbed his hand, and he pulled himself together.

"'Who are you? Tell Cap'n I was blown out of my room, and that all my gear, including the emergency set, is wrecked. . . . Tell him my eyes are wrecked, too, and I've got no emergency set,' he babbled.

"I pushed him on to a hatch.

"'Sit there, Jimmy, and don't budge,' I said. 'I'll come and put you in a boat if we have to abandon ship. I won't forget you,' and then I stumbled up on to the bridge, and reported to the Captain that the wireless was done in.

"'Blow four blasts on the ship's whistle,' he replied—that being the signal to lower the boats.

"And then I noticed that we were still going ahead at about twelve knots, and realized that either communication with the engine-room had failed, or that the engineer on watch had been unable to stop the engines. Probably the latter, owing to his own sudden and unexpected 'stoppage' by the torpedo, or engine-room explosion.

"Anyhow, we were forging ahead at a rate that made any boat-lowering a mighty risky business, and that forced water through the great gap in the ship's side.

"We were settling down fast.

"The starboard boat, being on the lee side, was somewhat protected, and was occupied without mishap. I ran to where poor blinded Jimmy was sitting, nursing his head, and told him to come along.

"He got up. I led him to the boat, and helped him into it.

"He immediately sprang over the side, and that was the last I, or anybody else, saw of Jimmy. I suppose he preferred a quick death to a living one—or perhaps he was mad with pain.

"I thought, for a minute, that it wasn't going to make much difference, for, as the boat pushed off, she swung so close to the propeller that all the oars on that side were smashed.

"The port boat had worse luck.

"By this time, four men had tumbled into her, the heavy rise and fall of the sea carried away the painter, and, breaking adrift, she floated right under the propeller, which was, by this time, clean out of the water. It was like a sausage machine in action on four mice in a match-box.

"Meanwhile I had opened up a chest, and served out cork jackets to the remainder of the crew. It looked as though we were going to want them, for our large cutter was blown to bits, and there was only a small dinghy left.

"However, it seemed that there were only six of us alive on the ship—the Captain, the Fourth Officer, the Second Engineer, a greaser, a trimmer, and myself.

"'Who's coming home?' said the Captain, and we lowered the dinghy.

"I was glad to see the propeller thirty feet up in the air—but was less glad when I realized that the fore-part of the ship, to which our painter was made fast, was correspondingly below water."

"Why?"

"Because we had no axe in the dinghy, and were being dragged under! See?"

"Hard case!" I murmured. "*Vanity Fair*. 'What should A do?'"

"'A' swore," continued Nemo. "Swore hard and well and truly, at the criminal fool who had removed the axe from the boat—the axe that is, or should be, in every ship's boat, for the purpose of cutting her adrift if necessary. I need not point out that it is utterly impossible to untie a three-inch painter which has the strain of a sinking ship on one end, and a floating boat on the other.

"The Captain, who was badly shaken and cut about, sat down in the stern of the dinghy, while the Second Engineer, the Fourth Officer and the two seamen got out the oars—and '*Cut the painter!*' was the cry, even while everybody searched for the axe, and I was shoving off in the bows.

"'Who's got a knife?' was the next almost simultaneous shout; and knowing quite well that I hadn't one, I thrust my hands into the pockets of my coat. As I did so, I remembered that I had felt for my knife when my pipe 'stuck', the moment before we were torpedoed.

"Had I felt for it—and found I had not got it—or did I only feel in one pocket?

"'Bite it, old thing. There isn't a knife among us,' giggled the Engineer, just as my fingers closed on that old knife that you were trying to break.

"And then I knelt down in the bows and sawed away with that feeble old thing at the three-inch painter that was dragging us under.

"It was like digging up a tree with a tooth-pick, or trying to shame a War Hun with fair play and chivalrous honour. The rope seemed to be made of iron and the blade of cardboard.

"And as I sawed away, I grew desperately terrified. I hadn't felt the least sensation of fright until that moment—hadn't had time to—but as I hacked away at that fat trunk of a rope, I felt all my strength going in sheer paralysing terror, and I nearly burst into sobs and blubberings of rage and fright.

"The greaser began to pray aloud, and the trimmer to swear louder.

"'Go it,' said the Fourth Officer to me; 'we're nearly under.'

"And then water ran over my hands.

"It did not splash over them—it ran over, and the nose of the dinghy was *under water*.

"The praying greaser fell over backwards as the stern of the boat rose, and the trimmer smote him a couple of useful clouts, and addressed him with impropriety.

"'We are going home,' said the Captain, and, as the sea poured in wholesale, and I was sawing away, up to my elbows in water, the strain of my cutting took effect and the rope parted—about a second before it was too late—and we came up with a jerk.

"'Will you have nuts or a cigar, Sir?' asked the Engineer, and then a big sea lifted us up and nearly smashed us on to the ship's deck.

"It seemed for a few minutes, struggle frantically as we might, that we had only escaped being dragged under by the ship, to be shattered against it by the waves.

"However, our luck held, and, by a miracle, we grazed her side and struggled clear.

"And then the ship's whistle gave a long, piercing shriek, precisely as though it were her death-scream, and she plunged from sight, her propeller whirling to the last.

"I suppose, however, that uncanny scream of her whistle was caused by the portion of the bridge, to which the whistle was attached, breaking away from the ship and pulling the wire by which the whistle is operated.

"My feeling of terror passed and changed to a great sadness, a desolating sensation of grief and bewilderment, at this sudden and complete vanishing of my floating home; this substantial and beautiful thing of which I had been a part; in which I had lived and moved and had my being, eaten and slept and laughed and worked.

"And, oh, how I hated the skulking brute of a Hun, the fiendish, callous devil that had done this thing hundreds of times, and drowned fifteen thousand civilians, men, women and little children—those German 'comrades' of some of our politicians.

"How I wished that some of our British Bolsheviks could have been in that dinghy with us, and had a taste of the 'destruction' they admire so vastly. But you don't find that sort running into much danger. . . .

"As soon as we found that we weren't going to be sucked under, and follow the poor old *Aquamarine* to the bottom, we just sat still and stared, stunned at the realization that our ship, which a few minutes ago had seemed as permanent and abiding as a lighthouse and as indestructible as a rock, was gone—obliterated. . . .

"Suddenly, we were very effectually aroused by the gurgle and plop and swash of an emerging conning-tower and whale-back, and there was our enemy not a hundred yards away.

"I don't believe one of us had given her a thought from the moment we were torpedoed—possibly not one of the seven men who had been on the look-out had seen either her periscope or the wake of the torpedo.

"Her conning-tower opened, and up came the head of a German officer. He was a fat, pig-faced brute, with a dirty muffler round his neck and a sort of pill-box, peaked cap over one eye. He hailed us in good English and ordered us to approach.

"'Where's your Kapitan?' he said, as we came alongside.

"The Old Man stood up.

"'I am, you dirty, slinking dog,' he said; 'and if I'm to be drowned or murdered now, I'd sooner be me than you, you cowardly swine'—which I considered a tactless speech under the circumstances, though constrained to add '*Hear! Hear!*' by the pluck of it.

"And then, suddenly, the German dived like a seal, and the lid shut down on him as though he were a Jack-in-the-box.

"A destroyer was racing up, and the submarine fellow knew that he was 'for it'.

"Oh yes, the good old usual 'pool of oil' on the face of the waters, after three depth charges had gone down. . . ."

Nemo fell silent.

"Had you ever been torpedoed before?" I asked.

"Three times."

"H'm. Did your nerves a lot of good, I should think."

"Oh, I don't know . . . though I admit there are times when I am glad that torpedoing is not one of the hazards of life in the Legion.

"And, but for that knife, I shouldn't be here, or anywhere else on this amusing world. . . ."

I handed Nemo back his knife, after carefully, and somewhat reverently, cleaning its long, worn, but unflawed, blade.

ONE GOOD TURN

"One Good Turn" is the last story Wren wrote about Michael "Beau" Geste. In this story, Michael does a "good turn" for an Arab woman, and then receives a "good turn" in return when he is captured by Arabs during a battle. "One Good Turn" first appeared in Flawed Blades *(1933) and was reprinted in the* Scholastic *magazine (March 10, 1934) and in* Dead Men's Boots *(1949).*

Quite frequently "the movies" hold the mirror up to Life and reflect it without unbearable distortion.

Occasionally Life, returning the compliment, copies "the movies."

When it does so, we are prone to observe that Truth is stranger than Fiction.

§2

Sergeant-Major Lejaune, his honours thick upon him after the battle of El Rasa, and on the eve of promotion to the rank of Adjutant, was a happy man—though none would have suspected it—happy in the attainment of ambition, happy in knowing himself to be the squarest of pegs in the squarest of holes, and particularly happy, at the moment, in the execution of a job after his own heart.

His orders were to reconnoitre an Arab *douar*, of which a scout of the *peloton méhariste*, mounted on a swift camel, had brought information; to reconnoitre it, and to act in accordance with his discoveries.

There was intentional and definite vagueness about the instructions issued to him, a certain euphemism, and wide room for the use of discretion, or, should circumstances indicate, of indiscretion.

What Sergeant-Major Lejaune quite clearly understood was that no inhabited Arab *douar* was to be left intact, useful and practicable, from the Arab point of view: a menace and potential danger on the flank of the advancing Brigade; a rally-point, retreat and stronghold whence the desert horsemen could sally forth for a whirlwind charge at dawn, and whither they might safely retire with the spoils of victory, or to lick their wounds and rest awhile to gather strength after defeat.

As usual, the Legion was in advance of the Brigade, its eyes and ears; and, as frequently, Sergeant-Major Lejaune, with a picked section of three sergeants, six corporals and fifty men, was in advance of the Legion, and a week ahead of the Brigade.

*   *   *   *   *

Warily, skilfully, and with desert cunning equal to that of the Arabs themselves, taking advantage of every sand-dune, *wadi* and fold in the ground, Lejaune brought his little force into position for attack.

"Place seems absolutely deserted," he growled to Sergeant Dupré, after long and careful study of the *douar* through his glasses.

Sergeant-Major Lejaune glanced along the line of men, lying prone and thankfully resting, beneath the crest of the sand-dune over the top of which he had been observing the *douar*.

"Here, you," he called suddenly, and beckoned to a soldier.

The man, crouching low, hurried towards him.

"See that *douar*? March straight towards it. If you are not fired at, march straight into it, and go on until you are fired at. . . . And don't be fool enough to get killed first shot. Let's hear plenty of shooting if the place is occupied."

Michael Geste shouldered his rifle, saluted and marched off.

There was a gleam in the eye of Sergeant-Major Lejaune and a twist of his lips that might have been the ghost of a sardonic smile.

"'It is expedient that one man should die for the people,'" murmured Sergeant Dupré, an educated man who was said to have been a priest.

Sergeant-Major Lejaune grunted.

"More useful dead than alive—if he manages to start that hive buzzing before he dies," he growled.

Straight for the village, steadily as though on parade, Michael Geste marched on, expecting at every step to hear the crack of a rifle and feel the thud of a bullet. . . .

Perhaps the first shot would miss him. . . . In that case, he would instantly throw himself flat—having done his job of establishing the fact that the silent and apparently empty *douar* was occupied. . . .

But no shot came.

A thousand metres, five hundred, two hundred, one hundred—they could not miss him now, surely, at little over fifty yards—if hidden riflemen were lurking in the stone-and-baked-mud houses. . . .

A nerve-racking trial of coolness this, marching up alone against the sinister place, silent as the grave and still as the dead, that yet seemed to watch with a thousand eyes, and might be alive with fierce fighting men. . . .

Fancy falling into their hands unwounded—to be tortured unspeakably—and with the added torture of knowing that one had failed one's comrades. . . . A blow on the head, from behind, as one passed along an alley, and one would be in their power.

Not a warning shot fired. . . . The village . . . No shot . . . No sound. . . Deserted and empty.

Michael Geste went through the *douar* from end to end.

As dead and derelict as the deserted cities of India, of which one had read; as empty and abandoned as Pompeii itself.

One might return now, and signal that there was no enemy in sight—though the very fact of the absence of any firing, and of his emerging safely, would show Lejaune that all was well, that there was no trap, and that he might advance without further precaution. . . .

Might look into one or two more of the empty houses, just to "mak siccar," as old McSnorrt would say. . . .

No, nothing. Nobody, apparently.

Presumably the inhabitants had fled after the battle of El Rasa, as soon as it was evident that the accursed infidel *Roumis* were going to penetrate yet further into the desert.

Michael Geste, from force of habit, closed the door behind him, as he stepped out from a dark interior into the dazzling light of the white-washed, white-hot "street," and, sloping his rifle, turned to march back to rejoin his comrades.

Hullo! What was that? Something had moved. . . .

Something white had moved—behind the bars of an un-glazed window. . . .

Now for it! Now for the *bang* and the rending crash of a bullet in the chest or head. . . .

Michael threw up his rifle and covered the dark, barred aperture. . . . He was there to draw fire and to shoot—not to escape unhurt, and then lead his comrades into a trap. . . .

Why did nothing happen? Why couldn't the skulking Arab shoot—or show himself to be shot at? . . .

Why should he? . . .

Seconds that seemed like minutes passed. Minutes that seemed like hours.. . .

Michael could bear it no longer, and fear, as usual, made him angry.

"Can only die once," he said, and, his rifle at the "ready," he approached the window.

Nothing happening, he looked into the room, or, rather, tried with shaded eyes to penetrate the gloom of the dark interior.

He could see no one . . . nothing of interest. . . . Just the usual bare, dirty and comfortless interior—apparently last tenanted by goats and fowls.

Nevertheless, something—something white—had undoubtedly moved in the room, had shown itself at the barred aperture, and had disappeared. . . . Almost certainly a human being. . . .

Was there a concealed sharpshooter in the house? Was there one concealed in every house in the village—perhaps more than one—waiting for the Infidels to walk into the trap?

Anyhow, this house should be searched pretty thoroughly.

Going round to the front of the place, Michael put his shoulder to the rickety door, burst its feeble fastenings, and, finger on trigger, entered, his heart beating fast, and speculation in his mind as to whether the sound of the shot that might kill him, and his shot in reply, would reach the ears of his comrades.

If wounded, he must try to regain the street and fire his rifle in the open air, so that its report would be heard. . . .

Nothing in the front room. Not even an article of furniture, a cooking-pot, a garment, nor anything else—nothing but bare, mud floor, filthy walls and smoke-blackened roof.

Yes—a door in one of the walls, a door that did not lead into the room, shed, or out-building of which he had already examined the interior.

"Well! Here goes," quoth Michael, and, at the second heave and thrust, burst this door open also.

A swift movement . . . a rustle . . . a gleam . . . someone or something in the far corner.

As he threw up his rifle, Michael, his eyes now accustomed to the interior gloom, realized that there were two Arabs in the room—that they were crouching in the corner. . . .

No, that one was lying on the mud floor, and the other crouching beside him . . . an old man and a young girl . . . the girl clutching a long knife, and evidently prepared to protect the grey-bearded ancient who lay staring and muttering incoherently.

Like a snake about to strike, the girl sprang to her feet, raised the knife above her head, and, her glittering eyes fixed upon Michael's, waited—a picture of desperate and devoted courage.

"Fear not," said Michael in Arabic, as he lowered his rifle. "I will not hurt you. . . . Nor your father. . . ."

"I will kill you if you come nearer," replied the girl.

"I am not coming nearer," answered Michael. "Do not fear."

"What do you want? . . . We have nothing. . . . We are starving. . . . My father is dying of thirst and of hunger."

Stepping back a couple of paces, Michael unslung his *bidon*, and placed it on the ground.

"Give him water—and drink yourself," he said, and returned to the door.

Thirst overcoming fear, distrust and bewilderment, the girl, without taking her eyes from the terrible invader, or lowering her knife, edged forward and seized the water-bottle.

"Do not fear," said Michael Geste again, and retreated to the door.

The girl poured water into an earthenware cup, and then raising the old man's head, held the vessel to his lips.

Not until it was empty did she slake her own thirst—evidently a consuming fire and torture.

"Here is food," said Michael Geste, and produced from his haversack two army biscuits and some cooked macaroni, the sight of which unattractive mess caused the girl's eyes to gleam.

Obviously she and the old man were, as she had said, suffering, if not dying, from starvation and thirst.

"Have you no friends? No one to help you? Why are you alone in the *douar*?" he asked, as the girl, still afraid to approach, held out her hand for the food.

"All have fled," replied the girl. "Scouts brought news of a great *Roumi harka*. . . . My father was too ill to go. . . . They said 'Let him die', but it was not the will of Allah, and he lives. . . . I cannot draw water without help, for the well is very deep, and they have taken the rope. . . . What do you want? . . . Shall we now be killed? . . ."

"No. Do not fear. Pour the rest of that water into the jar. . . . The *Roumi harka* will pass on, and your tribe will return. . . . Farewell. . . ."

*   *   *   *   *

On receiving his scout's report, Sergeant-Major Lejaune, being pressed for time, did no more than march through the *douar*, and give directions that, here and there, fire should be set to a house that looked a little more important than the rest.

Michael Geste, one of a small demolition party, contrived, after hasty communication with his brothers Digby and John, and his friends Hank and Buddy, to leave a further small supply of food and water in the outer room of a certain house, one of half-a-dozen marked down for destruction by Corporal Gontran. . . .

Evidently haste caused the failure of any incendiary efforts that may have been made in this case, as no flames were seen to burst forth from this dwelling-place, though Corporal Gontran observed that a reasonable amount of smoke issued from it.

"Come on," he bawled from the end of the street, as Michael emerged from the house . . . "or do you propose to wait for the sacred fire-engine to arrive, you . . ."

II

A week later, the Brigade halted to rest in perimeter camp, the Legion bivouacked a few miles to the south of it, while Sergeant-Major Lejaune and his scouts entrenched themselves a few miles to the south of the Legion, and slept, when sleep they did, with one eye open.

For most of the hours of most of the days, the majority of the special Section were engaged in scouting, patrolling, and keeping communication with the battalion.

*   *   *   *   *

"We'll have a look over the next ridge and then return," said Corporal Gontran. . . .

"Here, you two, Brown and Schneider," he added, turning to the *légionnaires* nearest to him, "four eyes are as good as forty. Scout over that ridge—and do it thoroughly. . . . Remainder fall out and sit down. . . . You, Schwartz, get on that rock and watch all round. . . ."

Le légionnaire Schwartz, scowling, obeyed—Corporal Gontran was too fond of picking on him for everything. Hadn't he earned a rest as much as any? . . .

"Up!" he bawled . "*Aux armes!* Here they come!" and opened fire as he shouted.

The thunderous rush of the small raiding-party swept away the two scouts who were approaching the ridge over which the Arabs had so suddenly appeared, and seemed to trample them into the earth.

One, Schneider, lay still for ever, beneath the spearman who had stabbed him through the chest—and received Schneider's bullet through his brain in the act of doing so. The other, "Brown", lay unwounded, but unconscious, knocked down, trampled, and kicked on the head by the horse of the swordsman whom he had shot, as he parried the sword-cut with his bayonet.

After the fight, the rearguard action, the dogged slow retreat, and the final escape of the survivors of the patrol, this man was picked up, bound, slung across a riderless camel and carried off for question, torture, and terrible death by the decimated Arab raiding-party.

*   *   *   *   *

When Michael Geste, alias *le légionnaire* Brown, recovered

complete consciousness, he found himself lying on the ground outside a village, trussed like a fowl, while a crowd of Arabs stood near and wrangled as to his fate.

A group of women waited with deep interest and eager anticipation their lords' decision; and a band of children eyed him with fear and hatred, and, according to age and disposition, sucked thumbs, spat, shouted unchildish threats or flung stones.

An avaricious-looking old man babbled of ransom, but was bidden to hold his foolish tongue, inasmuch as no ransom would ever be paid for a *légionnaire*, and could not safely be collected if it were payable.

Resolutions and amendments put to the meeting varied from proposals for crucifixion, burning alive, impalement, stoning, burying alive, slow and progressive mutilation, starvation, pegging-out in the sun to die of thirst, down to just ordinary plain decapitation.

"Hand him over to the women—and leave it to them," growled a savage-looking warrior whose thumb had been shot off in the day's fight, whereat a yelping chorus of approval rose from the group of crones.

Several of them had provided themselves with kitchen-knives—domestic utensils as useful and effective for the flaying and filleting of a *Roumi* as for the slaying, skinning and quartering of a goat or sheep.

"Peace!" boomed the deep voice of a big, important-looking man who now joined the group. "Let the women dig his grave—narrow and deep. He shall be buried alive, all but his head.

"In the night the jackals will come and tear the ears from his cheeks, the scalp from his skull, the flesh from the bones of his face—and in the morning he shall still be alive.

"Yes, and the sun shall rise and shine upon the thing that was his head . . . until he dies."

And all the congregation said "Amen!" and the old women forthwith got joyfully to work with mattock, spade, hoe, pieces of iron, shards of pottery, and their bare hands, vying with each other—despite a heavy day's work already done—in the delightful work of digging an infidel's grave beneath the horrified gaze of his living eyes. . . .

Occasionally a man dispassionately, and, as it were, almost

absent-mindedly, kicked the infidel, struck him with a stick, prodded him violently with the haft of a lance or the muzzle of a gun, spat upon him, or threw sand and dirt upon his face and into his eyes.

Now and then a boy or girl successfully flung a stone at his head. . . . Once, a woman—perhaps she had lost a son or husband fighting the *Roumis*—knelt beside him and proceeded to gouge out his eyes with a stick, an attempt which would have succeeded, in spite of Michael's struggles, but for the interference of the important man who had pronounced his doom.

"Cease!" he shouted. "Who gave him to you for a plaything? Leave him his eyes that he may see the jackals come for them. . . ."

And, willing hands making light work, the grave was quickly dug, Michael was flung into it, feet first, and the grave was speedily filled in—so that, though his body was buried to the neck, his head remained above ground.

There, after a little stone-throwing, buffeting, kicking, and the infliction of foul indignities, his capacity for suffering undiminished, his ability to protect himself entirely abolished, in fullest possession of all his faculties, and of the dreadful knowledge of what he must endure through the night and perhaps throughout the next day, he was left alone to face his hideous fate. . . .

Had hours or only minutes passed?

Hours surely. . . . "How long, O Lord, how long?"

Cramp almost unbearable—suffocation well-nigh insupportable—an impulse to shriek, scream, howl, nearly unconquerable.

A slinking shape, just visible against the stars.

Was that the first of the jackals—or only a village cur?

Could one keep jackals and pariah dogs at bay, by shouting at them?

Could one bend one's head back, and then jerk it violently forward, against the snout of the prowling, starving beast that came to . . . came to . . .

God! What was that behind him . . . behind his head? . . .

"Well? Comfortable? Still possessed of ears to hear, *Roumi*?

Listen to me, then. . . ."

It was the voice of the head-man who had pronounced his doom.

"We caught two of your people a year or so ago, and we buried them alive as you are buried now. . . . I came to them by night as I have come to you, and offered them their freedom . . . rank, money, horses, camels, women . . . all that makes life and freedom worth having—on terms.

"One of them joined us—and now rideth at the right hand of the Sultan of the Mountains, a warrior, the leader of a *harka*, rich, respected, strong. . . .

"The other did not join us. His body—all but the head, is still in the ground—somewhere near you now. He lived for a day and a night and a day. . . . Long before he died his skull was red . . . and then black. One knew it was a skull because it had teeth and eye-sockets. . . . That man was a fool."

"That man was a good soldier," replied Michael Geste. "True to his salt. . . . A brave man. . . . What Arab would have the courage to do that?"

"Will you join us?" continued the Arab. "Have a soldier's life instead of a dog's death?

"Come and serve as instructor of young soldiers in our leader's army, and rise to rank and power? Or shall I take one of your eyes away on the point of a bayonet and give it to . . ."

"If you were caught by the French, would you join them and fight against your people?" asked Michael Geste.

"That is not the question at the moment," replied the Arab.

"Give me time to think it over," temporized Michael Geste. "Give me until the moon rises—or until I shout, '*O Sheikh, come*,' with all my strength."

A good idea that. While there is life there is hope. The village might possibly be surrounded and attacked by the Section during the night—and when the jackals came to tear the flesh from his head he could bawl for the head-man with all the strength of his lungs.

The coming of his human enemy would then save him—for the time, at least, from the less cruel beasts. Yes—while there's life there's hope. . . .

The Arab rose to his feet.

"At the rising of the moon I will come for your answer," he said. "And if you refuse my mercy once, it will be but once—or I will cut out your tongue.

"Jackals can smell blood farther than camels can smell water," he added as he strode away.

Minutes that seemed like hours. Or were they hours that seemed like endless nights?

How quiet and still the village!

Was that to encourage and hasten the coming of the jackals, the scavengers of the desert?

In which direction would the moon rise?

Was there a faint lightening of the sky already above the distant hills?

What was that? . . .

Prowling, ravening beasts—or the head-man returning already?

Faint sounds . . . an odour of camel. . . .

And suddenly the Fates amused themselves by making Life imitate the "movies" in acknowledging perhaps of the fact that the "movies" do quite frequently imitate Life.

"I knew you at once," said a woman's voice. "I was milking a goat and looking out through the bars when they brought you into the village. . . . These are my father and my husband. We will soon dig you out. The sand is still loose. . . . My husband will ride with you to a place where you can see the *Roumi* camp."

*   *   *   *   *

"Oho! So you have not deserted then!" growled Sergeant-Major Lejaune as Michael Geste marched into the Section's bivouac. "You filthy scum—you look like a corpse that has been buried and dug up again!"

"I have been buried and dug up again, *mon Commandant*," replied Michael Geste, saluting.

Made in the USA
Middletown, DE
19 January 2015